I0673119

TRΛITOR

Red Fever Book 2

C R Macfarlane

Copyright © 2018 by C R MacFarlane

All rights reserved. This book or any portion thereof may not be reproduced or used in any manner whatsoever without the express written permission of the publisher except for the use of brief quotations in a book review.

ISBN 978-1-7753564-2-4

www.blueponypress.com

For Avery, who always believes.

GALIANT IDIM BALANCED HIS FEET at the top of a hill made of old, worn space debris on the planet Junk. Behind him by a few hundred metres, five Augments scoured the planet for repair parts. Thousands of kilometres above, his ship, the UECAS Ishash'tor, hovered in a slowly decaying orbit. Not that the old ship could do much more than float helplessly, waiting for gravity to suck it to its inevitable death. It orbited Junk the same way the past orbited Gal.

Closing his eyes, he inhaled deeply. The sweet, fresh air sparked in his lungs, seeming to jolt him back to life at the same time as the nearby solar body warmed his skin and transported him to a different time.

With his eyes closed, he imagined rolling, green hills, and sustainable communities with children playing under the sun. In the distance, instead of piles of scrap, were piles of food—real food grown and harvested here instead of reproduced in a laboratory. This version of Junk wouldn't have been so different from Indaer, his home, in ten to fifteen years once trees started to take root. In his mind, modular houses dotted the landscape, and as the trees grew, homes were replaced by hand-made, wooden farmsteads. A father chased his giggling boy down a hill.

The way Indaer had been.

A spot of grey caught his eye, ruining the illusion he had created. A figure, half the size of a human, with drooping grey skin and hair rotting from it's misshapen head, stood on the grassy hilltop. A demon. The settlers in his vision transformed, even the father and boy, until the community was ruined with grey.

His eyes opened, and he frowned at the rusted metals under his worn grey boots. UEC grey, meant to crush Hope.

The wasteland planet in front of him once held so much potential. Three years ago, Gal led the Exploration team that charted this entire region of space. Planet A24-alpha—now called Junk—was ideal for habitation: standard gravity, nearby solar source, rich mineral soil, rotation of 22 hours. With accelerated terra-forming techniques, it should have been ripe for human life. Now, it was no more than a dumping ground. That's what the Speakers designated it, and that's what it became.

There had always been good and bad planets, you learned that when they first sent you on Exploration. There were proper parameters that made a lump of rock habitable, and characteristics that made a planet completely unsuitable. But it was never so easy; it was difficult to tell which ones would become a new cradle for humanity, and which would hold the Speakers' most dangerous secrets.

Secrets like this planet's clandestine research facility that housed three-dozen Augments and the researchers who continued to experiment on them, long after the war was over.

Gal snorted. The war wasn't over, it never would be, it had just settled down from a rolling boil to a gentle simmer, enough for the folk to trust in the protection of the Gods again.

On the far side of the planet, the research facility—or what was left of it—still smoked and burned. Three-dozen

Augments—child soldiers who were dangerous enough the
Central Army had led everyone, including Gal, to believe that
they were dead—took refuge on the Ishash'tor. Thousands of
kilometres above, the engineers tried desperately to repair the
ship so they could at least leave this Gods-forsaken planet.
And countless galaxies away, the UECAS Warship Comrade
would be receiving her orders to hunt Gal to the ends of the
stars, words that would come from the Speakers of the Gods
themselves.

Protection of the Gods, indeed.

His mind blurred reality and dreaming—as it so often did
now—painting the green hills over the scrap piles as he stared
into the dismal horizon. The demons were everywhere,
multiplying, filling the hills and obscuring them, a growing,
exponential mass.

A hand fell on his shoulder. His old friend Aaron stood
beside him.

"I thought you'd gone," Gal said gruffly.

Aaron smiled. Only it was not Aaron, Aaron had died
years ago, probably on a planet not much different from this
one. "You must need me."

Gal frowned. There was no point in fighting the
apparition; it could only make it worse. The doctors thought
his JinJiu addiction induced hallucinations had dissipated, but
Gal had only learned to live with the demons. He shrugged
and sat amongst the debris.

Aaron sat down beside him. "What are you thinking
about?"

Picking up a shard of scrap, Gal scratched absently into a
lustreless sheet of metal. "It would have been beautiful."

"The planet?"

"A lot of things." He drew a low-slung farmhouse, fields of
maize in the background. And in front a stick-man and his
wife waved happily.

"Is that what's-her-name? Your girl?"

Gal scratched the drawing out quickly. "It doesn't really matter, does it?"

Aaron shrugged. "Everything matters."

Gal scribbled over and over the place where the picture had been, obscuring it completely.

"Why didn't they inhabit this place, keep terraforming until it was ready?" Aaron asked.

On the hills, the demons shifted, the hoard creeping closer.

"It doesn't matter. It was a long time ago," said Gal. But there were dozens of habitable planets that should have been colonized, but for reasons unknown, never were.

"Maybe it still matters."

Gal pressed his lips together. The reasons were becoming far too clear in the last few days. "Hap wanted it for himself." For his secret Augment research facility.

It seemed like too much, even for Hap Lansford, the First Speaker and direct descendant of the God Strength. But then, with what his father did, Gal couldn't pretend to know the limits of the man he once thought about calling friend.

Aaron shook his head. "It doesn't make any sense. They need more space. Etar is too crowded."

When the Earth was lost at the end of the Augment War nearly four years ago, humanity moved to its closest habitable base: Indaer. Indaer had absorbed the thousands of refugees, all of its landmass swallowed until the planet Gal had grown up on was covered in slate. Even the name had been changed to Etar. The folk lived over and under each other, in conditions that made a starship look spacious and terribly sanitary.

There were plenty of other options available, like body A24-alpha before it became Junk, but the Speakers said none of them were the Will of the Gods, and the colonies they did start all failed. "I thought you would have figured it out by now, Aaron. Hap Lansford can do what he likes, no one will stop him."

The wave of demons that had slowly been encroaching across the green hills reached them. They weren't real, of course. They were the demons of lost potential, demons of things that could have been, if only Gal had tried harder, if he had done more. They turned sinister, beady yellow eyes tracing Gal hungrily. Instead of being worried, he felt a placating calm. They *should* be mad, they *should* be angry.

"Why aren't you stopping him?" said Aaron.

"It's impossible. Dangerous. We're better off here."

Demons closed in, teeth gnashing, preparing to rip him limb from limb. He would rather face that than the Central Army's beloved Speakers. Aaron knew better than most, it wasn't nice what they did to traitors.

"Captain," a solid voice disturbed him and Aaron disappeared. Gal turned, looking into the cold face and vibrant blue eyes of an Augment soldier. "It's time to go back."

Gal sighed, climbing to his feet. He followed the Augment, climbing aboard the shuttle with the others. Demons packed in around them, three-deep, squeezing right up to the ceiling. No one else seemed to mind, but Gal gasped, squished in place. His chest collapsed, fighting against the insurmountable, crushing pressure. The demons tittered gleefully as the shuttle lifted off, making its way back to the ruined freightship.

ONE

Kieran Wood banged his fist on the engine. The gravity drive housing shuddered, reverberating with the sound of cold steel. There was a clunk, and another clunk, followed by a tinkling-grinding noise, and silence—the worst sound of all.

He raised only an eyebrow, too tired and frankly not surprised enough to yell. That was the way things had been going: half the ship was torn apart, a large part of the port-side exposed to space. The shielding array was melted, most of the surge-protectors completely fused. Maneuvering thrusters were operational enough to nudge them around in space, but nothing more. There was only one working airlock on the ship and that was the shuttle hangar. The ship's hull plating was destroyed too, so there was no chance of landing on a planet with any kind of atmosphere, which was too bad because they'd vented half the ship's oxygen, and the air constantly felt a bit too thin.

Out of the frying pan into the fire. Only they were about twelve layers deep right now, the fire a distant ember of hope far above where they were sitting.

Feet shuffled in the doorway to the long, narrow room that housed the long FTL engine separate from the main Engineering bay. He rested his head on the engine, not trusting himself to turn around and be able to stay pleasant. "I told you I needed ten minutes to look at this engine."

"It's us." Hoepe stepped into the room, followed by Grant. They picked their way over torn conduits and open floor panels. Grant craned his neck around, taking in the chaos that was their best chance at leaving Junk before the warship returned to find them alive and finish tearing them apart. His lips pulled into an O and let out a low whistle.

"Report?" Hoepe said.

Kieran turned, wiping his hands on his grey coveralls as he leaned back on the engine. "Well, what you see just about sums it up."

Hoepe frowned, his brows hooding over his already hawk-like glare. "It's been a week."

"I know. We've stabilized life support, reconstructed the water-sanitizers, run new electrical wires through most of the ship for grav-plating and lighting. We're still working on restoring the power generators and the ion thrusters. And then this baby"—he smacked the engine casing again—"I'm still tryin' ta figure out what to do with 'er."

"Her?" The corner of Grant's mouth lifted up.

"What about the sensors?" asked Hoepe.

"Workin' on 'em. Should be ready later today, if everything goes according to plan. That's a big if, with the way things have been goin' lately."

"I want those sensors," said Hoepe. "I want to be able to see what's coming for us before it gets here."

Kieran wiped a heavy hand across his brow, taking a deep breath. "I know. We're workin' as fast as we can. But the ship took a lotta damage, and—"

A new figure appeared at the door, moving quickly. A blue-eyed Augment strode quickly towards them. He was slighter shorter than Kieran, but twice as thick and ribbed with muscle. Kieran forced a smile across his face. "Hey, Rami."

Working with the Augments in Engineering hadn't been without its tensions and outbursts. Kieran was, after all, a Lieutenant on a United Earth Central Army ship, and they had been UEC prisoners and testing subjects most of their lives. Grant had been his biggest supporter, and with Hoepe's help, had convinced most of the other Augments to at least give him a chance.

Most.

Cold, angry Augment eyes glared at him before pushing a tablet into his hand. "Conduit repair notes."

Kieran took the tablet, not daring to mention that he had asked not to be disturbed while he looked at the FTL, or that he was obviously meeting with Hoepe and Grant. As part of his Observer training, he'd studied hundreds of psychological techniques in order to gain trust and earn information from the people he met while he was on his sojourn in Earth-time. He was good at making friends, but Rami had been a tough nut to crack.

The screen of the handheld device showed a number of careful diagrams, and Kieran obligingly focused his eyes to scan the numbers.

Beside him, Grant reached for Rami's shoulder, the two embracing roughly. "Good to see you."

"Your wounds appear to be healing well," Hoepe noted, in his clinical tone.

Rami grumbled, muttering, "I'm fine." He turned, angling his face to hide the fading red ion burns he'd suffered when he forgot to open the pressure valve before discharging an ion overload in one of the thruster engines. The result had been catastrophic ion burns to his face and chest. Unfortunately, Rami's ego hadn't healed as quickly as his skin, the mention of the accident looked more painful than the injury itself.

Kieran shoved the tablet back into Rami's hands, before the Augment could mention how the safety protocols had been deactivated, or how the ion load should never have been allowed to build up to such a level to cause his accident. "Looks all right," he said. "But I was hoping you could help with the sensor array repairs."

Rami scowled. "Sensors? We need the FTL."

Kieran tilted his head towards the tall hawkish Augment beside him. "Hoepe's asked us to make the sensors a priority. And I need some time to come up with a plan here." He waved his head vaguely at the mess all around them.

"You need to repair the conduits to repair the FTL," Rami said sharply, as though he was reading from a textbook.

Kieran shrugged. "It won't help to repair the conduits if we end up not needing 'em." The Kepheus Drive—which had plagued them since they first left Etar was borderline melted already and had a fifty percent chance of making it through one space-folding gravity jump, let alone two or three. "I have half a mind to bypass the whole thing if I can just figure out where the power's gonna come from.

Rami scowled. "You need the engine connect to the grav-drive if you're going to jump."

Kieran shifted uneasily on his feet.

Grant reached out, patting Rami on this chest. "Sensors are the thing right now, Rami. Thanks."

Rami looked up into Grant's eyes, but instead of arguing he bent his head and turned from the room.

"Friend of yours?" Hoepe nodded at Rami's retreating form. "He doesn't seem to like Kieran too much."

"Yeah," Grant nodded. "We had cells beside each other in Junk—before they took me up to solitary."

"How'd you get him to agree so fast. They all listen to you. They won't do what I ask them to, but if you tell them, they don't hesitate to follow orders. Even Rami, and I'm pretty sure that guy hates my guts."

"He hates all parts of you equally," muttered Hoepe.

"Are you the head honcho or something?"

"The what?" Grant stared before sharing a look with Hoepe.

It caused Kieran to blush, he'd done it again: wrong phrase, wrong time. It had been happening more and more the less sleep he got. Luckily no one seemed to question it that much anymore.

Before Kieran could explain it was just another stupidly-said turn of phrase, Grant sighed. "It's because they see me as the strongest. Because the researchers saw me as the strongest." He gestured vaguely to his back, where Kieran knew a grotesque protective-skin implant lay under the skin, barely hidden by never-ending scars. "And as for Rami, he'll come around. You have to understand, he's tough as nails, and he never gave up hope that we would get out of there. He kept trying to fight his way out, even after he made too much noise and they started taking him for experiments."

Kieran grimaced. In Evangecore, where the Augments had been held from the time they were children, they had been subjected to dozens of experiments—he had yet to discover exactly what, but he had seen the forty-three procedural marks running down Sarrin's back, and the surgical implants in her hands, and the toll it had taken.

When she returned from Junk, after being hunted and captured, she would tell him only that the experiments had continued, that the entire experience had been part of the experiment, and that the torture was worse than ever. Grant was probably the same.

"Rami probably kept the rest of us sane, at least focussed," Grant continued. "He'd rally us up—sending whispers through the cell blocks, or more often shouting loudly—even when the guards took him and they brought him back, and he couldn't even get off the floor he was in so much pain. I have no idea what possessed him to do that, but he did. He'd remind us to stay strong, that we would escape, find a ship, and—" He stopped short, looking at Kieran.

"Take your revenge on all the UEC soldiers you can find?" Kieran finished for him. "It's okay. You can say it. I get it."

Grant shoved his hands in the pockets of his coveralls. "We don't mean you."

"I know." But he couldn't help but wonder how it felt for Grant to be dressed in UEC coveralls, which had been the only they had. Was it better or worse than the worn, white hospital clothes they'd been wearing when they escaped the research facility?

He was trying to form the question when Hoepe interrupted his thoughts: "Is anyone giving you a hard time?"

"Nah, nothing I can't handle. Mostly, they question the repairs." Few of his engineering patches were standard UEC issue—they simply didn't have the resources, so he had to be creative. It bordered on breaking the first rule of being an Observer: don't interfere.

Hoepe put a hand on his shoulder. "Whatever you need to do to repair the ship, I want you to do it."

"Sure."

"Kieran," Hoepe squeezed. "I mean it. All means necessary."

Kieran gulped. "All?" He held millennia of knowledge from the dozens of rises and falls of civilization he had witnessed aboard the Observer ship. Laws like Relativity that allowed him to age far more slowly on the near-light-speed Observer ship than the people in Earth-time, a theory that had been entirely forgotten in this iteration of humanity. But to give even a little information if the folk weren't ready for it could have dire consequences. Consequences that shaped events even thousands of years later.

"Whatever you have to do to get this ship working."

"Of course." Kieran nodded, and Hoepe stuck out his

hand, grasping Kieran's forearm the same way the Augments greeted each other. Grant offered one too, and Kieran took it.

An idea sparked for repairing the FTL.

A working FTL meant they had half a chance of leaving Junk before the warship returned. And as soon as they left the planet and the little freightship was operational, Kieran would find a safe zone for the Observer ship to pick him up, and he would go home and finally get a nights rest.

"You okay, Kieran?" Grant waved a hand in front of his face.

He blinked rapidly. "Yeah, why?"

"You spaced out for a second."

Hoepe took Kieran's chin, tilting it up so he looked directly into his eyes. "Acute delirium," he noted, turning Kieran side to side. "Have you experienced other lapses?"

"What? No." Kieran slapped his hand away. "I was having an idea for the engine, is all."

Hoepe proceeded to move his hands around Kieran, examining quickly. "Are you sleeping?"

"Stop it, Hoepe." He grabbed the hand and pushed it down. "As much as I can, yeah." And the rest of the time, he had a drawer in his office full of stims. Sleep would be nice, but the repairs took precedence, Hoepe himself had said it when he gave Kieran the injectors.

Hoepe sighed. "I suppose we're all a little tired. I don't want you next on my medical table, I've seen enough of your team with burns and lacerations today already. Tired engineers making tired mistakes."

Kieran pressed a lopsided smile onto his face, nodding. But the burns shouldn't have happened. He should have been paying attention, should have seen when they wired the power converter backwards and initiated a feedback loop. Kieran knew it was a risk, but the three-hundred percent power return if they were wired properly was too good to pass up. And he had stopped it before it turned into a serious fire, but Rami had been right there, shoving Kieran's repair drawings into his face, all but shouting, 'I told you so.'

The Augments, genetically altered survivors of the Red Fever virus, were supposed to be hyper-intelligent and hyper-aggressive. So far, all he'd seen was a bunch of scared, starved, tired kids—even though most of them were the same age as him, they'd spent their entire lives inside a lab and reminded him painfully of the younger kids he'd looked after at home. He spent as much time watching them as he did explaining repairs, and it was a reminder that Sarrin—quick, brilliant, terrorized Sarrin—was exceptional, one of Evangecore's most prized subjects, and not the norm. So far, Rami's burns were the only serious injury out of the engineering bay, and Kieran aimed to keep it that way.

"You're doing it again," said Grant.

"What?"

"Acute delirium. Are you sure you're sleeping?" said Hoepe.

"I don't have acute de-uh…."

"Acute delirium. You're spacing out."

"I was thinking about Sarrin."

Grant let out an exaggerated, ohhhh, waggling his eyebrows.

Kieran frowned. "What's that supposed to mean?" Hoepe held an equally perplexed expression as they both looked to Grant for explanation.

Grant sighed. "Never mind."

"I am planning to encourage Sarrin to return to Engineering today," said Hoepe.

"Good luck, Doc." The repairs would be much easier with her help, but he'd been trying without success all week, and Kieran refused to get his hopes up.

"Leove says I have been too lenient in her medical care."

"She needs the time. With everything that happened, and her brother…." He let his words trail off. Her brother, Halud, was most likely dead. After losing his own sister, it had taken Kieran a long time to adjust. Heck, he was still adjusting.

But he tried to have a little hope—sometimes siblings could be found, like Hoepe's identical twin brother. "How is Leove?" he asked, changing the subject. "It's neat to see the two of you together. Must be nice."

Hoepe stared at a blank space on the wall, his thoughts taking him far away—Kieran was about to comment on his 'acute delirium,' when Hoepe spoke: "It has not been what I expected. We spend a great deal of time in the infirmary removing tracking chips from other Augments."

"Yeah, but you won't do mine," huffed Grant.

"It's too dangerous without a complete neural scan. We don't know how your second-skin implant ties in."

Grant folded his arms, but thankfully said no more— Kieran had witnessed that argument too many times before where Grant gave every reason he could think of, and Hoepe put down his doctoral foot and simply said, 'no'.

"We are brothers," said Hoepe, "but there is a wall between us."

Kieran shrugged comfortingly. "You just met the guy a few days ago. Give it time. My sister and I had a lot of rough patches too—." There was more to say, but he found his chest suddenly constricted.

"You have a sister?" Grant asked.

Kieran pressed his lips together and nodded once. More correctly, *had*, but that explanation was too complicated to try —she'd died of old age, nearly 200 standard Earth-time years ago. He had a brother too, Andy, still on the Observer ship. Andy had been a year younger than him when Kieran left, but it had been four years for Kieran, and Andy would have only aged a few weeks.

His mom and dad were there too, waiting to hear from him. He'd been unable to write a letter home since they'd first found Sarrin—initially because it felt like too much to send in a short, broken-phrasing communique, and then because their communications system, like everything else on the ship, had been ripped apart.

Maybe he would add the communication array to the list of priority repairs. It was time, he thought, to let them know he was ready for extraction.

"Kieran?" Grant waved his hand in front of Kieran's face.

"You sure you're okay?" asked Hoepe.

"Yeah." He waved them off. "I'll see you guys later. I'm gonna figure out this engine."

* * *

Gal stepped off the shuttle, taking a deep breath as the grey demons fanned out around him, finally giving him space to breathe. The Augments disappeared slowly, carting their finds to the engineering bay, until he was completely alone.

Rayne poked her head through the doorway. "Hi."

"Hi," he sighed. His body felt lighter than it had in a long time, lighter even than when he had been on the planet. She came forward, and he wrapped his arms around her, inhaling the faint soapy scent of her curly, brown hair.

Too soon, she pulled apart, batting at his chest and checking the door behind her. Satisfied no one was watching, she curled back into him. "How was your trip?"

"Good." Not as good as this.

A demon tittered, but Gal shot it a glance and it obediently scampered away into the shadows. "The fresh air was nice," he admitted, wrapping an arm around her waist. "And the sunshine." He led her out of the tiny shuttle bay towards the bridge. "How are you doing?" he asked, halfway along one of the grey corridors.

Her muscles tensed. "Okay. Kieran says the repairs are going well. Hoepe reports nearly all the Augments are recovered enough for duty. He's removing their tracking chips so the warship won't be able to find us—so far none of them are active, but—"

He took her wrist and stopped her as they reached the two stairs that led to the command bridge, partly because he didn't want to push through the demons that crowded the landing, partly because he wanted to savour this sweet moment. Her chin tilted up to him as he pressed a single of finger to the edge of her jaw. "No, I mean, how are you?"

She sighed, shakily, brushing away his hand and ascending the steps in a single stride, the demons bowing out of her way. "I'll be better when you're okay."

"I'm sorry." And he was, for all her had put her through, for all of the things he had done to land them in this situation —things he would never be able to tell her—and for everything and every way he had ever been less than perfect for her.

"Hoepe says you're doing better. No more hallucinations."

He glanced to the side, beady yellow eyes peering at him from the corners of the corridor. "Nope."

She pulled on his hand as the doors opened, tugging him onto the bridge and to its centre, to the place where the padded, grey captain's chair taunted him. "Go on, sit," she said.

The bridge was empty, the constant murmur and soft pings of consoles their only company. And a dozen wrinkled grey demons. He fell back, butt hitting the seat with an oomph. "I don't know," he said. "Hoepe's in charge now. The ship is full of Augments. They don't even like us."

She shook her head, pinning him down with her warm hands on his wrists, beautiful body leaning over him. "It's your ship, Gal. A Central Army ship. It needs its captain."

He leaned up to kiss her, but she moved away in the instant it had taken him to decide to do it.

Demons pressed controls on the computer access panels that wrapped around the walls of the bridge, giggling.

"Soon," said Rayne, staring at the blank view screen, "it will all be back to normal. You and me. Flying planet to planet. The way it's supposed to be."

The demons crept closer, pointing and tittering at the screen, but Gal ignored them, pushed them as far from his mind as he could. He gazed instead at Rayne, overwhelmed with the warmth that poured from his chest. Aaron was right: something mattered, Rayne mattered.

Whatever it took, he would keep her safe. Things would be okay. He would get better, the demons would disappear, and it would be just the two of them. A low slung farmhouse on an uninhabited planet far away.

"I thought we could discuss a plan," Rayne said quietly.

"A plan?" His throat suddenly grew tight, his voice strained. "A plan for what?"

"To go home."

His entire body stiffened.

"When was the last time you set foot on Etar?"

He knew exactly, it was the day the Speakers had told him never to come back. The day they realized he knew more than enough to be dangerous, and yet they could not get rid of him as easily as they had gotten rid of Aaron.

"We need to go back, to tell them about the Augments."

"Rayne...."

She wrapped a hand around his shoulder. "No, listen. I know how you pretend not to care, but all you do is watch over the crew and me and these Augments. We have a chance to make a real difference here. The folk have been living in fear for years, worried that the Red Fever will return and there will be new Augments. But we were wrong before; they're not vicious killing machines, they're kids."

"They're not kids, Rayne, they're in their twenties."

"I know, but they act like kids, they were in the hospitals so long. My point is, they smile and talk the same as you and I do." She rubbed his arm. "This is our part to play in the Path. Think of the fear we can alleviate, the millions of lives we can improve if we just help them understand. I bet when we arrive, the Speakers will be waiting for us, the Gods having already told them the Path."

They would be waiting, that was certain. If Gal could lie down and forget it all, he would, but his bottle of Jin-Jiu—the only thing that had ever worked to numb the memories of every mistake he had made—was disastrously empty. "Rayne, it's not that simple."

"Of course it is. In the Gods we Trust."

"Rayne…." He expected her to interrupt him, but she sat still, waiting. "Why do you think we need to go back right away? Can't we just take our time out here, under the stars?" He looked to the currently blacked-out viewscreen, the sensor array currently non-functional, and realized he liked that even better than a sky full of stars.

"The general will be worried." She pressed her lips into a thin line. "I don't want him to think that I, that we…. I don't want him to think that we're defecting and helping Augments, not without knowing why at least."

Sometimes, Gal could forget that Rayne, beautiful and sweet as she was, was related to the general for the Speaker of Strength. Oleander Nairu had been the general to Hap Lansford's father before him and now to Hap. He had been the general of Strength during the Red Fever and during the Augment wars. There was a pretty good chance he already knew everything he wanted to know about Augments.

Gal shook his head to clear the thought, ignoring the

demons that had crept close on all sides, watching with their big, yellow eyes. Instead, he said to Rayne, "He doesn't have to approve everything you do."

"I know, but."

"I think you are a wonderful officer, tactician, human being." Far better than him. "And I can't say how glad I am to have you with me."

The demons tittered excitedly.

Rayne bent down, kissing him on his cheek. "I'm glad you're feeling better."

And, just in that instant, if he ignored the demons and the arrival of Aaron who glared at him from the Navigation console, he was.

* * *

Sarrin DeGazo woke with a start, scanning the room quickly: six escape routes and twenty-three objects that could be used as deadly weapons.

Stop, she yelled inwardly at the dark clouds that crowded the edges of her vision. There was nothing here in the quiet, grey, lieutenant's quarters for the monster to defend against, and it slowly slipped away.

Her heart pounded unnecessarily in her chest. In sleep, she had dreamed of Evangecore, it's blinding white walls and glaring surgical lights. The monster had been born in Evangecore, as much a part of her now as breathing.

The white-walled memories slowly gave way to the grey sheets that billowed around her, to the grey walls and grey furniture. On the wall was a star chart of a system she couldn't name—which she originally found troubling because she recalled every starchart she had ever seen, but now merely fascinated her. On the bedside table, a colourful frame with a picture of a smiling brother and sister. The sister was long-dead—old-age, Kieran had said.

A neat set of blankets laid on the floor, undisturbed.

Kieran hadn't come by to sleep in a day and a half.

An image flashed in her mind: Kieran darting across the engine room. It was real, she knew, a vision of him in that exact moment, and she pushed it out of her mind as fast as she could, drawing her knees into her chest. The prescience was a side effect of the experiments she had been subjected to in Evangecore—one of many unnatural abilities bestowed to her by the monster that made her something other than human.

Some invisible arm pressed against her chest, pushing her down and down until she laid flat on her back, then down beneath the sheets. She curled into a tight ball at the foot of the bed.

A gaping hole inside her chest pulled from the inside like a gravitational anomaly, threatening to crumple her weak frame onto itself. In the hole was the space normally reserved for Halud, but he had left her. And with good reason: why stay for a monster if what you were looking for was a sister?

There was no way to know where he was, if he was alive or dead—except…. Steeling herself, she tried to reach out for a vision of Halud, but, as with every other time she had tried, she saw nothing except her own hands in front of her face. Perhaps he was dead, only it didn't *feel* like he was dead.

When he'd left, it had been in the middle of a firefight, the warship Comrade attacking the limping freightship. Everyone else was convinced his shuttle had been torn apart by the laz-cannon beams searing between the two ships. If not, then surely the UECs had destroyed him the instant he stepped aboard the warship. But, if he had made it across, and almost certainly the Gods would have helped, there was no doubt in her mind they would have taken him back to Etar, to the Speakers.

Her mind drifted to the UEC trap that had been set on Junk to capture her. Dr. Guitteriez had called her the answer

—to what problem she didn't know, but it meant she would never be safe. They had hunted her across the galaxy once, just to see what secret abilities still laid dormant within her. Luis Guitteriez was dead, but his experiments had torn open her fragile mind, and she had used her secrets to escape. No doubt it had been recorded and transmitted.

And Halud would almost certainly be used as bait. He would never be safe. No one aboard the little freightship would ever be safe.

Only Kieran had half a chance to escape back to the Observer ship he came from, a place completely out of time, untouchable by the Speakers and the Central Army.

Her eyes went the small puzzle cube, a bright beacon hidden between the grey sheets. She'd fallen asleep trying to solve it, and it must have slid to the foot of the bed during her dreaming. A seemingly simple toy, the "Ru-bex" cube had proven frustratingly elusive.

The mechanics were simple—twenty-six rotating cubes affixed to a central axis—but the interconnecting pivots, layers of complex moving pieces, required her full attention. The puzzle required complete focus, forcing all her other thoughts into the back of her brain and offered her some peace.

Where it laid between the sheets, she could see a row of yellow lining one edge, but the other six squares were mismatched. Perhaps a clockwise rotation of the right arm would benefit. She reached out to turn the cube, but gasped, her arm freezing part-way. There in front of her, where her hand should have been, was a silver skeleton dripping with blood.

She had killed forty-six guards during her escape from Junk only a week ago. The memory played out unbidden, her heart racing as though she was there again: guards screaming, walls tumbling, everything burning, burning, burning. Life ripped from body, molecular bonds disintegrating before her eyes. Brutal, brutal. A true monster. Of course she was, how could she be anything but?

Kieran said it wasn't her fault. It was self-defence. They would have killed her, she had to do it to stay alive. But self-defence would have meant escape, self-defence would have meant incapacitating the doctor and guards and running away. But she had killed them all and razed the building to the ground.

The silver skeleton flexed, and she choked back the bile that rose in her throat. She never wanted to become a killer —it was against the Gods, against all she believed was good. But the hands told her all she needed to know: they had made her. They had ripped out the bones and replaced them with titanium, stripped the nerves so she couldn't feel. She was a monster. More machine than human. A weapon. Her life belonged to them.

She stuffed her hands into her armpits, sealing them there with her body weight, so they couldn't do something unbidden.

Her eyes searched out the cube, heart thumping erratically. If she could just solve it—the same way Kieran had, spinning it around, hands a blur, until all the sides matched, then twisted it up again and tossed it to her with a carefree grin— maybe she had a chance against the rest, a chance to do something normal, to be human.

She had to solve it—there was no other way. The right side required a clockwise rotation—her humanity, whatever tatters were left, depended on it.

The cube turned, her hands still buried firmly.

A gasp left her lips, but the cube remained hovering between the sheets, inches from her face. The top layer now turned anticlockwise, lining blue up with blue. Then the bottom, green to green. Moving objects with her mind was as unnatural as her titanium-skeleton hands, as unnatural as being able to watch Kieran through solid walls two decks above.

She wanted to shove it away like the horrible mutated thing it was, but as the cube spun, as the simple toy followed her simple thoughts, everything else melted away. The cube took all of her focus, the need to solve it overwhelming.

Her metal hands she tucked under a pillow and wrapped tightly in sheets. The memories too she stuffed far from reach, and set all of her concentration on the toy.

Slowly, as she worked, her body stretched, opening and relaxing so that she laid comfortably on the bed beneath the unfamiliar stars. The side spun, now lining up yellow with yellow. Two lines came together, perhaps it wouldn't be so difficult. Perhaps none of this would be so difficult.

The door slid open unannounced, and the cube fell, bouncing across the bed.

Hoepe strode in, long legs taking him around the side of the bed in three steps.

Sarrin held her breath. Had he seen? What would he say? Or think? Who would he tell?

"How are you feeling?" he asked. He set his data-tablet on the nightstand, raising a single eyebrow at the colourful picture frame, then kneeled on the bed. He said nothing about the cube.

She shifted to the far side. He was unnecessarily close for an idle conversation. Not that Hoepe or Sarrin ever indulged in idle conversation.

He reached across and palpated her trigger points and lymph nodes. She fought her instinct to shove him backwards and run, gritting her teeth against his touch. Hoepe was a friend she had known for years, but he was still a doctor, and she never wanted to be in another medical suite or operating theatre ever again.

Dr. Guitteriez had always worn protective black gloves

when he touched her overly sensitive skin, but Hoepe had no idea of the danger he was in. Where his hands brushed her, energy crackled, snapping through her like lightening, and she could sense all of him, every cold, calculating, medical vibration. She could almost hear his thoughts.

She bundled her own energy and forced it to be still, locked deep in the core of her being. In the past, the monster had done things, terrible things of its own accord. Another thing that made her less than human.

He pulled apart the twisted sheets that wrapped around her hands, and she jerked them back. Thankfully the skin was back in place. They were whole again, pink and clean, blood nowhere to be seen. The only sign something was amiss was the almost imperceptible micro-suture lines that criss-crossed the flesh.

"It's time for you to get out of this room," he said. Hoepe turned his attention to his tablet, typing something quickly on the screen. He stood to leave, but paused at the foot of the bed, pointing at the door. "Come on, Sarrin. Doctor's orders."

She gulped. He thought... he wanted her to go through there.

The door stared at her every day. Three-inches of hollow plastique held together with a magnet lock. Three-inches that separated this safe room from the rest of the ship and the hustle and bustle of curious bodies. Three-inches that when open, even for a second, threatened to swallow her whole and chew her into nothing.

Three-inches kept the monster locked in its cage. Kept the others safe.

She shook her head.

"Sarrin," Hoepe said again, waves of impatience rolling off of him.

The hole in her soul tugged, stealing all her breath. She

laid down, pulling the blankets to her chest.

"Sarrin." He sighed and leaned against the wall. "You have made a full recovery. Your presence is needed in Engineering. The warship could return any day."

The warship that had taken her brother away—it left a sick feeling in her empty hole.

"Gods." He squeezed a hand into his hair, messing up the tufts that had grown in the last month. A wall of desperate emotion hit her as it rolled off of him.

She tugged the sheets all the way over her head, as though it might protect her. Protect him.

Hoepe sighed. "Come on, you have to go out. You can't stay in this room forever." His feet padded across the worn carpet until she could nearly feel him leaning over her. "You're the only one that's keeping you in this room. You're not a prisoner anymore, so stop acting like one," he said, and then his hand was on her arm, lifting her up with strength she forgot the doctor had.

She bolted up, scrambling to the far side of the room. The door opened as she passed its sensor, threatening to swallow her whole.

Hoepe watched from where he stood beside the bed.

Wary, she shifted back until the door closed.

"You might want to clean up a little first," he said.

She retreated to the latrine, the only place where she could avoid Hoepe's penetrating gaze. Pulling herself up to the sink, she blinked several times before she realized the haggard creature staring back in the mirror was in fact her. She no longer even looked human, more like a corpse: thin and grey, shaded hollows around her eyes and cheeks.

She scrubbed her hand over her face, although it made little difference. Her hair hung in matted sheets, and she tied it back haphazardly. An old memory caught her, slamming the air from her lungs:

Sarrin sat on a hard bunk in Evangecore, age six-standard. It was night, the room dark and quiet, punctuated only by the muffled sleeping sounds of a dozen other girls. Her friend, older, maybe ten, sat behind Sarrin, combing through her long hair with her fingers. Silently, the friend smoothed her hair over and over, knowing Sarrin would never brush it herself.

Sarrin reached her tiny hand for the girl's outstretched leg, and the girl wrapped her arms around Sarrin quickly, before they parted. Sarrin leapt to the upper bunk, laying in her own bed just as the door creaked open and the night nurse came to check on their unit.

Warmth tingled where the girl's arms had been, reaching in and filling Sarrin's chest, until she creaked open her eyes and found herself standing once again in the grey latrine. She slammed her eyes closed, begging for the memory to come back, but it was gone.

This was her life now. Her brother was gone, her friend long dead. And so was sweet, innocent Sarrin. In her place was a killer, a confirmed monster, and there was no comfort for her to find.

Stumbling back into the main room, looking no less corpse-like than before, she found Hoepe waiting by the open door. He stepped around her, long arms outstretched, herding her through.

TWO

Hoepe pushed her through the quiet corridor of the crew quarters and into the main hall. Two women passed, and Sarrin jolted back, pressing into the wall, somehow thinking she could hide there. Beside her, Hoepe chuckled. In Evangecore, she would have been shot for stupidity.

The Augments spared them only a glance, nodding quickly at Hoepe as they passed. Their hands danced back and forth in lively conversation. One laughed.

Sarrin found herself fixated, her jaw dropping open at the sight of their backs and the loose, torn fabric that exposed the lines of procedural tattoos. "What are they doing?" she gasped.

Hoepe shrugged. "It doesn't matter if their marks are exposed here, everyone knows they're Augments. While you've been hiding, it seems to have become a bit of a status symbol."

In Evangecore, they wore mandated jumpsuits which covered all but the barcodes printed on their necks and arms. In the war, they found clothes that ensured even the IDs were covered, because to be recognized as an Augment meant death or at least a lot of trouble. But here, these girls wore their marks with pride. They wore their marks without fear.

Her foot stepped forward.

A man rushed past, nearly brushing against her, the barcodes on the backs of his arms clearly visible. "Hurry up, we're already late."

She turned to Hoepe. "Late for what?"

"Grant and Rami called a meeting in the canteen. I don't know what about, but I thought you should be there." He encouraged her forwards again.

"Me?"

"Yes. People listen to you."

She stopped in front of the doors to the canteen, just far enough away not to trigger the sensors. There were nearly three dozen Augments in the room, she could feel them through the walls—all their nervous fidgeting excitement. "Why?"

"Because of who you are, your reputation, and"—he glanced at her back—"you have more marks than anyone else."

Cold ice settled in the pit of her stomach. "I don't want them to know." No one should listen to a monster.

"Fine. I still want you there." Hoepe lifted his arm, waving it, and the doors slid open on their pneumatic mechanism.

The normal arrangement of tables and chairs had been pushed aside. A sea of marks and barcodes faced back at her. Muscles flexed, rippling under the pale skin and dark lines, but the bodies were relaxed. As they turned and shifted, talking to one another, Sarrin searched for familiar faces. Many she recognized from Evangecore, but, with the exception of Grant and Thomas and handful of others she had known in the war, she didn't know their names—she'd known most of them only as opponents in the training exercises the researchers called the war games, where teams of children hunted each other, and the memory caught in her chest.

The edges of her vision crowded in, and her hands found the seams of the nearest wall panel, prying it loose to make her escape. It had been eight years since she had been put into the arena, but her heart still raced. The others chatted casually, nodding and smiling. A peal of laughter came from the front of the room.

Hoepe leaned against the wall beside her. His expression remained customarily grim, but his eyes darted over the others with as much fascination as she felt. It sparked a new kind of thought in her, a tactical calculation like she had been trained to make in Evangecore: with this many Augments, they might actually have a chance for freedom.

A cheer went up, the attention in the room turning to a table at the far end and the man who climbed on top of it. He was short and stocky, heavily muscled. Sarrin didn't recognize him, but he was young. Maybe he'd never been put in the arena. The others around her certainly seemed to know him though, and listened raptly as he spoke. "We did it!" he shouted, and the Augments around her clapped and whistled.

Another, louder cheer built from the first, and Grant, stumbling as he was pushed to the front, climbed onto the table beside the other Augment. His back turned to them briefly, as he scrambled up, and Sarrin caught a spot of blood blooming through his shirt. It sobered her and quieted the rest, a reminder they were not together for a party, but to survive.   While captive on Junk, Grant had been experimented on, much like Sarrin, a gruesome second-skin implanted between his shoulder blades, and the blood oozed from the cracking scab where it had torn through the skin too many times before.

Grant faced the crowd grimly. He said, "It's good to see you all again, especially without bars in front of your faces." A pleased murmur passed through the crowd, some bringing their five fingers to their chest. "We know there are other Augments, other facilities. Rami"—he gestured at the other man—"and I think it's time we try a little offence of our own, and help them."

Rami stepped forward. The Augments watched him with rapt attention. "When we were prisoners on Junk, I told you that I would get you out of there, that we would walk freely. I don't want for us just to be free from captivity, I want us to be free to live our lives however we see fit. I want for us to be able to walk through the streets with our heads high."

Sarrin gasped, a spark of hope dancing in her brain. What would it be like to not be hunted? She met Hoepe's eyes, but the gaze that met hers was strained and wary. He knew it as well as she did: freedom like that was impossible.

"Let me tell you, it is possible!" shouted Rami. "The same as us escaping from their torture facilities not once but twice. We will walk free." The crowd cheered as he pounded his chest. Hoepe stiffened. Sarrin's chest pounded too, entirely different from the heady emotions that swirled around her.

Beside Rami, Grant nodded, lips pulled back in a tight grin as he surveyed the excited Augments. "When I was being held in solitary, I heard rumours about facilities on Jade and Porter, and I think it's reasonable to assume there are more. And there's one place I know of that will have the full database."

"We're going to attack the warship when it returns," said Rami.

Sarrin's limbs went numb, and she thumped against the wall, nearly sagging to the floor before she caught herself. Attacking the warship meant certain death. The energy in the room stood shock still as well, Augments looking between each other.

Hoepe pushed away from the wall beside her, sliding through the crowd to the front. "I thought we had decided it was a fool's plan. I don't want to have this argument again."

"Why not?" Grant stared down at the doctor. "Everyone should be involved in making the decision. We don't know when the warship is coming back, but it could be any day. It could be tomorrow. Kieran thinks the ship is at least a week away from being able to make an FTL jump, which means we're stuck here."

Rami grumbled, his knuckles cracking as he worked his hands back and forth.

"The freightship is in no condition to fight," Hoepe said, and pointedly looked at the myriad faces around him. "And neither are any of you."

"We're Augments," said Grant. "We've been through worse. We're strong."

Hoepe shook his head. "Sorry, but as your doctor, you're not. Everyone is suffering multiple mineral deficiencies and recovering from exhaustion. Not to mention psychosocial disorientation. And you want to have us board a warship with a hundred and fifty elite soldiers and try to conquer it."

"We're stronger than they are."

"Not right now. For all we know, there are Augments aboard on their side—we know they can control minds."

Grant turned a sickly grey colour—what went through his mind, knowing they had the ability to take control of him at the flip of a switch? Knowing what he had done under their mind control, and what he had chosen to do to similarly affected Augments in the past?

Hoepe said, "I still say our best option is to first let ourselves recuperate. That gives us the best possible advantage over whatever we may face. We'll run sensor sweeps of Junk's moons and the surrounding area—we may find somewhere to go where the warship won't be able to find us, at least not easily."

"The warship," argued Grant, "will have information

about all the UEC bases and their research facilities. If we can get that data, it gives us a map. Otherwise, we'll end up flying planet to planet, hoping to get lucky and find them. We're already stuck here, we may as well make the best of it and plan for the warship's arrival instead of hoping like fools that it won't come back."

A murmur of assent rippled through the canteen, chased by nervous whispers. Back and forth.

"You're infiltrated the warship before," said Rami.

Hoepe frowned. "That was a trap. They wanted us to board."

Sarrin shuddered. When they had snuck aboard The Comrade, it had been the beginning of a long and convoluted experiment designed by Guitteriez to learn more about her and try to bring out deep unlocked abilities. Sarrin had barely held onto herself. By the end, she'd lost control, attacking the crew and Kieran. She wouldn't do it again.

But the monster whispered to her: it could be different this time. The others wanted to destroy the warship. If she let it, the monster could destroy every last soldier, every computer, every system. No one would be able to stop her.

Another thought occurred: Halud had been on the warship. If, by some miracle, they could attack it and learn the information stored on its database, there would be a record of what happened to Halud—at least if he'd made it to the warship or not, and if he had, had he been killed or brought back to Etar.

Her heart raced in her chest, the black tendrils blanking out the canteen in front of her. Could she? Could she attack the warship to find her brother? That was what siblings did, what normal people did—like Hoepe finding Leove—they went to extraordinary lengths to find those they loved. Perhaps, once she found him, she would be human again.

The monster let out a surge of glee, a deep rumble that

came for her chest, a hunter preparing to hunt. It wouldn't be so much giving in and losing control as it would be asking the monster for help. For Halud. Just this one time.

But, like the coloured cube puzzle, lining up one row of blue meant confusing the green. And the red and yellow and white and orange.

If Halud was still alive, he was being held somewhere, and she would need to save him. That meant more killing, more destruction. And if Halud was dead.... The monster surged, its anger ready to lash out—she couldn't think of that possibility. Not now. Not ever.

A sudden crash sounded from the front of the room, jogging her awareness. Augments in front of her ducked, their reflexes nearly as quick as her own. Splintered plastic shards flew at her while she braced against the wall. Then the shards stopped, hanging in the air, inert.

Time slowed. Between one heartbeat at the next, Sarrin realized she had stopped the pieces, holding them with her mind.

Telekinetics. Monster.

The dark tendrils cleared, and she willed the plastic to continue forward, smashing harmlessly into her chest and making her grunt. At the sound, some of the nearest Augments turned. A girl Sarrin recognized frowned, then nodded in recognition.

"You fool," Grant shouted, drawing their stares back to the front of the room. "What are you doing?"

"Getting your attention, the only way I know how." Rami proceeded to kick the table he had just smashed, its broken legs toppling over easily, even as Grant reached for him.

Sarrin blinked sharply at the display of violence. Most Augments tried to bury any strength or ability they had in case the UECs took notice and made them a special experiment subject—but not this one.

"Gods, Rami, we're not in the prisons anymore," said Grant.

But his outburst had drawn the attention of the others, their gazes locked on him intensely, muscles coiled. Rami took the opportunity to push Grant aside, stalking back and forth.

"We need to talk about the real problem here: the commons. I know how you feel, but it's also something we all need to decide together."

Sarrin shifted uncomfortably.

"There are commons all over this ship, and I don't understand why we're trusting them," Rami shouted. "What's changed? For all the years we were held in that prison, all the years of the war, the experiments in Evangecore, we always said we would never trust anyone besides ourselves. We *couldn't* trust anyone besides ourselves."

In the war, there had been no one they could trust or depend on. The UEC propaganda had turned everyone, even the folk, even the little children, against them. But this ship was different. Halud had chosen Gal's ship for a reason. And Kieran—there wasn't anyone she trusted more.

Rami turned, looking into the faces of the Augments around him who were starting to nod in agreement. "Now, we're suddenly working alongside them, taking their orders, with our arms wide open. There's no reason for them to help us."

"And yet they have," answered Hoepe, voice iced with steel. "Times have changed. I know you've only been aboard a short while, but the men in my crew are no UEC lovers, and the others—I've never seen an engineer do what Kieran has done for us."

Sarrin leaned forward, ears suddenly burning.

"He's a common, a UEC soldier," spat Rami. "If you want my opinion, he's slowing us down. Making us run all our repairs through him, using unregulated designs. It's nonsense. And it's dangerous." He shook his head, addressing the entire group. "I'm an engineer—Evangecore trained me to fix all their machines and engines. And the things he's doing don't make sense. Look at this." He reached into his coverall pocket, pulling out a data-tablet, pushing it in front of Grant and Hoepe. Sarrin strained, but there was no way to see from this far back.

Hoepe peered at the screen and frowned. "This doesn't meant much to me, Rami. I'm a doctor, not an engineer."

"Same here." Grant shook his head.

"These are schematics I showed your 'chief'. Repairs for the power conduits that drive everything including weapons, shields, and the FTL—which I thought should be our top priority—but he turned them down. Asked me to work on the sensor array instead."

Sarrin's heart thumped in her chest, her eyes flicking from each of the three men with each beat, time slowing.

Hoepe's frown deepened, the lines on his face cutting sharply. "I asked Kieran to work on the sensors so we can see when and if the warship returns."

"But we will still need to be able to attack when it arrives."

"We're not going to turn on them, if that's what you're suggesting," said Grant, causing Sarrin's heart to falter for a beat, squeezing painfully. "He's the ship's chief."

"And we're not going to attack the warship," snapped Hoepe.

Grant glanced between the two of them, unsure. But he stepped up in front of Hoepe, making his shoulders broad. "We have to help the others."

"Not by getting ourselves killed."

The room erupted into shouting, the words blanking out under a heavy haze. Two Augments—trained to fight since they were small children—pushed each other, throwing the

room into chaos.   Dark tendrils wrapped across Sarrin's
vision, and she gripped the half-open wall panel behind her,
grounding herself. She had to get out of this room before the
monster took control. But as quickly as it started, the din in
the room quieted, only the sound of her heavy breathing and
now-rapidly beating heart audible.   She cracked her eyes
open.

Three dozen sets of Augment-blue eyes blinked back.   In
the middle of them, Thomas held up an arm, the finger
pointed straight at her. "We can't be fighting each other while
the real enemy is still out there. Let's ask Twenty-seven, the
bravest and strongest of us all, what she thinks we should do."

Sarrin gulped, biding rising in her throat.

"That's Twenty-seven?" Rami stuttered. She'd never asked
for the nickname, didn't like anything it symbolized, but Rami
was suddenly stilled from his rampage, his gaze filled with
awe.

Another Augment caught her attention: a young man
smiling reverentially, five fingers pressed into his chest. Her
heart pounded as their eyes locked, and her mind pictured
him as a boy. He was the same boy, she was sure, but how
was he here after all these years?

The memory played out unbidden as she stood frozen in
the busy canteen: *Sarrin—age twelve-standard—crept through dense
underbrush, hiding, counting the minutes until the 'game' was over. She
fingered a dull fork she had collected from breakfast and hidden in her
pocket.*

*She came, quite by accident, upon another child, a small boy curled on
the ground hiding under the leaves of a bush. His face was smeared with
dirt, his scent rich with fear, and his heart pounded so loudly she needed to
cover her ears. Tears left pale streaks along his cheeks.*

*She reached forward without thinking, to comfort him.   He flinched
away—a child afraid of another child.*

Whatever had possessed her, as she sat squatted next to him in the brush, the actions she took next were the work of a demon. It had changed her life instantly and forever.

Before that moment, she had been nothing, just another subject in an experiment. A kid walking through a simulated battlefield, hiding from other kids. They wanted them to fight, to hunt until there was one standing, but she hadn't so much as spit at another person, not once in the nine years before that day. There was no reason for anyone, any of the researchers to think she was anything special.

A group of teens walked through the artificial jungle, their faces smeared with others' blood, heavy clubs in their hands: hunters. Children of an opposing team, set to task for this particular exercise-slash-game.

Sarrin lifted her head, her gaze directed above the older children. They were watching, they were always watching—the doctor and his researchers would be observing them all, recording little notes on their little charts. She wondered if they had ever felt anything close to the fear the boy felt now.

She gripped the fork.

A tall tower, cleverly masked behind trees in the artificial landscape, stood in the centre of the arena. The training area was large enough you wouldn't notice unless you thought to look, but the colours didn't quite match the surrounding landscape, the shadows on the trees falling not quite where they should.

Wild, vision tunnelled and barely in control of her own body, Sarrin sprinted across the forest floor. She ran right in front of the hunters drawing them off the boy. They chased, but she was faster.

She threw herself up the side of the tower, fingers digging in as she scaled the side of it. She sensed the researchers on the other side of the one-way window debating whether or not she could see them, their voices tight with panic.

Sarrin drew back a fist and slammed the fork through the shallow illusion, permaglass splintering. Another two blows and it shattered around her. The fork went through a guard's eye, and she strangled two before picking up the shard of glass. Something pricked the side of her neck, barely noticeable.

The rest of the researchers fell in the massacre, her movements gradually fading until she collapsed in a slump, the world going dark. She had been inches from him, from Guitteriez, glass shard in her outstretched, bloody hand, when the drugs had taken her over.

When she woke, it was to Guitteriez's fearsome grin, a crooked scar fresh with stitches oozing blood that dripped onto her face. "You killed twenty-seven of my men, Sarrin. They were good men, they were just doing their jobs trying to help you because you're sick."

Her hands were chained. A gravity-trap pulled down on everything, crushing her chest into her spine. Her heart raced so fast she thought it was going to explode in her head.

"A nice girl like you shouldn't kill. Didn't your mother ever tell you that?"

A single droplet rolled down her cheek as she struggled to move.

"At least, not until she's told."

He stood, his ornate cane tapping on the floor, and dabbed at his face with a handkerchief, blood blooming through the white material. "I think you could be very special, 005478F. Now it's time to see how much you can do."

"Sarrin?" Hoepe called her name. The dozen of eyes were still watching, and she shifted in the uncomfortable silence.

A chime sounded from one of the consoles embedded in the walls, cutting through loudly. Someone answered it, an unmistakable drawl instantly clearing her dark fog: *"Engineering to Hoepe. Where are you? Where is everyone?"*

Hoepe glared around the room, as though daring the others to say anything against the engineer, before moving to the console. "I'm in the Mess. How are the repairs?"

"The sensors are online again."

"Thank you. Run a scan. We'll meet you on the bridge."

"all righty."

Hoepe clicked off the communications program. His voice carried an edge like a knife, "Kieran is our chief engineer because I don't know anyone else who can fix a starship like him. Should anyone disagree, you can come to me directly. Understood?"

"Or me," Grant added, folding his arms across his chest.

Rami opened his mouth to argue, but the others had already turned toward the door, shuffling out efficiently. Instead, he pressed his lips together and turned towards Sarrin, studying her.

She stepped back, ducking out of his gaze, letting herself get caught up with the Augments who filed through the door, into the hallway, and up to the bridge, their ripped clothes and black marks bobbing confusingly around her.

* * *

Gal stood comfortably beside Rayne, staring at the black viewscreen. It was nice to pretend that it was truly just the two of them in the universe, that the sensors weren't broken but the universe around them had ceased to exist.

The doors to the bridge opened, and Kieran bumbled in, ruining the illusion. Rayne stepped to the side, putting a professional distance between her and Gal. Definitely not alone in the universe.

Kieran headed straight for the engineering console to the side of the bridge, barely looking up. "Hey, guys," he mumbled. He tapped a few controls, and the viewscreen suddenly flashed, revealing a dense galaxy of stars around them.

Gal groaned inwardly, the demons lining up on the consoles, sitting as though they were ready to watch a vid.

Shortly, the doors opened again, and a stream of Augments poured onto the bridge, walking in an orderly line that screamed of military precision. Hoepe nodded curtly before seating himself in Gal's captain's chair.

But it wasn't really Gal's, he corrected himself, he was too cracked to command a starship. It was far better someone else be in charge. Besides, nothing really mattered in the end, so long as Rayne was with him and she was safe. He stepped off to the side, blending out of the way.

He stood amongst the Augments easily—he'd never believed they were ruthless killing machines, at least not because of the virus—it was only their presence that made them dangerous. At least there wasn't any way for it to get worse.

"Scans are almost done, Doc," announced Kieran.

"Let's see." Hoepe inclined his head at the viewscreen.

The display changed, separating itself into six separate views, each a zoomed in on a portion of the stars around them. The images changed quickly, showing a brief view of different regions. Gal found himself studying them, the same as he had years ago when he'd first come to this region working for Exploration and searching for new planets to terraform.

"Wait, what was that?" said Grant, pointing.

Kieran adjusted the controls, and the viewscreen cycled back to the last set of images. In the upper left corner, something drifted across the screen, big enough to see and fast enough to notice. The image shifted to fill the whole viewscreen.

Gal felt his heart stop. It wasn't possible.

Hoepe sat forward in his chair. "It's a planet."

"There's no tag on it," said Grant.

"This sector has been thoroughly explored," said Leove. "I don't understand."

"It can't be a planet." Grant squinted at the screen. "What's it orbiting?"

But it was a planet, Gal knew it even before Kieran tipped the controls, and the image zoomed in again revealing a green-blue dot dashed with white. Gal stared to shake.

"Run a detailed scan," ordered Hoepe.

Rayne stepped forward, her data tablet held in front.

"Look at these readings." She glanced at Gal, eyes filled with glee.

Gal shut his eyes and prayed. Parameters told part of the story, but there was no way to tell a good planet from a bad one without exploring it. And there was no way he would set foot on this particular body ever again.

"It *is* a planet," said Hoepe.

"Really?" Grant cried joyfully.

"It must be unexplored," said one of the doctors, "but this sector was mapped years ago."

"It must have an irregular orbital pattern," said the other twin.

Kieran let out a low whistle. "I don't know much about planets, but those readings look awfully habitable."

"Perfect," muttered Sarrin from behind Kieran.

Rayne shoved her tablet into Gal's hands, forcing his eyes to open. Her own eyes twinkled at him. "What do you think?"

He sighed, but it was inevitable, his eyes fell to the readings like gravity. He scanned the data with practiced ease, knowing what each would say before he read it. Each parameter read in the green. It was as good as Earth. Better.

But this planet was something else, something inexplicable entirely.

The tablet fell from his hands, clattering across the ground.

Beyond him, the conversation continued: "It could be a safe haven from the warship."

"How long for us to get there?"

"Without an FTL, a week maybe."

"No!" Gal screamed, stopping them short. The bridge went silent, dozens of eyes tearing into him. "No!" he screamed again. "Never. Never. Never." His eyes met Hoepe's, he had to make them see. "Never speak of it. They can't know. It's too dangerous."

"Gal?" started Hoepe.

Blindly, he stumbled from the bridge, tripping and leaning on bodies as he passed. Demons shrieked with laughter. "Listen to me. Never again. Never, never again," he warned them.

"Gal!" Rayne cried, but he pushed past her. The doors sealed behind him. He heard them open and close again, Rayne calling his name. He ducked his head and ran.

THREE

Hoepe shared a look with his twin brother, Leove, all the muscles in his broad back stiffening as the door from the bridge sealed and Gal—with Rayne chasing after him— disappeared. The captain's recovery from his Jin-Jiu addiction had seemed swift and easy, but he made a mental note to examine him again.

He glanced at the tablet in his hand. "I don't understand. How is there a planet out here that is completely unmarked?"

Beside him, Leove shrugged. "It would seem the Gods are on our side."

Hoepe raised a single eyebrow. "Indeed. An unmarked planet—somewhere the Central Army has never been to, never named or explored—it's more than we could have hoped for. We can hide on the planet and the warship will never find us."

"Wow," said Grant, stepping beside him and staring up at the screen. "We have to go there."

"Yes." Hoepe smiled.

"Agreed," said Rami.

"What?" Hoepe's good mood deflated instantly.

"It will be a perfect base for an ambush," Rami said to Grant, the other nodding happily.

"No." Hoepe clenched his fists by his sides. "We should use the planet to hide, so we can recuperate and finish our repairs."

"Hoepe, there are others out there who need our help. It isn't right what they did in Evangecore, and I'm telling you it's worse now than it ever was," said Grant. "I know we've already found your brother, but what if Leove was still out there? Would you want to play it safe and hide?"

Hoepe paused, flustered by the logic of Grant's statement. "I was unaware that I had a brother, let alone that he was being held on Junk until after his rescue," said Hoepe. But he had always had a hole he felt within him, a hole that had filled when he laid eyes on his identical other half. As though he understood exactly what Hoepe was thinking, Leove met his gaze with a quick quirk in the corners of his lips. Hoepe made an attempt to return the smile, although it felt awkward and unusual on his face.

"So? Think who else we could find." Grant slapped him on the arm, grinning. "Maybe you've got a sister."

Hoepe frowned, but he had to give the idea merit, it was possible if he had a brother he hadn't known about, he could have a sister he wasn't aware of either.

Leove chuckled once. "No, we don't have a sister."

"It doesn't matter," said Hoepe, blinking away his wandering thoughts. "It's not about whether we go to rescue them or not, but it's foolish to try to mount an operation with a ship that's barely holding together, let alone attack the Central Army's most powerful warship."

"What if the others can't afford to wait?" argued Grant.

Hoepe shook his head firmly. "We rushed into Junk and it was nearly a disaster."

"I don't want to run and hide," said Rami. "It's time to fight back."

"The ship is too weak," Hoepe tried. "We're one laz-cannon hit from being blown into space. Need I remind you that of everyone here, I am the only Augment who was never captured after the war? Jumping into things unprepared is what got us into trouble on Junk, and I'm guessing is what got you taken to Junk in the first place."

Grant stepped up to him, a growl escaping his lips to cover the slight dilation of veins in his face and the embarassed blush that followed.

Leove stepped between them. "Everyone wants to go to the planet, even if you disagree what to do when we are there. If Isuma"—he cast a fond gaze at the pilot—"sets a course, at least we can get away from Junk. There will be plenty of time for repairs and for us to decide on our next course of action."

Pressing his lips together, Hoepe begrudgingly accepted the compromise.

"No," a small voice called from the back of the room where she stood behind the Engineering console. Sarrin shifted nervously as all eyes turned to her. She still looked unwell, too thin and grey, but at least she was out of bed, at least she was here.

Grant stepped in her direction. "What, Sar?"

She shook her head, eyebrows knitting as though she was stringing together the words. Her gaze settled on the bridge doors. "Gal said no."

His heart sank, and Hoepe silently cursed Sarrin's unwavering belief in Gal, simply because—as Kieran had explained to him—Halud had chosen Gal's ship for a reason, and they couldn't give up on him.

"There must have been a reason he said no," she said, "for him to say it was dangerous." Her gaze dropped to the ground, and her chest heaved as she took a breath.

He was ready to say it didn't make any sense, that they needed to get to safety, but Leove said it first: "The captain is deranged. No one has set foot on this planet before, or else there would be a marker."

She shook her head sharply once, and Hoepe caught the tremor in her gesture, the strain in her hands. She was starting to slip.

Kieran interrupted quickly. "Gal worked for Exploration, he lead the team that mapped this sector. He knew what was on Junk. He probably knows this planet too, marked or not, and he doesn't want us to go. There has to be a reason."

Beside Hoepe, Rami scowled but kept quiet.

"With it's wide orbital path, it's possible it was not in this sector when Exploration was marking planets," said Leove.

"Then why did it seem he knew it?" argued Kieran. "The scans look good, I agree, but they can't tell us what's on the surface."

"If that cracked captain thinks there's a hidden facility or something on this planet that he doesn't want us to find, then that's more reason to go," argued Rami.

Sarrin fidgeted, her eyes fading in and out of focus. "He said not to."

"Besides," Kieran blurted, much too loud. He pressed his lips as he scared Sarrin, as though for confirmation. "That planet is at least a week away if our thrusters were at a hundred percent. As it is, we have enough thruster power for one big burst, the only way to carry us there at a reasonable speed."

Rami glared back at him. "And?" Hoepe too frowned, wondering at the significance of it.

Kieran scrubbed a hand over his eyes. "There's only power for *one* burst. What happens if the planet shifts trajectory? We don't know what it's orbiting around, we don't know where it's going. If we miss it, we're drifting through space— no FTL, no way to source parts, no food, no fresh O2."

"The warship will be back any day." Rami put a fist on his hip, face growing dark. His anger rolled across the bridge, the intensity of it surprising and causing Hoepe to take a half step away as though he was being pushed physically. "With their jump radius, it's three days to Etar and three days back: six days, and it's already been seven."

"I know." Kieran sat up stiffly, his jaw clenching.

Grant sighed heavily, throwing his head back so he stared up at the ceiling. "Fine. We won't go."

"What?" Rami snapped.

"I don't want to spin out into space, hoping to bump into something that is preferably not a UEC ship. If Kieran says we can't make it to the planet, then we shouldn't go until we know we can."

Rami pushed past Hoepe, right into Grant. "Are you kidding?"

Grant's jaw clenched. "No."

"I still say our odds are better trying for the planet than waiting here," Leove said, and Hoepe turned to him in surprise, trying to send a message with a brief shake of his head. If Sarrin—who could know things before they happened—said no, and Kieran—who could do things he had never seen anyone else do—agreed they couldn't go, then it was decided. They would wait and face the warship. But Leove met his eyes with a frown, and he shook his own head.

"We can't go," cried Hoepe. His heart thumped in his chest as he watched Leove's reaction and the disappointed that bloomed across his brothers face. They were brothers, twins, and while they were still getting to know each other, he'd never openly disagreed with him before.

"Why are we listening to this"—Rami gestured angrily at Kieran—"common?"

"Because he's the chief engineer," said Grant, exasperated, "and if he says the ship can't make it to the planet, I'm inclined to believe him."

"He's a common, and a UEC soldier. He had things he

wanted before all of this happened. For all we know, he wants the ship to stay here so the warship knows where to find us." Rami lurched forwards, advancing on the engineering console and the pale, green eyed engineer behind it.

Sarrin moved faster than Hoepe's eyes could track, appearing directly between Rami and Kieran, her pupils fully dilated, entire body coiled and prepared to fight. Hoepe reached a long arm to Rami's shoulder, pulling him back— Sarrin might be getting better, but seeing Kieran pull the auto-injector full of sedative from his pocket convinced Hoepe that he wasn't wrong; she was slipping, badly.

"If it weren't for Kieran, the warship would have finished us a long time ago. He's saved my life and yours," said Grant. "We listen to him because Sarrin says we can trust Kieran."

Rami blinked, his gaze fixed on Sarrin, curious.

"If Twenty-seven says for us to stay here, then that's what we'll do," called a tall Augment from the far side of the room —Thomas. He bowed his head, even as the Augments around him started to stir. "Sorry, Rami. There's repairs to do, and we're wasting time."

Rami only blinked as the Augments filed efficiently from the room.

Leove bit his lip, and Hoepe's heart pounded in his chest as he watched his brother uncertainly. But Leove merely put a hand on his shoulder as he moved past. "I'll see you in the infirmary, brother."

* * *

Grant felt a hand on his shoulder, stopping him as he went to follow the last of the Augments from the bridge. He turned to see Rami looking up at him.

"Was that really Twenty-seven?" he asked.

Grant shrugged staring at the floor, uncertain how much he could share. "Yeah, I guess. People have always called her that, but she doesn't like it."

"Why not?"

He shook his head to say he didn't know.

"I was there, you know, when it happened," said Rami, a reverence he hadn't seen from the Augment before shining through. "I saw her scale the wall and smash into the observation tower."

Grant had only heard about it, his squadron being in the classrooms during that particular war game. Sarrin had always been a good fighter, able to match him whenever they trained together during the war, no matter what they were doing, but he knew now she had held back. When she had lost control of herself sparring in the cargo bay, Grant had witnessed the sheer raw power she possessed. He could only imagine the scene in the observation tower.

"It was incredible. It inspired me," continued Rami. "Before, I felt powerless—my squadron leader always ordered me to guard the perimeter because I was the youngest and he didn't want me in the fighting. But when Twenty-seven scaled that tower, she showed me the power we had. Because of her, because of that day when she attacked, they never ran another war games again."

Grant frowned. "No, they found worse things."

But Rami was undeterred. "She, more than any of us, understood what the UECs were trying to teach us: fight is might. We have to attack first to survive."

He thought of Sarrin, thought of her haunted eyes as she fell into the trap on Junk, the devastation after she'd lost control in the cargo bay and attacked him, thought of her broken when they pulled her from the wrecked facility that she had destroyed single-handedly. "I don't think you've got it quite right, Rami. Sarrin isn't like that."

"She is though. We need someone like her to be bold and aggressive. That's the only way we're going to see our freedom, Grant."

In principle, he agreed. Grant had always known they would have to fight the UECs for their freedom, but he found himself stuck.

"She must be planning to attack the warship outright. We'll just sit here, the same as she did in that arena, and say, 'we're here, we're going to tear you into pieces'." Rami grinned, nearly vibrating in anticipation. "I can't wait, Grant. I'm excited. All we've ever wanted is to keep all of our friends safe, and she... she can do it."

Grant found his mouth hanging open and forced it closed. "Rami, I don't think...."

Rami slammed one fist into an open palm. "I'll see you down there. I'm going to find out what the plan is."

Stunned, Grant blinked twice. "Rami, wait." But the other Augment was already half-way to the door. He flung up an arm in a half-wave and exited the bridge, stomping after the others. And Grant stood dumbfounded in the centre of the deck.

* * *

Gal pressed through the sea of demons that crowded the hallway, tripping into the door. He slapped his hand over the biosensor, and in start later the door opened and he stumbled into his quarters. Aaron sat on the bed, waiting with his arms crossed.

"What?" Gal snapped. He stalked across the room, demons scattering out of his path, and reached into the cubby at the top of his closet where he kept his JinJiu. There was, of course, nothing—hadn't been for weeks—but it didn't stop him from hoping a stray bottle had rolled all the way to the back.

"Why not go?" Aaron shrugged his shoulders. "It's a beautiful planet, lush, serene, quiet. Everything you've ever wanted, right?"

Gal groaned, climbing up to scrape his fingers along the

back of the closet. "Go away."

"I can't. I'm with you, a demon, a memory trapped in your mind circling around and around. Forever."

There was nothing in the cubby. Gal's fingers probing each filthy, empty, grey corner. He jumped down, finding the mug on his nightstand. It was as empty as the closet, but he tipped it completely upside down, just in case. A drop of bitter tea rolled onto his tongue—a far substitute from his beloved JinJiu, but it at least mitigated the hallucinations.

He tossed the mug to the side. "The hallucinations are getting worse when Hoepe said they would get better. Why?"

Aaron shrugged again. "The answer's not the tea, Gal. You need to fix it."

"Fix what?"

"All of it."

He sighed, throwing up his hands. Real Aaron had never been this complicated.

Gal dropped onto the bed, legs unable to support him. "It's all happening again."

"What's happening?"

"Why was I ever so stupid?" He buried his face in his hands.

"I never thought you were stupid."

"Look what happened to you, you're dead."

"There are worse things."

"You thought I was going to protect you, but now you're dead."

Aaron sat down on the bed beside him, the apparition causing a subtle disturbance in the thin mattress. "Gal, who's Cornelius?"

Gal started, turning wide eyes onto his old friend.

"Don't be so surprised. I'm in your head." Aaron shrugged. "You've been practically screaming his name over and over again. I assume it's a person. A memory."

Gal groaned. He didn't want to remember. He'd managed to block it out all the years running freight in the Deep Black. He never should have visited the planet, never should have tried to make the deal, never should have tried to convince anyone it was good idea. Demons, he never should have even told the Speakers in the first place, just lied on his report and told them it was uninhabitable.

"Where did it all go wrong, Gal?" Aaron interrupted.

He closed his eyes. If only he knew, maybe he could fix it. But he'd been born stupid, and it seemed he was going to die stupid. He had three dozen Augments running around his ship for Gods'sakes.

Aaron sat patiently. "Tell me about the planet. I wasn't around for that one."

No, Aaron had been long dead. So had John P.

"Cornelius…." He gazed out his porthole at the dusty planet below. "The planet was gorgeous, green and blue, something the Artist Laureate would draw as a dream. But it wasn't what we thought. Then"—he doubled over, biting back a shout—"they attacked… he died!"

"Who?"

"Cornelius!"

"I'm sorry, Gal." Aaron reached a hand out. But it felt far away, Gal's memories dragging him under.

He was suddenly in the office of the First Speaker, his mind reconstructing it around him.

Gal stood alone, waiting. Hap Lansford—Speaker of Strength and the leader of the Five Speakers—entered through the single door. He walked the length of the wedge-shaped room, seeming to move slowly, intentionally highlighting each vivid scene in the gory mural painted on the long wall. A history of blood and death displayed proudly.

Gal forced himself to smile.

"Galiant, my old friend!" Hap greeted him, the same as he always did. "They tell me you've found something very special. Special enough

to meet me in person."

In his mind, he screamed for his younger self to stop, but the memory rolled on like a pre-recorded vid, and the words came tumbling out of his mouth.

Hap's reply echoed around him, even as the hallucination faded, and he was back in his dull, grey quarters: *"It's too dangerous."*

The chime sounded, tearing away the last of the memory. Gal jumped, pressing himself into the corner where bed met wall, pulling the thin blanket up to his chin.

The door buzzed again. "Gal!" the muffled call came through the thin plastic. A minute later, the door opened on its own as Rayne overrode the lock. She strode in, shoulders pulled up in a way that made her more imposing than most security officers and most Augments, but her expression softened instantly.

Gal pulled the blanket up over his head. Of course this wasn't normal behaviour, of course he was cracked, he knew it. But what could he do?

Across the room, Aaron shifted as he settled into the desk chair.

"Oh, Gal," Rayne breathed. The door closed, her feet padding gently across the floor, until the bed shifted with her weight. She adjusted his blanket, pulling to down so that he could see her face just in front of his. "Are you cold?"

He nodded; it was always cold in space. "I'm sorry," he mumbled.

"You're going to get better." She patted him on the leg. "This was just a set back, nothing we can't handle, okay."

Below, the grey planet rotated. Hap Lansford's voice echoed in his ear, *It's too dangerous.*

"The readings on this planet are perfect. I thought you would have been excited."

He refused to look at her. "I won't put us, I won't put you, in danger."

"We're already in danger."

He shook his head. "Not like this." Didn't she know some planets were habitable and some were not, and it was never easy to tell the difference?

Sighing, she stood, suddenly farther away from him, and his heart cried out. She busied herself by going to his closet and riffling in the top shelf. For a minute, he thought she was hunting for his JinJiu stash, about to dump it all into the waste receptacle, but she returned with another blanket.

Tears sprung into his eyes. "I'm sorry I've put you through all this. You don't deserve it."

She interrupted him, "Do you remember when we were on that planet in the Desousa system? What did they call it?"

"Yates," he answered instantly. He did smile once, a real smile. "I don't know where they come up with these names."

She laughed. A near perfect sound.

"Second planet from the orbital star, base temperature twenty-three-point-six centigrade. Oxygen thirty-five percent, Nitrogen thirty-six percent," he recalled.

"Sharp as ever," she smiled at him. "What happened to it?"

Aaron sat up in his chair, suddenly interested.

Gal looked away. He shouldn't have brought it up. The demon's watched him intently.

"It was so beautiful there, I thought for sure it would be the next colonized world," she said.

It had been perfect, with beautiful, giant flowers that glowed in the dark. He had taken Rayne to a lush grove, rich with transluminant plants and a view of the stars, late one night, when the colours were their brightest. He had held her hand as they laughed and talked together.

He forgot the danger of their conversation. Instead, he smiled, taking her hand as he did then. He reminded her teasingly, "You kissed me."

She raised an eyebrow, her face softening as it did then with a smile. "Yes, I did."

Aaron caught Gal with his eyes, waving his hand in the air, asking him to elaborate on the doomed story of Yates. Gal frowned and turned to stare out the porthole again.

"Gal, whatever is going on, I want you to tell me," she said, coming back to the bed and leaning forward. She took his hand in hers. "Even if it's more crazy, drug-induced hallucinations that don't make any sense. It can't be good to keep this all bottled up. Maybe I can help you figure out what's real and what isn't."

All of it was real. None of it was real. He shook his head, staring at the grey planet below to avoid looking at her.

"I followed you after the Earth was lost. I followed you on Exploration. I even followed you out here on this cracked freightship in the Deep Black." She gripped his hand harder.

He frowned. "Why?"

"Because I love you."

Everything he had ever hoped for, but it was wrong, terrible. He turned to stare at their intertwined hands. "Love me?" He threw her hand away. "You don't even know me." He rushed off the bed and stalked across the room, demons jumping as he passed.

Rayne's mouth hung open. "Of course I know you. We're going to get through this, Galiant. But you have to tell me what's going on."

He leapt back onto the bed, shuffling on his knees to the porthole, pressing his face into it. "It's too dangerous." He pulled Rayne roughly, forcing her to stare through the porthole with him. "Don't you see?"

"What? Junk?"

"Yes, Junk." But that wasn't right—Junk held secrets, yes, but those were the secrets of the Speakers. The new planet was something else entirely. "No," he said. He found Rayne again, pressing her hand to his almost hopefully. "What if there was something more?"

"More?" she frowned.

Desperate, he pulled on her arm tighter, so it couldn't slip away. Would she understand, could she understand? "More," he whispered. "They destroy them." But she didn't see, how could she? She was already slipping away. He stared out the porthole. "The planet is dead. All the planets are dead."

"What?"

There was no way to tell which planets were good and bad. "Yates. They bulldozed the entire thing." He leapt off the bed and started pacing again.

She blinked, swallowing heavily. Blinking again, she seemed to recover, or to forget. "You're confused. I'll bring some of your tea."

"I don't want tea!" he shouted, louder than he meant to. The world was spinning out of control around him. Demons shrieked. Cornelius. The planet. "They're going to destroy it. It's all happening again, again, again!" He clutched his head in his hands.

"Gal, I—"

"Get out."

"I don't understand," she squeaked. "What about the unmarked planet? We can talk about it."

"Out!" He pointed to the door. She didn't understand, and she wouldn't. It was too dangerous, she couldn't find out.

Rayne jumped, true terror across her stricken face. The room cast briefly in the light, and then darkness again as the door opened and shut coldly behind her fleeing frame.

Gal spun on his heel, nearly bumping into Aaron who had come up behind him. "What's got you so riled up, Galiant?" The demons had formed a weird audience, huddled together on the bed.

Gal pushed Aaron out of the way with a grunt.

"Come on." Aaron paced behind him with a dog-eared grin. "I'm your friend. If you can't tell your subconscious, who can you tell?"

"No one." Gal stared at the grey floor, revelling in the solid feel of it. But the floor changed, from grey threadbare carpet to brown cracked tile. He looked up. Impossibly, A barkeep stood behind a rough wooden bar. "What's happening?" he asked through gritted teeth.

"The stress is making you hallucinate," Aaron explained. He slid into a seat at the small, rough hewn table tucked into a dark corner, easily picking up a handful of cards and joining the cadets around him. "Do you remember this day?"

Gal stared. He'd lost all tack of the freightship and his room.

"Second term, first year at the Academy." Aaron pointed to his cadet uniform, as if he needed to remind Gal of the occasion. "We had been to Bo's Bar more times than we could count, but this time was different. You were different. We had just returned from leave, just come back from Indaer, hadn't even had a class yet."

"I don't want to see this," Gal said, stepping back.

"You forget that I've known you your entire life. You were late when we left Indaer, almost missed the transport. You'd never been late in your life."

"My shuttle crashed, I told you that."

Aaron smiled sadly and shook his head. "You were hours late, almost a full day. We had made plans to meet in town the night before, but you showed up as the transport was about to leave. The Gal I knew could fix a tractor with his eyes closed, a shuttle wouldn't have been that much harder. And besides, something had to have happened, otherwise what happened at Bo's never would have happened."

The memory played out like a 3D vid in front of him. *A younger version of himself played in the card game too, cards and chits and figurines strewn across the table. His friends laughed, sloshing their drinks.*

The lights in the room flickered, then went out for five seconds. When they came back on, the younger Gal was pressed up against the wall by a man in a dark mask, a laz-gun in his side. Young Gal stayed calm, talking quickly in hushed tones, and slowly, the revolutionary let him down, nodding in agreement.

"Why are you making me remember this?"

Aaron shrugged. "I'm not, but it must be important to you now." He was suddenly standing beside Gal. "We should have fought them off. That was our duty as UEC cadets. But you talked to them. You joined them. I joined you, and so did the others. We didn't know what was going on, not at all, but you seemed to. Seemed to know too well." Aaron cocked his head, staring into Gal's soul. "I died, Gal. Hermes and Andre and Coyne all died too. Something happened to you on Indaer. It changed you so that you saw things the rest of us couldn't see. It changed you then, it changed you with the Augments, and it changed whatever is happening with this planet."

"I never forced you to stay," he choked out. Gal had lead them all to their deaths without ever offering a true explanation, never the whole thing. He wasn't even sure he understood it. He had encouraged them to follow what they believed was right, but they put their faith in him and his subconscious still carried the guilt.

"This thing, it's happening again. I want to know what. We deserve to know what."

"You're right," he told Aaron. "Something did happen that day the shuttle crashed, something that changed everything I thought I knew. But I can't tell you. It isn't safe."

Aaron frowned, back in the grey room of the tiny

freightship. Demon's crowded around gleefully.

Gal whispered, "This is a secret too big."

"Bigger than all the others?"

"Yes."

Aaron blew out a breath. "You keep too many secrets, Gal. They're eating you up." The demons drew their long faces into frowns, fangs showing from the corners of their mouths.

Gal shook his head. He couldn't, he just couldn't. "You stayed with me all those years because you thought I was right. There's a reason they killed Cornelius. Why they destroyed the Augments, why they're paving over everything on Indaer. It isn't safe. I have to protect you, and Rayne, and everyone."

The demons backed away, somehow satisfied, if only temporarily.

"We can't let it happen again, over and over."

Aaron nodded, placing a firm hand on his shoulder. "And we won't."

Gal gripped his friends arm. "We have to keep them away from the planet."

"It's okay, Gal. We're not too late."

"Promise me!" he cried.

Aaron nodded, his expression drawn and tight with worry. "We'll do whatever it takes."

FOUR

"I'm not saying that I don't trust you, but I see no reason to avoid the planet," Leove said. "If I'm not mistaken, you wanted to go there initially. I don't understand the change of heart."

Hoepe wiped the elbow of his surgical gown across his forehead, rolling the tight muscles in his shoulders at the same time. "I'm not saying I understand the reasoning either, but I know these people and trust their judgement."

His brother stood on the opposite side of the table, monitoring the patient's vital signs. They had removed tracking chips from nearly all the rescued augments, and Hoepe's hands worked easily through the motions.

"You told me the captain suffers violent hallucinations."

"Suffered," corrected Hoepe. "He has recovered. Besides, I didn't mean the captain. I meant Sarrin." Hoepe gently pulled a one-centimetre-square chip from the patient's frontal lobe and passed it into a sterile dish that Leove held out. With a final glance at the display from the camera, he removed the laparoscope and began suturing. The procedure was finicky, but with the scope they could perform it with minimal invasiveness, making only a tiny hole in the cranium.

"Inactive," Leove commented as he studied the chip. They

had only found one active chip, and that was the one Sarrin had pulled out of her own skull. The rest were quiet. Still, it was worth the risk of the anaesthesia and surgery to be sure the warship couldn't track them with one again.

"Finished," announced Hoepe and he tied and cut the last suture.

Leove nodded, and pulled the syringe of injectable anaesthetic from the IV port. Inhalant anaesthetic would have been preferred, but their supplies were limited.

"I'll call the next one," said Hoepe.

Leove sighed. "I think that's enough for one day. We've done six already. And my back is starting to ache."

Twisting to stretch his ow body, Hoepe frowned. "I think we should do another. No sense waiting if we are able to do it now."

"Brother, I'm sorry, I don't think I can."

It was still strange to hear someone call him brother, and an unabashed smile crept up on Hoepe's face every time he heard the word. "Are you well? I would still like to examine you for injuries from your time on Junk."

Leove shook his head. "No need, I was merely incarcerated. But I am tired and do not see the need to push myself."

"The warship could return at any moment. Do you want to put off removing the one chip that might be active and lead them here?"

"The warship will likely not be surprised to find us here. But if we were to go elsewhere"— Leove quirked his eyebrows, surreptitiously mentioning the contentious planet —"it may be of increased importance."

The Augment on the table started to stir.

"I see your logic, but maintain my position." Hoepe pressed his lips together, praying he hadn't misjudged Sarrin, but she had never been wrong before.

Leove node curtly. "Then I will see you tomorrow. I have someone to meet for dinner." He check the monitors an turn away.

"I could join you," Hoepe blurted at his brother's retreating back. "Adequate nutrition is important to maintaining proper functioning of body and mind."

"I'm afraid it is a social call, if you know what I mean."

Hoepe frowned; he didn't. A meal was a biological necessity, he had never felt the need to seek out company for idle discourse. Not until his brother arrived, anyhow. "I'm sorry I disagreed with you earlier."

Leove's brown wrinkled in confusion, and he shook his head. "I said I would Isuma an hour ago. "I don't want it to come between us, Hoepe."

Hoepe frowned again—didn't want what to come between them? "Nothing could," he said, although his insides crumpled as his brother pulled further away. An intense feeling of otherness and separation welled up in him, the same as it had been growing for the last week.

"I am so pleased to have met you again." Leove stepped close, gripping Hoepe by the forearm. "We may have opinions that differ, but we're still brothers."

A pleased smile spread on Hoepe's face. But something caught his ear as it repeated in his mind. "Met again?"

"Of course. We were seven years old when we were taken. Surely you must remember."

He shook his head.

"Yes, of course you must." A confused look spread across Leove's features, mimicking Hoepe's own. "The ramshackle apartment, mother's root vegetable pies, father's favoured collection of leisure equipment neither of us had any interest in."

"Not at all," said Hoepe. He recalled only the white walls of Evangecore. He assumed he had been too young to remember anything else. "Seven?" he asked unbelievingly. He should have remembered something.

Leove's face fell in an almost unreadable manner. "Yes, seven."

"I don't remember at all," he admitted. "Do you… do you remember our parents, before they died?"

Leove's eyebrows knitted together in confusion. "Of course."

"How is that? I have no recollection of my life before we were taken to Evangecore. Not of you, not of our parents, our home, nothing."

"Oh." Leove looked away, focussing on the ground. He scratched a spot on his arm in a gesture that Hoepe recognized as avoidance of a difficult topic. "I suspect it was intentional."

Hoepe gasped, the words hitting him hard in the gut. "What?"

"Think. They had a facility full of orphan children on which they tested every parameter. They must have wanted to know what effect not having their parents would make on them. But everyone's brain biology is different, everyone is preprogrammed to react to challenge in a certain way. And then we showed up, twins with identical backgrounds, identical brains, identical bodies…. You must see the research opportunity they had."

Hoepe forced his hand to return to motion, wiping the surgical table.

"Martin and Laurie Fallows," said Leove tentatively. "They were kind people. Independent, so we never had much. They survived the fever for a time."

"Did you remember me?" Hoepe blurted.

"It was hazy. I couldn't be sure if it was memories of me or of someone else." He smiled a silly grin Hoepe was certain he had never made in his life. "Sounds spread now, doesn't it?

But we looked the same."

"So they let you remember our parents and me, while I forgot?"

"I'll tell you everything about them, if you'd like."

"You said they survived?"

"Yes, they were patients in the hospital," said Leove.

"You knew them?" Leove bit his lip, and Hoepe realized he was shouting. "I'm sorry," he said quickly, but a kernel of anger, foreign and uncharacteristic, flared. "How is it you had our parents, your memories, everything, while I was left with nothing?"

"I'm sorry, Hoepe. We'll talk about it later. I have to go."

Hoepe fought for breath as he watched the identical and so very different man stride across the room. They were nothing alike. He had been fool to ever think it. And the worst part was the hole that had always been inside of him, temporarily patched, ripped open wide than ever.

* * *

Sarrin side-stepped, arms wrapped tight to her sides, avoiding the jostling of dozens of Augments as they moved down the corridor. Skinny arms with heavy dark barcodes waved, deceptively strong. Blue eyes darted from one Augment to another, the corners crinkled instead of drawn, the light in them bright. There was chatter too—questions about the planet, about surviving the next few days, and even beyond. On top of their fear, their uncertainty and confusion, ran a different emotion: excitement, and above that, hope.

Big-letter, capital-letter-H Hope.

This was freedom, she realized. This was how they should live. And there was *Hope* that one day, they would.

Breathing deep, she crossed the threshold into Engineering. Others passed around her, but Sarrin paused. Kieran had briefed her on the damage, but there was no way to imagine the complete disarray of burned conduits, hanging wires, and ship components in various states of reconstruction.

It was too much, the monster dancing around, confused by the sounds and colours after so many days hiding. She longed to return to the safety of the room.

Someone tugged on her coveralls, the shock of the touch shooting up her arm, even through the heavy fabric. She pulled away, breathing heavily as she warily eyed Thomas. "You okay?" he asked. She blinked twice in response.

She'd known Thomas in the war, always appreciated his gentle yet firm nature. But more than anything, she appreciated the way he seemed to view her as a person no different from the rest, unlike the myriad of blue-eyed stares that descended on her now from around the engineering bay. Their curiosity tore into her, gazes carving pieces of her flesh for examination.

The monster clawed at the edges of her vision, and she darted away, leaving Thomas in the centre of the room. Head down, she made her way to the engine room, retreating as far as she could before she was stopped by the utter jumble of displaced engine parts and open floor panels.

Kieran had told her about the FTL too, about its melted wiring and the blackened conduits, the Kepheus Drive hanging free from its mount, the cracked screens and the broken pieces strewn across the floor, but nothing prepared her for the utter silence. The engine always hummed, sometimes out of tune when one of the thousands of parts was out of alignment, and it brought her comfort. But now, there was nothing.

She stared quietly, aware of his approaching footsteps and his still racing heart, even before Kieran cleared his throat to speak. "We'll fix it, hey." When she turned, a smile was on his face, but not a real one. The expression underneath was unreadable, emotions kept silently to himself, and she found herself studying him.

His bright eyes met hers, and her heart sped up. "I'm glad you're here. Thank you for staying."

She had tried to get away, to slip through a wall panel while everyone on the bridge argued, but Kieran had slammed the panel shut before she could disappear. Fear rolled off of him then, much as it did now, the angry emotions rolling around the bridge pushing her to the edge. Dark tendrils licked at the corner of her mind, and she turned her gaze to the engine.

"What was all that stuff about Twenty-seven?"

She blinked. The nickname had stuck for many years, but she hadn't realized the importance it seemed to hold for the Augments. After the day she attacked and killed twenty-seven guards, she became too dangerous to let loose, and she didn't see any of the others again until Evangecore had been bombed and they ran into the woods, war starting around them.

In the war, she learned that her clandestine leap into the observation station had grown entirely out of proportion, and the person who had done it became a legend, someone that kept them hopeful. They thought she could lead them to salvation, but she couldn't keep anyone safe, not even Halud. She was the most dangerous thing on the ship.

"I've heard them call you that before," Kieran tried carefully. "What does it mean?"

She shook her head, unwilling to bring back the memory. Kieran at least treated her like a normal human being, however naive it might be. Instead, she reached into her coverall pockets and removed a heavy spanner, a laz-gun, and a half-dozen knives she had collected from the canteen, holding them out.

Kieran stared at the tools in her hands, hanging in the space between them. Just as she started to fidget, deciding she had been wrong to reveal them and her dark habit of collecting weapons, he snorted. "O-kay." He took them from her, a bemused grin spreading across his face. "You don't happen to have a spare FTL in there, do you?"

She—whatever possessed her—pretended to search through the pockets, drawing her hands out to show they were empty, shaking her head apologetically.

Unexpected laughter burst from his lips, and her heart leapt. He used his thumb to wipe the corner of his eye. "I always thought you would be funny."

Her brow tightened in confusion, but her heart remained light, muscles on her face tightening in an unfamiliar pattern in an attempt to match his.

He dropped the knives in a haphazard pile by the door and came back to stand beside the long engine casing. "But, really, what are we gonna do with this?" He proceeded to list the status of each component, but Sarrin shut out her conscious recognition of his voice, instead stepping forward to put her hands to the silent beast. She lost herself in the feel of it, in the diagrams that drew themselves in her mind trying solution after solution.

Slowly, she became aware that Kieran had stopped speaking, and she looked to him, standing quietly in the corner, hands folded as he watched her.

"What are we gonna do, Sar?"

She pressed her lips together. The diagrams had failed to yield a solution for the engine.

"Are you sure it's a good idea to stay here? That planet seems awfully tempting. If its trajectory keeps coming this way, and if it's stable and not too unpredictable, I think we should go. We can fix the hull plating on the way and land on the surface—it'll make repairs easier."

Maybe it would be better. The readings had been ideal for all she knew about planetary exploration. It even had an oxygen-nitrogen atmosphere.

"I know what you said about Gal, but...." His hand

brushed over his face, pulling at the dark circles under his eyes. "I guess it's hard."

"I know." But they couldn't go to the planet, not if Gal said no. Halud trusted him. Gal was their best chance. She knew it as well as she knew anything, although it defied everything her logical brain shouted at her.

"The warship will come back," he said. "I don't know what the others are thinking, but there's no way to get the ship ready for that kind of fight. Even fully repaired, we wouldn't stand much chance. Our only option, I think, is to jump the second they show up. But that means we need a working FTL."

She nodded, casting her gaze once again over the long room of ruined parts, even though she had memorized and catalogued each burnt component the second she had walked into the room.

"I've been thinking about sourcing the energy for the gravity-generator from somewhere else in order to bypass the Kepheus Drive altogether. I just don't know where."

Her eyes closed, but the diagrams were blank. "The engine is the only way to get enough power to grav-jump."

His exhausted sigh rested heavy on her heart. "I know. I just don't think the Kepheus can take any more jumps, or repairs. It barely held together before."

"I'll see."

"Thanks."

She nodded confidently, even though she already knew it was impossible. Perhaps there would be a way to repair the drive or construct a new one, but gravity-jump drives were sophisticated pieces of equipment, each component specially designed and absolutely necessary for the ship to be able to bend space and travel instantaneously across galaxies.

"I'm going to go check on the others," he said, turning back into the main engineering bay.

Sarrin ran her hand across the engine again, intent on finding a solution. Only, she wasn't alone for long. A set of short, quick footfalls approached. "Twenty-seven?" The Augment, Rami, stood directly behind her. When she turned and met his gaze, it was intense and eager. "I came to talk about the warship, I want to help."

She blinked in surprise, an unintelligible sound escaping her mouth.

He pulled out a tablet, activating a set of diagrams. "I thought if we approach their ventral hull, the access to the hangars is there and would make an ideal docking port for the ship."

Blackness pulled at her, cutting away everything but the diagram. The monster raised itself up with glee. "What?" she managed, pushing through the darkness.

"You know," said Rami, "for when they return and we attack."

She shoved the monster down; even it knew attacking the warship was insane. "No."

"Okay." His voice shook, suddenly uncertain, and he flipped the tablet to a new diagram. "There's also the wings and the large thruster manifolds. The ion discharge disrupts the targeting sensors."

Her breath caught, the monster scheming, attack diagrams unfolding in her head.

"-Ello? Twenty-seven?" A hand flashed in front of her face. Startled she realized Rami still stood in front of her. "We're going to attack the warship, aren't we?" he asked.

She blinked, glancing at the door into the main bay. Is that what they thought? "No." It was suicide. The stack of knives caught her eye, her vision narrowing.

"But... but...," he stammered, pausing to frown at the floor. "You're Twenty-seven, aren't you?"

A loud drawl caught their attention from the door, friendly

enough although she caught the strain in it: "Hey, Rami."

Sarrin stumbled back, gasping as Rami's intense stare left her.

Kieran strode towards them, his jaw clenched but smile firmly in place. "Whaddya got for me?" He reached for the tablet.

Rami yanked it out of his grasp, turning back to Sarrin. "Surely, the weakness in the communications array?"

She shook her head, staring at the floor. The warship had no weaknesses, it was a perfect system. "We're not going to attack."

"What do you mean?" Rami snapped. "We have to to find the others. There must be a way."

The monster took her away again, reminding her she was wrong. The warship did have a weakness—one she had painted in once she realized what the UEC researchers were having her construct. Its multiphasic shields kept all energy-weapons at bay. It's reinforced duranium hull made physical weapons all but useless. But the gravity jump drive was the largest the Central Army had ever built. That made it the most vulnerable, the delicate resonance grids unstable. A pulse of the right frequency would disrupt the plasma stream and tear the warship end-to-end.

They wouldn't even have to get close.

The exploding ship would have enough time to sense the disruption and jettison the computer core. All they would have to do was retrieve it and they would have access to all the information the warship carried: information about other Augments, information about Halud.

She turned to Kieran, catching his eye. He met her with a single eyebrow raised, his head tilted to the side—he could already see she had a plan. "Harmonics," she said.

His brow wrinkled together. "We would need to know the frequency."

"We do," she assured him.   She had designed the gravity drive too.

One eyebrow raised again in curiosity, but he accepted the fact without her having to explain. "And the generator?"

"Electro-pulse," she said.   "Simple."   An effectively tuned electro-torpedo would do, it wouldn't even have to penetrate their shields—better actually if the frequency was absorbed by the shield to vibrate all around the ship.   Easy then: she would build a weapon.   To rip the warship apart.   To kill everyone on board.

"What's going on?" Rami's eyes darted between them.

Kieran ignored the Augment, catching her eye again, his expression drawn. "Do you really want to?"

"What are you saying?" Rami demanded. "Are we going to attack or not?"   He reached out in frustration, his hand landing on her arm, energy searing her flesh.

The monster flared to life—Rami's grip overwhelming her, cold darkness pouring from where his skin met hers.   Her vision blocked completely.   An unknowable time later, the hand left her, and she stumbled back, crashing into the engine casing.

Rami shouted, "Hey!"   He glared at Kieran, pulling his arm from the engineer's grasp.

"Don't touch her," Kieran said.

"What?" spat Rami.   "Don't touch me.   What's wrong with you?"

"Look"—Kieran held up a hand, the other in his coveralls pocket, tracing the auto-syringe—"trust me on this one. Just don't touch her. You don't know what you're dealing with."

Rami thrust a finger at Sarrin without looking, his glare pushed right into Kieran's face.   "That's Twenty-seven, I know exactly who she is."

Sarrin blinked, making herself as small as possible.

"Come on, Rami," Kieran said quietly.   "Maybe she's not

who you think."

For a minute, Rami relented, his shoulders came down and his features softened. He looked at Sarrin, blue eyes soft, filled with unfettered adoration.

Her own eyes went wide, and she pressed into the engine casing at her back. Rami looked at the same way Halud did: full of hope, full of expectations she could never meet.

Kieran reached a hand between them, taking Rami by the shoulder and starting to turn him to the door.

But instead of going, Rami scowled, his brow hooding darkly over the lines around his eyes. He looked between Kieran and Sarrin, and she could nearly feel the turbulent thoughts that wheeled around his head. His arm came up fast, pushing Kieran so he stumbled across the floor, landing on his back. Rami turned to Sarrin, his heaving chest and an accusing finger still pointed at Sarrin. "No, I know you. We have to attack first. What's going on?"

Sarrin clenched her eyes shut, squirming away. Her heart beat too fast. Even the monster didn't have an escape from these expectations.

"Twenty-seven?"

Kieran stood, she felt him as much as saw him stalking towards Rami, outmatched but it had never deterred him before. The monster flared to life, suddenly seeing a threat it could handle, calculating the precision it would need to eliminate Rami while minimizing damage to Kieran.

Grant appeared in the door, changing the entire scenario and interrupting the movement diagram the monster outlined in her head. "I heard shouting," he said. "Everything okay?"

Rami tensed, anger boiling inside of him and crashing across the room. "Something's not right here." The monster flared, still on high alert. Muscles coiled, preparing to strike.

Grant scanned the scene quickly. "Come on, Rami." He kept his voice light despite the darkness in his eyes. "Let's go check on the thrusters."

"No, this isn't you." Rami stepped even closer, so he was standing toe-to-toe with Sarrin, and she flattened herself as much as possible, squeezing her eyes shut even as the monster whispered to her. "Why are you being like this?"

Grant wrapped an arm around Rami, forcibly pulling him away. "Don't be a fool." He cast a wary glance at Sarrin.

Rami snarled, but he let Grant pull him to the door, glancing over his shoulder. "That is Twenty-seven, right? That filthy common is doing something to her!"

The dark tendrils retreated as Grant and Rami disappeared into the main engineering bay. She found she was holding a length of broken plas-steel and dropped it to the floor. Her hands uncurled, bloody where fingernails had dug into unfeeling palms.

"You okay?" Kieran asked. He glanced behind him at the empty doorway. "What was that?"

She blinked furiously, pushing back the last of the black fog. "He wanted me to attack the warship. He thought we could win in a direct fight."

"And could you?"

Maybe. Probably. *Definitely yes*, the monster whispered. She shrugged in response to Kieran's question.

"But that's what you agreed to do. To destroy it by overloading their gravity drive. Right?"

Slowly she nodded.

He bent down in front of her, not touching but close, his green eyes staring up at her intently. "Sarrin, are you sure you want to do that?"

She looked away. It was brutal. Of course it was. But she knew how to kill, not save. In Evangecore, the children cheered because she had killed twenty-seven guards the day she launched herself into the observation tower. That killing had brought them hope.

Maybe destroying the warship would bring them hope. Maybe she could do some good. It oddly brought her hope. "The warship will have information about Halud."

"Oh."

"And the other Augments."

He frowned. "We already collected a database from the Comrade."

She shook her head, recalling the dark, feverish eternity she spent sneaking aboard the warship with Halud, the strange and familiar presence aboard. She had been too wrecked to notice it at the time, but the database they had collected had transferred too quickly, abnormally small. "That was the database they wanted us to find. This will be everything, even what's meant only for the Speakers'."

He gulped audibly, but he nodded anyway. "I'll help you however I can."

FIVE

Halud climbed the familiar stairs through the familiar halls. He had lived in the Gods' compounds since he was a teenager, since Hap had risen to First Speaker and named him as his Poet. Graceful paintings lined the walls—the work of the Artist Laureate—and gentle music tinkled in the background—from the Musician Laureate.

The only unfamiliar thing was the armed escort and the laz-rifle that continually poked him in the back.

This was his home, and had been since they evacuated Earth and built the new compound four years ago. At the top of it were the offices of the Five Speakers—direct descendent of the Gods who had lived among them millennia ago, and who took the mantle of leading the folk. The First Speaker—the leader—was Hap Lansford, the descendant of Strength. He was the youngest, the same age as Halud, in his early thirties. The others had nominated him First Speaker when he ascended after his father's death. They had wanted him to be First because the ongoing war needed the power of Strength most.

There were four others: Faith, Knowledge, Fortitude, and Prudence.

The Dome was the only floor above the Speakers' offices.

It was perfectly round, a complete glass hemisphere designed to give the Speakers full view of the heavens and of the folk. They were the only ones allowed in the Dome, the place where they could be almost at one with the Gods.

Halud's old office sat below the Speakers' along with the other Laureates. The guards pushed him past it unceremoniously.

The receptionist, Joyce, smiled brightly, looking up from her overly large console. "Hello, Halud. It's good to see you again. You look refreshed."

Halud frowned, his steps faltering. He had been gone for weeks, surely everyone knew what he had done.

"How was your holiday?" she asked sweetly.

Why would she think he had been on holiday? He had defied the Gods, only death was certain in his future.

The guard stepped in front, obscuring Halud's view of the receptionist. "Ma'am, he has a meeting with Speaker Lansford."

"Oh, yes! I did see that." She checked the appointment block on her console. "Go right in then, he's expecting you." She smiled again.

The guards pushed him forward, up the round staircase to the circular landing. Five doors lined the walls, each equally spaced, marked only with a symbol specific to the Gods they represented.

Memory moved Halud's feet to Hap Lansford's door, his hand sliding easily over the familiar handle. The office was unlocked. Halud gave his customary knock, as he had hundreds of times before, and stepped in without waiting for an answer. The guard shut the door behind him.

The walls were decorated—one featuring a full-length mural depicting the victories of Strength, the opposite hosting trophies of unrecognizable creatures, perhaps once real, perhaps mythical. Over the door was a staff, a six-foot long steel club that was said to have belonged to the God himself when he walked the Earth with men. It weighed over one-hundred kilos and Hap had lifted it only once when he had been inaugurated to his role of Speaker. The desk was a dark mahogany—also an ancient artefact, the wood long extinct—riskily saved from the imploding Earth. Halud took a seat in one of the plush chairs, and waited for Hap to turn from the window and face him.

The tall wing-backed chair swivelled finally, and in it sat a large, powerful man. His shoulders were broad, the cording on his neck belying their strength, but the years sitting behind a desk had made him soft, fat enough that he was almost perfectly round, his hair thinning and his eyes small and darting. "Halud," the Speaker greeted him.

Halud braced for the worst. He had faced the First Speaker many times before from this chair, taken dictations and collaborated on newsfeeds for the folk. But Halud had defected and shown his true colours, and that made this meeting very different from all the rest.

"How was your holiday?" Hap said, mirroring the receptionist.

Halud blinked. "W-What?"

"I hope you had a lovely visit with your family." Hap smiled pleasantly.

Heart suddenly pounding in his chest, Halud glanced at the door—the only exit from the office—and found it still firmly closed, guards, no doubt, waiting beyond. He was alone with the Speaker of Strength.

The mask slipped from Hap's face, cold voice cutting like laz-fire: "I trust it was enlightening."

Halud gulped, sinking down, instinctively trying to disappear.

"You see," Hap said, rising from his chair and moving in front of Halud, leaning over him, "I saw that you were struggling with your faith in the Power of the Gods. You were unfocussed, unemphatic in your writings. Sometimes, it even seemed as though you intended to say something else, something more than what was written." The warmth of his breath soaked Halud's face, his entire body stiffening. "Imagine my surprise when I discovered Augment 005478F had the same surname as you. Imagine when I discovered you were an orphan, with no records before you were twelve. Imagine when I left Sarrin DeGazo's file on the computer for you to find, and you took it within minutes."

Halud swallowed with difficulty, the lump in his throat refusing to move.

"I looked after you, Halud. I took you under my wing when we were at the Academy together. I even made you my Poet. And now you've gone and done a stupid thing like this."

Halud gritted his teeth. "I only befriended you to find her." He never would have said something so brash, but what did it matter now? His life was forfeit, he knew it the minute he arranged passage on Gal's ship.

Pathetic, bumbling, drunk Gal.

And Sarrin—was she even safe? Had he managed to change anything at all?

"Look where it's gotten you: your friends are dead, the freightship destroyed. And you fled in your little shuttle only to find yourself standing in these offices once more. Everything has come full circle."

Halud gripped the arms of his chair, tearing into the soft plastic fabric. It wasn't true, he was no pawn. He'd risked everything to save Sarrin. "There were Augments on that ship," he spat at Hap. "They were left alive, which means you wanted them for something. And now you've killed them all."

Hap laughed sharply. "Yes, and good riddance." He turned, facing a particularly gruesome scene on the mural: Strength swung his long club against a pack of grey, shaggy creatures, their blood flowing freely like rivers across the ground. "The Gods are powerful, Halud. I hope your *holiday* will serve as an eternal reminder. We have your sister, and now, the researchers will find out just how powerful she is."

Anger flashed before Halud's eyes, bathing the room in white, hot light. He thought of Sarrin, broken and ragged. He thought of Kieran and Hoepe, dead on the moon. Already he felt weak, but Hap was unrelenting.

"Unfortunately, you have become the face that the folk trust. And I hope now that you have seen the error of your ways, your behaviour will fall into line."

Halud paused. Could it be that after all he had done, they wanted him to continue to write? That they needed him? "I could have been lost on that ship too. What would you have done then?"

Hap crossed his fat arms. "But you weren't. You're quite predictable, Halud, and the Gods know what you will do, long before you do it. Like finding Sarrin's file and travelling on Gal's ship, you will do this too."

"Why would I ever? I despise you. I despise what you've done to her."

Hap turned again, sharply, viciously grabbing the edges of Halud's chair, pinning him in place. "You will do this. You will cower in your apartments, and you will write the words of the Gods—as I ask you to and nothing more and nothing less. You will smile for the feeds and you will pray to the Gods for forgiveness. You will do all this because we have your sister, and this is the only way you can keep her safe."

Hap grabbed a tablet from his desk and shoved it in Halud's face. There, in a high-definition video, was Sarrin, held up by her arms, screaming. Her face contorted, she was barely recognizable. Halud recoiled, heart pounding, but it was impossible to tear his eyes away as she writhed and cried. The girl looked barely human.

The clip finished, and Hap took it away. Halud eyed him warily, bile burning in the back of his throat. "How can you call that safe?"

"If you do as I say, we won't hurt her anymore."

"That video means nothing," Halud said. "It must be a week old, they could have killed her by now." Thankfully, the words came out sounding much stronger than he felt. "How do I know she's still alive?"

Hap glared. He sat on the desk directly in front of Halud, leaning forward into his face. "This is nothing. She can survive like this for weeks." He showed him the tablet again, frozen on a scene of Sarrin screaming, blood trickling from the corners of her eyes and ears. He growled, "The warship will return to Junk, and I need to know what orders to send with it—her fate is your decision."

"You'll kill her."

Hap curled his lip into a menacing grin. "You don't know the first thing about your sister, do you?"

Halud frowned. Of course he knew his sister—didn't he? But the thing in the video barely resembled the girl he knew.

"When you stumbled so cleverly on her file, did you even bother to read past the first page? All you cared about was where to find her, never mind what sort of thing you would find."

Halud felt as though he was falling back through his chair. He hadn't. Hadn't wanted to know. "It doesn't matter."

"The doctor is just getting warmed up," snarled Hap. "Her body can withstand much, much more." The man leaned back, smugly. "Her mind is a different story. I'm told it will break long before the body does, and then she will be exactly what we need."

Halud's heart hammered around in his chest and breath refused to come. He tried to close his ears to the screams of his sister, his baby sister whom he had promised to always take care of. "What are you going to do to her?"

Hap shrugged. He activated the video again, her screams echoing until it seemed as though they were coming from the walls themselves. From the rivers of blood on the mural, from Strength himself.

Halud pressed his hands to his ears, but the screaming was in his own mind. Finally, he shouted out, panting. "If I do as you say, you won't hurt her?"

A cold smile told Halud he had nowhere to go. "That depends how well you play your part."

* * *

Commandant Amelia Mallor scowled as the traitorous Poet was brought out of Hap Lansford's office, shaken and pale, an entourage of guards escorting him down the circular staircase she had just ascended. Surrounded by her own entourage of crewmen, she waited until the summons came from within, and she entered the office alone.

Reaching the middle of the room, she snapped to attention. The full council had assembled in the minutes before her arrival: all Five Speakers and each of their generals. They watched her closely, eyes wide and wary. It was not unusual, her height and ferocity often made people nervous, a fact she frequently took pride in. But today, she felt the coldness of their glares, and she attempted to slouch and soften her appearance.

Hap Lansford asked for her report, and she saluted, five fingers pressing into the spot above her heart. "Augment 005478F has been successfully captured. The subject is being held on the planet Junk. The doctor, Guitteriez, remains to continue his study."

"And the others?" Lansford asked.

She paused, tongue pressed to the tip of her teeth. "Believed dead."

"Believed, Commandant?" Hap Lansford rubbed his belly

in displeasure, sending a frown over his shoulder to his general, Oleander Nairu.

A moment of uncertain emotion caught her by surprise, necessitating she clear her throat prior to continuing. "They escaped to the freightship, Ishash'tor." An unfamiliar empty pit opened in her chest, and she sucked in breath. "After engaging in a firefight, the freightship entered the debris ring around Junk. Their course was obscured by the debris and they lost control, crash landing on the seventh moon. Our readings showed they were travelling at over one-hundred-thousand kph. The entire crew is presumed dead on impact."

"Were there life signs?" General Nairu asked. Something in his expression caught her attention: his face sat in its usual stone, but the general's eyes had clouded, intensity shifting to vulnerability.

Hap turned a scolding eye on him.

She answered his question anyhow: "The moon had a powerful magnetic field which baffled the sensors."

Nairu—that had been the name of the pathetic commander of the Ishash'tor who had tried to surrender. Her features were similar enough to the general's.

Hap frowned again. "So, you did not confirm their death. I am disappointed, Commandant."

She bowed her head. Her heart hammered in her chest, another unusual sensation. "It was not possible to bring the warship through the debris field without almost certainly suffering crippling damage." She heard her own voice shake —impossible—what was happening to her? "My orders were to return the Poet to you as soon as possible. To perform a gravity-well jump or use thruster power to travel to the far side of the planet and examine the moon would have taken an additional day. Given the extreme odds against their survival and your stated urgency, I elected to return despite the uncertainty."

General Nairu hit his fists on his thighs in an uncharacteristic display.   His eyes gleamed, deep brown surrounded by red.

"Oleander," chided the First Speaker.

The general grunted.

Amelia dropped her head again, as was proper. She stared at the ground and sucked in air that felt harder and harder to obtain. She felt the laser-glares of the Speakers and generals fall on the back of her neck.

The grey carpet swam, morphing into bright white—a ceiling in place of the floor. A face loomed overtop, a surgical cap and mask. Her heart raced.

"Commandant?"

She gasped. It was not the first time her mind had played a trick, showing her things that weren't there, but it was unnerving all the same.

"I am sorry for your loss," she said to the general, blurting it out before she could think. Almost certainly, his daughter had been lost aboard the freightship. The ship her vessel had hunted and caused to lose control.   Nearly three dozen Augments had been held at Junk and escaped, only to be killed. That she had killed.

A strange emotion welled within her making her feel small and regretful. She had killed the general's daughter.

But she had killed hundreds before.

These thoughts were not her own. Something was missing in her mind. A wall, a support, something, and her neurons wheeled to get around it.   There was something more, something she couldn't see.

"Commandant!" the First Speaker snapped. Behind him the other Speakers shared worried glances. Hap stared at her, fists clenched by his sides.   "You will return to Junk to examine the moon."

A question fell from her lips before it even registered in her mind: "Sarrin. What will happen to her?"

The Speakers leaned back in their chairs, pushing as far from her as possible.

Sarrin—that was the girls name. A girl with long tangled hair and a sad smile.

How did she know that?

The Speakers all turned to face the First, their faces tight, accusing. "What's going on?"

Hap shook his head once, dismissing them as he addressed her. "The Augment is no concern of yours," he snapped. "Return to Junk, examine the moon and ensure everyone on the freightship is dead. The Augments are dangerous."

"Yes, of course."

"Strength," the other Speakers demanded his attention, and Hap spun to face them. "How does she know the Augment's name? Is this not concerning?"

"The doctor has assured me everything is fine."

Amelia nodded in agreement. She had been to see Dr. Davidson just prior to her appearance here. Her hand reached to the fresh sutures that lined her temple, the vile chip that connected her to the Augment 005478F removed successfully.

"Guitteriez reported a stronger connection that expected with the frontal lobe implant," said one of the Speakers.

"Dr. Davidson has worked extensively with Dr. Guitteriez on this project and assures that any residual effects will wear off shortly," Hap replied.

Amelia nodded once again. Memory bleed, Guitteriez had called it, when the visions of a dark medical lab had woken her in the night—005478F's memories. Fascinating, he had said.

She must still be experiencing the girl's memories.

"Is there a risk she's starting to revert? To remember more?" asked one of the Speakers.

What more could there be—the memory bleed was temporary—everything else in her life she remembered perfectly.

"No. I am assured. Likely Guitteriez used the name and she learned it there."

But she could not remember a time when the doctor had called the girl by anything other than her assigned identification.

Hap turned. "Commandant, you have your orders."

"Yes." She saluted with her five fingers pressed to her chest. Augments still roamed the stars. She would not rest until they had all been destroyed and the rest of humanity was safe once again.

"Your ship awaits." Hap held out a black data tablet. "Please pass this directly to Dr. Guitteriez."

"What is it?" she asked instead of taking it, the question, as before, slipping out unbidden.

He glared. "It is not for your knowledge."

She ducked her head submissively, an unfamiliar flush warming her cheeks.

"Do not disappoint me," he said, thrusting the tablet towards her again.

In an instant, she felt as though she was strapped down, in a place far away. A dark hand passed a black tablet over her prone body. Luis Guitteriez's crooked, scarred face swam in the darkness.

A scar Sarrin had put there—005478F had put there.

How did she know that?

The same way she knew Hap's had been the gloved hand.

She took the tablet, and raised herself to her full height, standing inches above him. She stared into his eyes. An intensity of anger that was not her own flared full force.

Beneath her, Hap Lansford, First Speaker and the Voice of Strength, caught his breath as he cowered.

Then, she came back to herself, and strode from the room without a word. There were deaths to confirm.

SIX

Kieran tapped on one of the consoles in the engine room. Behind him, Sarrin crawled through the long access tube running through the centre of the gravity drive, exploring the engine for salvageable parts—both to fix the ship and for her weapon to destroy the warship. Engineering was quiet, a crew sent to Junk to search for supplies, and the rest on a night cycle. Only a few Augments puttered around the main bay.

He fingered the memory chip in his pocket, double checking the engine room was clear, then took a chance and dug into the computer's programming. A quiet subroutine he had installed automatically recorded the ship's data. There was too much happening for him to write a simple report to send back to the Observer ship; he would collect the data and then go through it when he was home, safe.

And with a copy of the warship's database too—a grin spread across his face. The subroutine activated, lines of data flashing by too quickly to read.

Heavy footsteps echoed on the engine room floor, and he slipped the chip back into its hiding place at the same time as he cleared the computer screen. Rami grabbed him by the shoulder and spun him around, Kieran falling back against the wall. "I want to talk to you."

"What?" he snapped reflexively, pushing Rami's hands away. "There's easier ways. You don't hafta grab me."

Rami crossed his arms, and Kieran braced himself. Normally, he could slip on an easy grin and turn people into friends, but Rami had resisted all attempts for the last week. "I came to apologize."

"Really?"

Rami sighed heavily. "Grant's a good friend, and he hates commons almost as much as I do."

Kieran balked, but he pressed his lips together and tried to seem relaxed.

"He says I was wrong. So I'm apologizing for what I said about you on the bridge, and for what happened earlier."

Kieran blinked in surprise, realized his slack jaw was flapping open. "Yeah, I appreciate that." Regaining his composure, he stretched out a hand, clasping Rami's in his own. "I'm lookin' forward to workin' with ya."

Hesitantly, Rami pulled him in closer, initiating, however reluctantly, an Augment greeting.

Kieran shut his eyes, allowing himself to relax. Without Rami causing trouble, he could breathe a little easier. There was still the overwhelming amount of repairs and the constant threat of the warship, but at least he wouldn't have to worry about Rami interrupting the repairs.

"What's that?" Rami suddenly stiffened, pushing Kieran away and brushing past him. To the console.

Too late, Kieran realized the subroutine had not shut down entirely, a prompt screen still flashing on the display. He slapped his hand out to stop it.

Rami glared, voice laced with ice. "What was that?"

Kieran gulped. "Repairs."

"You were in the programming."

"Yes, I'm the chief engineer. We have to reprogram the

ship to work with all the modifications."

Rami's fingers reached across the screen, digging through the programming. Fortunately, the code was hidden deep enough that it was impossible to get to unless you knew exactly where to go, but Rami was sharp enough to know Kieran wasn't doing program modifications, and angry enough to keep looking.

Cold sweat dripped down his back.

The secret of the Observers, of Kieran's home, had been kept for thousands of years. A select few people over the millennia had found out. He had told Sarrin. But no one had ever let themselves be caught.

"It's encoded," Rami spat at Kieran. "Why? What were you really doing?"

His pulse raced, thready and too fast—what a sloppy mistake. Too many stims and not had enough sleep. He shook his head like he didn't understand why it would be difficult to access, secretly glad the Augment hadn't been able to deeper into his subroutine or all the data he had collected. "I told you, programming modifications."

"It doesn't look that way." Rami's lip curled up in a sneer. "I didn't really know what to think when I said all that stuff on the bridge about you and the warship. I almost let the others convince me to give you a chance. But you're actually a spy. A cracked, filthy UEC spy." It happened too quick for Kieran to see, but Rami had him pinned against the wall, feet in the air. "When is the warship coming? How much time do we have?"

Kieran clawed at the hand that was around his neck. "I don't know. I'm no spy."

Rami slammed him into the wall, his head pouncing off the grey panelling so hard his vision blacked out. "I don't trust your repairs for one minute," spat Rami. "You're asking us to wire energy convertors backwards…."

A tick went off, Kieran's entire cheek twitching. "To help the ship run better!" He clenched his fist, driving nails into the flesh of his palm. "We've been through the calculations. Those modifications bring our efficiency up three-hundred per cent. Without them, we can barely power life support."

"You're asking us to rig explosives for you, and we won't do it any more."

"They won't blow if you wire them right!" Kieran pushed Rami away, suddenly aware they had an audience. In the doorway to the engine room, a half-dozen Augments had gathered, spilling in and lining the walls.

Grant wrapped a hand around Rami's arm and pushed him to the other side of the engine room. "Stop it!"

Kieran dropped to the ground, a hand coming up to his bruised throat.

Sarrin, having come out of the engine, stood by the access hatch. She gripped the hatch, her fingers curling the metal around her hand.

Oh no. Kieran blanched, he recognized the distant, swimming look of her eyes.

Rami slipped past Grant, driving the heel of his hand into Kieran's thigh, and Kieran slumped to the ground, eyes watering.

Sarrin gulped, her breathing heavy. Her expression shifted, one instant slack with panic, the next her lip curling up in a sneer. She grunted, shifting back with effort. She was fighting it, but she was slipping.

"Stop!" Kieran held up a hand.

Rami growled again. Sarrin let out a matching growl.

"Jesus," he muttered, helpless as Sarrin balanced on the edge of a trance—not because she was in danger, but because he was.

"What?"

"Rami, I'm trying to help you, I swear. You have to calm

down. You don't know what she can—"

Grant rushed forward, catching Rami as he pulled back to strike Kieran once more.

Sarrin ripped the hatch from the engine block, the metal screeching. Grant and Rami turned at the same time.

"Sarrin!" Kieran leapt to his feet, ducking as the hatch flew across the room with enough force to knock Rami aside and then stick into the wall.

"What in the Deep?" Rami yelled.

Her eyes darted, meeting Kieran's for an instant before she turned and fled, jumping over the engine and disappearing into the walls through an open panel.

Rami lifted himself up, lunging after her. His hand nearly wrapped around her foot as it slid into the wall, but Kieran tackled his arm. "Don't!"

"Get off me," Rami shouted.

"You don't know what you're doing. You have to stop."

"What is going on with this ship?" Rami grunted, turning to Grant. "You expect me to believe she's Twenty-seven? That girl is cracked. She ripped that hatch apart and threw it as us." He lifted his arm, examining the bleeding gouge across the side of his bicep. "And you." He stormed towards Kieran.

"Are you insane?" Grant shouted, putting himself directly in Rami's path. "You can't upset her like that."

"Upset her? We're talking about a traitor, a UEC soldier."

Kieran climbed to his feet, his body suddenly far heavier than it had been moments ago. At least Sarrin had gotten away.

"Was that or was that not Twenty-seven?"

"Yeah," said Grant, "but she's not like they say in the stories, okay."

Rami threw up his hands. "This is unbelievable. First, she doesn't want to attack the warship, and now"— he gestured vaguely to the place where she'd disappeared—"whatever that was." He put his hand to his head as though he was feeling faint, but he charged around the small room, strong as ever. "You. Now Twenty-seven. Can't anybody else see it?

"See what?" Grant held his hands on his hips, making himself look solid and broad.

"That's not Twenty-seven, Grant. That's not the girl who knows that fight is might, or that we need to attack first to survive. That's some shell. The engineer's done something to her. The same as he's done something to you and everyone else."

Kieran shrank back, uncertain of what exactly he was being accused of this time.

"Remember what the UECs did to us in the war?" Rami shouted at the Augments in the doorway. "Well, there's a UEC soldier in front of us right now."

"Rami," Grant shouted, but Rami didn't flinch. His glare fixed on Kieran, dark blue eyes menacing.

"We're on the same side," Kieran said carefully.

Rami jabbed an accusing finger into Kieran's chest, hard. "UEC," he spat, then he pointed at himself. "Augment."

"The Army wants us to be enemies, but we don't have to be."

"Once a soldier, always a soldier."

"I'm not a soldier."

"You sure look like one." Rami took a menacing step towards him. "Where were you when we were fighting the war—curled up safe at your mission headquarters?"

Actually, he was a million lightyears away, travelling at nine-tenths the speed of light, circling around a massive black hole to slingshot for another return pass through this galaxy. But Rami didn't want to hear that, couldn't hear that.

"Look, I'm just coordinating the efforts here, because this is my boat." He said, hoping to calm the situation, his back already pressed against the wall. "I know this ship best and how to get her functional again."

"No, I know your game. Stalling us. You'll do anything to keep us here, served up for your precious warship."

"That's not —," Kieran tried.

Rami turned on him. "I've seen your mods, dangerous inversions and haphazard wiring. I know you're rewriting the programming and you're turning all the energy convertors into bombs, but I don't know for what."

Kieran took a deep breath. "I am trying to help you. We need to rewrite the programming to compensate for all the modifications—even the thrusters aren't balanced." He saw the Augments gesturing back and forth, considering him, but their postures were relaxed, unlike Rami's. "This is my ship, I've gotten us all this far. No one else seems to have a problem trusting me, so why do you?"

Rami growled. A real growl that came from the depths of his throat. "I thought the biggest danger we faced was out there, but I was wrong, it's right here."

Kieran's heart crashed around in his chest painfully, but he didn't dare take his eyes off Rami. The Augment was unpredictable. No wonder Sarrin had nearly slipped. He hoped she was okay in the walls wherever she had gone.

"Come on," Grant tried to pull Rami away, but this time Rami resisted.

"We're at war."

"The war is over," said Kieran. "Right now, the UECs think we're all dead, they don't know there's anything to fight. Let's not start the war before the warship even comes back."

Rami blinked incredulously. "I'm done with this. It's time we instigated the Rule of War."

"You can't be serious," started Grant. Behind him, the spectating Augments stirred uncomfortably.

"The strongest of us should lead, that's the way we've

always done it. Evangecore didn't give us much, but they tested us, and they marked those of us as strongest." Rami started to pull of his shirt.

Kieran gulped, and he thought of Sarrin and her forty-three procedural marks. "We don't need to do this."

Rami ignored him entirely. His shirt came off, revealing lines of black symbols and lines. The other Augments stared, as did Kieran. Many of the others had let their marks show through strategically ripped clothing, so it wasn't a shock to see the dark geometric patterns, but most of them had a handful. Rami had at least a dozen. "Evangecore selected me, tested me, trained me."

"That's fine," said Grant. "But you forget"— he pulled his own shirt over his head —"you may have had more marks when we went into Junk, but they kept experimenting on me." He turned, revealing lines of black tattoos along both sides of his spine, an ugly scarred mass in between. "I have twenty-nine now."

Rami's eyes blew wide as he scanned Grant's back. But his surprise was short-lived, giving way to an unfriendly sneer. "You have a chip in your brain that can control you. You're my brother, but I wouldn't let you lead me through the canteen. Nothing personal."

"Nothing personal? You're saying you don't know if I'm in control of myself. Of course I am."

"You're practically hugging this UEC." He shot a dirty look at Kieran. "It's me or the common."

Kieran stepped up as Grant and the others considered first Rami and then him. "I want to help you," he said, searching for the right words, "but if you want me to take a step back, I will. I'm not here to cause problems." No, he wasn't here to have any type of memorable impact whatsoever. "But don't give the Central Army the power to tell you what to think of me—they want us to hate each other. It makes their job that much easier if we tear each other apart before they even get here."

The small engine room sat in unnatural silence. Finally, one of the Augments, Thomas, stepped forward. "Kieran's right."

"What?" Rami stammered.

"We don't need to start a war. We don't need to organize into battalions. Until the warship comes back and realizes we aren't dead on that moon, we have a few minutes of peace. Let's focus on fixing the ship instead of fighting each other. Twenty-Seven trusts Kieran, and so do we. He's given us no reason to think otherwise." Around him, heads nodded.

Kieran nearly fell where he stood, knees weak with relief.

"Come on, Rami," Thomas said. "If he says he's rewriting protocols for all the repairs, I'm inclined to believe him. Gods know we're rewired most of the ship."

Face red, Rami sputtered. The Augments at the door had already dispersed. Thomas waved him towards the door. "We need your help to boost the thrusters. Don't become the problem here."

Grant came to stand beside Kieran, watching as Rami and Thomas disappeared into the main engineering bay. "That was close," Grant said, rubbing a hand over his jaw. "I didn't realize—he was always extreme when we were being held on Junk, but not like that. He'll try again. Don't give him any fodder. With this chip in my brain, he'll convince the others not to trust me either—Gods know I barely trust myself. He wants to take charge, to make himself the alpha—always has. You're lucky Thomas likes Sarrin, and the others like him. I'm just telling you like it is."

Kieran gulped, forcing his racing pulse to slow. "I gotta go find Sarrin." He wiped a shaking hand over his too dry mouth.

Grant stopped him with a hand on his arm. He stared at

the ground, his expression warring with something internally. "I need to know—I didn't think I did before, but now I do— did you fight in the war? Did you want to?"

Kieran searched his face—did Grant possibly believe that after everything?

Grant screwed up his eyebrows. "I need to know."

"No," he shook his head violently, "this is my first posting. Graduated last year."

Grant paused, frowning as he did the math. "But you joined the Academy before the war ended."

"No, I did it double time. First in my class. Graduated a lieutenant. I was nowhere near body 609-alpha during the war."

"Six-oh…?"

"Earth," Kieran corrected himself quickly. "I just wanted to work on a starship."

Grant searched his eyes for a minute, then he put his hand on Kieran's shoulder. "Okay."

* * *

Gal kept his head down as he worked his way through the maze of grey corridors, memorizing every inch of the warship's layout. The Valkas was still docked at Etar station, but they would disembark any minute.

Hap's words still echoed through his head: *It's too dangerous.* He felt that danger now more than ever, surrounded by elite Tactical officers whichever way he turned.

He shut his eyes, wondering what exactly he thought he could do, why he thought he alone could stop a warship. There were two planets out there, lush and green, breathable atmospheres, good gravity—but they weren't good planets at all, were they? They just looked the part.

That's why Hap had ordered the Valkas to find the planets instead of Gal's terra-forming crew.   The planets were dangerous. They had to be destroyed. But it didn't sit well with Gal—maybe because he still blamed himself for the death of planet Earth he couldn't stomach the destruction of these planets. He should have just left them alone.

"Gal, what are you doing?" Aaron appeared beside him.

Gal frowned, but answered anyway. "Looking around."

"For what?"

"A way to stop them, or it will all happen again, and Cornelius will die."

"Who is Cornelius?"

A memory of an old-fashioned man with round glasses and a kind smile jumped to the forefront of his mind, but he held his tongue from answering Aaron as a lieutenant came bustling around the corner, nose burning in a grey data-tablet.

"Hey, Cap'n," the lieutenant nodded at him.

Gal sighed, acknowledging the officer. "Wood." He gave him a stiff captain-ly nod. But Gal stopped; Kieran shouldn't be on the Valkas.

Neither should Gal—that was three years ago.

The grey hallways of the Ishash'tor materialized in front of him, similar but not the same as the corridor he thought he'd been standing in a moment ago.

"Good to see you up. How ya feelin'?"

"Yes," Gal stammered. "Well." He studied the walls and bulkheads of the freightship. They should feel more familiar, but they pressed in on him all the same, confusingly similar to the grey walls of every other UEC ship in existence.

"I think I saw Rayne headin' for the bridge not too long ago," said Kieran.

"Huh? Rayne?" Gal scratched his head. What would she be doing on a warship?

"Yeah." Kieran squinted at him, sharp green eyes peering in. "I thought you might be lookin' for her."

Gal shook his head. He didn't want her involved. The walls blurred and shifted around him. Was this the Valkas?

Or the Ishash'tor? Kieran was standing in front of him, but he was certain he was standing on a warship. "Kieran, what are you doing?"

Kieran glanced around quickly, and Gal saw the faint bruising that was blossoming on his neck. "Have you seen Sarrin?"

Gal's chest constricted around his thudding heart. Sarrin? An Augment. This wasn't Evangecore, he was sure of that. Where was he?

"Nah? That's okay," said Kieran. "I was gonna check the shuttle bay next. There's good hiding places there, but I don't know if she knows the shuttle will be on her way back any minute now."

"Sh-shuttle?"

"Yeah. Back from the planet, hopefully with some useful finds this time."

"The planet?" Gal yelped.   No, no, no, it was too dangerous.

"Yeah. Whatever we do, there's a lot of repairs still. I gotta find Sarrin though. Glad you're feelin' better." The lieutenant disappeared down the grey corridor, leaving Gal utterly confused and alone.

Grey demons jumped around.   Aaron appeared once again.

Gal tried to swallow but his mouth was too dry.

"Gal, who's Cornelius?" Aaron repeated.

Gal shook his head. "The shuttle's going to the planet, but they have no idea. We have to stop them before they realize what it is, before everything is destroyed."

"Is this what happened last time, Johnny?" asked Aaron, frowning at him.

"Yes."   Because they were on an infinite loop, all of it happening over and over again.

"Which planet are they're going to? Junk?"

Gal stalked forward, following Kieran, the corridors of the grey warship flying past. "No. Cornelius. It's too dangerous." He slipped into the shuttle hangar and into the unoccupied bay where the shuttle should be returning. He couldn't let the shuttle come back, not if it was going to tell the others what was down there.

Aaron crouched beside him, watching as he pulled at the wires, improvising a solution. "Are you sure you know what you're doing?"

Gal nodded. "Just a little trick," he assured Aaron. "No one will get hurt."

"That's not what I meant. This isn't a warship, Johnny. And that's not Navigation, it's a shuttle hangar's docking controls."

* * *

Kieran tried to make his footsteps as quiet as possible as he fingered the auto injector filled with high-powered sedative in his pocket. He was still shaking, and there was no telling what condition Sarrin would be in when he found her. The trance had been so close—she had actually attacked Rami—but then she'd run.

He felt like he'd let her down. She hadn't been out of the room in days, afraid of this exact thing, and she'd wanted to go back but he'd asked her, even knowing how close it has been on the bridge, to stay and help him in engineering. All he knew was he needed to find her—the repairs could wait— no knowing where she was left an empty ache in his chest, like he had lost something vital.

He pulled an access panel off one of the main walls, this one across from the shuttle hangar doors. His shoulders were too wide to fit in, but he craned his neck to peer around the dark space. "Sarrin?"

He was ready to step back and close the panel, when he heard a rustling. "Sarrin?" He tried again, squishing himself into the tight space.

More rustling, and then two shining blue eyes blinked in the dark.

"Oh, thank God." He sighed in relief. "Are you okay?"

She slithered down the wall, and he gave her space to crawl out.

"What happened?" he asked stupidly.

She stared at the grey carpet, hands crossed over her chest and digging into the flesh of her shoulders.

He reached out to her, making contact on the exposed flesh of her hand. An electric shock zapped up half his arm.

Gasping, she pulled away. "Don't."

He stepped back, stinging hand held to his chest. "Sorry. I just thought...." He leaned against the wall, adrenalin dissipating now that he had found her, and he slumped to the floor. "I was so worried."

After a minute, a light pressure passed across his thigh, and he looked to see her toes retreating from the light bump. She folded her legs and sat against the wall beside him. "I'm sorry. He was so angry...."

"It's okay," he said.

"I nearly hit you."

He shrugged. "I ducked."

She closed her eyes, head dropping to rest on her knees.

"No one got hurt. No one really even saw but me." He sighed, and they sat in silence for a minute. "Rami wants to instigate something called the Rule of War. What is that? He said the Augment with the most marks would be the alpha, the leader."

She nodded once, her eyes closed. "It's how we decided when we were kids, going into the war arena."

"Grant says he's trying to take over. What will you do if he does?"

Her lips pressed into a line.

"You have more marks than anyone else. Hoepe showed me." The image of the forty-three harsh, black marks marring her too-skinny body was burned in his memory.

If possible, her face turned even whiter than before, and she leaned her head back, knocking it against the wall. "I can't."

"I'm sorry," he said. "Maybe I shouldn't have…. I wasn't supposed to know that."

She refused to open her eyes.

"I appreciate it, you know, what happened in the engine room with you protecting me like that." He reached for her again. The foot tap had been a good sign, maybe she was warming to the idea. And his mama always said a hug or a touch was worth a thousand well-meaning words in times of despair.

She flinched away before he could reach her. "I shouldn't have."

He folded his hands in his lap, trapping them between his knees. "You picked up Rami's anger, didn't you? That's what you meant when you said you could feel everything. That's why you started to slip."

The colour drained from her face, blue eyes wide.

"Maybe I can help you." He lifted his hand again.

"Please," she croaked. "Don't. If…. If anything happened."

With every ounce of will left in his mind, he clamped his arms to his sides instead of wrapping her in them. "Okay." His lungs shook as he took a breath to steady himself. He was an Observer, he couldn't get involved. "Why don't you go to our room—my room. No one but Hoepe knows you stay there. It'll be quiet."

She nodded, both of them standing in the corridor.

Kieran prepared another apology—everything was so messed up, so cracked—but he never got the chance. A violent impact shook the ship, sending them both sprawling to the ground.

Sarrin was up first, tapping into the nearest console.

"Warship?" Kieran guessed.

Smoke poured out of the narrow gap between the doors to the shuttle hangar. A second later it started to retract, and the surrounding walls glowed, orange flickering light escaping where holes in the access panels melted away. Wall fire.

He climbed to his feet, Sarrin already running diagnostics. There was no warship on the sensor readout.

"What happened?" Kieran asked.

She shook her head, pressing more controls.

More flames burst around them—overloaded relays and burned out conduits. Suddenly, the fire nearest him went out. And another. His lungs suddenly couldn't quite catch enough air. "Atmospheric breach," he realized.

Smoke that had filled the hallway disappeared, sucked out into vacuum. Sarrin ripped panels off the opposite wall, pressing them into the largest of the holes that was draining their atmosphere.

Augments came around the cornier, running towards them. "We need to seal these breaches," Kieran shouted, and several hands leapt into action.

Hoepe arrived, his brother behind him. "What's going on?"

Kieran's eyes darted over the information pouring across the screen. "Atmospheric breaches through the hangar."

"The shuttle?" Hoepe said.

Kieran had to assume as much, but he wanted information first. "I don't know what went wrong."

"Can we get in there?" asked Hoepe, pushing at the doors. "There may be injured."

"The doors auto-lock when the vacuum seal is comprised." Kieran typed again on the console. "I'm only seeing a small breach in the hangar itself—we're losing point-three-psi per minute."

Rami pushed through the crowd. "What happened?" He shot Kieran a glare harsh enough to make his heart stop for a second.

"I'm not sure, but if I was to guess, I'd say the pilot overshot the landing. Bumped the seal on the inner door."

"Then shut the outer door," said Rami.

Kieran shook his head and pointed at the diagnostics that appeared on the console screen, Sarrin stepping out of the way. "They banged it on the way in. It's jammed."

Rami snarled. "Pilots don't just overshoot landings."

Hoepe's eyes flared wide. "Who's flying the shuttle?"

"Isuma," Kieran said.

Hoepe shook his head. "I thought she was a trained pilot."

"She is," snapped Leove, face unusually pale.

"Isuma's flown four flights today," Kieran said.

"Four flights? Who authorized that?"

"You did."

Hoepe now rubbed his hand over his eyes. "She's been sleeping though."

Kieran nodded, stifling his own yawn. "I assume, she bunks every night."

Hoepe shook his head, "I don't understand. She should be able to do that. Prolonged periods of wakefulness were standard training." He shook his head in disbelief. He turned to Kieran. "Can you fix it?"

Kieran shut his eyes. It would mean taking a space-walk, his least favourite activity under the stars. "Yeah, we're gonna have to. But I need a way to go out there. That was our only airlock.

Sarrin nodded, gesturing to either side of the corridor, hands sweeping side to side, miming the barriers they would need. "Force-shields."

"Yeah?"

She shrugged.

"Okay."

Rami crossed his arms. "What are you saying?"

She turned away, presumably to build them.

"What are you planning?" said Rami.

"I need a force-shield that can stand up to negative pressure fluctuations—one on either side of the corridor around the door. Sarrin says she can build them, then we can use it as an airlock."

"That's spread," Rami argued.

"Do you have a better idea?"

* * *

Sarrin took two gravity generators and fifteen laz-torches from Engineering, rewiring the first as she ran back to the shuttle hangar, schematics drawing themselves in her head. The dark clouds still fuzzed the corners of her vision, the morning's events too much for her cracked mind. She should retreat to the quiet safety of Kieran's room—that would be safest—but she couldn't leave the others trapped aboard the shuttle, the ship slowly venting what precious atmosphere they had left.

Back at the hangar, she dropped the pieces to the floor, and they were eagerly picked up by waiting hands. Ignoring the glint of silver from her own fingers, she demonstrated how to modify the torches to emit a high-frequency web. The gravity generators would help solidify the force-shields.

"Is this going to work?" one of the Augments asked.

Of the force-shields she had no doubt—she had designed the strongest force-shield ever known after all, the one that destroyed Earth. But what could bring destruction could also bring hope. Right?

The stronghold, the shaking, the realization the shield would cut into the Earth—her mind played the scene, the battalions moving across the frozen landscape, the sneaking retreat, the sudden race to find a way off world.

Kieran came up behind her, stopping her mind from reeling itself into oblivion. "How's it comin'?" He was nervous, his accent extra thick, and he was dressed in an EV suit.

"The seal will be incomplete," she told him. "You will have ten minutes-estimated before the oxygen reserve on the ship becomes too low for survival."

He shuffled in his suit awkwardly, and somehow she remembered or understood his fear of being sucked off a ship's hull and carried away into oblivion. "You will have gravity and you will be contained within the ship's walls," she assured him. "There is no need to be concerned."

He raised the other eyebrow. "You just told me I only had ten minutes to get the crew of that shuttle back inside."

She nodded.

"Is there a way to seal the force-shield completely?"

"There is a microscopic gap on all sides where the shield begins."

He knelt beside her, evaluating the apparatus. "Can we recess the generators?"

"We have."

"You doin' okay?"

She nodded, but the glint of blood and silver showed on her hands, and the monster whispered in her mind.

"These are a great design," he said.

Too good, her memory flashed, recalling the power the force-shield on Earth had managed to hold before it finally shattered.

Kieran's head turned. He shouted to someone, "I'll be there in a sec." He flashed her a smile and was gone. But the smile was hollow. It was not as it was before, only a shadow remained.

More blood appeared on her hands.

At his signal, she triggered the force-shields—one on either side of the corridor around the door—and watched Kieran disappear into the hangar.

An Augment leaned over her, and she flinched away. He'd gotten too close while she'd been distracted. Anger rolled off of him, his face blocky and red. His words were far away, only static to her ears.

She turned away, ostensibly to examine the force-shield, drawing a shaky breath. Not here, not with so many people around. Blood dripped from her and coated the floor. The shiny silver skeleton poked through. The edges of her vision fogged, dark and narrow.

A hand touched her shoulder, electricity tearing through her, filling her with his rage. She spun wildly and threw the Augment against the wall. The monster acted on its own, she was powerless to stop it. Too many people in the small corridor. Too many target points. A spanner in her hand and fifty-eight other objects that could be used as deadly weapons.

* * *

Kieran and his small team muscled the door to the hangar, opening it just wide enough for them to slip through. Ten minutes. The clock started ticking the second the hermetic seal cracked on the door.

The problem was apparent immediately: the permaglass viewing panel had shattered, the shuttle's port wing most of the way through it. The shuttle appeared intact except for some superficial damage, a hand waved through the dark, solar-protected windows.

"Expanding foam," said Thomas over the microphone in his helmet.

Kieran nodded, pulling the canister from his utility belt. Faces watched them from the shuttle's viewports as they tried to plug the hole. But the foam was sucked out into the shuttle bay and into space beyond.

"The pressure variation is too much," said Kieran. The current of atmosphere leaking around the edges of the force-shields was too strong for the foam to take hold.

The other teammate nodded. "The hermetic seal."

The three returned to the hangar door and forced it shut, Kieran retriggering the door seal. They waited until all the oxygen had escaped before spraying their sealant again, this time the foam holding.

Kieran tested, venting in a small amount of atmosphere and then more and more. The foam seal held.

They forced the door into the hallway open again. Kieran gave the thumbs up to the Augments waiting in the hallway. The hangar repair had been successful and relatively easy.

But their expressions were horrified. Hoepe pointed anxiously to the other side, and Kieran turned.

There were a dozen Augments pressed against the walls. Rami slammed into the force-shield, then crumpled to the ground. He stood back on his feet, unsteady, and leapt, flinging his arms around Sarrin.

"Jesus," Kieran swore.

Sarrin's eyes were far gone—she had slipped into the trance —a spanner swinging wildly in her hand. The only thing saving the people around her was their own intensive training as they ducked out of her way. Although if half the stories he'd heard were true, she could bury every last one of them.

He rushed forward, pulling at the seals on his EV suit as he went. "Sarrin!" he called, but there was no way for her to hear him through the helmet. He bounced off the force-shield, landing on his backside.

Sarrin focussed on Rami, slamming him into the ceiling. She pulled a fork from her coveralls and embedded it in his leg before he fell back to the floor. Rami picked himself up and made to run at her again.

"Don't!" Kieran screamed inside his helmet, the sound echoing around. He waved frantically for someone to drop the force-shield. "Sarrin!" he shouted over and over. She couldn't hear him, but it was a reflex.

Someone deactivated the force-shield. Augments stumbled past, moving back as he pushed through them, pulling off his helmet and dropping it on the floor.

Sarrin turned, the same wild ferocity in her eyes as the first time it had happened, when she had lost herself in the cargo bay after boarding the warship. Another Augment jumped on her from behind, and Sarrin knocked them away easily.

Kieran fumbled, finding the auto-syringe in his coveralls pocket under the EV suit and extracting it. He swallowed dryly. He had hated Hoepe for suggesting he always carry one, he had wanted to believe Sarrin was better.

He called her again, careful to keep his voice level and even. Would she recognize him and stop? He squeezed the auto-syringe nervously.

She turned, stalking forward. At least she hadn't leaped.

"Sarrin?" he tried again.

Before he could stop it, Rami lunged forward, wrapping his arms around her again. Sarrin spun violently, her hand reaching for his neck and squeezing.

Kieran rushed forward, grabbing her arm. A moment of recognition dawned in her crystal blue eyes, as his other hand slammed into her neck, the auto-syringe unloading its full dose.

He grabbed her as they fell, her body limp and small, his crashing on top. Below them, Rami sputtered, a hand protecting his throat. The Augments stared, leaning away from her.

Kieran clutched Sarrin tightly, squeezing his eyes. "You have no idea what you're doing," he spat at Rami. Carefully he lifted her up. No one said a word. They stared at her, at her ripped shirt, the lines and lines of black procedural marks marring her back.

He called out instructions to cut through the wing and pull out the Augments, not daring to look back as he carried her away.

SEVEN

Halud stepped gracefully through the doors of the research wing of the central hospital. It was a sterile place, cold white walls and echoing footsteps.

A vid crew came behind him. The same cinematographer and producer he had worked with several times before. A factician and a scientist were with them as well.

And a guard.

It seemed his life had returned to normal after all, at least from the outside. He still had his handmade wool bed and his antique writing desk. His apartments were the same, the view the same, the shops the same. Everything was the same as always. Except the guards and the new cameras tucked into the wall everywhere he went.

Each day, he would wander the halls and climb the stairs to the Speakers' Complex. He would exchange pleasantries with the secretary, and he would sit in his office. Twice he had been asked to compile a statement for Arthur Herrington, Speaker of Knowledge, and once for Renee Green, Speaker of Love.

There was no secrecy, no espionage or database hacking. The new camera in his office and a set of subroutines on his desktop console told him that would be a very bad idea.

Hap had not spoken to him since the first day of his return. The others assumed what they were told, that he had been on holiday. He told them he had a wonderful time visiting the stars and finding peace in centring himself.

But he felt far from peaceful. They had his sister. And they would spare no grace torturing her.

"Would you like to see the facility, Master Poet?" the factician asked.

"Huh? Oh, yes. That would be excellent," he said blandly.

She nodded and beckoned for him to follow. He had not been told much, but Ingrid Stol, Speaker of Faith, had asked him to report on the laboratory's latest research and a new vaccine.

He had done the same thing many times before. He would ask the scientist questions, the scientist would give a wordy explanation, and he would summarize for the folk, lead them in a prayer to the Gods, and be done.

He only half paid attention to the tour.

"... And here we have the incubation chambers for multiplying the vaccine."

He had accumulated a large amount of knowledge from reporting over the years. Vaccine production was standard: grow the vaccine, harvest the vaccine, isolate, purify, and dose the vaccine. Rigorous hours of testing to ensure its safety would have been done, but if they were having him report on it, it was already well past the approval stage.

"Are you ready, Poet?"

He nodded, and the producer showed him to a staged set of chairs, the location carefully selected for its lighting and clean laboratory backdrop.

The scientist sat opposite him. The cinematographer set up his machine and gave them a ready signal. The factician crouched in front with prepared large-font cards.

Like riding a hoverpad, Halud's face slipped into a long-practiced, trustworthy smile. "Hello, United Earth Citizens. What a fine day for innovation. The Speakers have asked me to share with you the latest great gift from our Gods. Faith, the Healer, has been very generous, providing us with a lifesaving vaccine. Dr. Trae Amanpreet from the research labs at Central Hospital is here to tell us more."

He nodded at the scientist who launched into his pre-prepared speech. "Hello. The Gods have bestowed upon us a vaccine for the virus, *Xenoralia nervosa*."

The smile fell from Halud's face. "Sorry?"

Amanpreet paused, surprised, and stared back at him.

Halud recovered. "A Red Fever vaccine?"

The scientist nodded and smiled. "Yes, that's correct. Twenty years ago, the Red Fever, also known as *Xenoralia nervosa*, devastated many of the populations of Earth."

Halud glanced up, and the guard gave him a stern shake of his head. A warning.

"An airborne virus, it spread quickly, and was nearly one-hundred-percent fatal. A completely devastating disease. But we are not to understand the Will of the Gods."

Halud nodded his head, touching his five fingers to his chest at the long-familiar prompt, "Yes, the Will of the Gods." He read the next cue card: "But we are fortunate, the Gods say we have passed their test, and have given us this reward."

"The new vaccine will protect us against the devastating effects of *Xenoralia nervosa*."

"But isn't there always a reversion rate with this type of vaccine, Doctor?"

The scientist's eyes opened wide, and he paused, jaw opening and closing. "The vaccine is ready to be distributed to all of the Gods' population."

The factician pointed furiously at the prompt on the cue card.

The guard reached around for his holstered laz-gun.

"Of course," Halud said quickly.   "Tell us about the distribution."

The doctor began to speak, but Halud's mind wandered. The scientist had told him it was a modified live vaccine— they had taken the virus, changed some of its RNA programming, and made it benign. Except RNA was a fickle thing, each new generation of the virus would have subtle changes, incorrect copies of the generation before. Some of the vaccines could revert back to the Red Fever.

The disease that had killed so many adults. And changed children forever.

The producer tapped on the card, alerting him that he had missed his cue. "Marvellous!   A vaccine against *Xenoralia nervosa*.   Simply marvellous.   Let us pray to the Gods in thanks."   He forced his fingers to his chest and bowed his head.

They hadn't seen the virus in years. After it had ripped through the pockets of affected population in three devastating months, it had never been seen again. They had no idea where it came from, having appeared in hundreds of disconnected pockets around the globe, touching one suburb but leaving the surrounding ones unharmed. It never spread beyond those suburbs, never spread to other planets. And there had never been a hint of anything like it before or since.

Why create a vaccine now? How had the Central Army researchers even found the virus and isolated it?

He turned his gaze to the lab behind him, eyes locking onto the glass cages of the research animals. They stared back at him, eyes a terribly intelligent, haunting blue.

The guard shifted, holster creaking.

He said quickly, "In the Gods we Trust."

He read off the prompt card, barely registering the words that came out of his mouth. "The Gods are good. They have chosen to protect us against this terrible threat. So that the Red Fever will never again curse the citizens of United Earth. Thank you, Dr. Amanpreet. We are so thankful and anticipate this life-saving medication."

The doctor nodded and gave a final smile at the camera.

Without thinking, Halud's face did the same.

The cinematographer switched off the camera and grinned at them with a second thumbs up.

The guard shook his head.

EIGHT

Grant approached the infirmary, helping the last of the Augments who had been rescued from the shuttle. The steady ping of monitors and the shuffling of so many people crammed into the tiny room met them even before they turned in.

Rami sat on the exam table while Hoepe ran his hands over and around him. "Hurry up, Doc, it's just a broken bone."

"Dislocated, actually." Hoepe's scowl deepened. "And I'm checking your reflexes."

"They're fine."

"They're too slow." Scanning the others lined up along the walls, Hoepe admitted, "Everyone's are too slow."

Grant hadn't felt slow, but Hoepe was one of the best doctors under the stars, and if he thought their reflexes were slow then they must be. Funny how he didn't feel it. What else could he not feel?

"It's not Isuma's fault the shuttle crashed," said Rami. Of the eight Augments who had been trapped in the shuttle, it was Rami who had suffered the worst injury, and was appearing to be the worst patient.

"I'm not saying it is," said Hoepe. He glanced in the

direction of the pilot, Isuma, who huddled stricken in the corner at the far side of the room. "Your responses are still twice the speed of a common human, but they are slower than they should be."

Leove frowned from his spot beside Isuma where he held her hand, and interrupted his quiet reassurances to ask the same question that shouted in Grant's mind: "Why?"

Grant caught the subtle but annoyed glare Hoepe sent his brother, but the doctor turned back to his patient, replacing his professional mask of calm. "Sarrin suffered serious zinc deficiency when she arrived. I am seeing similar but mild skin and hair changes in everyone."

"Easily corrected," said Leove.

"Yes, but why in the first place?" responded Hoepe.

Rami squirmed under Hoepe's touch. "Shuttles don't just crash. Someone tampered with the shuttle and the landing controls. We have to see what happened, investigate the accident."

"You are injured," replied Hoepe, the muscles along his jaw straining.

"Then fix it already!"

Hoepe's eyes flashed, veins in his neck bulging, and Grant stepped forward. "Rami," he chided his old friend. It was meant for the doctor too, but Hoepe at least had the practice of controlling himself, he wasn't sure how much control Rami had.

Rami glanced at him, eyes still tight with pent-up frustration, but he stopped moving at least. "It wasn't even the girl that did it." Rami pointed to his dislocated shoulder. "It was that cracked engineer falling on me."

"That *engineer*," muttered Hoepe, "probably saved your life."

"He's done something to her."

Grant leaned back against the doorframe, his arms crossed

over his chest. "I told you not to touch her."

"What does that have to do with it? She shouldn't turn spread mad just because I touched her."

"You think you know her—," Grant started.

At the same time, Hoepe answered, his voice clipped: "Sarrin has been unwell from zinc deficiency; she was not in control of herself."

"Not in control?" shouted Rami. "Of course not. That engineer is controlling her, changing her." He leapt off the table, out of Hoepe's reach, waving his one good arm for emphasis— the same as he had done when tried to get the Augment's riled up in their prison on Junk.

"Rami, calm down!" Grant yelled, glaring at Hoepe. Rami was spread enough about Sarrin and all the commons on the ship, he didn't need Hoepe giving him any more reason.

The Augments around them stirred, some of their eyes lighting up with understanding. Alarmed, Grant realized Rami's wild ramblings were getting through to the others.

Grant grabbed Rami by the sore shoulder, Rami grimacing with pain. "Doc needs you on the table unless you want to hold up the whole line." He waited for Rami to climb back onto the medical bed, Hoepe's eyes meeting his with worry, before he turned to the others. He eyed each of the others in turn, conveying his seriousness. "He's not controlling her," he said as simply as he could. "You know I'm no lover of commons, so believe me when I say I wasn't very nice to Kieran when I came aboard either. But Sarrin—Twenty-seven—trusts him, and so do I."

But Rami would not be appeased. "Of course she does," he snapped. Before he could say more, Hoepe clenched viciously on Rami's arm, jarring the shoulder back in place. Rami doubled over, gasping. A smug smile crossed Hoepe's face.

"Kieran's unusual, sure," Grant said to the others, "but he's helping. He helps her. They have this weird understanding. He's the only one who can stop her when she——."

"Stops her?" Rami growled between heavy breaths. He clutched his shoulder, face unnaturally pale, but it seemed he still had strength to argue.

Grant gulped—he'd been as careless as Hoepe. "Not like that, but... you saw what happened today. Kieran had to intervene; she wouldn't have stopped otherwise. And you'd be dead."

Rami sat up, but Hoepe twisted a tight sling around the man, strapping the arm to his chest more forcefully than needed. But Rami turned away from the doctor, huffing unsteadily as Hoepe periodically tugged across his chest. "I don't trust him at all. He had a sedative ready for her, like he knew it was going to happen. "

"Kieran carries a sedative," retorted Hoepe, "because I asked him too."

"Why?" Leove asked from the corner.

Hoepe glanced at his brother, completely missing the sharp shake of Grant's head. "Because we've had to sedate her before."

"This has happened before?" snapped Rami. He turned to Grant. "Why haven't you done anything?"

Hoepe paled, but he still managed to answer faster than Grant could think of a helpful, non-inflammatory response: "It is not a physical ailment."

"Of course it isn't!" shouted Rami, face violent red.

"Calm down," said Grant, stepping in close to his friend, blocking him from the keenly listening Augments in the room.

"Why should I? You're not taking this seriously enough. You're got Twenty-seven acting like a lunatic, with a UEC engineer the only one who can control her. Do you know how spread that sounds?"

"No, you've got it wrong...."

"If Twenty-seven was of her right mind, she'd have destroyed all the commons aboard the ship," Rami called out, leaning around Grant so his voice carried to the others, "the same way she killed all the researchers in that observation tower in Evangecore, and destroyed the facility on Junk. That's the Twenty-seven that I know, that I follow, that I've modelled my own life after." He leapt off the table, pacing back and forth in the small room, his torso and arm wrapped in white bandages. "They used to make me hide in the bushes during the war games—they thought I was too young, too little to do anything—but I was there, and when I saw Twenty-seven, a girl even younger and smaller than me, leap into that tower, I vowed to never let myself be put in a place of inaction again. And I certainly won't now. We need to help her. If she's not of her right mind, if she's being controlled, we need to act."

Grant crossed his arms. "We don't need to do anything."

The Augments lining the wall looked bad and forth between each other, their brows creased. There had been a time on Junk when they all looked to Grant as their leader, but Grant had spent nearly a year in solitary confinement— who would they listen to now?

Rami placed a gentle hand on his back, his voice low but still strong enough to carry: "Am I talking to Grant right now or the chip in your brain? He's done something to all of us. Controlling Twenty-seven. Controlling you. All of us having slow reflexes—we were fine when they tested us on Junk, so what's changed?"

The Augments shifted uncomfortably, a bead of sweat rolling down Grant's back. Kieran was one of the good guys, he was helping. Couldn't they see that? But with the chip in his brain, there was no way he could convince them—Rami would explain away any argument he made.

"I'm going to investigate the hangar, figure out why the

shuttle crashed," announced Rami.

"You need rest," said Hoepe.

"I can't rest, not when we're in a situation like this. You're all convinced Kieran is helping, but he was the first one there —don't you find that suspicious?"

"Rami," Grant tried, even though he knew he was already losing, "if Doc says you need a rest, you need rest."

"We don't have the time to wait. I'll get to the bottom of this, and then you'll see. Don't worry, Grant, even if you don't see it now, I'll help you."

Grant reached out, but Rami was already gone. A pit of dread settled deep in his bowels. Hoepe's expression was as worried as his own. There was no explaining Kieran, no understanding his strange accent, strange habits, strange expressions, unless you took into consideration Hoepe's theory that Kieran was not from here, that he was from somewhere else: a God sent to aid them in their times of greatest struggle.

If Rami convinced the others, he would get rid of Kieran. And if they got rid of a God, there was no telling what would happen to them.

* * *

Aaron stood in a dark bunker, the walls made of dirt with rough shelves filled with spools of wire and old, broken machines. The air was damp and stagnant. Familiar. Gal blinked at the scene.

Grey demons watched from all corners as his mind slipped and slid.

Aaron called him, his face haunting int he faint glow of the single overhead light. "It's not over. We have to press on." It was then Gal saw he was packing a backpack.

"No," sniffed Gal, deep in the memory. "We just lost someone. Coyne was our friend. He was following me."

"He followed you because he thought you were right. He believed in what we were doing. What we are doing." Aaron's face was ashen, as

shocked and tired as his own. "We have to go now. If we wait, it will be too late."

They had just one chance, one moment when they would be able to access the database that housed the Speakers' private, most classified communications. One chance to figure out what was really going on.

Numb, Gal stood, going to the desk—the grey, plastic desk in his borrowed quarters on the warship Valkas—waiting for the demons that gathered there to make space for him to sit. His eyes scanned the thousands of lines of code that scrolled down the console screen.

"Do you think it will be enough?" asked Aaron.

"Of course it will."

A tentative rapping sounded on the door, followed by a chime and a familiar voice. "Gal, it's me."

He smiled and glanced knowingly at Aaron, who stood in the bunker while Gal sat in the warship and answered the door on the Ishash'tor. "Come in."

The doors slid open revealing the corridor just outside his quarters and the most beautiful woman he'd ever seen. Rayne wrung her hands as the door closed behind her. "I came to check on you."

Confused, he asked, "Why? Not that I'm not grateful." He stood and approached, eager for an embrace, but a fleck of grey caught his eye. A demon perched on her shoulder: the demon-Rayne with pretty brown curls and a UEC jumpsuit and a matching smile. It mocked him, making a kissy face, and then fell over backwards, dead.

Rayne furrowed her brow, watching him. "I thought all the commotion and the klaxons might have been … difficult for you."

Gal turned, impossibly, from his starship quarters to the bunker on Earth.

He was hallucinating, that much was clear. Was he on a ruined freightship with his beloved Rayne? Was he on a warship protecting Cornelius? Was he on Earth with Aaron preparing for a raid?

Aaron shrugged, and Gal turned back to Rayne.

He called her name uncertainly.

"Yes, Gal?"

"What are you doing here?" He glanced behind him where Aaron organized supplies. He couldn't tell her what he had been doing in the bunker. Not now, not ever. She would never understand.

As if to highlight it, she tugged at the open collar of her UEC jumpsuit. "So, you're doing okay? The shuttle crash didn't bother you?"

Shuttle crash? His eyebrows hooded darkly. Only his closest friends, the ones who had grown up with him on Indaer and travelled the same transport to the Academy, knew about his shuttle crashing over the forest preserve on Indaer, knew that it was what caused him to start questioning everything. How had Rayne found out? "I'm fine," he said cautiously, curious to know what else she had learned. Could she, hope against hope, have come to join them?

"I'm glad." She sat comfortably on the bed—the bed in his freightship quarters. "It gave me a fright. I thought the warship had come back. Hoepe says no one was injured, at least not badly."

Gal frowned. "The shuttle—the Ishash'tor's shuttle—crashed?"

"Yes." A puzzled look came over her face. "They're still trying to figure out what happened. We vented a lot of atmosphere, and that airlock was the only way to get supplies and people on or off the ship."

So, they were on the freightship. The bunker was the hallucination. Gal felt a little bolder, now that he had something concrete to work with.

"They're working through the calculations now—trajectory,

speed, thruster burst. We'll go as soon as possible. I would prefer to go straight to Etar, but this seems like our best chance right now."

A cold dread nearly dropped Gal to his knees. "What's our best chance?"

"To go to the planet. I know you said—"

"We can't go to the planet!" he shouted, clutching his chest again.

She jumped up, blurting, "I'm sorry!"

"It's too dangerous!"

Her lip trembled, eyes wide.

Gal hadn't meant to shout. "It's too dangerous, Rayne! Don't you see?"

"It's our only option. With the shuttle and the hangar ruined, Kieran can't get the parts to repair the FTL."

"I thought I was clear. Who decided we would go to the planet?"

She gulped. "Hoepe and the Augments."

"Augments," he despaired. They were back in the bunker. *Indaer, Augments, bunker, planets.* Rayne was with them. He drove the heels of his palms into his eyes. "No, no, no. You don't know what's going to happen. They'll destroy everything."

"The Augments? They've been working with us. They're just kids Gal. The rumours were wrong."

"No, Rayne."

"Yes." She grabbed him around the middle. "It's going to be fine. We'll go back to Etar and tell the Speakers. The Gods will be good to us. Sometimes hardship is part of the Path."

But that was the problem. They—the Gods—already knew. Gal pulled back. Across the room, Aaron watched him. The demons crept close, tangling in his feet. Even in the safety of the bunker, the truth was dangerous.

"We can't go to the planet," he repeated.

"Why not? You're not making any sense."

"Because." The lines of code scrolled across his console screen, a program he'd written just in case. But for what? For the bunker and their mission to infiltrate the Speakers' compound, or for the Valkas as a last, final measure to ensure they never made it to the planets and that Cornelius would be safe?

"What is so bad about this planet?"

"It's all part of it. It's all connected. Don't you see?"

She shook her head and stepped back.

"If we make it to the planet, they'll destroy it."

"Who? What?"

"The Augments, the planet." He shook his head, reality slipping through his fingers like water. "The Speakers! It's me, I'm in the middle of all of it. Me and Hap Lansford." She took another step back, towards the door, but he grabbed her wrist. "We can't let them take over. Can't let them destroy everything."

"You're scaring me, Gal." She jerked her wrist away.

"You should be scared. You have no idea what they're capable of." He reached for his desk, for the tiny chip attached to the console. "Take this." He pressed it into her hand, curling her fingers around it.

"What are you doing?" Her voice shook. "Tell me why the planet is so dangerous. And what do the Speakers have to do with it?"

"I can't. They would kill you, like they're killing me."

"Who? The Augments?" Of course she thought it was the Augments, not the Speakers. Never her precious Speakers.

"The Augments aren't the enemy." He shook his head. "I'm the only one left. The only one to be tortured with the knowledge of what I did."

"Gal, I don't understand."

He muttered, his head pressed into his hands, "No, and why would you?" He pressed the controls on the console, ejecting the thin data card he had been working on. "Take the chip. You need to deliver it to the main Engineering computer. Just plug it in and the rest will happen automatically."

"What?"

"Rayne, my love, the war isn't over, not for them. This program will stop it. It will keep us all safe."

"I thought you said the Augments weren't the enemy. I don't understand." She looked at the chip. "You made a computer program? How do you know how to do this?"

"I've made several. I need you to upload this one."

"I can't, Gal." She held out the chip to give it back to him

He took her hand, curled her fist around the chip again, and shoved it into her pocket. "I know too much. We need to stay away from the planets. Promise me."

"Planets?" she squeaked.

"Yes." He held her wrist until she nodded, her face ashen. "Trust me."

He let go, and she turned and ran for the door, pausing only until it slid open wide enough for her to squeeze through sideways.

Gal turned, striding into the dark shadows of the bunker with Aaron.

"That's one complicated relationship, Johnny," Aaron said.

The demon-Rayne lay prostrate on the floor, the others crowding around it to see. Just a hallucination, but the image died in his memory again and again. "I have to keep her safe."

"What's that program going to do?" Aaron strapped a laz-rifle across his back, peering at Gal questioningly.

Gal shrugged. A raid, a warship, a freightship—they were all the same desperate struggle. It was all happening again and again. "Are you ready?"

"I'm with you to the end, Johnny."

* * *

Sarrin woke slowly, pushing through the heavy blanket that four—hundred-milligrams of telazol left in her system. Groaning, she rolled over in the bed. She had lost control. The monster had taken over. The memory flooded her of a violent machine relentlessly attacking Augments in the hallway.

What was she? She could hardly say human, though she tried. A monster through and through, there was no escaping it. These were her friends. If she couldn't live with them, where could she live?

It was too dangerous. Hoepe had said she was getting better, but it seemed farther and farther from it. The more her synapses restored, the faster her reflexes, the quicker her trigger. The more she healed, the worse the trance would become.

She kicked out again, trying to straighten her leg, but it was stuck. Cracking her eyelids, she realized why: a hunched figure sat at the end of the bed. Kieran.

He turned, feeling her kick. No pretending she was asleep now. He smiled at her, but his eyes seemed to do the opposite. "I'm sorry, Sarrin." He wrapped one of his hands around her foot.

She gasped and pulled away.

If possible, his eyes seemed to get sadder. "I—I'm sorry. I didn't know what else to do. I—" He stopped and pulled his hands back into his lap and stared at them.

She remembered his face, filled with fear, in the second before he injected her. She remembered the feel of the other Augment's trachea, squeezed inside her grip. She stared at her own hand, blood dripping, silver glinting.

"Go away."

He stood obediently. "Sarrin, just…."

"I don't want to hurt you."

She heard him swallow from across the room. "You're not going to hurt me."

But she could hear the shake in his voice, feel the fear emanating off him. "You're afraid."

He paused. She glanced at his hanging open mouth.

"Yes. That's true." He sat down again. "But, I'm not afraid of you."

A fool. He had seen it. He had a bruise on his arm from Gods-only knew what she had done. Didn't he have any sense of self-preservation?

Her thoughts stopped abruptly when he grabbed her foot.

She yanked away, but he held on. What was he doing? Her eyes went wide with panic, as he held on through another kick.

"This isn't hurting you," he said, the sternness in his voice causing her to pause.

"Don't touch me," she said as icily as she could manage.

He let go, at least. "Why not?

She rolled over, squeezing her eyes shut. She felt him staring down at her, heard his exasperated sigh. When she opened her eyes again, she saw his back as he stomped to the latrine.

He slumped at the sink, pouring water over his face. Poor, sweet Kieran. If anything happened to him, if she lost control just for a second, she would never forgive herself.

She sat up and watched until he made his way back.

"I know you don't like to be touched. I respect that. But I'm trying to help. You can't go forever never touching a living human being."

"I can feel everything," she said.

"I know. I see it. I know you picked up Rami's anger, and probably the panic from everyone in that corridor—that's why you lost control, you got overwhelmed." His eyebrows knitted together in pain. "I don't understand why you're so afraid of me. I've touched you before, like when I carried you here, or when I carried you back to the ship—no one exploded or anything."

She tried again, owing him an explanation he could understand. She could barely understand it. "Every thought, every emotion—I feel them." She cleared her throat. "Rami, he's so full of anger. He touched me, and that's all I could feel. I took it into me."

Kieran nodded. "I feel it too. He walks into a room and my heart starts to race. But I'm not like Rami."

She shook her head. "I feel, and I take." A shaky breath left her body. "She was trying to help, too. And I killed her."

Kieran's face paled. He sat down on the bed and wrapped a hand stubbornly around her foot, the thin sheets the only thing between them, saving him. "Tell me."

Sarrin squeezed her eyes tight, bundling all her energy in her core. It was too much, and the words came tumbling out. "I didn't know it would happen, but I was so tired. She gave me her hand. I didn't know, I didn't know! She died. I touched her and she just died. All the life taken from her."

The memory of Nurse Adelaide's warm body falling lifelessly to the cold, hard floor of Evangecore threatened to make her vomit. She remembered the sensation more than the vision: she was filled up, renewed, left vibrant with life, and the horror as she looked up and saw the life drain from the nurse's eyes.

Kieran was staring wide eyed, fear and confusion rolling off of him.

But he wasn't staring at her.

He was staring at the floor. "Did you see that? All that stuff went flying." He stood to examine it, the warmth of his hand suddenly leaving her foot. "It was like it just hovered in the air for a second, and then blew across the room."

Sarrin's mouth was suddenly dry, the nurse forgotten. She licked her dry lips. "I didn't see anything."

Kieran scratched his head. "I coulda sworn."

She wrapped her hands in the sheets. It was impossible to swallow.

He picked up the stuff, and came back to sit on the end of the bed. "This was the nurse you told me about, the one who brought you books?"

She released a breath, at first relieved he hadn't asked again about the objects she had unwittingly manipulated. Then, hollow at the memory he had recalled in her once more. "Yes," her voice barely came out. "You can't touch me. I'm a monster. That's what they made me."

He grabbed her foot again, his voice serious. "No one can make anybody anything."

"Don't." She pulled away from him, curling into a tight ball at the opposite end of the bed.

"Sorry!" he shouted and leapt up, as far from her as he could. He paced, driving his hands through his sandy hair. "You remind me too much of my sister. I just want to help you."

Sarrin glanced at the photo on the nightstand, at Kieran's sister who had already died of old age. They looked nothing alike to her, Lauren was so full life, and she was so full of death.

But still an idea formed in her head.

"Take me with you," she said suddenly to Kieran, "when you go back."

He frowned. "What?"

"Can you do that? Can you bring someone with you when you go back to your ship?"

His eyes widened in understanding. "Yeah. You would want to come, be an Observer?"

She nodded. Maybe she could escape it.

He stared, expression frozen, before a real smile cracked through the surface. "Yeah," he laughed. "They always remind us to bring people back if we find someone. It's good for—" He stopped suddenly, and turned to her, his face pink. Then he looked away, gripping the back of the chair until his knuckles turned white. "No."

She sat up out of sheer surprise. "I can learn. Help with the engines, the research."

Confusion rolled off of him, and something else she couldn't name. "It's not that." He shook his head again, staring at the wall.

"I can't stay here."

He turned, his green eyes filled with sadness.

"They'll hunt me. I have something they want, something dangerous, and I'll never be safe here."

He stared at her with wide eyes. "I just…. I don't know."

She felt her heart start to fall.

He closed his eyes. "Maybe it would be okay. I'll have to write a letter."

She lifted an eyebrow. The emotions rolling off of him were so confused, but none of them were bad, none of them stirred the monster.

He smiled up at her, a sad smile. "all right. I would probably miss you too much anyhow." Then he flashed one of his goofy smiles that made her heart thump around, much differently than anything else. "I should warn you that my mom hugs everyone."

Sarrin swallowed. She hadn't thought of that. But it didn't frighten her half as much as the UEC experiments.

"It's not so bad. Mom gives the best hugs." He reached for her.

Automatically, she flinched away. But that was the problem wasn't it? She glanced up at him. He held his hand out, patiently holding it still. Always trying to help. Gingerly, she reached forward. Her fingers began to hum as they came close to his.

Too close. Too intense.

She gasped and pulled away.

Behind her, she heard Kieran sigh.

He moved past her and headed for the door. "Come on, we still need to get the ship out of here, and I need to write home—it's been a while, too long, probably."

She stayed firmly in place. "We should go soon."

He frowned. "You mean home? To my home?"

"There's nothing left for me here."

"What about Halud?"

She looked away.

"Sarrin," he said seriously. "He's your brother."

"He's already dead."

She felt his eyes on her, searching her. "You don't know that."

But it was hard to hold out hope when everyone else knew it too.

"You told me he was still alive, that you could feel it."

She shut her eyes. She felt so many things. If he wasn't dead, then he was bait in a trap.

If she went looking for him, they would catch her. If they caught her, he would be dead or worse. At least if she never showed up, they would keep him alive. Eventually, he might become useless to them, and they would let him go.

It was the best she could hope for.

"Don't give up on him."

"I'm not a fool, Kieran."

He frowned again, leaning away from her.

Not a fool, but maybe she was a monster.

"There's still a lot of work to do. I need your help."

She shook her head. "I can't."

"It's only going to get harder the longer you hide in here."

"That was the last of the sedative. If I ... if I lose control again, no one can stop me. I have to stay in here."

"Oh, right." His face turned white and she heard him gulp from across the room. He took a step forward, emphasizing his words: "I'm not afraid of you."

"I know."

He sat down on the bed.

"What are you doing?"

"I haven't slept in four days, what does it look like I'm doing." He pulled his boots off and dropped them on the floor. "Besides, Rami is investigating the shuttle crash, and until we know the extent of the damage, there isn't much to do."

She wrinkled her nose. "You trust him?"

Kieran shrugged and laid back. "He's a good engineer, despite everything else. A little trust will go a long way with him, I think." A moment later, soft snores sounded from his slightly open mouth.

* * *

The Rubik's cube shifted idly in Sarrin's hands as she made a half-attempt to solve the puzzle, curled up in the room's only chair. Her attention was focussed more on the sleeping figure on the bed. Kieran's chest moved steadily, his arm—still clad in singed grey coveralls—hung over the edge, and he snored. Loudly.

A gentle warmth stirred in her, knowing that he felt he could fall asleep with her—a monster—a few steps away. The afternoon felt peaceful, almost lazy. Nearly as though none of the rest of it existed.

But of course it did.

The door chimed, cutting loudly through the serenity. Sarrin froze, listening and counting three sets of shifting feet in the hallway. The gentle rhythm of Kieran's snoring was interrupted, and she swallowed a sudden urge to scream at them for being so thoughtless, but he remained asleep, falling into the cadence once more.   She blew out a breath and relaxed. They would go if the summons was ignored.

But the chime buzzed again.   Kieran snorted, rolling over. Sarrin held herself perfectly still, not daring to breathe until his body had relaxed again.   Then she leapt to the door, opening it before they could ring again.

Three sets of Augment-blue eyes blinked at her. Two males and one female.

Sarrin blinked back.

Thomas stood at the back.   "Can we come in?"   He glanced up and down the corridor, worried.

"No."   She stood in the door, toes curling back at the line between corridor and room. "You should go."

"Please," said Thomas.   The rest looked at her with pleading eyes.

Sarrin glanced at Kieran's sleeping frame, and stepped into the corridor, the doors sealing behind her.   She cast a wary look first at the group huddled together, warring between whether to lean forward or away from her, and then to the empty hall.   The edges of her vision darkened—it was not safe for her to be out of the room, the events of her last excursion fresh in her memory.   But Thomas had been a friend.   And beside him was the boy she had found cowering in the simulated war game so many years ago when they were all children.

Their eyes met, time dilating and folding in its strange way so that Sarrin was simultaneously in the corridor and in the jungle and slaughtering researchers in the hidden tower.   The monster clawed at her, asking to come out.

The girl coughed, and stepped forwards.   "Twenty-seven?"

Sarrin started at the nick-name.

The boy she had saved smiled quickly.

"I- I saw your marks," the girl blurted. "When you were fighting Rami and your coveralls ripped."

Sarrin stared. The girl looked the same as her: dark hair, blue eyes, the same sunken cheeks, tired eyes, and haggard frame that had greeted Sarrin the latrine mirror. Another Augment, another experiment.

"We've come to ask you to be the alpha," said Thomas.

It took a minute for his words to register through the encroaching fog. She had always hid the marks, letting others with fewer marks take the position. Sarrin stepped back, shoulder bouncing into the now-closed doors. "No." She wasn't fit to lead.

"Why not?"

She fumbled for the door controls embedded into the wall beside her. "It's not a good idea." She knew how to kill, not save. She was, after all, mostly monster.

"Please," said the boy. "You saved us before."

"We"—Thomas stepped forward, gesturing in a circle around to the four of them—"don't like what's happening. Rami is rallying others around him. At first it was a just a couple, now it's nearly half."

Sarrin frowned.

"He's trying to put himself in charge," said the girl. "I heard him talking in Engineering. How it doesn't make sense to have a common chief engineer, how nothing he does makes any sense, and he's trying to sabotage us."

"We like Kieran," Thomas interjected. "We're worried."

"Rami said he'll space all the commons," the girl said.

Sarrin's head swam, acutely aware of the serene, sleeping figure on the bed just on the other side of the wall.

"We're tired of all the fighting," said the boy she had saved. "Rami's convinced the commons can't be trusted, but if you say they're helping us, then we'll believe that."

Her hand found the controls, and the doors opened behind

her. Sarrin stepped back into the room.

"Wait." They all lurched forward, hands on the frame blocking the door from closing.

"I can't," she said.

The boy leaned forward. "I saw Rami grab you. I know you wouldn't hurt him normally, that you saved me."

The dark edges of her vision clouded in tighter and Sarrin was suddenly dizzy.

"Sarrin," Thomas said, his voice clear. "Rami is right about one thing. Whatever happened to you"—he gestured loosely at her back—"they did all that because they thought you were special, that you were stronger and smarter and quicker than the rest of us. None of us want to go back, we don't want to live in cages or wonder what they'll do to us next. You already killed Guitteriez. You could be our answer. Promise me you'll think about it."

They pulled their hands back, touching their five fingertips to their chests, saluting her as the doors sealed between them.

Kieran breathed softly on the bed beside her. Her head swam. Kieran spaced. Rami in charge. One thing was right though: she had attacked Rami.

Guitteriez too had called her the answer—to a problem she didn't know or understand—and she had killed him, ripped him molecule from molecule. What was to stop her from doing the same to everyone else? Her arms tingled with the remembered heat of the facility on Junk imploding around her, because of her.

A particularly sharp snore cut into her consciousness, breaking the whirlpool of thought that threatened to drown her. She stared at the sleeping form, her feet digging into the grey carpet of the old freightship. Kieran had shared his quarters, his bed, even his secrets—Gods knew why—and all she could offer was danger. Her vision still swam murky at the edges. The monster was close. Too close.

She stepped to the nearest wall, quickly removing a section of paneling, and slipped into the space. She squeezed between the structural supports, crawling on her elbows and pushing with her toes, wedging herself into ever tinier spaces, until she was scarcely able to move her chest. The space suffocated her. It was good, it was right. The place where a monster should be. All her focus was needed for her breathing, each inspiration and expiration marked by a ragged effort. Just like the puzzle cube, it made it easier to remember where she was.

Not perfect. The memories of Guitteriez surfaced, Junk burning in her minds eye. She pushed it away, but not to be silenced, her mind pulled up a fresh memory: An image of the boy, terrified and dirty, as he crouched, hoping to hide himself from his hunters. A flash of his pale blue eyes in the instant he saw her, saw her for what she truly was: a monster. A child hunting another child.

She gripped a metal beam in her hand, bending it. Her body drooped and she fought to suck in air, the cramped space suddenly more than she deserved. She pushed herself forward, squeezing into the increasingly narrow space. She pushed until she had to wedge herself, her shoulders firmly pressed into the metal.

She stopped, the pressure crushing her chest enough that it forced her body to focus on being alive, instead of everything else.

Her mind calmed, and there was the vision of the boy again. Half-standing in front of her, awe in his adult eyes. Half crouched on the ground, screaming.

No, no, no. She tugged on the mats of her hair. It triggered another memory, calm washing over her. A girl brushed her hair, humming softly—a variation on the latest aria from the Musician Laureate. The same girl muttered in her ear, then ran skittering fingers up her ribs, causing young-Sarrin to shriek with laughter until the girl snatched her close and whispered in her ear to be quiet.

Sarrin gasped. Definitely no.

The memory shifted: the same girl, years later, attacking full force while Sarrin scrambled to stay alive and not hurt the girl she had long considered a friend. And young-Sarrin wailed for what had been lost between them.

She forced herself to breathe. What would it have been like if she had never heard of the Red Fever?

She drew an image of the orchards by her house, one of the few memories before everything had changed. The breeze gently dropping the lavender blossoms to the ground. Spring was always her favourite time of year, when the trees started afresh.

One of the branches rustled heavily, sending a swarm of petals swirling in the air. Halud grinned back at her from inside the tree.

No, she couldn't think of her brother.

But he had always been there, permeated her childhood until the disease had ripped them apart.

Someone else's childhood, what would that have been like?

The copper bulkheads designed themselves easily, taking her by surprise. A green-eyed girl chased by a green-eyed boy ran past. They giggled, and when he caught her at the end of the hall, he hugged her tight as they both shrieked with laughter. No one told them to be quiet, there was no reason to.

She slammed back into the space between the walls, unable to breathe. What was happening? Was she pulling memories from people now? The copper bulkheads were the same as the ones in the photo on Kieran's nightstand. The green eyes were his too.

Kieran, marked an enemy, even though he hadn't been anywhere near during the war. He was an Observer, a simple historian who came for exploration. Nothing more.

Her vision swam again, the black tendrils reaching across.

Suddenly the deep of space on the other side of the hull was crushing. The hull had an irregularity to it, the telltale mark of an auto-seal. Another mark to the left and, a little farther away, to the right, the pockmarks were everywhere. The ship was held together by patches. Small miracle it hadn't been torn apart like everything else.

A small slit between the bulkhead and sheet of interior panelling let in light. In it she could see her hands—the normal, pink flesh surprised her. It hid—but didn't prevent from being—the glittering monster skeleton underneath. No matter what happened here, there would always be that. She would never be free. Never be normal. Never be trusted to touch another without bleeding them of their life-force, of being out in the open without a chance of attacking innocents around her.

She was not the answer.

NINE

Gal nodded solemnly at Aaron.

The other man nodded back and they slipped unseen into the night. Stop the destruction at all costs. They had agreed. From the bunker on Earth they had come, sneaking through the ship corridors and grey city streets. This was the mission where they had discovered it, the secret the Speakers tried so hard to protect.

Gal braced his hand on a clammy con-plas wall in the dark alley as he tripped over a piece of engine. The demons crowded around, tittering in their horrible high-pitched voices. He was not okay, he reminded himself. This was not the central city, not the Speakers' compound. This was a ship. But it was getting harder to tell the difference.

A ship that was about to destroy something—another piece of the secret—if he didn't put a stop to it. Something else the Speakers would do anything to suppress.

Aaron pulled a panel from a wall and they slipped inside, squeezing themselves into the Speakers' compound. Gal vaguely pushed aside the thick wires and ropey conduits that belonged more in a starship than a building. The demons clung to them, giggling as they swung back and forth.

Gal stopped them. "This is the spot."

"Why are we in the walls, Gal?"

"We're finding the Speakers' database. Remember?"

"Yes. But why the bomb?"

Gal stared down at his hands and the device he was patching into the ship's main power supply. "No." He blinked twice to ground himself. "I'm hallucinating again, Aaron." But now, at least, he could be certain they were on the warship.

"I know."

"We have to stop them from getting to the planet. It wasn't enough last time."

"You're still hallucinating, Gal."

"This is important, we can't fail. Not again."

"Because of Cornelius?"

"Yes. I didn't understand it, I still can't see the reason why the Speakers' did what they did." He bit his lip. "It's too dangerous. I can't lead them there. I never should have."

Quietly, they moved to the next location, and Aaron handed him another laz-rifle. Gal pulled off the casing, redirecting the connections.

"You almost beat them, you know," said Aaron. "You could do it, if you wanted to."

"Someone else will have to carry on the fight."

"You're the only one who can finish it, Gal."

Gal shook his head. "Not anymore." He paused, taking a deep breath as he studied the connections his fingers had made thousands of times before. "I miss you."

"I'm right here."

"No. I miss the real you."

"What are you getting at?"

"I couldn't stop the warship last time. I couldn't get our voices out. The truth…. I didn't do enough. I have to make this bigger."

"Bigger?"

Aaron helped him push a wall panel out, catching it before it fell, and climbed onto the floor below. The room was small and narrow, engine pieces dangling from the ceiling, the floor littered with scraps in the places it wasn't ripped open all together, but in his mind it was the pristine engine room aboard the Valkas.

"I can't make the same mistake as last time," said Gal. "All costs, remember?"

"Are you sure?"

He fought the torrent that threatened to bring him down, and nodded. "I can't watch it again, I can't see the same pattern over and over. You died for this. I'll die for this."

Aaron dropped the bag he had been carrying. Out of it spilled another laz-rifle and a magnified spanner. Gal set his face in a scowl. He picked up the rifle and the spanner, approaching the engine. Aaron watched as he worked, the grotesque little demons perched right on his head.

"Don't forget your mission, Johnny."

Gal twisted wires around each other. He connected his tablet to the circuitry, reading the hacked passcodes as if from a newsfeed. His fingers flew easily, the same as the day they'd accessed the restricted database, learned things they could never unlearn.

"You're meant to save people. Don't do this."

"What do you know about it, you weren't there."

"I know what we found in the Speakers' Compound. What we learned about the Augments. I was there with you."

"You're dead."

"And you will be too."

Gal grunted. "What does it matter? We all are, just varying degrees."

Aaron sat quietly, the silence hanging in the air so long that Gal turned to see if he was still there.

"You're important, Gal."

"I'm a cracked old fool. In all the years, we never helped anybody. We never saved one person. I only made it worse. And somehow I'm still stuck here. I'm only half alive, Aaron. You get to be all the way dead, but I'm still living this."

He turned to Gal, voice harsh. "I didn't go with you all those years just so you could blow yourself up. There's more you have to do."

"My life is forfeit. I've been dying since the day my shuttle crashed on Indaer, the minute I saw things and understood things I could never un-see."

"What about Cornelius?"

The demons jumped up and down, screaming in his ear.

He clamped his hands over his ears as though not hearing it would ease the searing ache across his gut. "I'm doing the best that I can."

Cornelius had trusted him, and Cordelia. Cornelius was dead and Cordelia was stranded without her companion.

Aaron grabbed him. "Think about what you're doing."

"Don't you see? They'll never stop."

"Will you ever stop?" Aaron pushed him, so he slammed against the wall, breath knocked from his lungs. "You go on and on about it happening again, but it doesn't have to be like this. I realized something, all of it *is* the same, it *is* happening over and over. Remember how I died? Remember when Earth was lost? It's the same. Good intentions, always, with unrealized side effects. You have to stop this. Stop protecting them from the secrets. That's what's killing you."

Gal gasped, the tickle of truth bothering at the back of his brain. "I can't let them find the planet." This was bigger than him, bigger than all of them. "No matter the cost."

"You don't know who you are anymore," Aaron screamed. "This isn't the Valkas! It's not the restricted database! And your friends are not Hap Lansford!"

Another voice surprised him, deep and booming: "Gal!"

He blinked, standing in the engine room of the tiny freightship, debris strewn across the floor. Among the debris, a spanner and a laz-rifle casing. How had he gotten here? Hands grabbed him, lifted him up to his feet. He stared at a tall, hook-nosed man, an identical man behind him—the Augment doctors.

Aaron spoke from the corner, "Gal, you don't know anymore. Think about what you're doing."

"I know what I'm doing!" But it felt futile, wrong.

The doctors grabbed him and pulled, shouting.

Gal struggled in their grip.

"Galiant," Hoepe grunted as he tried to hold him.

The cold sting of an auto-syringe pressed into his neck.

"The withdrawal effects are worse than we thought," said one of the doctors, talking to the other.

But Gal knew better, this was something deeper. His head swam as the drugs spread through his system. "Don't you see, they made you." He looked deep into the crystal blue eyes, eyes that haunted him every night. "They made you."

The doctor shook his head and turned to the other. "We'll have to secure him."

Gal felt himself slipping away, disappearing into oblivion. The past was trying to eat him alive. It was succeeding.

* * *

"What did you do, Gal?" Aaron sat on the chair in Gal's quarters, head hung in his arms.

Gal rolled over in the bed, head groggy. Demons jumped all around him, across the bed sheets and on the floor. He lifted his hand to the memory of the cold syringe, the hiss that pressed into his neck.

Behind Aaron was the bar. The other side of the room was the bunker, destroyed. Gal's hands settled on a set of old shuttle controls. He blinked. "Where am I?"

"You're here with me," smiled Hap.

Gal did a double take. Yes, it was Hap. Much younger, years ago. Tall and lithe. "What's going on?" Gal asked.

"Strength guides us," Hap answered.

Gal shut his eyes tightly, willing away the cascading memories that threatened to drown him. Hap had never understood.

He stumbled out of bed, thumping to the grey floor. He blinked. It was the impact of a shuttle, his shuttle, crashing to the ground—he pushed himself off the brown dirt and leaf litter. Tall trees surrounded him. He looked down, finding himself clad in his old cadet jumper, a scarf tied pretentiously around his neck in the style of the time.

Aaron was gone.

The demons were too.

A voiced called out to him, unseen, "You've forgotten us, Galiant."

He shook his head.

"I am disappointed," said the man in the forest, his accent thick and heavy—a man who never should have been, not if what the Speakers said was true. "I spared your life. I thought you were different."

"It was hard."

"All things are."

Gal dropped to his knees. His head spun violently, his stomach threatening to vomit. "I never asked for this."

"No one ever has. No one asks for the hard way, no one asks to do what is truly right. They think they want to, think they are prepared for the work, but no one truly understands what it means until they are faced with their own path."

Gal sobbed, pounding his hands on the dirt. But it was no longer dirt, it was grey carpet. UEC grey.

Aaron stood in front of him, leaning down.

Gal wrapped his arm around Aaron's leg. "What's happening?"

"The sedative they gave you is making it worse."

A soft hand comforted him. "Shh," she said.

A bolt of panic shot through him, soothed instantly. "Cordelia, you shouldn't be here." But she wasn't here, he was there, in a grassy green meadow, blue sky overhead.

She smiled serenely at him. "I'm not, dear. But you were so upset. I missed you."

"You're not mad?"

"Why would I be mad, dear?"

He blinked in bewilderment. In answer, a spectacled man wearing an antique suit strode into the clearing. "Cornelius?"

The man nodded, acknowledging Gal in his regal way.

"I— I thought you were gone," stammered Gal.

"Whatever do you mean?" the man said, a man who also could not be. "Stay here with us, it will be safe, you will be comfortable. We can take care of your every need."

Gal felt his heart soften, the panic melting away. "You're still alive."

The two smiled at him in return. "We're your friends," said the woman, eyeing him curiously. "It is remarkable, we've never known another being before. Come with us, enjoy food, rest yourself."

And Gal smiled. All around him, a great feast rose up, as if from the earth. Real food, potatoes and maize, field greens and persimmons. His mouth watered at the sight. So did his eyes.

He sat himself on the bench that lined one of the long sides. Cordelia sat at one end, Cornelius the other. They laughed and raised glasses high overhead. A strange custom, but Gal followed.

It was silent as Gal gulped down bite after bite, his body crying out in joy at the taste. It was more than perfect. He exchanged a furtive glance with the two others, and they all burst into laughter.

But something else, some dark memory pulled at him. He felt it coming. He blinked, and the warm meadow with its feast was gone. Gal's chest still rose and fell—it felt good to laugh again after all this time—but his mind came to tell him something was very, very wrong.

He saw the mural first, the story of the Gods painted across the wall. Bloody battle scenes played out in paint, the blood becoming rivers, torrents spreading across the floor.

Demons lay dead in the painting.

He turned.

The fat man, no longer lithe and spry as he was in his youth, made comfortable and large in his station, watched him with beady eyes from behind his desk.

Gal took a deep breath. "I won't apologize for what I did."

The First Speaker stared back at him darkly.

"Hap, say something."

Slowly, he rubbed his hand over his ever expanding belly. "It has never been for you to determine the Path of the Gods, Galiant."

Gal bit his tongue to keep from screaming out that the folk should have free will, that the Gods would never choose the Path that Hap had sold them.

"You caused significant damage to the Valkas, destroyed her entire weapons bank. What were you thinking?"

"I—" He couldn't say it was an accident, couldn't say he didn't know what he was doing. A fit of madness—maybe, it was that, wasn't it? "These planets were perfect. I couldn't let you destroy them."

"We've been friends for years. I've always trusted and respected your opinion, but as First Speaker, I have a duty to protect the folk."

"They were trying to help us!"

"Don't you see. These people who live on the planets do not believe in the Gods. They are dangerous.

Unpredictable."

Why couldn't Hap see? He'd not always been like this. Gal raked a hand through his hair. "They're not dangerous. They didn't even fight back when we went out there and destroyed one of them."

"Keep your voice down," snarled Hap. "What has happened to you, old friend? Perhaps the rigours of Exploration have been too much."

Gal's heart sank. He had expected it, expected this would be the end, but some part of him believed, foolishly, that Hap would turn a blind eye, that he could escape his crimes as he had done so many times before.

"I know what you did," said Hap. "But our official reports say the explosion was the fault of the engineer. A good man will pay for your crimes, but you, my friend, will be spared."

A slow keening had started in Gal's ears, a cry of disbelief, of selfish joy, of terror.

"I have arranged a posting with Freight for you, out in the Deep Black where you can't put yourself in too much trouble. The Gods thank you for your Dedication and Service."

An unseen weight pushed all the oxygen from Gal's chest, and he struggled just to stand.

Hap stood from his chair. "If you'll excuse me, I must convene with the Five. There are now very tricky matters to attend."

Gal watched him go, helpless. He would be spared, but so far from the central planets it would be as if he had ceased to exist. Except he would still exist, he would still be there to serve the Gods, because Hap was right and his name was known. People knew him: Galiant Idim, devoted friend of Hap Lansford, war hero, and surveyor for the Gods.

Demons poured from the mural and swam in the blood that covered the floor. Hap walked through them as if they weren't there, kicking and pushing them out of his way.

When he reached the far door, his pants and shoes were magnificently crisp, unsullied by the blood of millions.

The mounted heads of animals long since extinct stared back at Gal from the opposite side of the room. Hap hadn't hunted these animals, but his ancestors did, and so they were his prize too, displayed in all their glory.

Gal took a step closer, examining one and reading the brass name tag below: 'Beagle, *Canis familiaris*'. It was a strange feeling, touching something that was once so alive but now so still and hard, as though it had never been anything more or less than a bit of rock covered in moss, delicately sculpted.

'familiaris'—familiar.

Gal looked down the line. A beast with massive sticks shooting out from its head: 'Reindeer, *Rangifer tarandus*'. A shaggy creature with sharp teeth as big as a grown man's fingers: 'Grizzly Bear, *Ursus horribilis*'. An entire creature mounted sideways like an upturned smile, its body sleek and muscular with only tiny veils in place of arms and legs: "Perch, *Perca fluviatilis*".

Once all these animals were known to people, familiar, but now they were nothing more than decaying statues.

More creatures, more demons.

This was what the man in the forest had feared, all those years ago when Gal's shuttle crashed there and he discovered an idea more important than any other.

And there, in the middle of the row, standing in his hallucination as though it had been there all along, was a human head, its face permanently twisted into a scream: "Man, *Homo sapiens*".

Gal stumbled backward.

The human race was dying, going extinct the same as everything else.

Years of expedition and terra-forming had failed to yield a suitable planet to replace their Earth. Indaer—Etar was good, but the atmosphere was thin and the gravity too heavy.

Hap was wrong.

Gal ran out the door, climbing the circular steps to the Dome, the secretary chasing after him. But she stopped at the foot of the stair—it was forbidden for a mere human to enter the chamber, lest the Gods smite them down. Gal pressed on, Gods be damned, this was the human race.

His head breached the Dome, the perfectly round permaglass sphere that looked over every inch of the capital city and directly to the heavens, to the domain of the Gods, above.

The Speakers fell silent and stared at him. They stood there, their mouths hanging open: Faith, Knowledge, Prudence, Fortitude and Strength, all staring at this captain who dared to enter their Chamber. Arthur Herrington, Speaker of Knowledge, dropped his data pad on the floor.

Hap lurched forwards, and Gal braced. "Galiant, what are you doing? Get out of here now." Hap glanced up to the sky and kissed his five fingers.

"No," Gal heard himself shout. "I have to talk to you about the planets. It's too important."

The Speakers glanced nervously at each other, surprise and fear laced into their features.

Prudence spoke, nervous, "You should not be in here, it will upset the Gods."

Hap snarled, "We have already made our decision."

"You haven't seen. The planets—planet," he corrected himself, "is beautiful. Lush, green, There's fresh water and good soil, crops ready to be harvested. Everything we could ever want."

Knowledge held up his hands, asking him too quiet. "There are too many variables."

"Too much possible danger—what good is fulfilling our needs in the short term, without care for the consequences," said Prudence.

"We need somewhere to go.   Humanity is dying!" Gal cried.

"We have several colonies—many you helped set up yourself, Captain Idim.   Humanity will thrive once again," said Knowledge.

"We aren't surviving out here. Earth was our home."

"We have been through a difficult time, and difficult times are ahead," answered Fortitude, "but the Path will lead us to salvation."

"What if this is the Path? What if the planets were sent to us for our salvation? We can still make it work."

Hap braced, setting his shoulders. "The Gods do not speak to you, Galiant. We are the Voice of the Gods. And these planets are obstacles on the Path."

Gal gasped.

A hand rested on his shoulder, and behind him stood Aaron. "Gal, what are you doing?" he whispered.

But Gal was caught in the deep undertow of the memory-hallucination. "You destroyed Cornelius. All he ever wanted was to know us, to help us."

"The planet was against the Will of the Gods. It never should have been."

"Maybe we just have to have Faith."

Hap rose to his full height, his expression menacing, body towering—for a minute, Gal almost believed that there was truly a god inside him. "The Path of the Gods is never to be taken lightly, Galiant."

Suddenly, the Five stood around him, heads basked in the light of the dome, refracting around them like halos.   "We know what you have done. Your life has been spared as your disappearance would cause too many questions, but should you ever show your face on the Central Planets again, we can destroy everyone you have ever cared about."

Gal fell back, Aaron pulling him down so they landed in a mess of flailing limbs and grey carpet. Gal scrambled to get to his feet, but Aaron stopped him.

"You don't understand," shrieked Gal. "They'll destroy them."

"Who? Destroy what?" said Aaron.

"They don't see."

"See what?"

"They just destroy—Augments, Indaer, Cornelius—anything that's different, anything that threatens the Gods. They'll destroy me." Gal looked up at Aaron, into his eager, dead, very much alive face.

Aaron rocked back on his heels, afraid. "Cornelius is already gone, Gal. Years ago"

"No." He shook his head. "It's happening over and over. It will happen always."

TEN

Kieran soldered two wires together, stifling a yawn.

He blinked. Blinked again.

Something wasn't right. The connections were crossed— he was holding the wrong wires.

Another blink.

What was he building?

He stepped back, looking up and down the open storage locker. He recognized the device—a signal capture machine, a computer to process the ghosts and fragments of signals sent from too far away that were too eroded to be meaningful without the machine. What he didn't recognize was how he had come to build it.

If there was anything not to build, it was this. A machine not even imagined in this epoch. A machine designed specifically on the Observer ship to collect the transmissions of centuries.

He pressed his lips together. Hoepe's words echoed through his mind, taunting him: *tired engineers making tired mistakes*. He doubted he meant this kind of mistake. He scrubbed his hand over his face. The last thing he remembered was waiting for Sarrin to wake up, and then crawling exhausted onto the bed—he didn't remember lying down or falling asleep.

This machine had something to do with Sarrin.

She wanted to join him on the Observer ship. A guilty warmth started in his gut and spread out to his fingers and toes. Maybe she could. He would show her all his secret hiding places on the ship—the tight spaces behind the engines, and the weightless sections where the grav-plating didn't quite reach to the outer hull.

Would Sarrin like music? The Speakers had a Musician Laureate, but it paled compared to the rock and roll they played over the ship's speakers.

He grinned to himself.

Not only had he found some of the lost Augments, but he was going to bring one back with him. They were always encouraged to bring people back if they found anyone suitable. The Observer ship was massive, but it had been flying for generations. Any new blood would be welcomed.

So why the machine? He looked up at down at its long, cylindrical form and glowing blue power light.

She had been missing from his quarters when he stumbled out of the bed—gone without explanation, although he knew the things that plagued her mind. Dread tapped at his chest. If she came home with him, it would be forever. It would mean leaving her brother behind.

But the signal capture device could easily pick up transmissions from the warship to Etar, even if it was three-days FTL jumping away. That was how it was designed. If Halud was still alive, they would find him. And Halud could come to the Observer ship too.

The thought sat strange with him. Full siblings were non-existent on the Observer ship. It narrowed the genetic pool too much. But Halud, like Sarrin, wouldn't be safe anywhere either. He was an Augment, he had defied the Speakers. He would have to leave with them, and the Observers would just have to live with it.

The geneticist would have his work cut out for him, was all.

The geneticist. He frowned.

Kieran had a sister and a brother, but they were half-siblings—his sister and he shared a mother, his brother had the same father. And all the children were raised collectively. He knew his sister's other sister, and his brother's sister, and all their siblings. No doubt they were probably all related somewhere in the family tree, but it was too complicated to try to figure out in his head.

The geneticists had long algorithms to trace the genealogy. When he returned, they would determine the best match—they would use his genetics to contribute to a child, and a second one—every person two children. And he would help raise them with everyone else on the ship, the same as he'd done with the younger kids before he left.

But his part was easy—a lab sample. They would expect the same from her, only the children lived with their mothers, were borne by their mothers—and she had new genetics, they might want more offspring. The thought of Sarrin ever in a hospital again, undergoing another procedure, another scar—he clutched the locker door.

The machine stared out at him, its soft blue light pulsing gently. He should rip it out, pretend it never existed. But he couldn't. They needed to find Halud. And then... and then what?

What would happen after that was too much to think about. She had asked to come, he wanted her to come. But bringing her to the Observer ship might be the most selfish thing he had ever considered because he hadn't told her what it would mean. His chest sagged, the weight of his body suddenly crushing.

He glanced over his shoulder—the storage area was hidden from the rest of the engineering bay, but not separate. He could hear the dings and clangs and the muffled talk of the Augments working on the other side of the wall, but it was the middle of the night-cycle and the bay wasn't full. No footsteps came towards him.

He would finish it. Quickly. Lock it in the locker and let it run.

His fingers found the multi-dose injector in his pocket, dialling it for a double and pressed the cold stims into his neck.

* * *

"He said, 'they made you'. They made us what?" Hoepe rubbed his temples, slouching into the stiff, grey plastic chair in the canteen.

Across from him, Leove sat next to Isuma. She picked idly at the now-cool ration container in front of her, casting curious glances at Hoepe. Leove shifted, his arm coming off the backrest of Isuma's chair and into his own lap as he grunted and tried to fit himself into the too-small seat. "I've not seen such advanced withdrawal before. You were right to sedate the captain."

"But what did he mean?" Hoepe poked at his own cold ration dish—something with protein noodles and a sauce that looked like purulent discharge.

"He probably meant the UECs trained us, made us into their soldiers and pilots and surgeons—it's not that hard to figure out."

"He said 'made,' not trained."

"The ramblings of a confused addict, Hoepe."

"But what if it's more?"

Leove tore his empty ration container into little uniform strips. "The captain's symptoms go beyond mere addiction. There is a neurologic disorder at work. A brain lesion of some nature." A piece disappeared into his mouth and he chewed it roughly. "The captain could pose a danger, Hoepe.

I know you believe he knows more about this situation than he lets on, but we need to investigate his condition further."

Hoepe forced his jaw to unclench. "I'm not the only one."

"Yes, yes. Sarrin and the engineer."

Sitting up, Hoepe opened his mouth to argue, but thought better of it. The same argument had passed back and forth between them in so many ways already. It wasn't an argument, though, he told himself, they were brothers. They were identical brothers. They simply needed to get to know each other outside the stress of the infirmary, to 'bond'. That was why Hoepe had chosen to take his sustenance break with his brother, even if Isuma was present.

"You should consume the entirety of your meal," he told her, noting her barely touched rations. "The ratio of protein and complex carbohydrates is suitably balanced to help you recover from your recent trauma."

She paled, the muscles in her throat constricting.

"Are you nauseous?" Hoepe reached reflexively for the injector in his pocket, certain there was an anti-nauseant among the doses available.

Isuma shook her head once, turning instead to Leove at the same time as she started to stand. "I think I'm going to go."

Leove stopped her, gently tugging back on her wrist, and to Hoepe's surprise, Isuma sat back down. The long, narrow muscles in Leove's forearm flexed as though he was squeezing her hand as it disappeared under the table, and he held her gaze for a second before turning to Hoepe. He cleared his throat, starting apprehensively. "Tell me how you came to be on Contyna with your men."

Hoepe sat back. The expression he recognized on Leove's face told him he had inadvertently stepped into dangerous territory, but Isuma was a patient, one who had been through significant trauma, shock, and suffered not only burns but a concussion and memory loss. "I simply meant it would be beneficial for her recovery. It would be wise for her to obtain more rest."

Isuma's mouth dropped. "I am going to go." She bolted from the chair. "Sorry." She bent, her lips brushing quickly against the side of Leove's cheek, calling, "I'll see you later," as she exited the canteen.

As the doors closed behind her, Leove turned to Hoepe with a scowl.

"I was only looking out for her health, as should you be."

"I was pleased when you asked to come for supper with me, I thought you were interested in meeting Isuma."

"Isuma?"

"I told you I had hoped it wouldn't come between us."

"I came to be with you. The pilot needs rest, not further examination."

Leove blushed, a deep shade of crimson creeping up from the collar of his shirt that was so incredibly foreign Hoepe felt he was looking at a perfect stranger. "My dear brother, are we not human after all, at our very core, allowed these feelings and imperfections?"

Hoepe could only stare, his mind so jumbled that it was nothing but a complete blank. Of course they were human. He had imperfections, he had been blatantly reminded of that every time a child had died in his care. But Leove was talking of something entirely different.

"We were cell neighbours when we were held on Junk," he started to explain. "We formed a friendship, supported each other through difficult times. She's very special to me."

"I don't understand."

"Have you ever been in love, brother?" His brother's face had gone pink.

The question startled him. "Love?"

"Yes."

He frowned. No, of course not. There had never been

time. As long as he could remember, he had been saving lives. Where would he have learned about love, anyhow? It wasn't a medical condition, wasn't in the textbooks. You learned about love from the people around you, from your friends, your family. He scowled.

Of course, Leove knew what love was, he had known their parents. Spoken with them, treated them, while Hoepe had been alone. Another rift tore open in his heart.

"What is it, brother?" Leove asked, his voice laced with an artificial concern. His brother loved Isuma. And Isuma could feel love too. How was Hoepe ever to compete with that?

"You"—he stumbled on the word—"*love* her?"

A silly grin passed over this face, so foreign that it was nearly repulsive. "I believe I'm starting to, yes."

Hoepe frowned. "Then perhaps we are too different after all."

The expression on Leove's face softened and his arm reached across the table. "Of course we are different."

Something shattered within Hoepe, like a physical deflating followed by a million shards of sharp glass probing into every organ. When he had found Leove, he knew it was the thing he had always been longing for, the piece of him that he had always been missing. Now his brother sat in front of him, as distant as though they had never met at all. Or met again, as Leove remembered it.

"There you are." The harsh voice, followed by the closing of the canteen doors and the short Augment racing towards them, snapped Hoepe out of his reverie. A dozen Augments trailed behind Rami. "The shuttle wasn't an accident, and I have the evidence to prove it." He slapped a handful of wires and a large circuitry chip on the table in front of them, knocking Hoepe's rations over so the purulent gravy splashed across his pants.

"Rami!" Grant shouted, pushing through the Augments in

pursuit.

"I found this in the shuttle bay." Rami pointed to the circuit board.

Hoepe stared at the components. "This means absolutely nothing to me."

"It interrupted the positioning signals the shuttle uses to land, and provided enough feedback that the navigation controls in the shuttle exploded. We're lucky the explosion didn't rip the hangar apart or there would be no sealing it, and we would all be gasping for air right now."

Hoepe gulped. "It must have been an accident. Someone making an error with the wiring, like the convertors?" He looked to Grant.

Grant sighed and shook his head. "It's not likely. The work is detailed, there are too many crossed circuits for it have been an accident."

"Who would have this kind of knowledge?" asked Leove.

Rami looked pointedly at Grant.

"You think I did it?" Grant said.

"I don't think you did it, per se. You said you don't know when they're controlling your mind."

"I keep telling you, it wasn't me. And it wasn't anyone controlling my mind either."

"We can't ignore the possibility. You know more about demolitions than anyone on this ship."

Grant crossed his arms. "Apparently not. It wouldn't have even occurred to me to use the auto-landing controls to overload the shuttle. I've never seen anything like it before." The last of Grant's words came out slowly as he repeated the now too familiar phrase.

"Then it could have only been one other person," Rami said. "The one you always say you've never seen anything like." He turned abruptly, his dozen Augments following him out of the canteen.

"Rami!" Hoepe stood so fast, the bench he was sitting on tumbled across the floor. He bolted after them, Leove immediately following.

Hoepe pushed his way to the front of the pack, his long legs moving him faster than the others as Rami led them through the corridors straight to the engineering bay. Grant flanked him on the left, Leove on the right, but Rami stayed squarely ahead.

"This is cracked," Hoepe tried. "Kieran is helping us."

Rami snarled over his shoulder, "We can't afford to be so soft. What if he tries again, and this time he's successful?"

"There's no evidence it was him," said Hoepe.

"You have to admit there is some evidence, Hoepe," Leove said calmly beside him.

He turned to his brother. "You can't be serious."

"I know you feel indebted to him for the work he's done in the past, but your theory that Kieran is a God is ridiculous."

"You think he's a what?" Rami shouted.

Hoepe felt a burning creep up his neck, but he held himself steady. "We need Kieran. I've never seen anyone do what he can do. It's no secret that he's strange—he acts strangely, he says strange things, like he's not from our time. The Gods have come before to help humanity in our greatest need. Why couldn't Kieran be sent for us?"

"But to say he's a God is blasphemy," said Leove. "It's the most cracked thing I've ever heard."

A knife twisted in Hoepe's central nervous system. It had been placed there by his brother, by his identical brother, who was supposed to be his friend.

The doors to Engineering parted, and they entered the bay. "Where is Kieran?" Rami snarled. Three Augments huddled around the central console pointed simultaneously to the back of the bay, and the pack pushed Hoepe forwards as they made their way to the small storage area.

"This is spread," Hoepe called out, even though he felt the futility of his words as they came from his mouth. "Kieran has saved our lives multiple times."

"Too many times," Rami shot back over his shoulder. "We've been foolish to trust the soldiers—we should have left them at the first chance."

Hoepe ran a disturbed hand over his mouth. He had never been part of the war games in Evangecore, but he had a sudden sickening feeling that he was about to become part of one.

"There's no getting around it," said Rami. "He constantly makes unusual designs, always flipping things around in engineering. This bomb isn't something any of us could have come up with. It has to be Kieran."

Leove shot Hoepe a concerned glance, but they followed obediently, the mob drawing the other Augments in the bay to their flank.

Hoepe bade his feet to stop, bade everything to stop, but like some horrible vid, it just kept rolling. Rami shouted for Kieran as they rounded the bulkhead into the wide storage area.

Kieran extracted himself from one of the lockers that lined the room. "Jesus," he muttered as a spanner went clattering to the ground. He shut the locker door behind him, leaning against it. "You nearly gave me a heart attack." Kieran brushed a hand through his hair casually, but Hoepe noted his hand was shaking. And the pulse in his neck was strained and far too fast—a myocardial infarction, however facetious, was not out of the realm of possibility.

"We have to ask you —," started Grant.

Rami stalked forwards, fists clenched at his sides. "What are you doing?" In one rough motion, he threw open the locker door, sending Kieran stumbling to the side.

"No—." Kieran tried to stop him, slamming the locker

shut again, but it was too late.

There was a machine inside with a long cylindrical shape and a pulsing blue light—they had all seen it. "What is that?" Hoepe asked.

"It's nothing." But Kieran's wide, dilated pupils, and the new tremor in his voice said otherwise. "Leave it alone."

"No, really, what is it?" Leove turned to Hoepe worriedly.

Rami wrenched the locker open again, and Hoepe stepped forward for a closer inspection.

Kieran paled, his mouth hanging open. The dark bags under his eyes and the sickly pallor of his skin only grew more evident. "Really. It's nothing. It's a ... personal project. I was talking to Sarrin, and—"

Rami scowled, shooting a look at Hoepe. "We're low on resources, trying to repair a cracked ship as fast as possible. What are you doing?"

Kieran paled. "A few spare parts, some of my rest time. It's nothing." Kieran sent a pleading look in Hoepe's direction.

But now Hoepe was more confused.

Leove was beside him, implacably calm. "What is it, Kieran?"

Kieran pressed his lips and glanced back, a heat coming into his face. "I can't tell you."

"Is it for Sarrin?" Grant tried.

Carefully, Kieran nodded.

"So, what is it?"

He gave the machine a sidelong look, a shiver running through his entire body. "You have to trust me," he blurted, the air whooshing out of him. "It's nothing." He buried his head in his hand and muttered something that sounded like, "Oh God,"—just one God. "Please. Just forget it. It's not hurting anything."

"It's a bomb," Rami scowled.

"What?" Kieran's eyes snapped open.

"Just like the one in the shuttle."

"Shuttle?"

"Yeah," snarled Rami, "Just like the one you set in the shuttle."

Kieran's face turned white as the sterile rooms in Evangecore.

There was a loud shuffle behind them, and Thomas pushed his way through the group. "What's going on?"

"The shuttle was no accident," said Rami. "I found a bomb, a strange bomb like nothing I've ever seen before."

Hoepe felt his knees go weak. "Rami, stop."

"I didn't set no bomb," Kieran said, voice shaking as obviously as the rest of him.

"Then what is this?" Rami pointed accusingly into the open locker.

Kieran's eyes met Hoepe's, pleading, but like his brother, the eyes he looked into were not familiar. A barrier had fallen between them.

"What does Sarrin say about this?" asked Thomas, his face contorted.

Rami jutted his chin defensively. "Why?"

Thomas glanced between the woman and two men who had come in with him. "Because... because she should be our alpha."

"What?" Rami snarled. "She's spread-mad. And a common-lover. She's sleeping with the enemy. He's blinded her like he's blinded all of you."

Hoepe gulped. Sarrin stayed in Kieran's quarters because somehow he seemed to be the only one she trusted— that, along with her forty-three procedural marks, were secrets, known only by Kieran and Hoepe.

With a roar, Kieran leapt at Rami. "She's not crazy!"

The Augment didn't fall from the impact, but he stumbled

backward. Kieran was on him again in an instant. Hoepe stared, feet rooted in place.

Thomas rushed forward and pulled Kieran back.

Leove held an arm across Rami's chest, pressing him into the lockers.

Hoepe stepped between them, his body numb. "Stop," he said. But this close, he saw for the first time how bloodshot Kieran's eyes were, the inconsistency in his pupils, the slight tremor of fine muscles in his chin and brow.

Kieran hung his head. Thomas released him and he thumped into the wall, muttering at the floor, "I don't know what I'm doing anymore."

"How many stims have you taken, Kieran?" Hoepe put his hand over Kieran's wrists, checking his pulse. It was erratic, empty and stringy, too fast and too weak to possibly be good. "Gods. Kieran, tell me how many?" He realized he was practically holding the engineer up, and Kieran sagged down the wall as Hoepe released his grip.

Beside them, Rami pulled the machine from the locker and it crashed across the floor. Its blue light sputtered out.

Kieran sucked in, a horrible, stilted sob. "It's not hurting anything," he said. "It's not a bomb, just a stupid, stupid mistake."

"We ought to space him," shouted Rami, "for being a traitor, for wrecking the shuttle, for planning to explode this entire ship."

Hoepe stood between Kieran and the rest of them, a barrier. "He didn't set the bomb. He's sick." The words felt hollow even as they left his mouth. Could Rami be right? This was his friend, couldn't they see that? Or had it all been orchestrated?

"Brother," Leove laid a hand on his shoulder, "I know you care about the engineer, but we have to face facts."

"No," Hoepe whispered. "We don't have proof he caused

the shuttle accident."

Leove stared back at him, his expression cold and stony—the same expression Hoepe would have made if someone was being dangerously unreasonable. Because there was evidence. All the signs he had tried so hard to ignore and explain away, were too much. Kieran wasn't a God, he wasn't even his friend. A trillion shards of shattered heart stabbed into every inch of him until Hoepe wanted to cry out in pain. Kieran, like his brother, wasn't at all what Hoepe had expected.

He pulled himself to his feet. It seemed harder than ever, an eternity before his frame straightened himself.

Kieran was bent over, his head in his hands, watching through his fingers as Rami pulled the machine apart. "It's not a bomb," he croaked.

A tiny bit of hope stitched some of the fragmented pieces together, and Hoepe bent down. "Then what is it, Kieran? Just tell us."

Kieran shook his head. "I honestly can't tell you. I can't even think of an explanation that will make sense."

Hoepe pulled back. How could that be? "Try."

Beside them, machine parts clunked on the floor as they ripped it out.

"You understand how this looks," Hoepe urged. He wanted nothing more than for Kieran to give him an explanation. Kieran might be a God, maybe it was something to help them. But Kieran only slumped further, his hand clutching at the shirt over his chest.

"Hoepe, we can't trust him," said Leove. "Look at all this. Grant says it's the most complex bomb he's ever seen. He doesn't even know where the trigger is."

"It's not a bomb."

"Kieran, if it's something to help Sarrin, tell us."

He shook his head.

It was irrational, but Hoepe looked up at the others all the same. "It's not what it looks like."

"What about the bomb in the shuttle?" said Leove. "He's the only one who could have done it."

"No," said Hoepe.

"I didn't set no bomb," said Kieran.

Grant frowned, poised between rushing forward to help and teetering back with fear.

Hoepe chose the only thing that he truly knew anything about, and he pulled the auto-injector from his coveralls, dialling it to the last dose of sedative. Kieran had taken enough stims, combined with long-term exhaustion, to actually overload his heart, and Hoepe had been trained to never let anything die. "Kieran, you're high on stims. When was the last time you slept more than ten minutes?"

"I didn't set no bombs." But Kieran's face scrunched up, his eyes unfocussed.

There was no other option. The injector hissed against Kieran's neck, and Hoepe lifted him. "I'll take Kieran back to his quarters," he said to Leove.

Leove put a hand on Hoepe's arm, but Hoepe only flinched away, the touch less than meaningless. "I think Rami's right. We can't ignore this threat. I'm sorry. I'm going to put my vote behind Rami and the Rule of War. We need him to check over everything in Engineering."

Hoepe pushed through the Augments, nearly all of them pressed into the small space, despite the late hour, despite not seeing that many in engineering ten minutes ago. He didn't dare look at them or their expressions.

Grant caught up with him as he entered the corridor, pacing silently beside him.

"Usually it's Kieran carrying Sarrin around," Hoepe said.

Grant managed to override the door lock, and they stepped into the empty quarters. "Where's Sarrin?" He asked. "Is this really where she's been staying?"

Hoepe set Kieran on the bed gently.   "I don't know."
Sedated, the engineer was nothing like his usual bright self, he
was just another body, another human machine.   "Do you
think he did it?"

Grant bit the inside of his cheek.   "No, I don't.   I didn't
have a chance to really look at the thing in that locker—I tried
to stop them but they just tore it up faster.   It wasn't like
anything I'd ever seen before, I couldn't see any kind of
trigger or detonator, no feedback loops, nothing.   I know how
to make things go boom.   That machine wouldn't have
exploded—not more than anything else at least.   Truth be
told, most things will explode if they're overloaded or mis-
wired.   It's because of Kieran that nothing has.   Not the other
way around."

"You saw the shuttle.   Do you think Kieran could have
done that?"

Grant rubbed his jaw.   "I'd never seen anything like it,
which is what we say about most of what Kieran does.   But he
wouldn't have, not on purpose.   And if he had actually
wanted to tear the ship apart, that's what would have
happened."

"If not Kieran, who else?"

"I don't know."   Grant hung his head.   "But we all make
mistakes.   I actively tried to blow up the ship when you landed
on Junk the first time—you've forgiven me."

Hoepe sighed.   "So what do we do?"

Grant hesitated again.   "You have to take my chip out.
Rami has enough evidence to make everyone in that engine
room follow him.   Even your brother agrees.   The Rule of
War is inevitable.   I have more marks than he does, but he's
convinced the others that the UECs are controlling me, and
that Kieran is controlling Sarrin—neither of us are fit for the
job, so he becomes our leader by default.   But if the chip is
out, I can be the alpha.   I can at least keep Kieran from

getting spaced."

Hoepe's heart dropped.   "We can't remove your chip. There are too many unknowns."

"You have to take this chip out of me, or I think Kieran is going to die," Grant said. "And then what happens to us?"

"We need a full neural scan. We don't know how the suit is tied in, or how the mind control element works."

"If Kieran is really what you say, we have to take the chance. Rami has gotten more extreme. He idolized Sarrin, the idea of her at least. Now he's confused and angry that she's not what he expected, and he thinks its Kieran's fault she's not the same."

"But Sarrin's always been like this."

"I know, but Rami saw her leap through the observation tower during the war games, and he's never forgotten. He says she's the only one who really understood we had to attack to survive, 'fight is might'." Grant pointed at the sleeping figure on the bed. "Kieran might be a God, but he bruises the same as us. If something happens to him, we'll all die. Or at least be smote down."

Hoepe took a steadying breath. All his instincts, the years he'd spent as a trauma surgeon, told him this was a very bad idea. Inspire of that, he nodded once, they would remove the chip. There was nothing else they could do.

ELEVEN

Sarrin pushed open the grey panel, catching it before it fell onto the grey floor and sliding out into the grey room. Kieran laid on the single bed, silent and unmoving except for the artificially slow rise and fall of his chest.

Certain he was asleep, she rounded the bed and peered down into his face. Unbruised. She pressed her five fingers to her chest in thanks. The terror that had flooded the ship, the images of Kieran surrounded by angry Augments, had overwhelmed her—sent her vision spiralling into blackness, the monster screaming at her to run. Only there was nowhere to run. The tight spaces between the walls of the ship held her, squeezed her tight, the weight pressing on her like a grav-trap in Evangecore. She spent unknown minutes —hours?—simply suspended. She would have stayed had it not been for the call of a particular biological function—a remnant of being human.

The latrine was standard—shower, toilet, sink, and a small mirror. She ducked her head, averting her eyes as she passed her reflection. Palms pressed into her eyes, shooting stars across the emptiness. Another bathroom in another time: *Amy stood at the sink, soaking the edge of a ripped shirt in the running water. "Gods, Sarrin," she said, reaching out to dab at Sarrin's cheek, "why didn't you protect yourself?"*

Sarrin, age eight-standard, sniffed, sucking up her quivering lower lip.
Pain seared as Amy cleaned the blood from her already swollen face, the
split in the skin stinging as the cloth brushed against it.

"I didn't mean to hit you so hard. I thought you were going to move."
And why hadn't she?

"The next time they put us against each other, I want you to fight,
okay. I know you can."

She shook her head. "Why do we have to fight? I don't want to hurt
you."

Amy bent down in front of her—at age twelve she was nearly a head
taller than Sarrin. "Because I don't want them to hurt you."

A fresh round of sobbing rose from the knot in her chest. "I don't
understand."

Amy drew her in, wrapping her arms around Sarrin's little body. "I
don't want them to think you're weak. You're strong, I know you are.
But you're also kind, and that... that doesn't seem to mean anything
here." She pushed Sarrin to arms length, looking intently into her face.
"They will make us fight again, Sarrin. They know we're friends, and
that's the reason why—they want to know if we will still hurt each other.
When they do, you have to promise me you'll try. No matter what
happens, no matter what they make you do or me do, I will always be
your friend. Always, always, always."

Sarrin blinked, sitting once again in the little grey latrine.
Amy had protected her, even when Sarrin was too stubborn to
know the price of not obeying in Evangecore. And Sarrin
had been unable to return the favour when Amy had needed
it most. No doubt she was dead, a childhood memory long
gone.

She returned to the main room, intent to slip out the way
she came, but Kieran was sitting up in the bed, scrubbing a
hand over his face. "Hey," he called out, making her pause.
"Where did you go?"

His speech was off, his eyes too droopy. She took a step

closer to the bed, examining his pupils. "Sedative?" she realized, surprised he had agreed to take one.

His eyes darted to the side. "Yeah. Hoepe...." His hand brushed wildly through his hair. "God, I feel awful." One leg reached out of the bed, pushing uncertainly against the floor. He wobbled, nearly falling forward as he stood. Instinctively, Sarrin reached her hand forward, jerking it back before she made contact. Their eyes met in a horrible, terrifying heartbeat. Kieran fell back instead, plopping onto the bed.

"You haven't metabolized the drug yet," she said.

"Yeah." His hands rubbed all over his head and face, and he groaned into them loudly. "What have I done?"

She straightened, scanning the room for evidence— something significant must have happened while she was lost to the monster and trapped in the walls. There were three escape routes and thirty-six objects that could be used as deadly weapons.

No.

The console screen flashed an intermittent green light— powered on but the screen was dark. She stepped to it, activating the console with a touch of her finger, and it lit up. A program she wasn't familiar with shone out at her, on it was a string of words and short form abbreviations. It was difficult to read, but she picked up enough: 'Evangecore', 'alive', and 'continue study'. Kieran was writing a letter home.

The Rubik's cube spun in his hands, its multicoloured surfaces flashing quickly.

"How do you do that?" she said.

He frowned, gaze steady on the cube, and grunted harshly, "Practice."

The gruffness was so unlike him, it nearly pushed her into a trance. She looked for escape, but her feet stayed rooted in place. Instead, she said, "You were writing a letter to the

Observers."

His vibrant green eyes lifted, suddenly wide in panic. "What?"

She turned to the console—what else could it have been?

He was beside her in an instant, then brushing past and leaning into the screen, his movements clumsy but agitated. He cursed under his breath, a word she didn't quite recognize. Eyes darted across the screen, his pulse bounding loudly enough she could hear its rising pace. "This is bad." He huffed and paced to the opposite side of the room, returning only to stare at the writing again. His finger hovered uncertainly, then withdrew and he paced again.

Sarrin pressed herself into the wall, pushing out of his way.

He stopped in front of her, white. "What do I do?"

She shook her head. Wasn't he supposed to write a report home?

"If I leave it there, someone will find it eventually. But Rami will be watching, and if I erase it, he'll have a tag to find everything." He lifted his wrist, looking as though he normally kept something there, and then turned his head to the clock on the console. "How long have I been out? Long enough for him to hack my computer." He cursed again.

She took a tentative step towards his hunched shoulders. "Why would Rami be watching?"

Kieran sighed. "The shuttle crash wasn't an accident. Someone set a bomb. They think I did it."

Her foot took another step. "Why?"

"It was stupid. The thing is, I can't be sure I didn't." He paced across the room, throwing his arms into the air, and she stupidly followed. "I don't remember writing that letter, Sarrin!" His hand flew out, nearly bumping into her. "I was building something in Engineering, and I don't remember starting that either. Rami found it. He thinks it was a bomb, the same as I set in the shuttle, the same as I rewired all those convertors." He let out a rough roar and fell back on the bed, head once again in his hands.

"The solution with the convertors was sound."

"Well, Rami didn't think so. Someone rigged one wrong and it blew up." He sighed again, straightening. "Like, not really blew up, just fizzed a bit. Problem is, Rami has the Augments rallied against me. Even Hoepe thinks I caused the shuttle to crash. And, I don't know, did I?"

"No."

"How do you know?"

Because she had visions of him working, and never had she seen him in the shuttle hangar. Because she had been with him when it happened. Because Evangecore had opened up too many extra senses in her mind and the idea of Kieran sabotaging a shuttle rang completely false. "It's not in your nature," she answered simply. She took the final step to him, bending down.

His eyes were red, uneven from the sedative, and a thick layer of moisture collected on the lower lids. "I'm scared, Sarrin," he said, his voice cracking. "He's going to come for me. This rule he's set up so he's in charge, is it... is it normal? Is there a different way?"

"It's how we commanded our war teams in Evangecore." She frowned. Amy had been their leader most often, her tactics calculating and deadly.

"I asked you before what you would do...."

She shook her head to stop him—a monster couldn't lead.

"Please. Rami is in the engine room, tearing all the repairs apart. Gal still says the planet is a bad idea, and we couldn't even get to the surface if we tried. We expected the warship two days ago, and by some grace of God they haven't come back yet, but they're gonna." A fresh wave of emotion rolled off of him, so foreign she lurched back: anger. "They'll listen to you, Sarrin. But you're too scared to go out there and face them."

Everything flinched, her vision clouding around the edges. "I can't. What if—"

"You can't keep running away, hiding in the walls. Wanting to come back to the Observer ship—it's the same thing. But this is your fight. No one is going to make your life better but you. You're the best one for the job, don't you understand?"

Something flew by in her peripheral vision: a data tablet.

"Did you see that?" The weight of Kieran's anger lifted, and he turned his head left and right. Memory chips and old ration containers flew around the room. The bright Rubik's cube went spinning through the maelstrom.

She gasped, letting it all fall.

"Sarrin?" he whispered hoarsely. "That was you, right? Because I got so upset. I'm sorry." He rubbed his fists into his eyes. "I haven't been sleeping, pumping myself full of stims and now seds. I'm probably as messed up as Gal."

She picked up the photo frame that had fallen at her feet, staring at the smiling faces. At a man who was not the same as the one in front of her. Her lips pressed together. "I told you I'm dangerous. I can't control it. I'm a monster."

Silence followed, and when she finally chanced to look at him, his gaze held her. "You're not a monster."

She bit her lip.

"I'm sorry I yelled," he sighed. "I... had a rough day... week... month...."

She nodded.

"I mean it," he said. "You're not a monster. You never were and you never will be. Got it?"

She turned away. "You need sleep."

"Say it with me," he told her. "Say, 'I am not a monster'."

She turned the photo in her hands to avoid his gaze. "It's foolish, Kieran."

"Sarrin, it's true. Just once. You can't keep telling yourself you're a monster, you've got to change it and change the way you think. These things that happened, they were terrible, but none of them were your fault. The only thing you are in control of is what you do now, what you do with the cards you've been dealt."

How did the girl in the photo smile that way? Gleaming white teeth on full display, only her green eyes brighter.

"Please, Sarrin."

Her eyes squeezed shut and she pushed the words out in a rush: "Iamnotamonster."

"Close enough."

"Kieran, what's 'cards'?"

He barked out a laugh, sharp and hard in the tiny room, and collapsed back on the bed. "Just tell me it's all gonna be okay."

Her mind flashed an image of Amy, leading their battle group, as they stood around, heads bowed in defeat. *"It will be okay, Sarrin," she said, but it was a lie, Sarrin could feel it in her tiny bones. They should not have lost. They never lost—none of the kids ever really lost or won, they just beat on each other until the sedatives permeated the air in the room and they all laid down to sleep and were transported to their dorms, or the infirmary—but this battle was particularly poor.*

In that moment, Amy lied, but Sarrin understood the reason: hope, so she nodded, a smile on her face.

Amy laid down, beckoning Sarrin to follow, and she did, allowing the drugs to take her into sleep.

They never saw Amy again.

"Yes," she told Kieran. "It will be okay. I'll stay while you sleep." Like she should have stayed with Amy. Like she should have stayed with Halud.

His eyes fluttered closed, exhausted. "Thanks." A minute later, soft snoring echoed around the room.

* * *

Hoepe threaded the large bore needle directly into the vein as Grant held his arm out. The infirmary was quiet. It needed to be that way. The last thing Hoepe needed was for Leove to see what he was about to do, to remind him what a very bad idea it was. "Tell me there's no other option," he said.

"Not a good one," said Grant. "We'll be a lot better off if there's no way for anyone to control my brain, for a lot of reasons."

Inhaling, Hoepe centred himself, shifting his perspective from friend to surgeon, Grant melting away into a faceless patient. He pressed his five fingers to his chest, eyes closing as he prayed. "Ready?"

"Someone put it in me, which means you can take it out. I know you can, Hoepe."

Hoepe pulled his hands back, wiping them on the back of his shirt so that Grant wouldn't see the shaking. "Okay." Hoepe pushed the dose of sedative—a strange concoction he had scraped together from incompletely dispensed vials and cartridges—through the needle into Grant's vein. Grant blinked up at him once, then slumped sideways, and Hoepe guided him gently to the table.

Normally, Leove would assist by attaching the myriad of monitors, but his brother wasn't here, so Hoepe did it all. The machines started to beep in their comforting rhythm. He palpated Grant's skull, marking the telltale indent with a surgical pen. It seemed far back, not in the same place as the others, but this was a very different kind of chip. He swiped across the skin with sterilizing solution.

What was Grant melted away, becoming nothing more than a body, a medical machine that always followed a certain set of parameters.

Hoepe's blade cut through the skin easily, a drop of blood oozing out of the small incision. He pushed the soft tissues out of the way with a pair of blunt scissors, exposing the shining white cranium. The bone saw made him grimace as it whirred against the bone—forever reminding him of Evangecore, of emergency surgeries and resuscitations—but the craniotomy was quick.

Hoepe glanced at Grant's monitor readings—steady. The chip was visible, resting prominently on top of the grey matter. He blew out another breath.

The laparoscope camera slipped easily into the opening, resting on the edge. Slowly, Hoepe fed the forceps and grasped the chip. The chip would slide out easily, the same as all the others. He prepared himself, and gave it one, steady tug.

An alarm went off with a shrill beep. In an instant, Grant's body danced, and the sickly limpet flesh exploded from between his shoulder blades, wrapping around him, pulling the camera and tools from Hoepe's hands. The body stood for a minute, and then crashed to the floor.

Hoepe stood for a second, too shocked to move, his hands still held up, poised for surgery. "Grant!" He darted around the table, kneeling beside his friend. Alive or dead? With the ugly suit, there was no way to tell. Only one eye was exposed, rolled backwards in his head. Hoepe fumbled for a light, tugging at the eyelids until he could see a fragment of the cornea, and shone the light in. The pupil contracted: alive.

"What's happening?" Leove appeared in the door, dropping to his knees beside them. "I heard the monitors and then you shouting."

In the doorway, Isuma stood watching, holding back. The bottom of Hoepe's stomach fell out from under him, his diaphragm spasming so badly he couldn't breathe. They had been on a social call.

Leove rolled Grant over. "Help me get him onto the table."

Dumbly, Hoepe lifted. Isuma came forward to help, and

the three of them put Grant back onto the procedural bed.

"What were you thinking?" Leove connected probes to Grant's skin suit, pushing angrily. "I thought we agreed it was too dangerous."

"You don't understand," said Hoepe.

"I don't understand?" Leove shouted—an outburst of emotion with a myriad of expressions Hoepe had never shown in his life. "He has a chip that we know is tied into the depths of his consciousness, that's tied into an implant we know literally nothing about."

Hoepe's chest jerked, drawing a short gasp. "We had to try," he growled. "There wasn't any other option."

"What? Because of Rami? Because you're worried about your common friends?" Leove gripped the edge of the table. "You cracked fool. Grant was the only one who Rami might have listened to."

The monitors beeped, cold and steady. Hoepe stared down at Grant, unconscious, the suit wrapped around the laparoscope that jutted form his head. "He wouldn't have listened to Grant with the chip in his head. He wouldn't have listened to Sarrin. He wouldn't have listened to anyone."

Leove took a deep breath. "I see that this is difficult for you. But have you considered Rami is right?"

"You can't tell me you agree with him," Hoepe snapped. His hands slammed on the table, and he instantly regretted himself as Grant's body rocked from the force, the limpet suit drawing tighter around him.

"I respected that you have known these people longer, and you have your crew of trusted men. But they're UEC soldiers. We have always fought to be out from under UEC control, and yet we were happy to subjugate ourselves to it here." He rubbed his hand over several days worth of stubble he had allowed to grow—another foreign entity. "I know you have your reasons, but perhaps it is time to let them go. Look at the evidence we're faced with."

"What evidence?"

"The captain was found hallucinating in the engine room. The first officer is a devout follower of the Speakers. The engineer has been setting bombs. A shuttle was tampered with and nearly tore the ship apart."

"You don't know he was building a bomb," Hoepe said through gritted teeth. "I don't understand why you're being so difficult. You are supposed to be my bother. Identical."

"We have identical genetics, Hoepe. But we were raised very differently."

"Thank you for the reminder. It seems you have to remind me of a great many things since you remember it all, and I was made to forget. You had a family at least, someone to teach you how to love. Kieran was one of the only friends I had, and you want to space him. And now Grant's... like this." He gestured to the grey-brown, unconscious form.

"You did this to Grant. And I never wanted to space Kieran, but it's hard for me to trust him," Leove said, voice tight. "Don't think your life was so much more difficult than mine. You got to forget. I remember every day. Did you know they survived for a time—with the hideous and painful boils, disfiguring tumours, all of it. They were my patients, Hoepe. For five years, I watched them suffer, trying to save them from a disease for which there is no cure. Father went first. I still hear mother's pain, see the scars. I can't get the sound of her voice out of my head as she told me to stop. To stop trying to save her. To let her go." He seethed, breathing heavily, eyes dark with pupillary dilation. "It was the UECs that did that. Forgive me for not trying harder to embrace them."

Hoepe's mouth worked to find the words.

"It's not my fault you feel alone. It's you, you've decided you're alone, you're hurt, you're wounded. But you forget, I am your family. No matter how we disagree, I am your family. I'm sorry we're not the same, Hoepe. I truly am. I'm sorry that our lives were different. But it doesn't mean we have to hide things, it doesn't mean we can't talk about our disagreements."

"How was I supposed to make you understand?"

Leove threw his hands up in the air. "If I knew taking out Grant's chip was this important to you, I would have helped. I would have. But you never told me."

"You always said it was a bad idea." And in hindsight, it really was, but Hoepe was too worked up to admit it now.

"I wanted to take his chip out, I did. But there were too many unknowns. It likely threads into his amygdala, into his hypothalamus. You might have killed him."

"So what do we do?" he growled.

"I don't know." Leove reached a hand towards Grant's head and the laparoscope that jutted out the side, but he stopped himself. "Gods, of all the horrors I've seen from Evangecore, this is the worst."

Hoepe's jaw clenched, the fear taking hold of his gut and twisting it in a knot.

"We need to tackle this fresh in the morning, I think. Everyone's cortisol levels are dangerously high. We need to pause, cool down. There's no more room for rash decisions or errors."

"It wasn't a rash decision."

"Promise me you won't do anything more to him before morning," Leove said. He glanced at the monitors, eyes darting rapidly as he took in the steady if not slow heart rate, the adequate blood pressure and blood oxygenation, then he turned and left the infirmary.

Isuma glanced up at Hoepe, turning her lips up into a sad smile. She touched his arm quickly before following Leove. "Everything looks brighter in the morning," she said.

And Hoepe was alone with the grey-brown mess of limpet suit and medical paraphernalia who used to be his friend.

Not a little alone. Truly alone.

* * *

Rayne swallowed as she walked into the engineering bay, data tablet under her arm. Engineering had a different sort of feel to it, something she couldn't quite put her finger on but that made her breath come in little forced gasps all the same. The engine room was mess, more so than before, the engine in a complete state of disarray as pieces were flung out of it and across the room. "Hello?" she called.

An annoyed grunt met her first, before a red faced Augment stuck his head out the engine block itself: Rami. "What do you want?"

She held the data tablet like a shield. "Where's Kieran?"

Rami pushed himself out of the open access tube and was across the floor standing in front of her in an instant. "Why are you looking for him?"

"Uh." She glanced at the tablet, reminding herself. "I'm the First Officer, I'm in charge of work schedule and ship resource allocation. I came to see if there was anything that he needed."

"Yeah, there is something we need," he said. "I need for that crackpot everyone believed was an engineer to not have done this to the engine."

The tablet slipped in her arms from the shock of it. "Sorry?"

"We found the bomb Kieran was setting. He's not in Engineering anymore, and neither should you be."

Her pulse raced erratically—a bomb? Kieran?

Rami pushed into her. "We don't need you in here," he said. "Now go."

All her instincts told her to flee, but she held her ground. "I'm a soldier of the United Earth Central Army, and this is a

Central Army ship. I'm here to help."

"Oh, like when you locked us all in Evangecore, to *help*?"

"I—. We didn't know." Rayne pressed her lips together.

"You're lucky I don't lock you away like I did him." Rami turned away, grabbing a piece of the engine block. With a roar, he ripped it from its mooring and sent it bouncing across the floor. "The engine has to be completely stripped. I don't even know if it's fixable." He stormed across the room, with his arm draped dramatically across his head. "It's completely insane that he was allowed to even be in here. These circuits are all wrong, the connections totally botched."

"I-I've always though Kieran was a very good engineer," she managed.

"No," he shook his head, still pacing. "That's what he wanted us all to think. But he was a traitor, a saboteur."

Rayne bit her tongue. *In the Gods we Trust.* "Central Army officers have the necessary training to run this ship."

"This is an Augment ship now. Go back to your quarters, Commander."

"I've been aboard this ship for years. I can help you."

"Get out," Rami snarled.

A firm hand gripped her arm, tugging her backwards. "I'm sorry for what happened before. We didn't know," she said.

Rami stepped up to her, even as the hand pulled her away. "Don't for a second think we believe you didn't know what was going on. You UECs are all the same, with your cracked little Speakers. Who tortures children? Who holds them captive for decades and pits them against each other? Get out!" he snapped. "We Augments have been working together a long time. We take care of ourselves."

The hand dragged her from the engine room, Rami's angry, red face left behind a wall of grey. "It's not safe for you here," whispered the man when he finally let her go, his blue eyes darting warily back to the engine room. "You need to go."

Her breath caught, and she turned to run, any bravado long since used up in front of Rami. She pressed her data tablet into the Augment's chest, trusting him to catch it before it fell. Her hands dropped into her pockets as she ducked her head,all but running across the bay.

Her fingers caught on a data card, small and tucked away, nearly forgotten. Gal's chip.

In the time she'd known the Augments, she had come to realize the UECs were wrong—they weren't cold, heartless killing machines. But Rami was different—he left a fridgid darkness in her after only a few words. He could not be predicted, and he had taken control of the ship.

It couldn't hurt to have an extra layer of protection. Just in case. It was still their ship. Gal was the captain and she was still his first officer. Regardless of how complicated the mess became, she still served the Gods and the Central Army.

Carefully, so no one would see, she paused at an open console right beside the exit doors. She tapped into the system and plugged the chip into a data receptacle. An icon appeared, the program uploading rapidly, then it flashed to tell her the transfer was complete.

She pulled the card from the console and left quietly, crushing the data chip between her thumb and forefinger. Gal had always been trustworthy, a good man to his very core. It was something she'd known about him from the very first moment they'd met, and never doubted. This was the same.

TWELVE

The receptionist, Joyce, nodded with a serene smile as Halud passed her desk. He gripped the handrail of the staircase. The summons had come not five minutes ago, and Halud had already delayed too long. It was an honour to serve the Speakers and they demanded immediate response.

He knocked once and pushed open the door to Hap Lansford's ornate office. His feet made soft thumps as he walked across the room to the desk.

The Speaker watched him the entire way. "I heard there was almost a problem with the report on the Xenoralia vaccine, Halud."

Halud clenched his hands on the arms of his chair. "I was surprised, was all."

Hap swirled a large cup of brandy in his hand as he sat behind his massive desk. "Why? The Red Fever was devastating."

Halud fought to keep his tongue in check.

"Speak up."

He pursed his lips, choosing his words. "It was such a long time ago, I suppose I hadn't thought there was a vaccine in development."

Hap frowned. He leaned forward, arching over his girth

with great difficulty, and started a queued recording. On the vid, Halud asked the question about vaccine reversion.

"I thought I had shown you that lying does not work. You're scared about the vaccine causing the disease."

Swallowing heavily, Halud's cracked voice came out as less than whisper: "Yes."

Hap stood, a smile bloating his once handsome face. "The Gods are good, Halud. This vaccine is a wondrous gift."

His mouth too dry to swallow, Halud could only blink.

"Do you have so little faith?" Massive hands reached out and shook Halud's chair. "Do you believe us only to be creations of evil? Look at all of the things the Gods have achieved."

Hap turned away, moving to a particular segment of the floor-to-ceiling mural. He beckoned for Halud to join him.

The mural depicted the Rock of Antiche, the Five Gods standing around it. It was the story of the beginning, and Halud knew it well.

"When our ancestors first came to Earth, it was a terrible, barren place. Most of the world was dust and stone. Beyond the mountains lay the seas, the only water too sulphuric to drink. There were no grasses, no grains, no plants of any kind. Human beings emerged, cold and thirsty and hungry, but there was nothing to satiate their needs. They lay dying.

"Then, the Gods came to them. Faith lifted them up and turned them to work, even when they could barely stand. Knowledge showed them the way to plant the crops that would feed them. Strength dug the well that would water them. Prudence built the shelters that protected them from the heat and the cold and the storms and the light. Fortitude healed them of their wounds, and showed them all they could achieve despite the many hardships."

The words were as familiar to Halud as his own breath.

Hap moved to the next depiction, a baby surrounded by

shining light. "The Gods departed, but they left a piece of themselves for us, so that we could always be guided. For generations, this has been passed down, the gift passing from father to son, mother to daughter."

The next image was of a battle, one of Hap's ancestors holding a bloody spear. "Through the ages, the Gods have always prevailed." The rest of the painting was dedicated to Strength, his, and sometimes her, muscular body on full display, tearing and lifting and shredding and stabbing.

Physically, it was a far cry from the man Halud saw before him.

"What are you going to do with the vaccine?" Halud asked.

"It is the Will of the Gods, Halud. We will do what they ask of us."

Halud frowned.

"You will do it too." Hap turned on him, his face darker than any night or warped vaccine Halud had ever seen. "Need I remind you the Comrade is on her way to Junk as we speak?"

Halud pressed his fists to his sides to keep the from shaking, mustering as much bravado into his voice as he could. "My sister is not a thing for you to play with. She isn't a tool to make me do exactly as you say. Tell me what you plan to do with the vaccine."

"Oh, Halud." Hap chuckled and returned to his chair. "The infection that changed your sister was not my fault. But what happens to her next will rest squarely with you."

THIRTEEN

The **UECAS** Comrade tore into space, shooting out of its gravity hole on the far side of Junk. Commandant Amelia Mallor stood at the central control hub, her hands tensed on the metal railing.

There was something here that unsettled her. It was not simply the shame of completing a job haphazardly, the certain death of the fallen freightship not confirmed. Nor was it enduring the surreptitious stare from her first officer. It was a quiet and unnatural thing in the back of her mind.

The ship glided soundlessly through space, the small magnetic moon rotating rapidly on the large view screen that surrounded the front wall of the ship. There was a disturbance on the surface, a long crack that was a darker colour than the rest of the moon, but the rotation made it impossible to see more clearly from this distance.

Amelia caught herself drumming her fingers on the edge of her console, and quickly suppressed the nervous movement.

The pilot shifted the steering sphere, the thrusters adjusting their course slightly. The view screen changed from the magnified image to a clear window, showing them actual space.

"Scan the moon," she ordered. She kept her expression stony, but her hand opened and squeezed closed repeatedly.

The Operations officer replied: "There is too much magnetic activity, Ma'am. I'm not getting a clear reading."

She glared at the man. She considered ripping out his trachea, but the magnetic field of the moon was not his fault.

The pilot eased them up to the moon, synchronizing their path with the rotation.

"Take us over the crevice."

The ship moved slightly, the view of the moon in the clear windows above them changing. And there it was, the long, dark gouge in the surface. At the near end, scorch marks covered the trench, small specks of littered canisters and deep furrows outlined their trail.

She followed it, craning her neck. Her teeth ground together anxiously as the grooves grew deeper where the ship had ground into the grey soil. And there at the end, at what should have been the final resting place of the freightship Ishash'tor, was a hole, unsettled dust still floating above the surface.

She gripped the console so hard it cracked. A growl escaped her throat. They had been fooled, bested by a ship full of filthy Augments.

She could feel the eyes of the others on her. Pathetic underlings. She didn't bother looking at the officer who suggested there was no way the freightship could have survived. They obviously did. She gestured once in his direction, heard his pathetic squeak and the rustle as two Tactical officers took him away. At least he had the good sense to be quiet, preserve some dignity before they sent a laz-beam through his skull.

"Take us to the surface," she said after he had gone. "We must consult with Dr. Guitteriez."

"Ma'am?" questioned the pilot, his annoying voice shaking

slightly.

"Take the ship down."

The pilot swallowed audibly, but he did comply. The warship was capable of landing, but it was so large it had been built in space and it was meant to stay in space. However, a visit of this importance to the good doctor deserved some fanfare.

Her head ached. A great tear of emptiness had opened in her. Certainly it was the stress of the disappeared freightship containing two-dozen, still living Augments. It had nothing to do with the absence of the mind tether which left an ache in her soul. Nothing to do with her concern for the passengers on the freightship.

She shook her head. The very thought was preposterous.

But Sarrin DeGazo had impacted her more than she was willing to admit, even in the brief few weeks they had been connected via Dr. Guitteriez's chip.

The ship groaned as it entered the gravity field of the planet. The pilot frowned, but kept her hand on the controls steady as the ship descended.

Perhaps the doctor could remove these last fleeting thoughts of the Augment that still swam around her head, nearly making her nauseous with contradictions.

She felt the lieutenant's apprehension before he started to speak. "Uh, Ma'am."

She lifted her eyes, heavily hooded by her throbbing brow. Her tongue, she pressed against her teeth in annoyance.

He gulped audibly and gestured to the screen.

She turned her gaze, hearing him relax.

The compound was scorched. Razed to the ground.

"No," she gasped, slapping her hand on the console. Where was Guitteriez? Her heart thudded erratically as her eyes searched the screen. "What happened to the facility?"

No one would answer.

"What happened? Where did the warship go? Where is the Augment? Where is Guitteriez?"

Her first officer stepped up behind her, his demeanour annoyingly placid. "It appears the warship fooled us and escaped. My guess is they attacked the facility."

She slammed the console again, widening the crack with a loud split. "I want a team down there immediately. Retrieve the databases. We must find out what happened."

Two officers left the bridge quickly.

"Scan the area. We need to find that freightship."

* * *

Kieran slapped a hand up to his face reflexively, falling immediately back into the rabbit hole of sleep. But an instant later, another ping landed on his cheek, and he rolled over heavily. His eyes creaked open in the half-illumination.

A shape hovered over him, and Sarrin's face, worried, came into focus as she dropped another torn piece of ration container on him.

He sat up, dizzy at the sudden movement. "What is it?"

She shook her head and turned, pulling a panel off the wall.

"Sarrin?"

She motioned at the new access hole, expecting him to get in. "Something's wrong."

"What do you mean 'something's wrong'?"

She gestured again at the opening in the wall.

"Sarrin, I won't fit in there."

The space between her eyebrows creased, and she scanned him, measuring. "Collapse your shoulder." She demonstrated, tilting her one shoulder down and in.

"What? No. What's going on?"

She shook her head, eyes staring into the unknown. "Something strange, but familiar."

"Familiar?"

"Something I've felt before, but I'm not sure." She sent him a pointed look. "Something that's not the same."

"Like what?"

"We have to go." She pointed again at the wall.

He pointed at the door.

"There are five Augments stationed outside your quarters."

"Oh. And we can't just —?"

"We need to get to Engineering."

"You can go." He shrugged, settling back into the bed. "I've had it. If they want my help, they can ask. Besides, I'm only here to observe. I shouldn't be helping this much in the first place."

She pressed her lips together, looking down at the open panel, suddenly looking very small. "I can't," she said. "There's no sedative. I need...."

"Sarrin?" He leapt to his feet, a sudden knot of worry propelling him to her side. "What do you think is going on?"

She shook her head again, blinking rapidly, then crawled into the wall.

Kieran swore as her feet disappeared. He poked his head in—tight spaces didn't bother him, but even with his shoulder collapsed into his chest, he had to push with his legs to squeeze his torso through the tight space. It opened up a little when they reached the horizontal plane between decks, and he caught Sarrin half-sitting up, watching for him. She scrambled away, and he crawled on his elbows to catch up.

Engineering wasn't far when they travelled this way, but it was slow. "Sarrin, what's going on?" he tried again, but she refused to answer, darting up a connecting bulkhead.

The panel fell out where she pushed it, filling the dark space with light. She crawled out, and he scrambled after her into the empty and throughly wrecked engine room.

"Oh my God," he gasped. "What have they done?" His feet carried him to his beloved engine, now entirely stripped.

If it was broken before, it was irreparable now.

Behind him, Sarrin muttered, "I don't understand."

"They must really think I've got it in for the ship, to pull apart everything."

But Sarrin was focussed on one of the screens built into the wall, tapping the sensor controls. Her hand came up and rested on her temple, over the same spot she had pulled the tracking chip from, the same spot that had ached every time the warship arrived.

"Sarrin?"

She shuffled forwards to the main engineering bay and into it. The bay was busy, but she ignored the commotion as she made her way to the large central console. Kieran followed, one eye open for Rami. Pulling up the 3D display on the console, an image of the freightship and its surroundings flickered to life. The display zoomed out, showing Junk and its moons and the thick band of scrap parts spread out like orbital rings.

Kieran stooped, aware that there were now multiple sets of eyeballs turning his way, and they weren't friendly. "Sarrin," he whispered, "I shouldn't be here."

Ignoring him, she peered deeper into the display.

"What's happening?" he said. But she never answered, a blip flashing on the display, a hulking starship materializing on the far side of Junk.

Sarrin jumped back, her eyes wide.

"Shit," Kieran spat. Then—regardless of who saw him—he yelled, "Warship!"

"They haven't seen us," said Sarrin.

"How do you know?"

A sharp shake of her head.

Kieran blinked. It didn't matter how she knew the warship was about to arrive before it did, or how she knew they hadn't seen them. What mattered was there might still be time. He turned, dodging Augments as he ran to the engine room. "We're gonna have to hot-wire the engines if we want a chance to escape."

A cold voice stopped him in his tracks. "What are you doing here?" Rami stalked towards them, face red and fists clenched so that every massive muscle stood menacing. Kieran found himself surrounded by a wall of Augments. "Space him," Rami ordered, and a pair of hands wrapped around each arm.

Eyes wide, he looked at Sarrin, but she turned her head, looking to some unknowable distance. "They've seen us."

* * *

Gal fell from his bed, crashing on the grey floor in a tangle of sheets as everything shook underneath him.

"Johnny?" Aaron sat up abruptly from his casual seat by the desk.

The ship shook around them. It could mean only one thing. Gal tripped over the tangled bedclothes, blinking away the pall of deep sleep. "They've found me." He stumbled into the door, barely catching himself. He pounded on the mechanism, but it wouldn't open. "What's going on?"

"They found you in the engine room," answered Aaron. "They were afraid. They locked you in here."

His head whipped around. "How do you know that?"

"Because you know it. You saw it, even if you don't want to remember. I'm not really here."

The walls around him were grey—a pleasant tan-grey that did not belong on a starship—and sunlight streamed through the open window. A photo stood above the mantle of an old stone fireplace—he and Rayne, standing on the planet Yates. With a gulp, he recognized his old apartments on Etar.

They would destroy him. They would destroy everything he ever loved.

He looked to the standard issue desk, at the cabinets with

their false bottoms and fake doors. "Destroy everything," he told Aaron. Years of records—paper records that were completely untraceable, unhackable—went into the fireplace. Pocketbooks and diaries, manifests and lists, hastily copied blueprints and oaths sworn on napkins. All of it had to go.

"Send a feed out. They're coming for me."

Aaron shook his head. "None of this is real."

"They have to know!"

"This isn't happening. I'm dead, Gal."

It couldn't be. Gal shook his head.

He ripped the panel off the door controls. He switched the wires around until, satisfied, he pushed the switch again and the door opened, the panel lighting up in a mini explosion of fire.

A guard let out a shout of surprise and turned.

They were already here. UECs. Hap's men.

He threw his fist into the man's genitals as hard as he could and ran. The demons chased after him, shrieking down the never-ending grey corridors.

* * *

Sarrin steadied herself against the wall, pushing away the dark clouds at the edge of her vision. Her heart raced fast, even as she sped up.

Kieran lifted himself up off the floor, loosed from his captors when the warship's first shot raked across their bow. "Rami, listen. You need my help to repair the engine if you want half a chance of surviving this."

"Get out," Rami shouted, darting over and stomping a boot into Kieran's side. "I don't want you anywhere near these engines. You'll probably hand us straight over to the UECs."

Clouds condensed again, Sarrin's hand shaking as she shut her eyes and forced herself to inhale slowly.

Kieran shuffled back on his knees, away from Rami. "I

don't care what you think I did, but no matter what my motives are, I need the ship to stay in one piece to stay alive, just like the rest of you. There's a warship out there—they thought they'd killed us once and I bet they're none too impressed that we're still floating."

"That's who you're working for, isn't it?" sneered Rami, his wide frame dwarfing Kieran. "Why you've been wasting all our time with these ridiculous modifications? You just wanted us stranded here until your friends on the warship could return."

The ship shook under them again. Sarrin gasped, grabbing onto the nearest bulkhead. The clouds, and the strangely familiar feeling, warred with her senses.

"That's insane," shouted Kieran. "I'm trying to survive this, same as you." He was far away to Sarrin's ears.

"You want us to get caught," Rami accused.

"We don't have time for this. We need the FTL working now."

Rami reached for Kieran. The weight of the fog pushed down around Sarrin. She felt herself lunge forward, grab Rami by the collar, and throw him to the ground, twisting so his one good arm bent awkwardly across his back and he landed under her knees. Rage poured through her hands, both hers and his coming together in a violent clash. The monster purred in her mind, and in her rage, she encouraged it right back.

Two green eyes blinked at her, making her pause. A hand grabbed the back of her clothes and sent her flying. She landed against the engine block with a thud—enough to clear her senses.

Kieran flashed her a worried look.

Rami, his face nearly purple, scrambled to his feet.

"Stop." Thomas appeared, his deep voice booming across the engineering bay. He was flanked by the boy she had saved and the same girl who had shown up at her quarters and asked her to be alpha.

"Get rid of her," Rami screamed.

But Thomas stepped in front of him. "You put us all under the Rule of War, but you're not the alpha, Rami. You never were."

Sarrin blinked, a different monster washing over her: dread, and she scrambled back against the wall.

"You can't be serious," said Rami. "She's insane. She tried to attack me."

Thomas shrugged. "If she hadn't, I would have. We need to make a jump away from here, we need the FTL. You've spent the last day pulling it apart. Now, Kieran is probably the only one who can put it back together."

The girl stepped forward. "I've seen her marks."

"We won't follow you, Rami," said the boy. "Twenty-seven has saved us before, and if she says you're dangerous, then I want you nowhere near any of this, especially not with the warship already firing on us."

As if for emphasis, the ship rocked under them again. Sarrin reached for her head, for the intense pressure that built there, something tearing wide apart. She had never wanted to be in charge, never wanted to be alpha or for anyone to know how many procedural marks had been etched on her skin or how she had earned them. She only wanted to be normal. Her vision turned nearly black.

A hand wrapped around her arm, pulling her to her feet. She twisted, but the arm held, and she stared into Kieran's green eyes. She caught a glimpse of a memory: a young girl brushing the hair of an even younger girl. Then they were running, Kieran pulling her into the engine room.

"This is bad," he said, letting her go.

She gasped and pulled away, he had come too close.

Kieran pushed a hand through his hair, but he wasn't

talking to her or anyone else, he was talking to himself as he studied the massive, ruined engine block. "All we need is a gravity pulse, it doesn't even have to be a big one. The grav-generator is functional, checked it first thing, but with the engine in pieces we'll never get enough energy to make a jump."

She watched him closely, his every feature outlined in extreme detail as she watched him think. Her mind was speeding up.

Another hit rocked the ship, and all but the emergency lighting went out, leaving engineering in a pale red glow.

"The pulse frequency," she said. The weapon she had designed to tear the warship apart, it would save them now.

Kieran pressed his lips together. "Sarrin…."

Her eyes caught on the wrecked engine room. "It's our only option."

He stared at her for a minute, long enough for her to shift under his gaze, but he gave her a grim nod and turned away. "I'll check the torpedo launcher."

A desperate yearning welled up inside Sarrin as he left her, but her gift, and her mission now, was to kill. She followed him into the main engineering bay, past the collection of worried looking Augments, to the torpedo tubes. A memory flashed: this was where she had first met Kieran, the first time they had escaped from the warship.

She pulled the cap off one of the weapons, adjusting the frequency output on the electro-torpedo by feel. Her head swam. The warship held a crew of one-hundred-fifty-six. How much of a monster would she be when it was destroyed?

Dark clouds obscured everything in front of her, the engineering bay falling far away as the monster took hold. From somewhere nearby, Kieran called out her name.

She blinked and she was on the pristine white bridge of the warship Comrade.

An instant later, screaming pain ripped through her bones.

* * *

"We can't trace gravity-wells," said the Operations officer aboard the pristine white bridge of the UECAS Comrade.

"I don't care."

There was silence as the ensign started the scan. The commandant stared at the smoking rubble on the screen.

"Oh," gasped the ensign.

She whipped around to face him.

"They're here."

She whipped back to the view screen where he pointed. Floating serenely in the black of space was the freightship. Its hull torn apart, transmission lights blinking painfully slow— they were injured. "Hit them with everything we have."

Amelia gripped the console with renewed intensity, a snarl on her face. The tacticians fired multiple volleys of laz-cannon fire at the pathetic freightship. She should have felt pleased, the familiar adrenaline of the hunt slid through her easily. But another part was apprehensive, her stomach fluttering.

Computerized flashes lit up on the display marking each hit. Though there weren't as many as she liked. There were more than she liked—half of her cringing, warring with the other half.

The Augments were abominations, direct insults to the Gods. With a growl, she ordered, "Activate the negative pulse beam." No doubt it was an Augment pilot dodging their cannons—Amelia silently cursed the ineptitude of her own pilot and tacticians—but the Augments could be subdued.

"Are you sure?" asked her first officer.

She gripped the console, nodding sharply as her only response.

Guitteriez's weapon, the pulse emitter was activated. It was an uncomfortable sensation she had felt many times a s

Guitteriez had built and tested the machine, but it seemed particularly debilitating to Augments.

Hit by a sudden, devastating sensation, Amelia screamed, dropping to the floor. She blinked, a hazy vision of a cluttered grey room filled her senses until the fire burning through her bones consumed every thought.

She was vaguely aware of her bridge officers turning to look, their expressions painted with only dull surprise. The first officer leaned over her. He didn't seem surprised at all. He met her eyes, staring down at her with disdain. "You're too close to them," he said. "Guitteriez warned me this could happen."

"W-what?" In her head she felt like a small child, cradling her arms around herself as she shook in fear. Where was the pain coming from?

Her eyes fell on the tactical console where a lieutenant was manning the weapon. It should cause mild sensations of discomfort, nothing more.

And yet. Guitteriez said he had designed it for Augment 005478F, had used it in her capture. "I don't understand," she panted. And yet she did, she had been connected to the Augment. She could feel what she was feeling.

But how? The chip had been removed. Their connection should be severed.

"It appears you are still connected to the girl," the first officer said. He reached his hand for the controls. Amelia shot a hand out to stop him, but it was too late. Her body clenched in pain as his hand dragged over the controls, only bringing the intensity higher.

"Stop," she croaked. She panted, her vision going grey. "Stop."

He raised a single eyebrow. "I cannot. My orders were quite clear—to keep an eye on you, to monitor you for any strange deviation in behaviour. This was a known possibility."

What was a known possibility? Did Guitteriez know the connection would remain? If he wasn't dead, she would kill him herself.

"I am taking command of the Comrade," he announced, turning so the others could see.

The officers nodded, scarcely blinking.

He reached for the controls again, increasing the intensity.

She screamed. Her mind pulled her away, visions dancing in her head of old dreams. Of a little girl who taught her how to pull away from pain, how to survive.

A girl with long brown hair she hated to brush herself and a sad smile.

FOURTEEN

Screams echoed around Sarrin's head. They weren't hers.

Blinding white light, the quality of it ethereal. A set of polished black boots walked up to her, her face on the ground staring up at the man.

Something was said, and something else—she couldn't hear any of it.

All she could hear were the screams. And... and... was that humming?

Her ears strained for the melody. It was familiar. She'd heard it so long ago it was difficult to place.

Her vision started to clear, but she was not in the engine room on the Ishash'tor, she was in some bizarre dream. As she lifted her head, she saw she was surrounded by consoles, all gleaming white—the colour of purity, of prosperity, of the Gods.

The humming melody grew louder than the screams. It was a four bar stanza, a children's song.

A young girl brushing an even younger girl's hair. Humming.

She gasped.

What was this place?

But she knew it. The central command station, the wraparound consoles, the elite officers. Even the starfield in the view screen was familiar.

As was the crumpled little ship set in their targets. She gasped, her mind slamming backwards. This was the UEC warship.

But how? She was on the crumpled little ship.

The humming roared in its intensity.

And she knew too the familiar but strange feeling. This was not her body, not her screams, not her arm reaching out in front of her.

This was Amy.

Amy was alive.

Amy was on the warship.

* * *

Kieran stared at Sarrin where she had fallen to her knees without warning.

Her face contorted in a grimace, every muscle defined as she strained.

"What's going on?" he asked out loud. He glanced behind him.

Thomas answered, his face ashen, "They have an energy weapon."

Kieran put a hand to his chest, pressing against the chasm of emptiness that opened there. "Is this what it feels like?" It wasn't physical pain. He hadn't felt like this since his sister died. He shook his head to clear it, but it wouldn't go. "What can we do?" he jutted his chin in Sarrin's direction.

Thomas shook his head. "Nothing, but wait for it to stop."

That wasn't good enough. "We don't have time," he said. "We have to stop them now."

Thomas nodded roughly. "I'll retrieve Sarrin's weapon."

Kieran pressed his lips together. It would be their only option. He had no doubt the machine would work exactly as Sarrin said it would, that the warship would be torn end to end. What he didn't know was how it would affect her, if she would ever recover from killing a crew of over a hundred-and-fifty people.

But Sarrin flinched and groaned on the ground next to him, her eyes distant. He had used the last of the sedative, if she got lost in her trance, there would be no way to stop her, and she was just as deadly as the warship.

He shouldn't have yelled, shouldn't have let Rami get him riled up. Again. Rami stood on the opposite side of Engineering, watching and scowling, and Kieran pushed down his sudden violent urge to scream. He was losing sight of what he was here for: to observe, to not interfere, to not get involved.

He leapt to his feet, glancing back at Sarrin's prone form as he followed Thomas.

* * *

Gal forced his legs to run faster. He felt them close in around him. Felt their laser targets fixed on his back. The demons screamed and leaped, running with him like some feral pack of animals.

Aaron wasn't with him. Because he was dead. It had only been Gal's wishing that had brought him back.

So much had been lost already.

He slammed into the wall as the ship shook out from underneath him.

It drove a renewed sense of urgency. If they were fighting back, there was still time. Cornelius could be saved!

Except this wasn't real.

They had killed Cornelius years ago. In his mind he still saw it, still saw the explosion. Felt the heat in the conduits as he pulled them apart.

He stumbled, falling to the ground. Demons jumped on him, pressing him down, forcing all the air out of his lungs.

Soldiers were coming to arrest him. There was no hiding

what he did on the ship. But he refused to be captured. Refused another cycle on the merry-go-round.

It was all happening again. He could see the future coming around on him, preparing to sink its rabid teeth into his flesh once more.

Hap would sit in his office. Pretend to offer Gal mercy when he announced he would let him live despite his actions. Gal would plead insanity, a temporary confusion of the Gods. Gods that had abandoned them all years ago.

A sick sense of relief would twist in him. Relief that Hap thought destroying the ship's weapons array was the worst thing Gal had ever done. Relief that he wouldn't have to face looking over his shoulder, wondering when and how it was going to happen. The Gods always punished those who disobeyed, it was made to look like an accident, but it was the hand of Strength.

Gal pressed his hand against the access panel. It read his hand print, the silver-grey panel popping out and up from the wall.

He pushed it the rest of the way up. A dozen laz-rifles stared back at him, lined neatly in their row, ready for any foreign threat.

What threat did the UECs think they were going to encounter in space. Everyone followed the Gods. Peace was rampant. At least on the outside. A product of complacency, blind belief.

He took a laz-rifle. He would only need one.

There were a dozen ways to use the components in the rifle besides the one the Central Army suggested. All of them deadly.

Gal pulled the panel off, exposing the delicate circuits.

Vaguely, he remembered the hackers showing him this trick.

"What are you doing, Johnny?"

Gal glanced to where Aaron had appeared. He shook his head. "Super charging the laser."

"I know. Why?"

"It's time to get off this ride."

* * *

Sarrin came back into herself, on her hands and knees, staring at the cold grey floor. Amelia was alive.

She was supposed to be dead. How did she end up on the bridge of the UECAS Comrade? But if she was there, could she help them?

The ship rocked under her as the warship made contact with multiple rounds of laz-cannon fire, their biopulse weapon paused for now.

Kieran was not beside her, and immediately the black clouds started to close in. But she heard his voice, and turned to see him and Thomas loading the modified torpedo into the chute.

"No!" she cried, but her voice got stuck.

Her legs were weak, everything wobbled as she tried to stand. Instead she crawled.

The jolts of landed laz-fire came more frequently now. If what she had seen on the warship was true, they were getting closer. And they would destroy them without hesitation.

Kieran and Thomas braced themselves, working even as they fought to stay standing. They were making connections, she realized, repairing the tubes so they could fire her weapon.

Cold shock cleared the clouds from her vision instantly, made her draw in ragged breath. If the weapon fired, everyone on the warship would be killed instantly. Including Amelia.

"Stop," she called out. But she sputtered and wheezed, the cry ending on her lips.

They only had two more connections to make and it would be ready.

She never would have drawn the plans if she'd known. Amy who had brushed her hair and held her and stood in front of her so Sarrin wouldn't have to fight.

She tried to call out again. Tried to stand. None of her limbs worked. What was happening to her? She crawled determinedly forward, hoping someone would notice her. But the flashing emergency lighting and the rocking—everyone was too busy to see.

She reached the torpedo chute as Kieran slammed the second-last conduit in place. One more and they'd have it.

"No." She dove in and pulled the connections apart.

"Sarrin, what'rya doin'?"

She shook her head, panting. "No."

He frowned at her, his green eyes searching. "Sarrin, they're gonna tear us apart in the next five minutes."

She pulled the wiring from the launch controls, destroying the delicate internal workings of the machine that would take hours to solder back together. She took a handful and threw it across the floor.

"Sarrin!" he screamed.

She felt the darkness close in, heard the hummed melody. "I owe her my life."

"Gods! What's she doing?" she heard Rami scream. "I told you she was insane."

Her every nerve fibre lit on fire—the biopulse weapon. At least she had time to save the warship.

* * *

"Checking out, Johnny?" Aaron asked.

Gal's blood boiled. "Don't call me that. It's not my name."

Aaron shrugged. "It's who you are."

"Were."

The demons crowded around. Sick grins of glee plastered

on their hairless, scabbed faces. They watched as Gal fussed with the wiring, hands steady from years of practice making the fine connections.

He had failed all of them. The demon's hairless heads turned, staring at the far end of the corridor.

A soldier. Dressed in standard issue, grey jumpsuit. A commander at least.

They had come for him. It was all happening again.

She said his name.

She would drag him in front of Hap, capture him and start the ride all over again.

"I won't let you hurt them," he warned her.

"Hurt who?"

There was no way for her to understand. To the soldiers and the folk, everyone, the Gods were everything. "They're not going to hurt us," he said. He clicked the access panel back in place on the rifle.

Her voice was muffled. His vision was hazy too, the demons somehow taking all of it. "Th-the Augments? I know. You have to make the warship understand."

"They'll never understand," he told her, as much as he told himself. It was true after all. "They'll just keep coming and coming and coming. They're afraid."

He stood, using the wall for balance. "There's nothing we can do." Eyes closed, he swung the laz-rifle around, feeling the cool muzzle against his skin. For some reason, the design of the rifles had always been the perfect length, with the trigger in his hand, it stretched to the hollow beneath his jaw. "Over and over and over." He tensed against the trigger, feeling its resistance.

"Gal!" Aaron shouted. His friend lunged toward him.

Gal's eyes flew open, and he saw the demons staring at him. He dropped the rifle to point it at Aaron.

"What are you doing? This isn't the way," Aaron panted.

"What about all of them?"

The demons jumped up and down, their eyes wide, terrified.

Could he just leave them?

He swallowed, mouth dry.   "Just because you can't understand it. It's not wrong. I can't live on this merry-go-round Hap has set me on, to watch them die over and over again." He begged Aaron to understand, just a fraction.

His friend's face fell, resignation darkening his features. They would be together again, not just some figment of Gal's wrecked mind. If it worked that way. Who knew.

He swung the rifle back to himself.

"Gal!" the soldier called out, her voice sweet and panicked. She took a step towards him, arms outstretched, reaching.

His eyes slammed to hers. He poured his hatred for the UECs into his gaze—if he was going to go, at least someone would know. He hated what they had done to him, what they had done to his friends, to Aaron. He hated the demons they had created, the thousands of people who died who never had to.

He pointed his gun at her. "You can't hurt them."

Her hands came up. "I'm not going to hurt anyone, Gal."

He almost believed her. "No!" he screamed, pressing his hands to his ears, the laz-rifle caught haphazardly in his arms. "You're all the same."

The demons spun in his vision.   They multiplied exponentially, filling the corridor, drowning him.

The soldier rushed forwards, as he collapsed to the ground.

He fired the rifle.

She fell, hard, straight back, crashing to the floor with a thud.

The demons paused at the sound.

He stared at the familiar olive skin, the dark curly hair, the strong facial features. He stared at the smoking hole in the soldier's chest.

Rayne.

The world spun, his vision narrowed and became dark and blurry.

The demons were quiet. One by one they started to fall. Corpses littered the corridor, their weight pressing in, crushing him. He gasped for breath that wouldn't come.

One demon remained standing, and he recognized it: the demon that looked just like Rayne, haggard and ruined, but there was no doubt what it meant. He had destroyed her life, dragged her with him into the abyss, and then shot her.

His stomach churned, bile licking the back of his throat.

Demon-Rayne fell over, dead.

He scrambled to his feet, demon bodies flinging away as he pushed through them wildly.

Rayne's body was still.

His heart raced, as though it was trying to make enough beats for the both of them. As though it was trying to make up for the thousands of people who had died because of him. But the demons lay dead.

* * *

Kieran stared at Sarrin as she pulled out handful after handful of wire, tossing it to the ground. Her eyes were glazed, and she was humming. Honest to God humming.

He looked to Thomas, but the Augment looked just as shocked as he felt. "What's she doing?"

"I have no idea." But one thing was clear: Sarrin didn't want them to fire the weaponized torpedo. There was something on the warship that had changed her mind, there had to be.

Thomas cringed as each handful of connections plummeted through the air. "That was our only chance."

Rami appeared beside them. "Gods, I told you she was insane."

The FTL engine was beyond repair. Their only option was to go around the whole thing. The energy they needed to open a gravity-well through space and time was astronomical. Another jolt shook the ship, the lights flickering with the sheer power of it. Kieran paused. "How many megavolts do the Comrade's laz-cannons have?"

"Three-thousand. Why?"

A terrible idea formed in Kieran's head. "Do we still have the gravity generators Sarrin used to stabilize the force-shields after the shuttle crashed?"

"What?" barked Rami.

"Yes, but they're micro-generators," answered Thomas, shaking his head. "We'll never be able to open a grav-hole with them."

"I know. We'll use them to stabilize the shields."

"Are you insane?" snapped Rami.

"The surge-protectors are melted. The grav-generators will hold the shields for a while, but eventually the energy will overwhelm and the field will collapse," said Thomas.

"I think we can use it, harness the power in the shields to make our grav-jump," said Kieran.

Rami looked at Thomas. "This man is a lunatic. When the field collapses, it will blow up the ship—the same as our force-shield in the North tore through the Earth."

Kieran swallowed a sudden wave of nausea—he'd known the Earth was destroyed in the war, but never how. It didn't matter, it was the only way to build enough energy for the FTL jump drive to work.

"He's going to kill us all. Himself included."

Thomas glanced down at Sarrin, and Kieran knew Thomas was helping him only because of her. But at the moment, his faith was stretched to its limit.

"We should have thrown him out the airlock when we had the chance," said Rami.

Kieran bit back his angered shout. "You might not like me, but you're the one who pulled the FTL apart beyond repair. The most advanced warship in the fleet is out there, and it wants to destroy all of you. There are two ways this ends: one, they blow the ship to pieces. Two: they catch and board us and capture you. If that happens, I've heard the best you can hope for is death, but that probably won't come. Me, I'm not like you, they won't fuss with me too much—bang, I'm dead, peaceful-like." He stalked over, jamming his finger in Rami's chest. "I don't work for the UECs, and I never have. I'm sick of all this and you and… at this point, I don't care if we get caught, but I'm trying to avoid it for you."

Rami gritted his teeth, pressing into Kieran's finger with his chest and bending it away.

Thomas stepped between them. "There isn't time for this. We can't be fighting each other." He sighed, glancing at Sarrin, still humming and pulling wire. "We don't have any option but to try Kieran's plan."

* * *

Bright lights dazzled Sarrin's eyes. She heard screaming— a woman, a horrible high-pitched wail of pain.

She heard a deeper voice screaming her name, somewhere closer and more immediate. Green eyes caught her gaze and she fixated on them, used them to ground herself. "Stay with us."

Below her she felt the cold hard floor, the solid grey surface of Engineering, the tangled mess of wires still clutched in her hand. Felt the burn of the bio pulse weapon in her bones.

Around her she saw the pristine white consoles of the warship's bridge. She focussed here, everything else fading away.

The pilot tapped quickly, calmly at his control panel.

Two tacticians worked in unison, their heads bowed over a single large console, a large 3D holographic display shining in between them.

She—Amelia—was still in the command nest. She was kneeling, holding herself up by her arms. On the other side was a man, his face painted with distaste.

The crumpled up little freightship floated helplessly on the display, close enough now to take up nearly the entire view screen.

"Destroy it," she heard the man say, his voice emotionless.

No, she thought, and heard the woman's voice say it.

The green eyes aboard the Ishash'tor swam back into focus. Her heart leapt at the sight. Everything would be okay. She was exhausted, her body in so much pain, but she could just disappear in those eyes and never surface again.

"Sarrin?"

Vaguely she registered that she had been turned over, was staring up at the ceiling instead of down at the floor. Hard to tell, they all looked the same. Something held her head.

"Is she okay?"

The green eyes blinked, turned away, tearing the blissful calm away with them. "I don't know."

The freightship, they were on the freightship. "You have to jump," she told him.

"What?" he turned back to her, her heart skipping again.

"I can't hold them much longer."

"Sarrin?"

He was gone, the whiteness blinding her again.

"Stop," she said. "Amy."

The woman gasped, her own voice looked up at the man and said, "What's happening to me?"

The distasteful man frowned down at her, and Amelia coiled, making herself small.

The green eyes, the grey ceiling peered down at her, and Sarrin gasped. Why wasn't he moving? "You have to…," she panted, "get away."

Amelia wasn't going to help them. Couldn't help them.

She tried to roll herself over, heard herself shout out as she did. The pain threatened to make her vomit and she rolled up on to her elbows.

With a grunt, she lifted her arm. In the other half of her mind, she saw the arm lift from where she crouched on the warship, saw it make contact with the master console as her own hand slapped down, randomly, on the console in engineering.

She held on for dear life.

Kieran was quiet. "Wire the gravity drive into shields."

Madness.

"You can't be serious," said Rami.

"We don't have another option."

A pause, footsteps as the others ran to switch over the conduits.

"Kieran, come on."

A pause. "I can't leave her."

She turned her head. Green eyes shone with concern as he stared at her.

"Go," she breathed. "We don't have long."

"Sarrin, what happens if…?"

She shook her head. "There's nothing you can do."

"Are you okay?" His face looked sick.

She shook her head again. "I can't do this much longer."

His eyes flared wide.

She turned away. When she looked back, she was on the bridge of the Comrade, her arm outstretched.

"What are you doing?" the angry man demanded.

Sarrin felt the tenuous fibres of the connection, a bond that carried across time and space—weaker now than when they were children, but still there. She felt them strain, felt it nearly snap, but the tether held.

She stared defiantly into the eyes of the angry man. Noted

in him all the finest qualities of the UEC soldiers: dull, dark eyes, small cranium, slack face. The men who were the deadest also went the furthest.

She rose up to her full height, which, even when they had been young, was significant in Amelia.

Fear flashed in the captain's eyes. He turned away, pointing at two officers. "Secure her."

They moved toward her, throwing themselves on her. But Amelia was strong. Another two and then three leapt forward.

The angry man shouted, "Finish the freightship. It shouldn't take this long."

Amelia's hand reached for controls in her command nest that nullified all their laz-cannons, her palm signature all the code that was required to shut down the ship's offence.

Sarrin closed her eyes. *Hurry, Kieran.*

She was back in Engineering, the air frantic.

The ship rocked violently, throwing her across the floor.

"Sarrin!" she heard Kieran scream.

"Kieran," Thomas shouted behind him.

Everything moved too slowly.

The engineer blinked, staring at her.

She blinked back.

Rami ran up, dragging a conduit.

Thomas touched Kieran's arm, saying something that was lost to the buzzing in her head. He turned, taking the conduit from Rami. Their faces were too serious.

Rami argued, but Kieran took the conduit. His eyes grazed over her again, his face pale.

And he went to make the junction.

A shout erupted, the ship shook again. The electrifying buzz reached its fever pitch.

Kieran rammed the conduit into the plug.

A terrifying crack-sound bit through the darkness, charging

the air around them.

Kieran rolled away as white-blue voltage arced around the conduit, amplified in the dark emergency lighting.

She closed her eyes against the familiar feel of gravity swallowing her whole.

And then complete darkness, Amelia and the warship gone, the only sound Kieran's deep maniacal laughter that was miles away.

FIFTEEN

Sarrin blinked, white light blinding as she laid on the floor, staring up at the ceiling. For a minute she worried she was back on the warship, but her eyes settled on a strong, grey-brown lump set on an operating table, wires dangling from him. The steady sound of beeping came into her senses.

Grant.

She was in the infirmary.

The dark clouds were gone. Her heart beat steadily, rocking her body gently as it did so. Slowly, her senses and perception returned to her.

She stared at Grant, at the ugly suit that covered his entire body. Guilt washed through her, and regret. She'd held onto her hatred of him for far too long, left him alone in a dark cave in the middle of nowhere to fend for himself.

All because she was convinced he had taken Amy away and killed her. But he hadn't.

When they'd escaped Evangecore, there was no time to think. She had been in isolation for months, no idea if her squadron was still alive or where they were. Grant had found her, taken her into their group. They wandered, slowly meeting up with more and more of the Augments.

Sarrin had been overjoyed to see the girls from her

dormitory again, but Amy wasn't with them. She had fallen, had been captured while they tried to fight their way out, they told her.

But then Amy came, a year later, wandering across the desert with a group of others. They claimed they had been running for days, managed to escape from the UECs.

So the Augments let their guard down, ushered them into their secret hiding spaces. And the others, their minds turned by some trick of the Army, attacked. It was a trap laid out by the UECs: deadly weapons made to look like friends.

They lost many, their secret hiding places compromised, and they had been forced to kill all their brethren.

But Sarrin took Amelia, captured her and sedated her and smuggled her far away. Grant had helped. For a month they had fought the brainwashing. Amelia spent most of that time wildly vicious or heavily sedated. And Grant had gone along with it, knowing Sarrin needed more time to let go. Sarrin was certain she could bring Amy back. But they had run out of sedative. The programming had gone too deep, there was nothing they could do to bring her back.

One morning, when Sarrin woke, Amelia was gone, Grant returning guiltily to the cave. He had talked about killing her, euthanizing her to end the danger she posed to them and the horror she must have endured to end up so lost.

Maybe they should have killed her—a deep pang ripped open her gut. The brainwashing did go deep. Amelia had apparently returned to the UECs and become the Commandant of the warship, hunting Augments, hunting Sarrin.

Without thinking, Sarrin ran a hand over her matted hair. Amy had been the one to keep it straight for her, now it was a tangled mess.

"Sarrin?"

She turned, one of the tall doctors leaning over her,

scanning her. There was still an ethereal quality, her senses not fully returned. "You passed out," said Hoepe softly.

She nodded.

"How do you feel?" No, not Hoepe after all, Leove.

She didn't answer him.

"I didn't know it was for you," he said, "when Guitteriez asked me what I thought the effect of the weapon would be on someone so sensitized. I thought it was hypothetical—it never caused anything but mild discomfort to any of us. I'm sorry."

She frowned. Of course it wasn't his fault, Guitteriez had made them all do terrible things. "What happened?" her voice was gravelly.

He smiled a little. "Kieran managed to force a grav-jump so we could escape. You collapsed, but you haven't been asleep long. You're going to be okay, nothing physical, just the stress from the bio-weapon."

"Where is Kieran?" she interrupted.

"He's safe as well. Confined to quarters for now until we figure out what to do."

Her mind shifted, replaying a young girl brushing another girls' hair. And then Grant saying, "We can't take her with us, it's too dangerous. She doesn't even know what she is anymore."

Sarrin stared down at her hands, blood dripping off them. Shocked, she turned to Leove to ask if he could see it. He stared mildly back at her, his smock also covered in blood.

She blinked.

The blood on her hands disappeared, but his didn't. A new sound reached her ears, a quiet metallic clacking.

"Rest for now, Sarrin. We escaped the warship." He reached his hand out to touch her shoulder. She flinched away, seeing now his operating gown and gloves, the blood on him real.

She turned to the clacking. Hoepe was bent deeply over the short bench, his concentration intent. From beneath the drapes on one end were standard UEC-issue grey boots. On the other, partly obscured by Hoepe's frame and operating clothes, was the telltale curly hair of Rayne Nairu.

The only one who could reach Gal—the only one who had a chance of bringing the man back—lay injured, the doctor operating deep in her chest.

And somehow she knew it was Gal. Knew that Gal was too far gone, the way that Amelia was. Knew that Gal was never going to save them.

For all that they'd been through, all the sacrifice. In the end, their saviour would be the one to kill them.

"Sarrin, are you okay?" Leove asked, suddenly reminding her he was there.

"Fine," she answered reflexively.

But her mind was not. The edges of her vision started to narrow again. Her hands coated in blood and glinting silver.

Grant lay dying. Rayne lay dying. And Gal—who knew about Gal.

Abruptly, she stood, knocking the doctor back. Her feet carried her out the door and sprinting down the hallway.

But there was no where to run. The whole thing was a cage, a desperate trap laid by Guitteriez and the UECs. The infirmary, the ship, even the stars seemed to close in, her fate sealed as death followed.

Still, she ran and ran, circling the same corridors over and over. Hoping for something, anything. Blindly, she ran, until she was stopped, her path blocked by something—no, someone. They both went sprawling to the deck.

* * *

A stinking, grey demon appeared in the corridor ahead of him as Gal rounded a corner.

He wasn't surprised. They had died before, mass deaths

that occurred over and over again. But they could never really go.

He lost track of where he was. His mind flashed between the Valkas, his apartments, Hap's office with its wall of death, the Speakers' Complex, and the Central Army prisons. His feet moved one in front of the other, but he was trapped. He moved forward, but with no where to go, he circled around and around and around.

He had no idea how long. Long enough to relive Hap banishing him to the deep of space. Long enough to talk his way in the secret hacker organization and learn to set bombs for them. Long enough to hack into the UEC systems again and again, each revelation more damning than the last. Long enough to see Earth destroyed. Long enough to see the white walls of Evangecore and see them tumble to the ground.

It cycled over and over, no matter how he screamed or staggered or slammed his head into the wall.

So lost he was that he didn't see it coming: something slammed into him, something small and sinewy and dark that sent him flying back. His demons scattered to avoid being crushed.

Was it there to kill him, finally?

He climbed to his knees, gasping for breath only when his body forced him too.

Crystal blue eyes met his, fear wild in them.

They stared at each other, Gal and the skinny girl who this was all about.

She moved first, almost too fast for him to see. "You were supposed to save us." He didn't see her lips move, but heard her voice echo around his head.

"I—I—I —," he gulped. Her eyes had him locked in place. "I tried."

He tore away from her gaze, afraid. Instead, he looked at her. Really looked. Pale skin peppered with faint scars.

Ratty, dark hair matted in long strands. Dark circles and hollow cheeks the prominent features on her face. They contrasted her eyes, which were filled with a ferocious intelligence.

Another memory struck him: *explosions in the dark of night. Running amidst the chaos—it wasn't random to him, it was exactly as planned. Walls tumbled. Sirens blared, and hovercraft with search lights scanned the ground.*

He slipped unnoticed into a platoon of foot soldiers.

From the rubble, kids climbed and ran. A teenager poked her head over the edge, bewildered and confused, their eyes meeting.

His hand flew up, grabbing her arm.

They were the same eyes he stared into now.

Could it be? Was it possible that under all the stars, the girl he had seen across the rubble was the one right in front of him now?

Something inside of him cracked—not in a painful way, but like a crust, dead and burnt, had been peeled off, light seeping through.

Her eyes shifted, the fear in them plain as she glanced at his hand. She pulled away, leaving him sprawling on the floor—the kids always were strong.

"Wait," he called after her.

She disappeared into the wall, slithering away almost so quickly he could have imagined the whole thing.

He took a deep breath, filling parts of his lung that hadn't expanded in years, the crushing weight lifted. An Augment had escaped one of Hap's secret research facilities and found her way onto his ship. And from there, they had found more. Dozens of the kids, still alive. Saved.

But the UECs still hunted them. Hap would have sent his elite squad. He wanted them. But the question was why? What use could the Central Army, the Speakers of the Gods, have for so many infected children? What did they still want from them?

He sat alone in the middle of the corridor, surrounded by unfamiliar silence.   There was not a demon, not a titter joining him.

Only memories.

His mind worked slowly, he had been wandering.   The ship had been attacked and made a gravity-jump.   And before that?

Oh no.   His heart fell.   *Rayne.*

* * *

Gal sprinted, nearly slipping as he turned into the infirmary.

The twin doctors rose as one, staring at them with identical expressions of confusion.   "What are you doing here?" Hoepe asked.

Gal panted—had he really gotten so out of shape? "Rayne," he breathed, his eyes drifting automatically to where she lay, propped up on the bench that served as a makeshift second bed.   A large bandage covered her left chest and shoulder.

"You're meant to be locked in your quarters," said Leove.

Gal's feet carried him to her side.   "She's alive," he smiled.

"Gal?" Hoepe questioned him.

He took her hand in his.   "Please," he turned quickly to the doctor.

Hoepe stared at him—Gal knew why, he hadn't been himself for a long time, but he was now—and the doctor nodded.

He kissed her hand.

A chair shifted, and the doctor sat down beside him.   "We don't know what happened, Gal.   She caught a high voltage beam in the chest—possibly an electric arc surge from one of the laz-cannon hits.   It was inches from her heart.   She's lucky to be alive.   Luckier that she was able to trigger the medical alarm and we could get to her quickly. She will make a full recovery."

Gal heaved a sigh of relief, unable to hide it. He dropped his head to Rayne's hand. She looked younger, the worry gone while she slept.

He recalled their time on Yates. A beautiful planet, too beautiful for its fate. Like Rayne, too beautiful to have ended up tangled in his mess.

Her eyelids fluttered in the harsh light. She shifted beside him, groaning on the medical bed.

He pulled back, afraid to hurt her. Afraid to hurt her more than he already had.

"Gal," she sighed happily. She lifted her right hand, wincing as she tried to salute.

Quickly he grabbed her hand. "At ease, Rayne."

"What happened?" she asked him groggily.

His heart hammered in his chest. He licked his suddenly dry lips. Avoiding her gaze, he looked instead at the two doctors watching him intently. "They think it was a high voltage arc, triggered from one of the cannon blasts."

She nodded, grimacing again. "That's why it hurts so much."

"Rayne, I'm so sorry," he sobbed. "This is all my fault."

"Gal, shhh." She slurred slightly. "I know who you are."

He gasped and sat up, every muscle in his body tense. "You do?"

"You're a protector. That's why I've stayed so long. I don't know what's happened to you these last few years, but you look much better now."

He nodded, both relieved and disappointed that she didn't know who he really was. "Yeah, I do feel better. Hoepe's new medicine must be working." He smiled. Something about it was wrong, but what other explanation was there?

She smiled again, sloppy and sedated and radiant all at the

same time. "You'll save us, I'm sure of it."

Hoepe pressed in, checking her vital signs. He frowned, adjusted an auto-syringe, and injected her.

Gal watched, a sick sense of worry building in him. She might think he was a protector, but how could he possibly save them? He closed his eyes and a demon glared back in his mind's eye, grey and rotten, wearing spectacles and an antique suit.

Cornelius.

Gasping, he found himself back in the infirmary, demons disappeared. But they were only thinly veiled. They were stranded in space, heavily damaged. But there had been another option. A friend. A planet.

He frowned, maybe a friend.

The planet would not be dangerous to them. Only difficult.

Rayne blinked blearily, the pain killers taking her. "Gal?"

"I'm here, Rayne."

"I love you."

His heart stopped. His gasp set his thoughts back in motion again. "I promise I'll make it right."

She was asleep already.

He would keep her safe, keep everyone safe. All of them. The weight of it crushed him, far heavier than a sea of dead demons.

*　*　*

Sarrin dragged herself through the space in the walls. Weight crushed down on her, drowning her, making it hard to breathe.

Her stomach threatened to expel all its contents again. A horrible chill passed through her, a wave destroying every hope in its path—the same feeling as the instant Gal had grabbed her arm, his skin brushing against hers.

She pulled energy from people, and Gal's burden was

intense. The emotions that constantly boiled off of him, the ones that were heavy with regret and failure, poured in her, threatening to crush her from the inside.

The desire to escape intensified, doubled now. Only she couldn't bring herself to run. She had to fight for each drag of her arms as she crawled through the narrow space.

She passed out, slumped down and lost consciousness in the walls. When she woke, there was no way to tell how long it had been.

Long enough for her whole body to go numb, or maybe that was something else.

Her vision crowded in. Not in the way it did when she was in danger and the trance threatened to take over. But in the way it had done on Junk, when she was in pain and her mind had needed to escape it.

Blindly, she squeezed through the walls, barely aware of her direction until she reached a familiar space. The panel was worn from her repeatedly climbing in and out, and she pushed it. It clattered softly to the floor.

Her body was so cold. She was so tired. Her legs shook in desperation as she stood.

She needed something. Something warm. Something hopeful. Something to remind her she wasn't alone.

His warm body was curled on the floor, gently snoring, tucked into his make-shift bed so that she might take the real one. Kieran looked peaceful, happy. He looked everything she wasn't. And she fell to her knees beside him.

She reached out, desperate. Desperate to see him flash his grin, or hear him laugh. Desperate for him to grab her foot through the blankets and tell her everything was all right.

She longed to touch him, but stopped herself.

She had touched Gal, and Gal had walked away—But Gal had nothing left to lose. Kieran had everything.

If she touched him, she would kill him. It was the monster

that wanted her to do it, to save herself. But she wouldn't.

Her heart still pulled her down next to him. Carefully, she pulled the blankets up, keeping a thick layer of sheets between them.

The closeness wasn't comforting, but it was something.

Her body shook violently now. Pain coursed through her and she grabbed the blankets, stuffing the sheets into her mouth against the screams. It crashed up and down her arms and legs, worse than anything from a laz-rifle or scalpel or bio-pulse weapon.

It was unnamed emotional pain, pain that was not hers and pain that was hers. Pain that had no cure.

Tears slipped across her cheeks.

Pain consumed her until everything just stopped.

SIXTEEN

Kieran groaned, rolling over as a screeching tone tore him from sleep. It took him several long seconds to place the sound of the door chime. Longer to realize he was on the floor of his standard-issue lieutenant's quarters on the Ishash'tor.

With a rush, the memories returned to him: the desperate jump away from the warship, plugging a live conduit into the gravity-drive as Thomas shouted at him not to. In hindsight, he was lucky to be alive. He must have passed out, he remembered vaguely flashes of the dark engineering bay, and someone carrying him, and laying him down on the bed.

But he was lying on the floor. In just an undershirt and shorts.

The door chime sounded again, impatiently.

Everything ached, his body so heavy he wasn't sure he could get up. Something hard and knobby pressed into his side: a lump, no, a knee. His eyes shot open, heart racing. Sarrin's knee.

What was she doing?

Instinctively, his hand jerked under the pillow, where he had slept with the auto-syringe of sedative close at hand, but it was long gone. Sarrin didn't move, her body prostrate like a corpse, the only sign of life a sudden jerking rise and fall of her chest.

He slipped himself out from under the covers, careful not to disturb her. The bed was empty, the sheets pulled off and piled like a barrier between them.

With one last curious look at Sarrin, he opened the door as the chime sounded a third and very annoying time.

Gal leaned against the frame. He glanced in the apartment, his eyes scanning the lump on the floor and the dislodged blankets, before meeting Kieran's gaze with a single raised eyebrow. The expression on his face was amused. Alert, even.

Kieran immediately stood up straighter, his brain working to process. This was not the same man he had seen aimlessly wandering the halls a day ago. "Cap'n, it's oh-three thirty," he said.

"I need your help," said Gal. He turned without further explanation.

For a minute, Kieran stared at the form retreating down the corridor, but Gal had an air about him now, one that begged to be followed. Quickly, he grabbed his boots and ran after him.

"I know you keep track of everything," Gal said as Kieran caught up, hopping as he put one boot on and then the other. "Can you set a course to the planet?"

"To Junk?"

"No, C—. The other planet."

Kieran tripped over his untied boot, falling into the wall. "What? Like the unmarked one?"

"Yes," Gal said crisply.

Exhaustion or confusion taking over, Kieran found himself frozen in place, staring at Gal. He was completely unlike any version of the captain he had ever seen, drunk or sober. Gone were the worry lines and grey skin. His eyes were filled with an intense cunning. Gal looked alive for the first time.

"Kieran," Gal prompted him.

"Uh, yeah. I think so." He jogged to catch up again. "Why?"

"Good," nodded Gal curtly. "We need to go there."

"I thought you said it wasn't safe. That we couldn't go there."

Gal sighed, his head drooping. "We don't have many options at this point. It has been explored, but never catalogued. The planet isn't unsafe. As long as we keep our wits about us."

They paused in front of the Engineering doors. A shiver danced across Kieran's skin, exposed as he was in his boxers and undershirt.

Gal lifted his head and looked at Kieran from the corner of his eyes. "I haven't been myself for a very long time. But we are in too much danger for me to ignore it any longer. I know I said it was dangerous, but it will be okay."

Kieran nodded once, slowly, trying to understand.

"I'm sorry I left you. I'm sorry I tried so hard to go away and forget."

Before Kieran could form a response, Gal stepped forward, triggering the doors to open and bringing them into the engineering bay. The bay was dark, bathed in the eerie red of emergency lighting. A few Augments worked at the far end, inspecting what he realized was the conduit he had jammed into the overloaded shield relays to fuel the jump drive, and another shiver passed through him for how close he had come.

Gal led them to the central console. "Can you set a course?"

Truthfully, Kieran wasn't even sure where their emergency FTL had taken them. The sensors were luckily still operational, and he ran a quick sweep—just enough to orient himself. He had been tracking the planet, just as Gal said, watching its orbital path bring it closer and closer to Junk, so he had a good idea of where it was, he just needed to figure out where they were.

Gal seemed to be watching the display expectantly, and Kieran feared he would need to explain jump-drive mechanics to the captain again. "The jump drive is wrecked, it's gonna take a few days at least to get it together."

"It's okay. Just aim us there with the thrusters."

Kieran clicked his tongue. "Thrusters are all but toast, Cap'n. It'll take a hundred years to get back to Junk that way."

"I'm going to presume by 'toast' you mean they're barely functional." Gal caught him with a single raised eyebrow, and a curious smirk that made Kieran nearly jump out of his skin. "It's okay, it doesn't matter. Do the best you can."

"Are you sure? Just before you seemed pretty opposed."

Gal smiled sadly to him. "I don't know what I said before, Kieran, but I am sure now. Take us there, it's the only place the UECs will never find us. We need somewhere to hide, to make repairs. This poor old ship won't hold together much longer—actually I'm impressed any of it is still working."

"She's a good ship, Cap'n."

Gal put a hand on his shoulder. "Said like a true engineer." The hand filled Kieran with warmth. It reminded him of his dad, and by association, his sister. But the best parts. He couldn't help but smile. Too soon the hand retracted along with its reassurance, and Kieran found himself more confused than ever. Gal shrugged. "It will be okay, find the planet and set the thrusters toward it. Trust me, it'll work out if we need it to."

Kieran frowned, but he still forced a cheery, "Sure, Cap'n." Something else crossed his mind. "I hate to tell you this, but even if we get to the planet, we can't enter the atmosphere—

we're missing too much hull shielding. And the engines aren't strong enough to fight the gravity of even a small moon. I'd sure love to set down for a little while, but I don't know how we're going to land on a planet."

"Leave it to me."

"What're you gonna do? The laws of friction are pretty set. Same with gravity."

Gal shrugged. "Not always." Then he tapped the display, zooming in.

Kieran blinked. An object moved quickly across the display, a green and blue orb. "What the —? The planet's headed straight for us. It's halfway here."

The corners of Gal's eyes turned down. "Just point us there, okay."

Something interesting was going on. Kieran looked from Gal to the planet and back again. Licking his lips, he agreed, "Yessir."

"Thanks, Kieran. We'll get out of this." The hand came up to his shoulder again.

"What are you doing here?" A gruff voice cut through the moment: Rami. The burly Augment marched towards them. Slowly, the others trailed in, forming a part-circle that surrounded Kieran and Gal and the central console.

Kieran took a step back, suddenly very aware of how exposed he was in front of all of them and recalling the fight that Rami had started—or maybe he'd started—the last time they were in Engineering together.

But Thomas put his arms across Rami's chest, pushing him back.

Rami did step back, but his eyes traced over the console between them quickly. "What are you doing?" But he answered his own question: "You're turning the ship around —sending us back towards Junk. He's trying to get us back to the UECs so the warship can finish us of."

"No, look," said Thomas, pointing at the green-blue planet. Rami blinked in confusion.

"Forget it, Rami." A few of the Augments around the edges sighed and turned away, returning to their work. "Sarrin is our alpha, if she says we can trust him, we can. Besides, there's no way you can say he's working against us after what he did with the conduit to help us get away."

As quickly as it had swarmed, the crowd dissipated. Even Thomas shrugged and walked away, spanner in hand. Only Rami remained, staring daggers over the console. "I don't like you," he said.

Kieran took a step back, but Gal slid an elbow behind him, stopping him. "That's odd," said Gal, his feet planted and shoulders dropped casually, "everyone else likes Kieran."

"There's something strange about him."

Gal shrugged. "There's something strange about all of us."

"Who are you?" Rami's glare turned to Gal, scraping him up and down.

Unfazed, Gal answered simply. "I'm the captain. And you are on my ship."

"The captain? You're as cracked as the rest of them. You and Sarrin and—"

"You are aboard my ship by my good graces." Rami opened his mouth to retort, but Gal stopped him again: "I have been at war nearly as long as you have been alive. And you are a fool. Lieutenant Wood's engineering skills are unmatched, by far one of the best engineers I've ever known. We owe him, and the miracles he performs, our lives many times over, and we may need to count on him again."

"He set a bomb in a shuttle, nearly killing six of us."

A flicker of uncertainty passed over Gal's face.

"I didn't set no bombs," said Kieran.

Gal blinked, holding up a hand as though to tell Rami to stop. "You have no evidence."

"What about the one he started in the storage lockers?"

This time, Gal truly frowned.

"It wasn't…"—he turned to Gal —"it wasn't a bomb. It was something for Sarrin, to find Halud."

Gal's gaze met his, and he nodded once, the hand coming up to Kieran's shoulder again to say he understood. Then he turned back to the angry Augment on the other side of the display. "Rami, is it? I am the captain of this vessel, and I will not tolerate insolence and infighting amongst my crew. The Augments have long suffered—I more than most know the true extent of what they did to you—but this conflict you have created, you have created in yourself. Be more, now."

"What are you on about?"

Gal sighed.

It was Thomas who came up, finally, and dragged Rami back.

"What have you gotten yourself into?" Gal asked Kieran, a smirk hiding at the corner of his mouth.

Kieran shook his head. "I honestly don't know."

"I've never seen an Augment act like that, despite what the UECs would have you believe."

Kieran's ears twitched, and he stared at Gal, trying to read the expression on his face. There was something more to the mystery of Galiant Idim, but his exhausted, cotton-filled head couldn't get around any of it right now.

"Tell me honestly," Gal started, his expression suddenly drawn and nervous, "have there been bombs?"

"The positioning controls on the shuttle froze out and overloaded. That's all."

"Okay." He sucked in a deep breath. "And Sarrin—she's okay?"

Since when had the captain had any interest in Sarrin or the other Augments? But that could have changed in the last day too, along with everything else he thought he knew about

Gal. "Yeah, she's doin' good."

"I'm glad." A worried expression passed through Gal's eyes. "Is the course laid in?"

"Yessir."

"Thank you. Go get some rest. You look half-dead."

Kieran sighed. "So they keep telling me."

They walked together to the door, a comfortable, uncanny silence between them. For the first time, Kieran allowed himself to actually hope that maybe they would get out of it all right after all. He could see his Mom and Dad and brother again. Maybe, Sarrin had been right all along: they needed Gal.

As they parted, Gal called after Kieran, "And put some pants on—I don't know what Sarrin would say if she knew all the others got to see you in your skivvies." The captain laughed as he disappeared around the bulkhead.

Heat rushed across Kieran's face, cold air biting at his exposed legs and arms. Soon, he could go home. For now, the pile of blankets in his quarters seemed just as good. A bounce entered his step, and carried him through the corridors. He couldn't wait to wake Sarrin up and tell her about Gal—that she had been right never to give up—before he fell into a deep sleep for a year or two.

The door to his quarters opened with a whoosh, and a grin spread across his face. "Hey, Sarrin!" he called, stepping in. The pile of blankets on the floor was empty. "Sar?"

Dread overtook excitement. The wall panel laid on the floor. Had she disappeared into the walls again? Only she normally pulled the panel closed after her.

A sound came from the latrine, quiet and muffled. He spun toward the closed door, the lights inside turned off. He paused, his heart thumping too loud as he strained to listen.

"Sarrin?" He tapped the door gently, met by a quiet shuffling. She was inside. He slid the door open, fully expecting to admonish himself for being a fool when nothing was wrong, and for her to scream at him to get out like his sister.

Light spilled across the grey latrine floor, catching the edge of her foot and her grey coveralls as she vomited into the toilet. A dark pool of red crept across the floor.

"Shit!" He rushed forward. "Sarrin!"

"Don't touch me," she croaked, but he lunged forward the same. She curled up, dodging away at the last second. Her hands came to her face and he could see that was where the blood was coming from, the silvery skeleton shining in the dim light.

He halted, hovering just over her. "Sarrin," he begged— God, what was she doing? "You have to let me see."

"Don't," she mumbled, her voice far away, barely coherent.

"This is too much blood."   He looked from the thick puddle to her ghostly-pale skin.

She shook her head. "I need it out."

"I don't understand." His heart raced in his chest.

"That's where the monsters live."

He swallowed once, mouth too dry, eventually frozen in place.

"I won't die," she said, though it was hard to believe— anyone else would have. "The skin is already starting to heal. My bone marrow is already regenerating new cells."   Her voice was tinged with despair.

"Sarrin," he reached out.

"Don't touch me," she repeated, slumping back against the wall.   The small girl curled in the corner, blood smeared across her body like paint.

"I want to see is all, to help."

"Don't touch me, not when it's like this."

"Sarrin, I'm your friend. Let me help you."

She sniffed, burying her face in the corner. "It's too much.

I'll kill you."

He reached again. "You won't, I know it."

"It's not up to me. It's what they made me. I'm a monster."

"No, Sarrin." She was talking about the nurse, he knew it as well as he knew himself. "You're not a monster." The very sound her saying it, the very idea, scorched his heart.

He steadied himself with a breath, holding out his shaking hand, like he would try to coax a child. "Please let me see."

"No!" she screamed, throwing herself to the opposite corner of the little latrine. The blood splashed as she moved, her eyes melting in and out of focus. She had lost too much blood, her movements clumsy and slow.

He couldn't just watch her. He lunged, trying to trap her. She twisted and rolled, throwing his back into the toilet, but he clung on. "You're not a monster," he said through gritted teeth. "You're not gonna kill me."

She caught him in the chest and sent him flying. Scurrying back, her bloody, glinting hands came up to cover her head, to hide.

In the half-light of the room, he dragged his own hands through his hair. His stomach turned at the overpowering tang of iron coming from her blood.

With the fingers of one hand, she reached under the flesh of the other and pulled, more of the skeleton extracted from its cover. But the bones would not separate, the titanium slipping out from her grip no matter how desperately she tried. "They shouldn't be there," she cried.

"They're your hands."

"They aren't." She returned to picking at them, to trying to pull them off.

Kieran crept closer. He pulled the thick towel from the rack, stretching it between his arms, and launched again. He held her tight, wrapping her as she thrashed.

Another incredibly stupid thing to do, he thought as his back screamed and his arms strained painfully. But he was in it now. Sarrin was his friend, and, as much as he called himself an Observer, he couldn't let her die.

Slowly, the thrashing stopped. Her body shook with sobs instead of violence, screams subdued to jagged breathing. Kieran wrapped himself around her as much as possible on the hard floor. "It's okay, it's okay," he repeated, rocking gently. If she took energy from people, he let himself be full of light, of positive, calming energy, hoping she would feel it. "You're not a monster."

She blinked in confusion, her face softening, some of the colour coming back.

He reached for her hands, cupping them in the towel. She flinched half-heartedly, but let him rub them, nearly in a daze. "I wouldn't have died," she said.

He found it hard to believe, with long tears running down her hand, the silver skeleton glinting through, and with the amount of blood on the floor. But the cuts were already starting to knit themselves back together, her skin tone starting to improve from deathly white to its usual pale hue. "I wouldna either," he said. He wiped the blood off her face and arms.

"I don't understand."

She was like a kid in his arms—he'd never seen her like this. Terrifying and deadly, yes. Serious and solemn, yes. Elusive and quiet, yes. But not bone chillingly despondent. Not irrational.

"Sarrin," he tried, "do you know what happened to Gal? Why he's better?"

She turned away, her face burying in the towel. "I ran into him in the hall. He was..."—she swallowed heavily—"dark."

Kieran sighed. "Why'd you do it?"

She blinked, small and bloody. "Do what?"

"Gal's better. Looks great, like a huge weight has just been lifted. I know you pull energy from people, but you took his, everything that was wrong with him."

"I can't control it."

He sighed, rubbing a towel over the worst of the bloody steaks. "You have to let it go. It's not yours."

She blinked, motionless as he scrubbed. "Why didn't I take yours?"

"I'm tougher than I look," he joked.

But the joke fell flat, and Sarrin shut her eyes, collapsing into herself. "You could have died. I could have taken everything. That's what they did to me. I'm a monster."

He dropped back, leaning heavily against the wall as his heart rate returned to normal. "My mama always said, we need other people to survive. Sometimes we need ta borrow a little of their strength when ours isn't enough. It's not a bad thing. People need other people. That's just how it is, no shame in it." He rubbed his back, trying not to let her see as he checked for any extra crunchiness. "It's funny, at home, everyone knows this. Everyone just gets it, maybe not in so many words. But we care for each other, help each other. And we know when we hafta pull back, look after ourselves and not give too much away. If someone's havin' a bad day, you give 'em a hug, you give a little bit of your energy so they can take that and feel a bit better. If you're havin' a good day, you spread it around as far as you can."

Her blue eyes searched his, full of confusion.

"For some reason, people have forgotten we're all in this world together. Their energy's not the same. But you, I think you're more sensitive, is all. You just need to learn to control it." He put his hand on her back, and though she flinched away, he could feel the tug on him, feel her desperation clawing for more.

The life that swam in her was powerful, and he realized that was probably how she could know all the things she knew, how she could count enemies through solid walls. Even, probably, how she could fight so quickly. He let her have a little, but he knew enough to be careful not to let her take it all. He couldn't lose himself as he tried to help her.

"You're not a monster," he told her.

"You're not scared of me?" She blinked, rivulets of water dripping down her nose, but already her eyes looked brighter, clearer.

He smiled. "Never have been."

Leaning against the wall, she lifted her hands. "They're not mine. They're theirs. I thought that if I could cut them off, then I could be free of it."

He pressed his lips together, unable to offer more. "I get it." They sat in silence, the flesh on the hands knitting back together before their eyes.

"Come on." Kieran stood, offering her a hand. "We have to get you to Hoepe before that scars wrong."

She ignored his hand, but pushed to her feet. She glanced up at him, questioning.

He met her gaze, lips twisting into a grim smile. He would take her away from this place. Away from a world that would do... whatever they did to her as a little girl. He would keep her safe, bring her to the Observer ship, a world where she could simply be. In the end she would be okay.

He would make sure of it.

SEVENTEEN

Gal's heart pounded in his chest. The planet barrelled down on them, the same as it had been doing since they'd set their feeble thrusters in its direction. In a few minutes it would be in range.

The others stood around him on the freightship's small bridge, staring in disbelief, but Gal had known the planet would come for them. It always did. Returning to the planet was a last measure, one he would have avoided if there was any other way.

He considered taking their chances adrift in space. But this was the Deep Black—there were huge gaps of nothing everywhere you looked.

"What the…?" said Kieran.

They stared at the viewscreen for a minute, Gal's insides churning. "We should prepare to land."

"Cap'n," Kieran reminded him, "the hull-plating has multiple exposed sections. I don't know if we can pass into the atmosphere safety."

Gal put a hand on his shoulder. "I know, you told me already. It will be okay." If it had to work out, it would. That was simply the way.

A feeling of déjà vu gripped him. The last time he had

seen the vivid green and blue planet had been from the warship Valkas, and Gal had been terrified. Much like he was now.

"Are you sure?" Kieran asked.

Gal nodded once. "I know it's hard to understand."

Kieran pressed his lips, considering. Far more went on in that head than Gal had ever given the boy credit for. There was a lot that was hard to understand, but Kieran just might. And that could be a problem.

"Take us down," Gal ordered the pilot.

She turned to look at him, uncertainty clouding her face. "The thrusters won't be able to counteract gravity and control our landing."

"It'll be okay."

"Go ahead, Isuma." One of the Augment doctors appeared beside him. Gal studied the abnormally tall man. His kin was sallow, eyes tight—tired, scared—a fact he had failed to notice in the middle of all his own struggles.

The ship dove.

Kieran inhaled sharply, but didn't say another word.

Clouds parted, the atmosphere splitting and wrapping around them as they descended. The pilot set them down easily in large clearing, one that had appeared almost perfectly in their path. They had arrived.

The bridge erupted in claps and cheers, even Hoepe allowed himself a smile. Gal's chest constricted. Hopefully she wouldn't be there. Hopefully she would stay hidden.

Rayne touched his shoulder, bringing him back from the thoughts that threatened to drown him again. Her arm was heavily bandaged, but she used her free hand. She gave him a gentle smile. "Are you coming?"

The past clawed at him, but the demons did not appear.

This would be okay. It was only a few days. He knew what they needed, kept it solidly at the forefront of his mind.

There was no reason everything had to come crashing down.

He steeled himself and followed Rayne and the others through the ship, pleased that the doctors had given her something for the pain and she seemed to have a new lightness in her step.

The others congregated at the cargo bay door, eager to step off the ship. Kieran bent to remove the seal.

"Don't worry, Gal," said Rayne. "They ran the atmospheric scans three times—it's perfectly breathable."

He nodded. That had never worried him.

Would Cordelia be here, or would she hide?

The doors slid open, bathing them in wave of sweet, clean air.

What would she say?

Through the cargo bay, they descended. The Augments stopped, pausing at the jagged, torn-away ramp, staring at the scene in front of them. Beside him, Rayne gasped. She turned, her eyes wide. "Gal, it's beautiful."

He nodded grimly. Cordelia had outdone herself. He jumped from the ship to the ground, setting foot on the first planet he had been to three years that wasn't grey and dead.

Everyone around him chattered and laughed, excitement burbling through them as they jumped down. Still, it did not make him feel easy.

A woman stood in the centre of the field in front of them. She was plain, her look colonial, with a simple cap over her hair and a long dress laced up the back.

Gal grimaced and pushed through the crowd.

Cordelia smiled and folded her hands serenely when she saw him. "Galiant," she said.

"Cordelia. We need somewhere to stay for a few days," he said.

"I know."

He leaned close, whispering in her ear. "Nothing about

anything else," he said, partly to reassure her, partly to warn. Would Rayne ever understand it, if she knew what he had done? Would the others?

Her eyes went cold, only a flash, and then she stepped back and raised her arms to the others. "Welcome! You must have had quite a journey. Come and rest."

Gal drew his shoulders up as though he could hide, while the others came from the ship and streamed past him. His eyes traced Rayne as one of the Augments helped her.

"The compound is this way," said Cordelia, leading them across the field.

Gal grabbed her arm before she could go, his voice menacing. "Don't show off."

She smiled serenely. "I'm glad you came. I've been so lonely."

Gal hung back. His wary eyes traced the line of towering trees that surrounded them. Above, the sky was bright blue, fluffy white clouds gently gliding past. Only, he knew there was no star here. The light, all of it came from the planet itself.

His eyes drifted down to the ship, and there, beside it, standing as though he had always been there, was Aaron. The apparition walked over to him.

Gal turned away. He had promised Rayne he would do better. That he would save them after all. He couldn't afford to be pulled into another downward spiral.

Still, Aaron advanced. "Remember who you are," was all he said, sending a chill through Gal as he passed. In a blink, the man was gone.

Wide-eyed, Gal took a deep breath.

He caught Kieran staring intently at the ground, at the perfectly manicured lawn. The others passed him by, until he was the only one left. He looked up, staring at Gal. Gal recognized the look in his eyes, even as it flashed away:

intense, calculating, curious.

"Nice planet," said Kieran, in his laid-back drawl. "I can see why you didn't wanna come here." A smile bloomed on his face, practiced enough it was hard to know if it was real or not. He started toward the compound.

"Wait." Kieran was no idiot, not by a long shot, and the idea of him exploring and studying the planet was more than Gal could handle. "Get started on the repairs. I don't want to stay here too long."

Kieran frowned, seriousness and annoyance passing over his face so quickly they were nearly imagined. "Whaddya mean? I need a little rest before I get started, Cap'n. I'm wankered."

"No, this is important."

He rubbed his face, grey and pale. "Yeah, all right. Yessir." The engineer turned back to the ship, Gal watching him until he climbed back into the cargo by and disappeared.

It would be okay, Gal told himself. The planet was dangerous, just as Hap said. But it was only a few days. Not enough time to discover Cordelia's secret. Or his.

*　*　*

Sarrin followed as Cordelia led them across the clearing and through a path in the trees. A grey building rose up behind the tree line. It was the same grey as the UEC buildings, similar in its blocky design, but somehow there was a lightness to it. Sarrin felt lighter as well.

Hoepe's bandages had already come off her hands, the skin looking as though nothing had happened. Below the surface still sat a gleaming, inhuman skeleton, but today, it didn't bother her, not as much. Kieran had helped her, whatever he'd done. And while it still scared her to think about touching anyone, especially him, he thought that one day she could learn to control it.

There was no grey concrete wall surrounding this structure,

nor grass that constantly needed to be watered and fed with artificial UV lamps. Instead there were bright flower gardens, meticulously kept, with abstract statues and paths and seating benches. A ravine with a quaint crossing bridge ran through the centre. The Augments around Sarrin seemed to grow an extra inch, the fresh air and the sunlight creating a warmth deep inside.

Cordelia kept up a constant stream of chatter, pointing out the different tree species, different from anything Sarrin had seen on Earth. "You'll find a fully stocked medical bay in the compound," Cordelia said to Hoepe, gesturing to Rayne and her bandaged shoulder.

Hoepe turned to his brother, communicating something quickly. He turned to Cordelia, "is it possible you have a three-dimensional neural scan?"

Cordelia smiled knowingly. "Why, yes, of course."

"We will need to transport someone from our infirmary."

She nodded. "I can assist you."

"Thank you," said Leove.

"My pleasure. My aim is to please, it is so rare I get visitors."

Thomas beside them frowned. "Are you by yourself here, Cordelia?"

A stricken look crossed her face. She glanced back at Gal. "Yes. I am alone."

Gal looked up at his name, his expression seemed more like a warning.

"I don't understand," said one of the Augments. "What are you doing out here?"

She sighed, shrugging. "Exploring. Research."

"By yourself? Without a team?"

She nodded. "Do not be so concerned. I have been here for many years. I find the environment quite fascinating. Although I do wish I had more visitors."

"Understandable," said Hoepe.

"You are planning to stay a while?"

"Yes," said Hoepe. "If we are welcome, I think this will be a positive opportunity. Our ship is in grave need of repair."

"And you need somewhere safe to hide," agreed Cordelia.

Gal glared at Cordelia.

Something was amiss, prodding the monster inside Sarrin, but the warmth of the sun soothed it away.

"Not to worry," Cordelia continued smoothly, "the captain has told me about your troubles. It will be no problem. The Central Army doesn't bother me out here."

Hoepe smiled. "Thank you. That is kind."

She clapped her hands and smiled brightly. "We must see to your injured crewman, but first the rest of you look half-staved, surviving on UEC rations." She led them into the complex, the first room a large hall with rows of tables.

"I thought you were here by yourself," said Hoepe.

She sighed again. "It was meant for many more people." She glanced at Gal. "There is food in the kitchen, and fresh vegetables in the gardens out back. Please, the rest of you, help yourselves, while we take care of Grant."

Sarrin frowned. She hadn't heard anyone say Grant's name.

"Don't be silly, dear, your tall doctor friend mentioned it." The woman, Cordelia, reached her hand out to touch Sarrin on the shoulder. She smiled politely as Sarrin flinched back. "Relax, dear, you're safe here."

Sarrin stared as Cordelia left with the doctors. Gal's demons must still be in her head, and it was worse than she thought—she didn't even remember speaking her concern aloud.

The others dispersed, some running, some laughing, as they swarmed into the dining hall. They pushed into the kitchen, returning with breads and cakes. Others headed through the back door, returning with armfuls of vegetables.

Sarrin glanced around quickly, scanning and cataloguing the room. Kieran was missing. He would be in the engine room making repairs. A table laden with apples sat against the wall, the fruits not dissimilar to the ones her parents had grown in their orchards, in the trees where she and Halud had played. Her hand reached out, immediately taking two—one for her and one for Kieran.

EIGHTEEN

After a too long sleep, Grant sat up, rubbing his eyes. A firm hand pushed him back down. The steady monotony of beeping made his head throb in a matching rhythm.

Slowly, his eyes started to focus, lumpy silhouettes starting to condense into something recognizable. Hoepe's grim face greeted him. "How do you feel?"

Grant opened his mouth to ask how the procedure went, but he coughed uncontrollably. Each cough slammed his brain into his skull. He reached a hand up reflexively, meeting a massive line of sutures across his entire scalp.

Not well, it seemed. It should have only been a small chip.

"Don't try to speak," said Hoepe. He turned, gesturing to someone behind him.

As his vision cleared, Grant realized he was not in the same place he had fallen asleep. This room was large, almost cavernous. Grey walls were replaced by a warm white and gentle blue. On the far end of the suite was a full wall of monitors, images and 3D displays of a skull and spine.

"There was an incident when we removed your tracking chip," Hoepe said.

Grant frowned, opening his mouth only to fall into another fit of coughing. Hoepe's identical twin brother lurked into view, holding a cup of water, and Grant took it readily, tossing it into his mouth.   The cool liquid burned the back of his throat.

Immediately, his stomach turned and it came right back up into the dish Hoepe had somehow procured.   He'd never had an anaesthetic reaction this bad.

"Take it easy," said Hoepe.   "You've been in a coma for six days."

"Six?"   The voice that came from him didn't sound like him at all.

"When I went to remove your tracking device, it triggered your limpet suit," Hoepe explained.   "Any attempt we made to deactivate it or remove it, the suit dug into deeper.   It nearly killed you."   Hoepe looked away, a break in his otherwise unflappably-professional manner.   "We were lucky to find a research base, one of the captain's friends.   They have an advanced medical suite where we could image your central nervous system and the equipment we needed to remove the chip and release the suit.   But, Grant,"—he took a breath and shuffled in his chair uncomfortably.   Grant's heart started to pound, this was how Hoepe delivered bad news, and he wanted to tell him to just get on with it, rubbing at his sore throat instead.   "The suit is ingrained too deeply.   It's connected directly to your amygdala, to the fear centre of your brain.   I can't remove it.   Not without killing you."

A wave of violent coughing caught him by surprise, and Grant doubled over, clenching his fist.   The UECs had sunk their claws into him permanently.

"We did manage to remove the tracking chip, if it's any consolation.   They can't communicate with you or follow your actions any more.   It was quite a tricky procedure, necessitating a full craniotomy and nearly fourteen hours of surgery time.   Electrodes were wired directly from the chip into several areas of the brain and into the base of the limpet suit. The suit itself appears biological in nature, extending hyphae like a fungus deep into the recesses of the dura matter. We had to stabilize…."

But Grant stopped listening. He had this suit, this ugly thing that they put there. It was a part of him. Forever.

The UEC scar on him, forever.

There was no way to remove it. No way for him to be free. The suit dug its tentacles into him the same as the UECs had, into every single facet of his being, every facet of life. It would never be his again, not ever.

"Grant." Hoepe put a hand on his shoulder. He did a double take, not Hoepe after all, but Leove. Leove put his other hand on his brother, who was still rambling and pointing at various scans to illustrate his point, and told him to stop.

Now it was Leove's turn to try to explain, and he started the same way: "Grant," Leove sat next to him on the bed. "I know this is hard to process. It's not the outcome you anticipated when you hopped onto the table a week ago"

"No," he croaked. "It's not."

"I'm sure if anyone anticipated this as the outcome, you would have held off. You need to rest and eat a little bit when you can. After six days without supportive care, your body is low in nutrients, most of your systems shutting down to preserve strength. It will be a few days, but you will recover."

Grant nodded, his head throbbed and spun.

Hoepe stood with his arms folded over his chest. "We chose the best action at the time."

Leove sighed. "I'm not arguing with you, brother."

"But you are."

Slowly, Leove stood from the bed, running a hand over his brow. "Fine, Hoepe, you're right, I am arguing. It was foolish to try to remove the chip by yourself, without any scans or information. Against our oath to Faith, the healer."

Hoepe's fists clenched. "The chip needed to be removed."

"Yes, because you thought Rami was going to destroy the ship and Grant was the only way to stop him," Leove shouted. "He nearly died."

"Are you telling me we should have just let Rami take over? You saw the way he was acting, he would have gotten rid of Kieran. And then where would we be?"

"You were so focussed on that engineer, you assumed the worst. But everything turned out, didn't it? Rami's not even the alpha."

Grant's ears perked up.

"No," Hoepe said, casting a grim glance in his direction, "Sarrin is."

Another fit of coughing doubled Grant over on the bed, his heart pounding to keep up with the effort. His head felt like it was going to burst.

Hoepe flopped down in the chair by the bed, pulling on a tuft of hair as the muscles in his jaw clenched. "We're supposed to be brothers. Why are we fighting?"

Leove huffed. "We share a genetic code, Hoepe. We are brothers, but we can't expect to be the same. Not with what Evangecore did." His long legs strode quickly from the room, his arm catching briefly on the doorframe as he called out, "Let me know if you need help."

Hoepe sat motionless, head sunken in his hands.

Grant blinked twice, reaching a tentative hand to his friend. "Hoepe, are you okay?"

He pushed angrily out of the chair. "Do you require anything?" Hoepe asked, his medical monotone firmly in place.

He shook his head. He was starving and his chest and lungs hurt from being too dry and he desperately wanted water, but for all his problems, Hoepe looked far rougher. The doctor retreated to the far end of the room, his shoulders tight as he angrily swiped through several 3D scan projections.

Another thing Evangecore had taken from them.

* * *

Sarrin stood in the dark engineering bay, cataloguing each damaged and torn and burnt component. She nodded, only half listening as Kieran detailed the repair list. He was talking mostly for himself, organizing his thoughts.

She'd had a dream in the night, one she hadn't had in a very long time: there was a vast forest and strange ungulate creatures that ran alongside her. It was as though in that place each knew her and she knew them, a place she belonged. Even the thought of it now made her heart swell.

Kieran's hands moved fluidly through the air as he talked, making shapes and figures appear in front of him. It was mesmerizing. He paused in his stride, turning back to look at her.

She gasped as his green eyes met hers. She'd had her hands half-way to touching him, she realized. And her mind had gone blank, completely ignoring the repairs. Her hands snapped down to her sides. Gal's demons still screamed around inside of her, adding to her own. It wasn't safe. She wouldn't risk it, never risk it. Despite how he had helped her. It didn't make sense, that he had touched her for so long and survived. No one else had—but then no one else was like Kieran.

He smiled, reaching for her. Now it seemed he thought it was safe. She would have to be extra vigilant.

She side stepped out of reach.

He sighed and continued. "I don't understand why Gal is in such a hurry to leave," he said. "Do you have any idea?"

She shrugged when he turned back to look at her. The captain had been acting strange—but then what was normal? He seemed more stable than he had since she first met him, but he still lived in passive glances and tight lipped worry.

"I just hope he doesn't hang around the engine room all day like he did last night," said Kieran. Gal had constantly run between the ship and the compound, worried about what was happening where he wasn't. "Do you think we have time to go get some food, like some real food? I'm starving."

Sarrin nodded. Besides the fruit and a couple of reheated rations, they hadn't eaten since the afternoon before when they had arrived on the planet. The silence was easy as she led him through the cargo bay and across the lawns. Everything with Kieran seemed easy.

Kieran followed her to the compound. His eyes grew wide as they entered the dining hall. "Oh wow," he said. "Now that's somethin'."

The hall had been laid out with a massive feast, fruits and vegetables carved into ornate structures, piles of food running the length of each of the tables. Augments sat in groups, talking loudly, even laughing.

Sarrin, too, couldn't help but feel the cheer. It piled on top of her growing sense of anxiety, the two emotions warring with each other uncomfortably.

But then Kieran laughed, his bright eyes dancing as he smiled at her. "I'll go find us some grub."

She frowned, reluctant to eat insect larva and curious as to why he would be so excited, but he was gone before she could stop him. Leove sat at a nearby table, waving at her—if the doctor was here, that meant Grant's procedure was complete. The doctor's mood appeared to be good, so she made her way to the table where he sat with Isuma, eager for news.

"Sarrin!" he cried. A space was cleared, and she sat carefully—there were too many people too close, but their mood was good. The doctor smiled intently at her, the expression odd when compared to the normally dour face of Hoepe. "We were just talking about you."

She paused.

Another Augment leaned forward, a face whose name she did not know. "We were talking about when the warship attacked."

"How did you stop it?" another called out.

She inhaled sharply. Her heart rate quickened, thumping so loud the others must be able to hear it as well.

"Was it your weapon?"

"We heard you collapsed and were screaming."

"Thomas thinks you tore apart the warship with your mind."

Flashes of the warship came to her mind: the display of the ruined Ishash'tor, the militant XO. Most prominent was screams of Amy, trapped on the ship, fighting both fronts. The dining hall disappeared behind a wall of black.

Pushing away from the table hard enough to shake it, she extracted herself. Her vision was marred by dark and cloudy patches. Kieran was no where to be seen, no matter how far she looked. Someone called her name, but she ignored it.

She had to find Kieran.

A woman appeared in front of her, her bright green eyes cutting through the fog. Her hand was nearly on Sarrin before she realized it and moved away. Cordelia. "Calm, child," she whispered sweetly. "Let's go outside. There is a lot of commotion in here."

Wide-eyed, Sarrin followed, finding herself swept along into the gardens. The breathing was a little easier out here.

Cordelia stood beside her, hands clasped serenely in front, while Sarrin panted. "I find exercise is the best way to calm the mind," said the woman.

Sarrin stared at her, the monster still on high alert.

"There are trails that extend for miles in these woods. I use them myself often." Cordelia smiled. "Go ahead, dear. There's nothing to be afraid of out there, just trees and rocks.

Go for a run, you'll feel better."

Sarrin's eyes snapped to the opening in the tree line. She had told Kieran she would help him again today. But he would understand, surely. A run was what she needed, and a chance to run in the outdoors, in the woods was too tempting to pass up.

She turned to thank the woman, but Cordelia was already gone. Sighing, and pushing through the clogged edges of her vision, Sarrin let her legs move, speeding through the garden and across the field and into the trees.

* * *

Gal sat at a quiet end of one of the long tables, Rayne opposite him.

Her arm was in its sling, but the new painkillers provided by Cordelia let her move it enough to cut through the stack of flapjacks and cured meat in front of her. She said the doctors were able to help a lot with the equipment in the infirmary, speeding the healing almost ten times.

He didn't like it at all, but seeing Rayne smile and laugh in front of him, nearly healed, he had to admit he was a little grateful to Cordelia.

"What are you looking for?" Rayne asked him.

Startled, he turned to look at her again.

"You've been looking around constantly, watching for some monster to leap out. You haven't even touched your—I don't know what that is."

He forced a smile. He had told Cordelia not to show off, but she insisted the feast was nothing. The oblong grey and orange fruit sat untouched in front of him. "Gammot fruit, from Etar 3." They were his favourite.

Rayne smiled. "Cordelia has crops from everywhere under the stars."

Gal nodded.

"Amazing she can tend all these gardens by herself."

He nodded again, turning his head for another scan.

"But really, what are you looking for? We should take this opportunity to relax, you said so yourself, Cordelia is an old friend."

He pressed his lips. He did say that, but Cordelia was exactly who he was watching for.

"Hello, Captain. Commander."

The voice made him jump, soft and smooth and far too accommodating. "Hello, Cordelia," he sighed. The woman had appeared at the end of the table, pouring fresh juice for them both.

"This is simply amazing," Rayne said around a full mouth. "How do you manage it all?"

Cordelia simply smiled in return. "This place was meant for a large contingent, there is a large industrial kitchen, most of it automated." She glanced darkly at Gal.

Rayne didn't seem to notice. "A large contingent—what happened? It's so beautiful here, why haven't they colonized it? It's not even marked."

Cordelia stared at Gal for a long time, a cheery smile still painted her face but her eyes were dark and hard. In them, he could see a reflection of the planet exploding. "It's a long story," she said, finally turning to Rayne. "Politics and whatnot. Perhaps Gal would like to fill you in."

She turned back to Gal. "There is a lovely picnic spot just over the rise, not far from here. I could pack you a basket, and you could take this lovely woman to see some of the views."

Gal shot her a stern look. He was about to say 'no', when Rayne reached across the table, taking his arm. "That sounds wonderful. I think we've earned a little leave. What do you say, Gal?"

It was a terrible idea. He couldn't tell her why. "What about your shoulder, Rayne. We shouldn't stress it."

"It's feeling quite good actually." She moved it up and down in the sling. "Besides, fresh air and some exercise will be good for you. The ship is in good hands, take a little time for yourself."

The answer was still no. A definite no.

"Please, Gal." She blinked prettily, and he knew the no wasn't was firm as he thought.

"If you're sure your shoulder is okay."

She nodded.

He shot a dirty look at Cordelia, warning her again. So far, her secret was safe and by association so was his, but for how long? Cordelia smiled pleasantly and spun on her heel, quickly disappearing into the crowd, presumably to find them a picnic basket.

Rayne simply grinned at him, not a clue about how dangerous this place truly was.

* * *

Kieran tinkered madly with the Damn Kepheus Drive. He'd decided that was the official name, given how many times he'd repaired the thing. He was glad a few others had trickled in throughout the morning to help with the repairs, and happier still that they were on the opposite end of the engineering bay, so no one could hear the colourful words that escaped him. But Sarrin still hadn't returned.

"Hello," said a voice, "I missed you at breakfast." The colonial woman stood in front of him.

"Hi," he said reflexively. "I just came in to grab something quick, so I could get back here."

"I'm Cordelia," she extended a hand.

He nodded, wiping his own hand on his coveralls first. "Kieran."

"You don't want to take a rest?"

He shook his head, already turning back to the cracked drive in front of him. "Cap'n wants these repairs done A-S-

A-P."

She paused, thinking. "He doesn't want to stay?" her voice carried a note of sadness, which made Kieran look up again.

"No, we're in some trouble and need to move on."

"Where will you go?"

He shrugged. "Cap'n has a plan, I'm sure."

"What about you? Where do you think you should go?"

"We lost a friend a week back—I think we ought to see if we can help him." He frowned as soon as the words left his lips—why was he telling her this? But then again, why wouldn't he?

"Do you think you can find him?" she prompted.

He frowned again. "I do. But we have to get these repairs done, if we're going to do anything about it."

She paused, letting him get back to his work. "I could help, you know."

He considered her. "Help with what?"

"Repairs. Finding your friend. Whatever you need."

He shook his head. "Naw, that's all right. Thank you. I think we've got it." He looked up, seeing more people had joined the repair team in the engineering bay.

She nodded, falling silent again. She moved to the other side of the table. "How are the repairs coming?"

"There's a lot to do, but we're making steady progress. Shouldn't be a day or more with this much help."

She nodded.

"Say, have you seen Sarrin? Skinny girl, mess of dark hair."

Cordelia smiled. "I have. Poor thing looked overwhelmed, so she went for a run on the trails."

"Did she look … okay?" Or was she panicking, wild-eyed? He'd not been able to shake the fear that the busy dining hall had overwhelmed her.

"Yes, just needed some air, I think. She was looking for you." Cordelia smiled.

He sighed, lips relaxing ito a smile.

"Maybe you should see if you can find her," Cordelia suggested.

He looked at the half-repaired Kepheus in front of him.

"She did look like she could use a friend," she said, watching him. "There are plenty of people working on these repairs. You could take a small break, I'm sure. You look tired yourself."

He sighed, pressing his hands into his weary eyes.

He found himself nodding before he finally said, "Yes. Do you know where she went? Can you show me?"

"Yes, dear. There's a path in the woods."

NINETEEN

Halud followed the factitian and the cinematographer back into the research wing of the hospital. The vaccine was being revealed today—they would inoculate the first patient, and celebrate.

He gritted his teeth, forcing his feet not to drag. He had to stay professional, play the part. Otherwise Sarrin, whom he had seen still trapped in the secret research facility of Junk, would suffer.

He sat down with the same scientist he had interviewed before. They exchanged a greeting, and the factitian set up with her set of cards for Halud. After a moment the cinematographer waved his hand to signal he was ready.

Halud took a deep breath and glanced at the scientist, who also nodded to say he was ready. Halud started: "Hello, United Earth Citizens. The Gods have been good to us. I am here with Dr. Trae Amanpreet."

"Thank you for meeting with me, Honourable Poet." The scientist pressed his five fingers into his chest.

Halud nodded. "Of course. You are here to tell us of the gift from Faith, the Healer. The vaccine for *Xenoralia nervosa*."

"Yes, I am. As you will recall about *Xenoralia*…"

Halud zoned out, half watching out of the corner of his

eye for the factitian to flip a cue card telling him when to speak next. His heart pounded in his ears and the image of Sarrin strung up played over and over in his head.

The card changed, and he read it: "I understand this vaccine is now available to protect our citizens from ever again experiencing the deadly effects of Xenoralia."

He had been told precisely to call the disease Xenoralia or *Xenoralia nervosa* instead of Red Fever. Never Red Fever. The Speakers had been clear.

The doctor said something scripted.

"It is with great pleasure that I am here to witness the first human inoculation. The first step in a brave new age." He filled his voice with confidence and excitement, as his gut filled with fear.

The camera shifted slightly, bringing the additional two chairs into view. Halud watched as the subjects came towards them, a man and a woman. The man sat down first, followed by a woman cradling a small bundle in her arms swaddled in cloth: a baby.

Halud froze. He glared at the factitian, but she was watching the couple, a smile on her face. He forced his to do the same.

The swaddling was pulled back, a bright red, wrinkled skin baby. A newborn.

The mother was still swollen and pale from childbirth. But she had a bright smile on her face, her hands shaking in her excitement.

Halud glanced at the scientist who also smiled as he took a single syringe from the tray beside his chair. He cooed, admiring the child and praising the parents.

Suddenly, they had all their gazes focussed on Halud.

He nodded once. "The Gods have blessed you well," he said, and rose to give the baby the proper anointment. He passed his hand over the child's head and then to its chest, tapping the spot above the heart. Halud's arms moved on their own, his mind stuck, rolling over and over again at this brand new baby, the first ever human recipient of a vaccine for the most dangerous disease the folk had ever seen.

He passed his hand again over the head, the baby's eyes blinking at him once, a deep brown.

Quickly, he fell back into his chair, his legs all but giving out.

The doctor tapped the syringe, preparing. The long needle waved in the air above them.

The mother reached out her hand for the father, and together they held the child out. The needle plunged deep into the baby's thigh. A scream broke across the room. After a second, Halud was pleased to realize it wasn't him. He took a breath, gasping hungrily, as the baby cried.

The parents quickly fussed and the researcher made a show of comforting the child.

Halud watched the scene, fear growing within him, an anxiety he couldn't shake. A quiet noise grabbed his attention, and he realized the factitian was tapping furiously at the sign. He sat up in his chair. "Simply marvellous. Tell us, Doctor, how effective is this vaccine?"

"One hundred percent."

"And can we expect any side effects?"

"None, it is perfectly safe. Besides the sting from the injection, this child will grow up healthy, stronger than ever before, and safe against the *Xenoralia nervosa* virus."

Halud smiled again, but he wasn't able to stop his shaking.

"At this time, we are looking to vaccinate all children under the age of three. Vaccine centres will be set up in major residential blocks."

Halud caught himself before he shouted out. Instead he read the card, verbatim: "And so it shall be, the words of the Gods to the Speakers, all children must be protected." He stood again, mechanically, and anointed the baby, still wailing. As it cried, it opened its crinkled eyes.

Halud gasped and backed away, his arm only half way through the prayer. They were blue, brilliant crystalline blue. The same blue as the rats in the cages behind him. The same blue as Sarrin's.

The interview ended in a blur.

He fidgeted his hands together, waiting for the doctor to finish his goodbyes with the couple. The producer spoke to him, but his muffled brain couldn't comprehend it. He turned away from her as soon as the doctor had finished, the couple escorted out of the laboratory.

"The eyes," was all he could say.

"Yes, the colour change is the only side effect of the vaccine. We were unable to clear that from the virus." The researcher suddenly started to search him, more interested than before.

Halud cast his gaze down, hiding the pale blue of his own eyes. "Very good work." He rushed out the room as fast as he possibly could.

TWENTY

Hoepe brushed his hand through the holographic display, watching as the lines blurred around his fingers and then straightened. All this tech, the best the Central Army had at it's disposal, all collected in this one, remote facility. The Gods truly must be looking out for them, providing everything in their time of greatest need.

Footsteps clicked on the pristine floor, signalling an entrance. Hoepe turned, but he should have guessed the entrant from the long strides. "Hello, Hoepe," said Leove, wringing his hands anxiously.

Hoepe looked at his twin, his emotions a complete jumble.

Leove took a steadying breath. "I came to apologize."

"Apologize?"

"For my actions, and the things I said." Leove took a step forward. "I should have realized how it would make you feel. I didn't think. It's been hard for you, never having known your family. And harder still when you found out that I did, that I had the life you did not. I hope you can forgive me for this." He took a step forwards. "And my time with Isuma has been superfluous. You are my brother. You're all I need. Brothers are more important than anything."

Hoepe smiled.

"Will you forgive me, so we can be the brothers we were meant to be?"

Hoepe stepped forward, and they embraced. "I'm glad you understand."

"Me too," said Leove. "I've told Isuma I'm done with her. I never really cared for her, only for you, my brother."

They embraced for several minutes, Hoepe taking in all the warmth his brother offered, feeling as though he could finally breathe. As they pulled apart, the feeling stayed.

"How is your friend, Grant?"

"Doing well. His recovery is ahead of schedule and his neurofunction tests are nearly at normal levels."

Smiling, Leove said, "I'm so glad to hear. And you were right to operate on him when you did, I'm only sorry I didn't see it then and wasn't there to help."

Hoepe clapped his brother gladly on the shoulder, burying the twinge of confusion. "Let's go check his latest scans together." They walked into the main hospitalization area shoulder to shoulder.

Grant sat propped up in one of the beds. "Hey, guys." He waved a tablet at them briefly. "What do you know about this place?"

Leove sat down by Grant. "It is a nice facility, well equipped. The caretaker, Cordelia, is easy to talk with and very helpful."

"It's a massive place," said Grant.

Hoepe nodded. "We were told it was originally meant to house several hundred people."

"So why doesn't it?"

"It is unclear," said Hoepe, the uncertainty twinging again until he pushed it down.

"It seems to be a point of distress," said Leove, "We haven't questioned her further."

Grant frowned.

"What is it?" Hoepe asked.

"I just can't stop thinking about Junk, or the idea that more of our friends are trapped in other facilities." He tapped on the data tablet a few times. "So I was playing around, looking through different sections of the compound, and I found this." He held it out for them to see.

On the screen was a detailed schematic of the building: the main floor with the dining hall and kitchens, and the upper floor which housed the infirmary and living quarters, and a basement which was listed as storage. But there was an empty space. Grant tapped again, zooming in on the empty space, which contained an elevator shaft.

He tweaked the image. Another schematic appeared, another floor. This one bearing an uncanny resemblance to the maze of cells in Evangecore.

Leove gasped. "You don't think?"

"We know there are others out there. We know they put them on uninhabited planets where they think no one will ever find the facilities."

Hoepe licked his lips. "You believe it's a research facility."

Grant tapped again. A long list scrolled across the screen: names and ID codes. Many of which he recognized.

Hoepe turned to Leove. "Do you think Gal knows?"

"Is that why he refused to bring us here?" Leove finished.

"What about Cordelia? She's been nothing but helpful. Does she know?"

"Has she been hiding the secret all along, or is she unaware?"

Hoepe shook his head. "It doesn't matter, we have to be cautious."

"We can't leave them in there," said Grant.

The brothers nodded, Hoepe searching Leove's face to be sure they were on the same page.

"We'll rally the others," said Leove. "We have to move

quickly. We've already wasted time."

"I'm going too," said Grant.

"You're still recovering."

"You have to let me. Those are my friends."

"It's all right." Hoepe nodded at Leove.—If he knew his friend Grant would come whether they said he could or not. "Leove and I will talk to the others. We'll have to be quiet about it, we can't let Cordelia know. Find out everything you can about possible obstacles or security measures."

Leove nodded solemnly. Grant too.

More Augments, hidden on a lush planet. And they had nearly been so relaxed, so lulled by Cordelia's charms, they could have missed them entirely. "Good work, Grant." At least his brother was with him now. Together, they couldn't fail.

* * *

The trees parted as Sarrin ran. Her lungs stretched and her legs burned. The pace was frantic.

Breathe in.

Her feet landed solidly, surely, adapting with each stride over the uneven path. A stray branch slapped across her arm. She ran and ran, the demons slipping away through her fingertips as she trailed them across low-hanging leaves. The last of Gal's pain left her, and some of her own.

She hadn't had this much freedom since the war—no, not even then could she run in the open. This was the most freedom she had ever experienced.

The fresh air was cool and sweet. She breathed until it filled her, set her cell metabolism into overdrive, made her feel unstoppable. The path took her up a hill, overlooking the valley below, a great river winding through it. The trees were foreign, the leaves round, their branches spiralling up and up before the weight of the canopy pulled them back down.

There was a familiarity she could not place. The forest was

silent except for the soft turn of her feet on the leaves. This was living—a feeling she had all but forgotten, and the buzz of it made her giddy.

A smile broke out as she ran.

Movement in the woods caught her attention. At first startled, she turned her head to investigate without breaking her pace. Through the trees, long-legged animals ran along ahead and beside her, their long tails teasing her to follow. She gasped, her step faltering. They were the ungulate creatures from her dreams.

But there should be no animals here.

She pushed the thought down, too eager to have found the place of her dreams to let it go. The path turned down, the creatures bounding ahead, looking back like they knew her, like they called her a friend. She wasn't scared of them, and more importantly, they weren't scared of her. There was no reason to be.

* * *

Gal followed Rayne as she hiked up the path in front of them. Cordelia had outdone herself, he had to admit. The forest was beautiful despite the danger they were in.

That was the trouble. The other planet too was beautiful, together they could have provided everything the folk ever needed.

But Cornelius was gone now. And Cordelia unpredictable.

The path levelled out, opening into a flat meadow. Directly ahead of them, the trees parted. He didn't need to step forward to know the view was incredible. "Oh, Gal," Rayne said, "you have to see this."

He stalked forward, but his eyes were fixed on Rayne. Partly to be sure she didn't fall with her arm still in a sling, partly because the ambient light made her skin glow like honey.

She turned, smiling up at him.

He realized how close he was, too close to be professional. He turned away quickly, busying himself with the picnic basket. He laid the blanket on the ground and proceeded to unpack the food.

Rayne sat down watching him. A desperate itch started to tickle in his brain, but the demons did not appear. "You're doing much better," she noted.

He nodded his head once, refusing to look at her.

"I'm glad." She edged closer, reaching a hand out to touch his arm.

He met her eyes uncertainly.

"This has been an... interesting experience," she said. "I'm glad though. I'm happy I could be here. Happy you could be here." She wrapped her arm around his, leaning into him. "Happier still that everything worked out." Her arm was warm, already easing the uncertain feeling that plagued him.

"Why did you stay all those years?" he asked. "I was horrible."

She hugged his arm tighter. "I told you," she said softly, "I love you."

Pain shot through his head, mind whirring; he didn't remember her saying that at all. He had hoped to hear those words from her for so long. He had done nothing, could do nothing, but hurt her.

"Your arm..." he said.

"It's fine, I told you."

"No, I...." How could he say it?

"It's not your fault. A freak electrical discharge. But Hoepe says I'm going to make a full recovery."

Yes, that's what it was, a freak discharge. Entirely his fault.

She leaned over and kissed him. The warmth on his lips erased the last of his uncertain feeling. He pushed her down onto the blanket, the food disappearing, careful of her arm.

When he pulled back for air, she was smiling up at him. Her face was flushed, beautiful, and her hair slightly askew. He knew he would never deserve her.

"Gal? What's wrong? Your face is worried."

"Rayne, I…." He should tell her. Tell her everything, but she would never understand.

She half-sat, propping herself up on her good elbow. "It's okay, Gal. We're a long way from Etar."

He nodded, but it didn't ease the guilt that gnawed.

"Remember Yates?" she asked, teasing. "It was so beautiful there, romantic. I've never told you, but I think about that night all the time."

"Me too," he sighed honestly.

She gasped slightly, and he followed her gaze. There, on the yambucta tree from Irideon, bloomed a bioluminescent flower from Yates. A horticultural impossibility.

A wave of irritation flooded through him.

Rayne turned to him, melting him with her big brown eyes. "I'm glad you're doing better. I'm glad you've come back to me. I'm even glad we rescued all those Augments. They're not so bad, the Army is just afraid, that's why they said all those things."

He smiled. Maybe she would understand after all.

She reached for a slice of bread and cheese casually. "And we never had to use your failsafe program on them."

His smile dropped. What failsafe program? He looked around for Aaron, hoping for someone to ask, but the apparition was nowhere near.

Suddenly, Rayne pulled away. "Did you see that?"

He hadn't seen a thing.

"Hold on," she said, rising to her feet and pushing him back down, her expression a mix of excitement and curiosity. "I want to go see."

She disappeared into the forest before he had a chance to

stop her.

* * *

Grant put a hand up, quickly motioning to those behind him. The Augments moved efficiently, silently. It had taken no more than forty-five minutes for them to assemble. Only Sarrin was missing, but it didn't matter—so far they had encountered no resistance.

They were in the basement, ready to breach the staircase to the secret level.

Thomas went in first, then Rami.

Grant hung back, he had agreed with Hoepe he would do more commanding than fighting. Besides his head still throbbed enough to make him dizzy, or maybe it was the dehydration and muscle atrophy.

At least he didn't have to worry about the mind-control device taking him over.

Rami signalled the all clear, and Grant waved the rest in. They made a bit of noise on the stairs, Grant flinching at every soft clunk, but still there wasn't any resistance.

They broke into the antechamber, subduing the two guards without a single shot fired. Grant stepped to a nearby console, bypassing a simple lock and opening the heavily fortified door.

As the others went through to the cell blocks, Grant searched the console's archives. He found what he was looking for as they started bringing out the first of the Augments: three planets were listed as having other facilities —Junk, Porter, and Jade, confirming the rumours he'd heard on Junk.

Captive Augments ran past on their own feet. As quickly as they'd come in, and half as quietly, they ran up the stairs. Grant cleared the last step, taking up the very rear, glancing into the empty facility. A strange feeling settled on him: it was easy. It had been too easy.

TWENTY-ONE

Hoepe looked up from the data tablet in his hands, hearing footsteps in the corridor. Leove paused at the door to the medical centre, leaning against it. He stared at Hoepe, his long face contorting into an unknown expression. His gaze stayed long enough that Hoepe began to feel unsettled.

"Do you know where the others went?" Leove asked finally. "I was stocking the ship's infirmary. Isuma went to get food a few hours ago and never came back. And I didn't see anyone on my way over."

Hoepe frowned—Leove had been there when they discovered the underground bunker and Grant laid his plan to rescue the Augments. "Isuma?"

Leove's face set in defiance.

"I thought you were done with her?"

Leove's expression moved to shock. "Why would I be done with her?"

"You said…."

He shook his head coldly. "Isuma is important to me. I'm sorry you can't see that. I don't know what you think I said."

"You said, 'Brothers are more important than anything.' You didn't need anything else. Isn't that true? We are brothers."

"Yes, we are brothers."   Leove stood rigid, his face contorted into yet another expression that was foreign to Hoepe. "But it's not everything. We all need people, many people to make up who we are."

Hoepe frowned again. They were brothers, weren't they? Bonds by blood that could not be broken. And they were twins, literally a perfect mirror. "I don't understand, you said...."

"I'm in love with Isuma. That's not going to change. But you're my brother, and I love you too."

Hoepe felt his chest constrict. An itch started behind his eye. "Love?"

"I'm worried. Do you know where she is? Or anyone?"

Hoepe frowned again. "I don't understand, you were here when we rescued the others. We examined them and sent them for rest."

"Rescue?"

"Yes, don't you remember?"

"I haven't examined anyone today."

"You were there."

"Forget it, Hoepe. I'm going to go find her."

* * *

Rayne crept through the trees, her years of tactical training taking over as she searched the forest.   She had seen something out here, a glimpse too tauntingly familiar, but the trail had run cold. Whatever she followed left no trace, if there was anything at all. Hard as she looked, her eyes met only the dense forest of trees and scraggly underbrush.

"Good job, Rayne," said a familiar voice behind her.

She spun quickly, not believing her ears.

But there he sat, leaning casually on a boulder, looking neat and pressed as ever. His short, grey hair stood out on his dark skin, and his impeccable slate-grey uniform was buttoned all the way to the top, looking so tight it could choke him. The uniform carried four solid lines of gold piping, and the left breast was heavy with medals—the ones he wore for everyday use anyway.

"Daddy?"

He smiled. "Hello, Raynie."

She stood, dumbfounded.

"You should always salute a senior officer, Rayne."

Quickly, she tapped her five fingers to her chest and stood at attention. Her heart beat fast in her chest.

"At ease," he said, chuckling warmly. He stood, smoothing away invisible wrinkles in one crisp, clean movement. "I was worried about you, Rayne. I didn't know where you had gone."

Too excited, she ran, throwing her arms around him. "I missed you, Daddy."

He patted her back, and when their embrace ended, he straightened her uniform. She tucked her hair behind her ear —how dishevelled she must look with her uniform casually closed, hair flying out of place. But the general didn't say anything, merely helped her present herself.

"Oh, Daddy. I was so scared." She wiped her nose, tears had started to collect in her eyes. "I did things I'm not proud of."

He nodded patiently.

She took a deep breath. "I did things against the Gods."

He cupped her chin in his hand. "It's okay, Raynie, sometimes all we can do is stay alive. The Gods understand this more than anyone. Remember, 'All life is a struggle.'"

She nodded, continuing the litany: "But Faith will show us the Path, and Knowledge will tell us the Path. With Fortitude, we will stay the Path. And with Prudence, we will see the Path. And Strength will keep the Path clear."

"That's right, Rayne." He held his finger up as though he was giving a lesson. "Let us pray now."

She followed as he touched his hand to his chest and then his forehead. With a wink, he tossed his prayer to the sky and brought his hand back to his heart.

Rayne closed her eyes, imagining sitting safely in the main building on Etar, surrounded by the general and Gal, before throwing her own prayer to the sky and the stars beyond. She stared heavenward, as though she could see it floating away, disappearing into the stratosphere, and being collected by some giant fist.

"I don't understand," she said.

He pressed a finger to her lips. "I managed to track your ship. I'm glad I could find you."

She smiled. "Me too."

"Rayne," he said, "None of this was your fault. I never say it enough, but I love you, my Sweet Raynie."

She couldn't help the tears that leaked from her eyes, try as she might to hide the thing her father had always said was a weakness. She didn't realize how much she had ached to hear his love, or how much she missed the nickname of her childhood.

Instead of scowling at the tears, he smiled, his own eyes misting. He wiped the streaks from her face gently. "This is a UEC base," he said. "I need someone to take charge. I see big changes coming. Your Augment friends will need a place to stay."

"Oh, Daddy," she said, reminded, "The Augments are nothing like we thought. They don't want to fight, they just want to be normal, like us."

He nodded, "I know, Sweet Raynie. I've seen them. That's why we need this base."

"There might be more though, Daddy. We have to help them, the Gods would want that, I think."

Again, he nodded patiently. "And you will help them. The Speakers have told me this planet will become their new home, a safe place. They have asked that you lead the way, having seen your bravery these last weeks."

"Really?" A mission from the Speakers, for her.

"Yes."

"What about Gal?"

"There is a place for him here too. And he will receive a full pardon. What a nice, young man for you, Rayne."

"I love him, Daddy."

"I know, sweetheart. And I love you."

He hugged her tight, and she sighed against his chest. All life was a struggle but for those who persevered in their service to the Gods, life could become truly miraculous. The struggle was over, the running and the fighting and the fear was over. The Augments were safe. Gal was safe. And her father was with her.

* * *

A cool mist brushed Sarrin's face. Her ears had been tracking a rushing noise, growing louder the further she descended into the valley, and finally a waterfall came into view. It crashed down from above, pooling on the rocks below and feeding the lazy river that stretched beyond. Water droplets played in the light, glistening with a full spectrum of colour.

She breathed deep, letting the fresh mist fill and cleanse her lungs. She had spent too much of her life breathing still, recycled air. This was far better.

Gingerly, she probed the water with her toes, a perfect semi-circular wave rippling across the water. It was cold. She put both feet in, standing in the slow moving water, and then sitting, letting it wash the last of her demons away.

Peace, for the first time in a very long time.

She closed her eyes. A vision appeared behind her dark lids: Amy smiled through their connection. "I'm all right, Sarrin."

"Are you sure?" Sarrin said aloud.

"Yes." She laughed. "I know everything you did to help me. But I'm okay, I promise. I'm doing everything I can to help you here."

Sarrin blew out a breath, heavy with relief. "Will everything be okay?"

"Yes," Amy said with confidence, grinning infectiously. "I know it will, Sarrin. I promise."

There had been only one promise Amy had never kept, and that was her promise that they would see each other again. But it seemed they were seeing each other now.

The creak of crunching twigs and shifting branches sounded behind her, and Sarrin tore her eyes open to look. A figure emerged from the woods, brushing leaves from his clothes.

Halud.

She gasped.

Her brother smiled, holding his arms out.

Instantly she was on her feet, running, throwing herself at him. "I thought I would never see you again," she mumbled against his chest, pressing herself into the fold of his arm like a child.

He wrapped his arms around her, chuckling a little. "It's okay. I'm right here."

"I thought I would never get a chance to tell you," she said.

"Tell me what?"

The words tumbled out: "How much I love you. How much it means that you came for me."

He kissed the top of her head. "I will always come for you, Sarrin, you know that."

She nodded, her head still pressed against him, letting his warmth envelop her.

But. Something shifted, a weight clunking down in the depths of her gut. "Wait." She pushed back suddenly, extracting her arms and folding them tight to herself as she looked into his eyes. "I don't understand."

The part of her brain that never slept started to sound warning bells, the dark clouds rolling over the edge of her vision as the monster came to attention. "I thought you were taken, or dead."

"I managed to escape from the warship," he said, "and came on board when they attacked. Everything happened so fast, I didn't have a chance to find you until now."

The warning abated slightly. She took a long look at her brother, checking his features against her perfect memory. But there was no difference, right down to the scar on his left cheek from when he fell as they left Selousa.

But. "How can I speak to you now? So freely, when it's always seemed too much before."

He smiled at her, but there was something wrong, something that made her heart pound heavily.

Another person crashed through the bush and emerged: Kieran.

"Hey, Halud!" he shouted, letting his accent roll out thick and heavy, the way it was only when they were alone and he trusted her with the knowledge of who he really was.

Halud reached out and shook his hand.

Kieran rested a hand on her shoulder, his green eyes lighting up. "Isn't it great? I found him in the shuttle bay."

She looked between the two, bewildered.

"Sarrin," said Kieran, "this is good. The fight is over. We'll start a normal life, here, out in the open."

It was everything she had ever hoped for. It would be so easy to believe it all. But warning bells sounded, her heart racing, beneath the surface.

Kieran reached out, taking her face gently in his hands until his brilliant green eyes were level with hers. Slowly, he leaned forward, and Sarrin stood, too frozen to move. The feel of his lips on hers was soft and sweet.

And nothing at all like Kieran.

He smiled as they pulled apart, but Sarrin frowned. "I've wanted to do that a long time," he drawled.

She pushed away.

Halud wasn't there, he couldn't be, even though he was standing in front of her. She wanted him to be alive, but he just as easily could be dead. At the very least, he was being held hundreds of thousands of lightyears away.

And Kieran… she didn't even want to think about that.

Her feet pressed against the dirt. The monster pushed her forwards, told her it was right to run, to save herself, and for the first time, she agreed. She sprinted, moving faster and faster, as fast as she'd ever gone, away from the idyllic scene. The demons at least could be trusted.

* * *

Kieran crouched behind a tree. She was still as beautiful as he remembered. Younger though, her hair longer and floating gently in the breeze, lighting up like golden ribbon as the sunlight caught it through the trees.

She giggled. "Hide and seek. Where are you, Kieran?"

He winced, hearing her call his name, his heart leaping wildly. It wasn't Lauren, not really. But, God, did it ever look like her.

Every fibre of his being pulled towards her, screamin to go over there and hug her and tell her he loved her and make her come home. Or never leave in the first place.

But he couldn't. Lauren was dead. If she wasn't, she'd be a hundred-and-seventy-two. Not a child.

"Kieran, come on," she called, stomping her foot playfully. "Where are you Kare-Bear?"

The vision was cruel. There was nothing under the stars he wanted more than to see his sister again. But it didn't work that way, you had something for a time, and then it was gone.

The Lauren-vision set up a tea party at a table that appeared to shoot out from the ground, complete with a collection of toy-animal guests.

A rustle in the trees drew his attention, and he turned away reluctantly. Sarrin appeared, slowing as she ran out of the woods.

An unpleasant thought crossed his mind. "Are you real?"

"Yes."

He couldn't trust it. He reached his hand out to test.

She jumped back. "Don't." Her eyes were wild and her face flushed.

He sighed in relief. "It is you."

Sarrin turned her head, her eyes falling on Lauren. "Oh," she said, watching the vision as Lauren poured imaginary tea. "I'm sorry, Kieran, she's not real."

"I know," he smiled bitterly. "It sure is tempting to go over and just have a cuppa though."

She fidgeted a careful distance away. "I saw Halud."

He chanced to touch her on the shoulder. "I'm sorry."

She pulled away after a second, her face unusually flushed. "We have to find the others."

"Gal warned us it was dangerous, but it all seemed so perfect." He took one last look at Lauren before turning away from the vision for good. "Do you think its something in the air, a hallucinogenic compound or...?"

"Or the planet itself."

In front of them was nothing but a swarm of trees, the path gone. "How do we get back?"

Sarrin shrugged. "I think we see what it is we want most."

"Okay. Then I want nothing more than to get back to the ship. To the real ship."

The trees shifted before their eyes, a path appearing between them.

* * *

Gal watched as Rayne disappeared into the woods. She was moving quickly, stealthily, and she'd managed to go before he had a chance to stop her. He rubbed his face in his hand before rising from the picnic blanket, the warm impression of Rayne still beside him. His foot kicked the basket as he rolled over. There was a familiar tink and slosh as it shifted.

He paused, hating himself for what he knew was there. His hands reached forward and opened the basket. The label on the bottle was an elegant rich red with golden swirls. JinJiu. Warm.

There was a cup on the ground beside him. He had the bottle open and the cup full before he even realized what he was doing.

It would be so easy to just forget it all, to disappear into that oblivion where nothing mattered so everything was fine. So easy to forget about the past, and the things he'd done. So easy to forget how he ended up here of all places.

Ironic, really, he'd had his first taste of JinJiu when he sat in the Speakers' prison, after he visited Cordelia the first time. In that prison, his future seemed sealed: death by settlement colony. The Gods would never kill anyone, but they could let you die. The JinJiu numbed the pain and the fear just enough to get through the day.

But then Hap, his old friend from the Academy, gave him a pardon and a ship and a freight run. Death by another means. The pain was still there, and Gal numbed it with anaesthetic, because there were things Hap had never pardoned him for, things he had never discovered, that still haunted him.

Gal swirled the liquid around in the cup, inhaling the sweet, spicy aroma. He savoured the warmth of the cup in his hands. He even admired the honey coloured glow of the liquid.

And then, with shaking hands, he dumped it on the

ground.

"Cordelia," he shouted.

The colonial woman appeared behind him, her skirts rustling just enough to alert him.

"Where is Rayne?"

Cordelia stepped forward, her hands held out, palm up. "All you want is an escape, Gal. It could be here."

"No," he said, grinding his teeth. "Where is she?"

"She's with her father."

He tilted his head back. "You didn't."

"The people here, they're scared. Same as you. They just want what comforts them."

"Take me to her. Now."

Cordelia paused, her mouth open as though to respond but then thought better of it. The woods opened into a short path.

"Rayne?" he shouted.

His first officer was already walking toward him, a grin spreading ear to ear. "Gal, you'll never believe it."

He glanced warily at Cordelia.

"The general is here, my father." She spun around. And there, in all his regal glory, sat General Nairu, first commander of Strength's army. His dead brown eyes as hard as ever. "He's arranged a pardon for all of us," Rayne said. "And the Speakers want us to re-establish this base, make it a home for the Augments."

Cordelia beamed, taking Rayne's hand. Then she shot Gal a look of defiance.

"Rayne, it's not real," he said.

"What? Of course it is. He tracked our ship here."

She was so excited, how could he take it away? After all he'd put her through, she was smiling. "Rayne, you can't track a ship through FTL jumps."

She blinked in confusion.

The sound of breaking branches and quick footsteps drew their attention. Even Cordelia looked surprised.

Sarrin emerged first, followed by Kieran. Sarrin's eyes danced over everything, calculating.

Gal gulped.

"I want a clear answer on what's goin' on?" Kieran said, his eyes settling first on the general in his pristine uniform and then on Gal.

Sarrin's gaze fixed on Cordelia.

Cordelia stepped back, shaking. She turned to run, making it several steps before Kieran yelled, 'Stop,' and she was forced to freeze. "Please don't be mad." She turned slowly, her voice shaking.

Gal watched Sarrin shift uncomfortably. Kieran looked tired and pale. Rayne peered between all of them. "Tell me what's going on with this planet," Kieran said slowly, "why I saw my dead sister?"

Rayne gasped, turning to him.

With a sob, Cordelia collapsed to the ground. "I just wanted you all to be happy. I never have visitors." The sky turned a pale grey, and a light rain started around them.

"Cordelia, stop raining," Gal said. "I want it to stop raining. I much prefer sun."

The raindrops stopped, melting in mid-air, and they were bathed once again in bright, warm light.

Kieran's eyes met his, and Gal knew there was no hiding it anymore. "What's goin' on?" Kieran asked again.

"I'm so lonely," Cordelia cried. "Ever since Cornelius...." Her hand came up, wiping her nose. "I don't want you to go. Please stay with me." Cordelia's face melted, morphing into another woman that Gal didn't know. But Kieran did, jumping back with a yelp.

"Stop." Gal lifted her roughly, and she changed back into the colonial woman. There was no hiding it now. "None of it is real."

"What?" Rayne gasped.

"I'm sorry, Rayne. Not the grass, not the trees, and certainly not the general."

Her head whipped around as the apparition of General Nairu blinked out of existence. "Daddy?" she wailed. She turned back to Gal. "I don't understand, where did he go?"

He swallowed heavily. For a second, he considered telling Cordelia to bring the General back. But it was better this way.

Kieran, for his part, had started to grin, his eyes darting all around. He really was a lunatic. "You're the planet. None of it is what we see."

A light drizzle felling only around Cordelia.

"Gal?" Rayne sniffed.

He would have to start from the beginning. Gathering himself, he found an overly convenient boulder to sit on before his legs collapsed. "I was in Exploration. I found Cordelia and her companion, Cornelius, during a routine survey mission three years ago. Two planets, absolutely perfect for our needs. They hit every criterion for habitability, and were gorgeous too. But they don't make perfect planets. You learn that in Exploration, there is always a compromise for habitability. We soon realized these were no normal bodies—the planets seemed to sense our needs, and suddenly things would appear, things that we were thinking about wanting. We learned they were not planets at all.

"They had travelled far from their home on their own journey of exploration. But they thought we were interesting and wanted to study us. Their natural form isn't recognizable or understandable to humans, so they took our memories and created something that seemed like the best fit. The person you see in front of you is just a representation, a mouthpiece that we would understand. Isn't that right, Cordelia?"

She winced, wrapping her arms tightly around herself before she nodded.

The long silence was broken when Rayne shifted. "There was a second planet?"

"Yes." This was it, the heart of the matter, the moment Gal had been fighting since the Ishash'tor's scanners first showed him the planet. "It was destroyed." He waited for it to sink in. "The mission returned to Etar. I was eager to tell the Speakers about a planet that had everything we needed and could make whatever we wanted. Cordelia and Cornelius had been the ones to suggest it. The arrangement couldn't be permanent, of course, but they thought the idea of humans living on them for a few hundred years while they explored our galaxy could be fun and entertaining. And we were in need, so much need after Earth was lost.

"Some of the team was scared, they didn't know what to think of something they couldn't understand, something that didn't fit into the litanies of the Gods and their Speakers." He looked directly at Cordelia, who still sat under a cloud of rain. "They decided the beings were trying to trap them, to draw them off the Path. And they convinced Hap of it too. The Speakers labelled the planets a threat. Strength decreed the beings should be destroyed. I couldn't convince him otherwise."

Gal took a deep breath, seeing only Cordelia as he spoke. "There was nothing I could do, but it was my mission, my find, so I felt I had to go with them. Maybe I could get a message to the planets, get them to flee before we arrived. But there was no way. The weapon destroyed Cornelius." Now that he'd started, he had to say it all, the demons pouring free. "Cordelia, I'm sorry. You have to know I did everything I could. I destroyed the ship's weapons, overloaded the wiring and melted half the systems beyond repair. I nearly blew the whole ship up. But I was too late.

He was gone. I'm sorry. I tried."

For the first time, Cordelia lifted her head. She looked up at him coldly. "No, you're not."

He inhaled sharply, his chest already fixing to explode.

"Cornelius is gone. I'm trapped in this awful galaxy forever. Alone, by myself."

He reached for her. "I never wanted any of this to happen. I didn't think, I didn't know."

She started to cry again, horrible wracking sobs. Rain poured from the sky.

"If I'd thought for a second this was how they would react…. I knew they were afraid of anything that was different, but I didn't see how afraid."

"He's gone," she shrieked. "I'm all alone. All. A-lone."

Gal sat back, uncertain what to do next. It was all his fault, and there wasn't anything he could do.

Kieran appeared at her side, his hand on Cordelia's shoulder. "I'm sorry," he said, "I know how much it hurts to lose someone you care about." She looked to the engineer, nodding along with him, and then she collapsed, throwing herself into his arms. Kieran flashed Gal a concerned look. "But you need to be with your friends. Go home, be with them, not us."

She shook her head. "I can't. Cornelius and I were travelling together—it only works with two. I could never travel that far by myself. I needed him." Cordelia sniffed, burying herself in Kieran's arms.

Sarrin held a particularly angry expression on her face as she stepped forward. "You tried to trap us here. To trick us."

"I was all alone," sniffed Cordelia. "I just wanted someone to talk to."

"You showed me my brother."

Kieran still held Cordelia. "You let her believe Halud was here, but he's in trouble, he needs our help. You were going to stop us from that. Imagine if Cornelius was somewhere, and you were being kept from him."

"I wouldn't like that at all." Cordelia paled, pulling away from Kieran.

"Then let us go."

She stood, dusting off her smock. The woods parted again, this time filling the clearing with dozens of soft running footsteps. Grant, running in front, stopped short. The clearing had expanded to contain nearly a hundred Augments. "What is this?" he said.

Gal stared, bewildered at all the Augments. Three times as many Augments as they had arrived with.

Cordelia sighed, dozens of people fading away, leaving only the ones they had come to know in the last week.

Grant spun around. "What did you do to them?"

"They weren't real," said Gal.

"No, no, no!" Grant advanced on Cordelia. "She's not alone. There's a research facility here. We found all the Augments."

Kieran stepped forward, putting a hand on Grant's arm, stopping him. "It was an illusion," he said. "We all got tricked by something. It's over now."

"What?" Grant sunk down, squatting with his head in his hands. "I don't understand."

"We've all seen what we wanted to see most," said Kieran.

"My friends…," started Grant, then he sighed, dropping his head again. "I knew it was too easy." His gaze fixed on Cordelia. "Her?"

Kieran nodded. "It's taken care of."

Gal turned to Cordelia. "You understand we need to leave immediately."

She nodded sullenly.

"Kieran, get the ship in order. Only the absolutely essential repairs. I want us off this planet today."

"Sounds good to me." A path opened for Kieran, and he left, the others ambling slowly, confusedly, after him.

"Daddy?" Rayne said softly behind him, gazing into the woods. She hadn't moved, still staring at the rock where the vision of the general had sat.

He stepped up behind her, wrapping his arm around her shoulders gently. "I'm sorry, Rayne. It was just a vision. None of it was real."

She nodded bravely and sniffed. "He will understand though, when we tell him. Right?"

Gal sighed. In all the time he had known the general, he had never once seen him bend a rule or change his mind. "I don't know, Rayne. But if anyone can convince him, it's you."

She quivered.

He kissed the top of her head. "You should go with the others."

She nodded, wiping her eyes, even as she left him and walked down the path. The forest gradually opened up so Gal, alone on the hill, could watch them descend into the meadow where the ship sat.

"I never blamed you, Gal," Cordelia said, suddenly beside him again. "I know what the UECs did to you, I know you did what you could against them. But I hoped you would visit. It's rare to meet a person like you, good to your very core."

He stared at her, the words echoing in his head. But she was only telling him what he most wanted to hear. The truth was, he wasn't good at all.

TWENTY-TWO

"Kieran, are you in here?" a woman's voice called

Kieran slid out from under the impulse manifold. His breath caught as he saw Lauren, the same age she'd been when she left the Observer ship, standing in the doorway. He forced himself to breathe, his heart thumping erratically in his chest. Staring, he swallowed several times in his dry throat before his mind cleared itself. "Hi, Cordelia."

Not-Lauren smiled at him and came into the engine room.

"Can you make yourself look different—not like her, I mean."

She frowned, and then her face and body melted into the woman-shape he had come to know as Cordelia.

He breathed a sigh of relief.

She flopped down, sitting on part of an open panel, her knees curled up almost to her chin. "I'd give anything to see Cornelius again," she said. "I thought you would like to see her."

"You're right, I would. But not like this—it's not real. I have my memories, and that'll have to be enough."

She nodded a few times in understanding—but was it, how could he know what she felt? She wasn't even human, a fact that fascinated him. It was worth further investigation—the things she'd seen, how far she'd travelled, how long—if only he weren't so tired and admittedly angry, and if Gal hadn't given him explicit instructions to stay away from her.

She stood, bending down to examine the engine block. "What a strange way to travel."

"It works for us," he said. "Sometimes."

"But it's not how *you* normally travel, is it?"

He bit his lip—it was clear she could read their thoughts and their memories. "No, but that's different. That's secret."

She nodded, putting her hands up. "I know."

He didn't like her knowing. Though maybe she didn't like him knowing her secret either.

"I'm sorry I tried to keep you here," she said. "I realize that it was wrong."

"It's okay, I understand it," he forced himself to say. "I'm sorry about what happened to Cornelius. He must have been very special to you."

She sniffed, nodding. Her eyes glistened with tears, or the illusion of tears.

"The people in this epoch, they're different. You know," he said.

"You're certainly very different, Kieran Wood. There's more to you, something about the way you think."

He watched her, pursing his lips in annoyance, and wondering how much he needed to hope for something before she would do it.

"I learned my lesson," she said, throwing her hands up. "I won't be doing anything else just because someone thinks it. Unless they ask, of course. I can do anything, build anything."

"Do you have a new Kepheus Drive?"

"You know I can't just separate parts of myself, give pieces away."

He didn't know, but it made some kind of sense. He turned

away, preparing to slide back under the manifold.

"But," she said, and he braced himself for whatever temptation she could offer. "I was thinking about what you and Sarrin said about Halud. And I realized how I would feel if there was a small chance Cornelius was alive, and someone was keeping me from him. Well, I would be—how do you say it at home—*so goddamn pissed*." Her voice, like the words she chose, rolled into a perfect mimic of his dad. "I want to help," she said in her own voice.

He licked his lip, thinking carefully before asking, "Do you know where he is?"

She shook her head, "No. I only know the things you know. Sarrin wants him to be alive, but even she doesn't know anymore. But you could find out, couldn't you?"

He frowned. "What do you mean?"

"There's a device you want to build—I've seen it in your mind. You think it could find him."

He stared at her. He didn't like the idea of her in his head one bit.

"I can build anything," she continued, "if you show me how. Let me see the diagram in your mind."

Gal had warned him to avoid her altogether. But it was tempting. "How would you build it?"

She smiled. "I can make myself into anything you want, any shape at all, as long as you don't try to take it away."

He bit his lip again. "You would built it, and it would show us real transmissions? Not ones you made up."

She smiled brightly again, nodding exuberantly. "Yes."

"Is this a trap? You have to tell me."

"No. Please, I want to help. It's the least I can do."

He rubbed a hand across his mouth, considering. What would it mean if he trusted her again? She hadn't tricked them maliciously, she'd only showed them the things they wanted in hopes they would decide to stay, but she didn't force them. Years of training had taught him to see every situation from multiple perspectives, and he could understand her desperation not to be alone, the pain she felt from the death of her companion. It was the same as when he lost Lauren, and, like he had told Sarrin, they all needed somebody.

"Sarrin needs this," she said. "She need to know. You know that."

He closed his eyes. "You can build it?" He held an image of the full-size capture device from the Observer ship.

She smiled, and nodded.

"You can do it secretly, so no one sees?"

She nodded again.

"And this is just between us."

Again, a nod. "I promise, Kieran, I just want to help. I think you're the only one who understands that right now."

He sighed, he must be getting soft.

"Kieran," she said seriously, "I want you to know, Sarrin is out running. Don't worry, she's safe. She needs the wide open space, the wind and the grass and trees—it helps her stay calm, to remember the part of her that isn't a soldier. I know you understand these things, the same as you understand what I did."

Part of him went cold. "Don't touch her. Don't trap her with visions of Halud. She doesn't deserve to lose him again."

Cordelia shook her head. "She's too smart for that. I'll build your capture device so you can find her brother. Don't worry about Sarrin, all the trails lead back to you, because you can give her the thing she wants more than anything."

"Me?"

"Yes, you."

* * *

Gal leaned back in one of the wooden-looking chairs spread-out in the meadow beside the ship. Rayne sat beside him. He let his eyes close, allowing himself to rest in the sun for just a minute, no matter how artificial it was. Secrets had come out. Rayne hadn't even seemed that disturbed by the fact that he'd sabotaged a UEC ship—or she hadn't heard, too distracted by the disappearance of her father or the fact that none of what they were seeing was real, just a projection from an alien-being.

The very existence of something non-human was shattering. A being that didn't follow the Gods or the Speakers would change everything, open the door for questions, for disbelief—no wonder Hap ordered it destroyed.

But Cordelia was hidden, he knew because despite multiple survey missions, the UECs had never been able to find her again. Now, he and Rayne and a few dozen Augments knew, but he could be pretty certain the Augments wouldn't be telling Hap any time soon.

Perhaps, they would be all right after all.

Some fruity drink appeared beside him, and he shrugged, downing the concoction that didn't have a name, something Cordelia had designed on his first visit to satisfy his personal palette.

Without warning, a shout rang across the meadow, slamming Gal's eyes open and his heart into his throat. One of the Augments stood on the torn edge of the open cargo bay. "Where's Grant?" the Augment called out. "Kieran needs him to look at a problem."

Gal bolted to his feet, Rayne beside him. A problem Kieran couldn't fix had to be a big problem.

Grant ran past, leaping onto the ship. He was followed by Rami and a handful of others. Gal started running too, a pit opening in the bottom of his stomach though he couldn't say why. Rayne was a half step behind. The Augments, faster, pulled ahead as they climbed the stairs and weaved through the corridors of the ship. They were already gathered in the engine room when Gal stumbled in, breathing heavy.

Kieran stood at the centre, Grant bent down beside him. "I saw the glow when I turned the ship's computer back on," Kieran said. Grant mumbled in response, reaching in and examining something.

When they pulled back, Gal could see they were next to an open access panel on the massive engine block. Inside the engine, nestled between the machinery, was a laz-rifle glowing red. Its mechanism had been redirected, sitting backwards, a handful of wires spilling from it. With a start, Gal recognized the design—it was one of the first bomb-types the hackers had ever shown him.

Grant nodded. "It's got power to it, but it's not active. No telling how long its been there."

"Can you dismantle it?" Kieran asked.

Grant nodded again. "Shouldn't be too hard." He reached into the engine again. Gal fought back a sudden urge to tell him to stop, an uncanny certainty that it couldn't be removed, although he couldn't say why.

"Hey," Rami shouted from behind. He stood at one of the console screens set into the wall. They all turned, watching as the normal array of controls disappeared, replaced by a blank screen with a large insignia: a circle with two parallel lines through it. An instant later, a schematic of the ship appeared, a red diagram overlaid.

Gal stumbled back into the wall of Augments that was now behind him.

Grant swore, rising from the engine and coming to study the diagram.

Rami glared at Kieran. "What is it?"

"I didn't even see the connectors," said Grant. He blinked at the diagram twice.

Gal read the schematic in a heartbeat, his legs threatening to give way under him.

Grant told the others: "There's a dozen laz-rifle bombs throughout the ship. They're all wired into each other, like a giant web. I must have triggered a failsafe when I tried to dismantle the power-supply. We're lucky Rami saw this before I actually disconnected it—they're not charged or active."

"Can you still remove it?" Kieran asked.

Gal leaned in, curious. Could it be removed? Safely?

Grant bit his lip, eyes darting across the screen. "I think so. But I'll have to find the central hub. Otherwise, as soon as I disconnect one, the failsafe will trigger the others. Even with one bomb silenced, the rest will still tear the ship apart."

"What about the program?" Rami asked.

Grant shook his head. "I don't know. I've never used code to trigger a detonation. I suppose it's possible."

Rami's hand reached out before Gal could stop him. "Then we should be able to stop it."

The back of Gal's head burned, and he turned. Rayne stared at him, her eyes wide, angry. A sudden guilt made him shrink away, though he didn't know why. He had a suspicion though, based on the insignia that had first blazed across the screen—it was a signature of sorts, something to let the UECs know who was responsible. It was the symbol of the hackers, and later, the rebels.

Another shout called his attention back to the console. A scroll of code reeled across the screen, too fast to read. But Gal didn't have to read it; he already had a terrible suspicion he knew what it said.

"There's a program uploading," said Rami.

"Can you read any of it?" Kieran asked, pressing in close.

The code finished, replaced by a digital clock: 10:00.00. The first digit flicked to a 9, the others counting down rapidly. They had ten minutes before the bomb blew.

Rayne stared.

"Everyone off the ship!" Kieran shouted.

Gal stood rooted in place as Augments started to move around him.

"What did you do?" Rami accused Kieran. "I saw you in the programming. I knew it wasn't repairs."

"We have to get off the ship, there isn't time."

A hand grabbed Gal's elbow, pulling him as the Augments ran off the ship, and he sprinted to keep up.

Beside him, Aaron jogged. "What did you do, Johnny?"

Gal's lungs heaved as he fought to keep up, unable to answer. He had been good with bombs once. A long time ago. He had made bombs powerful enough to rip through four-foot thick reinforced plastic con-steel.

This bomb would tear the ship apart and everything surrounding it.

He stumbled, falling as his feet hit the manicured lawns. Cordelia.

Cornelius had died from a single laz-cannon blast. What would happen to Cordelia?

Behind him, the ship's thrusters rumbled, filling the air with a humid heat. The ship started to lift off the ground.

Maybe he was wrong. Maybe someone else had set the bombs. Maybe they weren't as powerful as he thought.

"How could you do this to me?" Rayne towered over him, arms crossed and her face as cold as ice.

A chill shot through him instantly, and he started to shiver. "What?"

"That's what you had me install, isn't it?" said Rayne. "You used me."

He shook his head. "No, I—" What had he done? There were rebel bombs on the ship that Gal knew could only have come from one place, even though he didn't remember setting them at all.

"You told me that program would help us protect the ship.

That we could take control if the Augments started to become dangerous."

"I—."

"You used me to set a bomb, Galiant!"

His heart hammered in his chest. "What program?" But he knew, he already knew.

She pushed him, hard, as he tried to stand, toppling him over.

"Rayne, no, it's not—"

"I don't know you at all."

He reached for her to explain—he'd been hallucinating, he'd had no idea what he was doing—but the words stuck in his throat. It wasn't him, not the real him. He didn't remember doing it. He had been so confused. Realization dawned. "It's all happening again."

Cordelia would be torn apart, a third planet lost in a violent explosion. This time—like the loss of Earth, like the death of Cornelius—it would be his fault.

Gal looked up into the steely eyes of Aaron. Behind him, an army of hairless, grey demons watched. "You forgot yourself, Gal," Aaron said. "You tried to run, but you only made it worse."

* * *

Sarrin jogged back to the grassy meadow, her mind feeling clear and, even, calm. She'd never run like that before, and her lungs burned joyfully. There were no flaxen ungulates this time—they weren't meant to be on this planet—but Cordelia had provided her with a wide open woods and a way back as soon as she'd wanted it.

But as she neared the green space, a worry crept in, and she looked just in time to see the freightship rise above the trees.

A group crowded together on the grass, huddled anxiously where the ship had stood not an hour before. Sarrin's mind counted rapidly. All the Augments, Hoepe's crew, and former UEC soldiers were present except, she realized, Kieran, Grant, and Rami.

Cordelia appeared in front of her as she approached. Her face was drawn tight in a human expression of worry. "He's on the ship, dear."

He, meaning Kieran. It was disconcerting how Cordelia could read her mind so easily.

"There was a problem," Cordelia continued.

Sarrin frowned. "Why are they leaving?"

Cordelia closed her eyes for a minute. "They are very worried. I think there's a bomb on the ship."

"Who's worried?"

"Everyone."

Hoepe appeared through the crowd, pushing his way forward, but he had no answers and they stared into the sky in silence. The little freightship disappeared rapidly through the cloud cover and into space beyond.

"Where are they going?" Sarrin asked him, although she already knew the answer.

"Grant doesn't know if he can disable the bombs in time. They wanted to put distance between themselves and everyone else," answered Hoepe.

A heaviness that had nothing to do with physical exhaustion or gravity traps crushed her chest and forced her to fight for every molecule of air. "I should have been there."

"There's nothing any of us can do. They're in the hands of the Gods now," said Hoepe. "Kieran's with them."

Sarrin shut her eyes. Hoepe thought Kieran was a God, but he wasn't. He was an Observer, human.

But Kieran was smart, bright, he wouldn't die. No, he couldn't die.

Cordelia shifted, her voice quiet as she muttered, "Something's wrong."

Sarrin's entire body jerked. "What?"

But Cordelia didn't answer. She took two running steps forward and then melted into a silvery tendril, reaching up into the sky.

* * *

Kieran flew threw the air across the engineering bay, registering the punch after he had landed on the floor. He gasped for breath, turning to see Rami.

The Augment's face was redder than ever.

He was back on his feet in an instant, holding a hand to his aching cheek. "You too. Get off the ship."

"No," Rami snarled, taking a menacing step towards him. "I won't let you do this."

"We have to get the ship away from the planet and everyone else."

Grant pushed between them. "It doesn't matter who did this, we need to figure out how to disarm it." He bent down under the central console, pulling the grey panelling away from its base so he could reach inside.

An image formed in Kieran's mind of a massive fireball consuming everyone, and he blinked it away. He stepped around Grant, reaching for the controls on the central console. "If you're going to stay, at least make yourself useful."

"What are you doing?" Rami grunted, but some of the malice had slipped from his voice.

"There's been too much damage to the thrusters. The auto-pilot can't compensate for all our rewiring. We have to take the ship up manually. It's too much for one engineer."

Hesitantly, Rami stepped to the other side of the console, a holographic image of the ship appearing between them. Together, they coordinated the thrusters, putting out enough burn to start lifting the massive ship. Kieran hoped Cordelia might give them a hand.

As the display showed more and more distance between the ship and the planet's surface, Kieran's lungs finally sucked in a deep breath. He looked through the display at Rami, the Augment's face pinched in concentration. "I'm glad you stayed," he said.

Rami only grunted.

"How's it going?" Kieran called to Grant.

Grant responded with a non-committal noise. "I've never seen anything like this wiring. I keep having to check everything twice and again. I'm still not sure I get it. It's the same as the re-wiring in the shuttle."

Kieran looked back, already aware of Rami's glare. "I didn't sabotage the shuttle, if that's what you're thinking."

"Someone did re-wire the shuttle," said Rami. "And someone rigged this. If it was you…."

"That bomb is going to blow us to kingdom come. Why would I ever set something that was going to kill me too?"

"Martyr," grunted Rami.

Kieran blinked. Another image of an explosion, throwing him and ripping the planet apart flashed in his mind. He shuddered. He didn't want to die here. "Look," he huffed, "can you keep the ship level? I'm going to look at this with Grant."

He expected argument, but there was none. Kieran ducked down, crawling under the console. The central hub was above them, dozens of connections spilling from it.

Grant's breath came in spurts and stops as he traced the lines with his fingers. "I was wrong, I have seen a system like this before. Just a picture they showed me at Evangecore. Something they pulled from the wreckage at the Lansford's cabin."

"What?" Kieran blinked. "Who set it?"

"The rebels—that's their symbol too, the circle with the lines. It was on the bombs that destroyed Evangecore, though

I never got a good look at that system."

Kieran blinked.

"You shouldn't be here," Grant said. "Take the spacesuits or try to get the shuttle clear. I know you hate spacewalks, but I don't know if I can stop this. If I can't.... Kieran, I have my suit at least."

"No. We're going to figure this out." Kieran focussed on the wires above their heads, forcing his mind to stop thinking about the fireball that was now less than seven minutes away, or about Lauren—at least if it went off, he would see her again. Maybe.

Sarrin would be somewhere down on the surface. *Please, God*, he prayed. He wanted to see her again too.

Methodically, he traced each wire—some of them real, many of them fake connections meant to throw off anyone who was trying to dismantle the system. It was working. He'd never seen a system like it before either, and for the millennia of tech he'd studied, that surprised him. Humanity hadn't come up with anything original in centuries.

His heart crashed around in his chest. He forced himself to release a breath he didn't realize he'd been holding.

Grant lifted a hand to his head. Blood seeped from the still-fresh line of suture. "I can't do it."

"Like hell you can't. Come on, Grant."

"Get out of here. There's less than a minute left."

Kieran flinched. "How do you know?" But it was the same way that Sarrin always seemed to be counting time. He pushed himself out from under the conduit, looking at the display.

"I think we're far enough from the planet," Rami grunted, his concentration still fixed on the controls as he tweaked each of the thruster banks individually, keeping the ship level. The countdown clock rushed past fifty-seconds remaining.

"Shit," Kieran muttered. "Grant, let's go." He banged on

the console. They were low on options. "Get to the shuttle. Hopefully its shielding will be enough to protect us from the blast."

Maybe it would, maybe it wouldn't. Rami ran ahead of him. Kieran waited for Grant, pushing him in to the corridor, running the short distance to the shuttle hangar.

Grant turned, eyes wide as his suit ripped out of his back, pouring across his skin.

In the same instant, Kieran felt the ship jerk and he went sprawling to the ground. Grant dove, covering Rami. The walls erupted as a massive fireball pushed down all around them—Kieran marvelled that it looked exactly as he had imagined. Lauren smiled at him. And everything went dark.

*　*　*

The tiny freightship exploded without warning, nothing more than a bright flash high in the stratosphere. Sarrin's body crumpled, and she sank to her knees.

But he couldn't be dead. Maybe they got away in a shuttle, or maybe they jettisoned the bomb before it exploded. Kieran was clever. Kieran thought of things that others didn't.

Gods, let him be okay. She pressed her fingers to her chest, tapping rapidly.

Beside her, the others stood, their slight movements slowing, or maybe she was speeding up. Her heartbeat pounded in her ears until it was overtaken by a high pitched whine. Someone moved their mouth, slowly, but she couldn't hear a thing. A voice started to cut through the static, "-Rrin." Hoepe's face was pale, his pupils dilated. He took a heavy breath and set his face in a frown. He turned back to the sky.

She followed his gaze—she had to watch, the shuttle would be coming down soon, now that the danger had passed. Kieran would climb from the hatch, find her in the crowd, and flash his smile. He'd reach his arms out, try to hug her. Maybe she would let him.

Cordelia's long, silvery tendril started to retract. Her human body rematerialized, charred and bloody. She staggered, almost falling over.

Hoepe pushed past Sarrin, knocking her to the ground. He cut through the crowd straight for Cordelia. In the hole left in his wake, Sarrin could clearly see the bodies at Cordelia's feet.

She had brought back bodies.

There was no memory or awareness of running forward, but Sarrin suddenly stood on the edge of the crowd, looking down. Grant kneeled on all fours, his limpet suit covering him as he heaved for breath. Rami twitched where he lay under Grant, burns visible on his arms and legs. Hoepe reached down to look at them. And Kieran.

Oh Gods, Kieran!

Instinct took over, her body leaping across the distance, unsteady legs crashing down beside him. Kieran was pink and raw, deep burns covering his entire body. He took a shallow, shaky breath.

She screamed for Hoepe.

He turned his head, his eyes scanning Kieran. Then he gave her a look she couldn't interpret and his head shook once, side to side, before he dropped his gaze, turning back to Rami.

"No!" She pulled Kieran's head into her lap, desperate. The seared flesh was hot to touch. He was too far gone, Hoepe knew it. He was keeping his focus on Rami— someone he might actually be able to save.

She could already feel Kieran slipping away, his body's energy desperately low, his heart rate too slow. Nothing like when she had touched him before, the beauty of his vibrancy gone. He took another incredibly shaky breath—some part of her brain told her it could be his last.

There had to be something they could do.

Her whole body folded as she sobbed, tears streaming down her face. It didn't matter that everyone watched. It didn't matter than no one cried in Evangecore.

She felt his heart shudder, felt it take two more slow, pitiful beats, and then stop.

A pain worse than any they had ever dreamed up in Evangecore, pain worse than Guitteriez's negative pulse machines, overtook her.

She needed Kieran. She needed him to understand her, needed the way he always saw her as herself instead of an Augment, needed the way his eyes, his smile, even his touch could pull her out of the darkness.

Her mind worked, solving problems as it always had: it drew schematics like an engine, except it was the two of them. Kieran had shown her the way before, when she was desperate.

She gritted her teeth, pulling together all the strength and courage she could find. Her hands spread wide on his skin, wincing at the heat and wetness from the burns that made her arms feel like were on fire too. She let the energy flow from her into him, giving all she had and then more.

Kieran said she could use the abilities for good, she just had to figure out how. She didn't really know the how, but this was the when. Her mind reached out, terrified to do it but desperate enough to try. She saw his heart in her mind, still in his chest, and gave it a little squeeze, willing it to carry on.

She squeezed again and again, forcing it to beat, until it gave a little thump of its own. It was working. She dug a little deeper, finding more and more strength to give to him.

His heart rate sped up a little, and he took another breath.

Come on, Kieran. She slammed into him with all of her mental might.

He gasped, a full, deep, startling breath.

Hoepe looked up, springing to his feet. He pushed her out of the way. His expression was still grim, but at least his hands worked quickly on the charred body in front of him. He didn't think Kieran was completely lost.

Cordelia appeared next to them. "What do you need?"

"Hypobaric chamber," he grunted, his hands and eyes focussed on Kieran, twisting into trigger points.

Sarrin clambered out of the way as a table erupted from the ground and lifted Kieran up, a massive medical device enveloping him. Hoepe and Kieran disappeared, as she stared at the outside of the chamber.

Someone touched her elbow, and Sarrin gulped. She still crouched on the ground beside the solid barrier that still contained Hoepe working on Kieran. Time seemed to have stopped altogether.

Grant looked down at her, his hand by her arm, limpet suit still covering his body. Only his one eye was exposed. There were deep burns there, but he seemed not to notice, staring with her at the chamber.

Slowly, Sarrin found her feet. Her legs still shaky, but not like before, not burdened as they had been, simply tired. Her hands flexed, pale pink skin looking so normal. She stared as though she had never seen them before. Such brutal devices, but maybe they had saved Kieran's life too.

TWENTY-THREE

Commandant Amelia Mallor sat on a medical bed in the centre of the bright infirmary. She had walked into the medical bay freely, but that freedom was tenuous at best. She picked at the piling on her sterile gown as the others talked around her.

"Commander Jameson told us she began screaming while on the bridge of the Comrade. She had to be subdued and relieved of duty," reported General Nairu.

The same doctor who had assessed her before read through her charts. "Her physical exams and psychological evaluation have all passed within normal parameters. I see nothing worrisome behind the strange outburst of behaviour." He shrugged. "We know she was close with the doctor, Guitteriez. Perhaps she was reacting to his untimely death."

Amelia clenched her fists under the folds of the thin fabric gown. His death had not been untimely. He had it coming to him for a long time.

No, she liked the doctor. He was a friend. One of her only friends. He had helped her recover after her accident.

The new doctor continued, "I see from the notes here she had been part of an unorthodox experiment, tying her mind to the mind of Augment 005478F. The Augment is presumed dead, her tracking and identification chip was found in the wreckage of the facility on Junk. There is no way for us to know how that may have affected her, how it would affect any of us, to be connected to someone as they died."

Hap Lansford grunted in disagreement. He paced the room, she could see his fat little feet stumbling in front of her, and her face contorted into a sneer, her mind overcome with hate.

Shocked with herself, she schooled her expression into one of bland complacency. Hap Lansford was the First Speaker and a direct descendant of the Gods.

But Sarrin was not dead. That much she knew. She no longer had her tracking chip, nor Amelia hers, but they were still connected. It was no more than a whisper in the commandant's mind—without proximity, she could no longer feel the same sensations as the Augment, but she was there.

"What is your recommendation, Doctor?" asked Hap.

"She appears to be in perfect health. I see no reason she could not continue her duties."

Hap paused again, his feet turning toward her. "Commandant."

"Sir." She saluted, lifting her hand by rote.

"Stand," Hap ordered.

She resisted the urge to lunge forward and crush his trachea.

"Jameson has made a report detailing your actions when the Comrade engaged the freightship Ishash'tor," he said, his voice flat, lifeless.

Amelia blinked. Even she hadn't been able to truly understand her actions. Familiar memories had played in her mind, and then her arms had moved of their own accord. Then, while she lay in shock, her XO had taken over the ship, and she had sat in the brig of the Comrade until they returned to Etar.

Hap stared at her for a long time, and she set her jaw, refusing to fidget under his glare. "Well?" he said. "Explain."

She tightened every muscle in her spine. What could she say? Should she try to explain the inexplicable pain she had felt, the connection to the Augment? The way the Augment had forced her hand to reach up and punch the controls? She swallowed once, praying silently to the Gods that they didn't see her weakness. "The recently deceased doctor, Guitteriez, implanted a chip—."

"Yes, we know." Hap slapped the table behind her hard enough to make it shake.

The doctor beside him jumped. "I removed it, I swear." His hand clutched an injector. Sedative, she guessed. He thought it could save him. Fool.

Hap glared at the doctor before he turned back to her. "The chip has been removed."

"S— s—," she stammered. What was happening to her? This was unbefitting, totally against her character. She paused, collecting herself. "005478F was still able to connect with me."

Hap raised an eyebrow. He shared a look with the general and then with the doctor. The doctor's wide eyes were perfectly round. He shook his head once.

Hap groaned, shrugging his massive shoulders. "That doesn't explain your actions. Jameson said you were screaming uncontrollably. A great deal of resources have gone into your development. I expect better."

She nodded, "Yes, sir. I—I felt the pain from the bio-pulse weapons as she felt it. It was terrible." A shiver ran through her at the memory, and she ran a hand over her arm.

"The pulse weapons are not said to be powerful."

She shook her head. "It was like…." But there was no way to describe the feeling.

The doctor turned to Hap, his shrewd eyes narrowing.

"Thew weapon was designed specifically for 005478F's altered neurocircuitry."

Hap leaned forward. "And you felt this. Through her?"

Amelia nodded. That must have been it. "She was able to control me. My arms, my hands, they moved of their own accord."

"She could move you?"

Amelia nodded. She never would have done those things on her own. Would she have?

Hap slammed the table again.

She braced, her chin held defiant. "What are my orders, sir?"

The general answered, "You are relieved of duty, Commandant."

"Why?" she snapped. Questioning a general of the Speakers was borderline treason. She stared into the First Speaker's dull, dark eyes. This made him angry, the lines of it clearly etching under his brows. "The doctor has cleared me for duty. I had an emotional outburst following the death of Guitteriez, but have recovered now." She knew it was a lie, but it was believable and convenient.

Hap turned on her, attempting a pose of strength that was obscured by his bulk. "We need to capture the freightship. I cannot afford mistakes or erratic outbursts."

"I am your foremost military commandant. If anyone should be on this mission, it is I." If she could find the Augment first, maybe there was a chance.

A chance of what?

"Captain Jameson will take your place," said Hap.

Jameson? He was nearly as vicious as the First Speaker, he would torture them, kill them!

Wasn't that what she was going to do?

"You wish to capture the freightship, not destroy it, sir?" asked the general.

Hap threw a sharp look at Nairu. "005478F is everything Guitteriez promised. We need her. She must be brought back alive."

Amelia frowned. "Let me go after her. I've served you for years. I've hunted countless Augments across the stars. You'll never capture her, but I can."

General Nairu spoke to Hap, ignoring Amelia. "Even if 005478F could do it, she's caused us so much trouble already. We have the second generation. She needs to be destroyed."

"Do what?" Amelia asked.

Hap turned. "Dismissed, Commandant." He feared her. She saw it now, obvious in the way he held his shoulders against her, hunched as though he was protecting himself.

"I have not questioned your orders before." She jumped off the table so she was standing before him. Taller than him.

He took an involuntary step back, his eyes wide. "Sedate her!" he screamed.

The doctor approached, Amelia glaring blatantly, her eyes locked with Hap. The auto-syringe pressed into her neck, the sensation horrifyingly familiar.

* * *

Halud wiped sweat from his brow, fidgeting before the door to Hap Lansford's office. If there was any reason to avoid it, he would, but he couldn't and so he plunged himself through the doorway. He sat in the same chair, opposite Hap, and waited for the Speaker to acknowledge him.

Hap swivelled in his chair, his expression darker than usual. "The warship returned this morning."

Halud swallowed heavily and waited.

"Are you going to ask about your sister?" Hap snapped. "Or perhaps what my orders to them will be on their return voyage."

Mouth suddenly dry, Halud nodded. He forced his mouth open, to form the question, but he never had the chance.

"Well, it doesn't matter now." Hap's rage was obvious, boiling off him as he pounded his tiny fists against the desk. "Look." He spun the viewer around faster than Halud could catch up with what was happening.

Bewildered, he watched the screen. On it, a dusty landscape decorated by pulpits of fire slipped by as the recording drone flew overhead. Darkened ruins came into view, jagged edges of con-plas sticking up from the ground.

"That's the facility on Junk," growled Hap, "one of our premiere research laboratories."

Halud's stomach clenched. Sarrin was in that facility. His eyes searched the video wildly for any sign of her. Anything at all. Even if he could think of words to say, he wouldn't have been able to.

"It's all your fault," said Hap.

Halud turned his wide eyes on the Speaker. "My fault?"

Hap queued another video roughly. "Watch," he commanded.

Now, the screen showed footage from what must be one of the internal security cameras, although the room was dark. Only shadows shifted in the vid, until a brilliant blue arc lit up the room, the unmistakable shape of Sarrin in the centre.

The room turned dark again. A flash of sparks, and emergency lights cast a dim red glow. The shadow of a wild animal dove across the room—a girl, Halud realized. It ripped out a guard's throat a split second before the hand reached up, tearing the camera down.

For an instant, the vid turned to static, then changed to another angle. The creature fired laz-bolts at six soldiers before snapping the spine of another, and tearing the face off the last.

She disappeared from the room, none of the guards so much as twitching. The horrible violence lasted no more than a few seconds.

Halud's heart thumped erratically in his chest. He knew, without a doubt, the vicious creature in the room was Sarrin, her telltale dreadlocks and brilliant blue eyes.

"Your sister did this. She killed every one of my men in that facility tearing it down on herself."

Halud blinked. If Sarrin could do that, what else could she do? "How do you know she's dead?"

"Her tracking chip was found in the wreckage."

"What about —?"

"She destroyed my facility, my labs. My head researcher was there with her. She killed him with a view screen." Hap rewound the video until it showed the exact moment the flash of blue went flying across the room.

Sarrin never even touched it, Halud saw as he studied the freeze-frame, she still hung tied in the middle of the room. He gasped. What had they done to her?

"Someone will pay for this. Strength must be maintained. This is your fault, Halud."

Halud shuddered as Hap slammed his fist on the desk hard enough to crack it. Inadvertently, he turned his head away, his eyes landing on the river of blood on the mural.

Hap did bear a striking resemblance to the God depicted above it, to the fist of Strength painted above the river of blood.

Halud's heart started to pound again, rapidly and violently inside of his chest. This was a game of survival. A game he had played his entire life from the moment his parents had gotten sick and begged him to run with Sarrin. He set his jaw, refusing to show even the slightest hint of weakness. "It is not my fault what you did to my sister."

Hap's face flared a deep shade of red.

Halud let a growl edge into his voice, leaning forward in his chair. "Not my fault you couldn't control your own weapon."

"If you weren't the Poet..." Hap threatened.

"But I am. And you need me. The folk look to me." He thought of the latest communique to cross his console. "You speak of renaming this planet again, but without me, the folk will never accept your plan. And if they never do that, how will they ever forget that there was an Earth before this one? How will they ever forget what the Gods allowed to happen to their home?"

Hap stared at him, mouth agape.

Standing now, Halud braced his arms on the desk, hanging menacingly over the Speaker who crumpled with each word.

Hap reached his hand under the desk, searching for the panic button that was hidden there.

"Don't do it." Halud bent his voice, calibrating it to control the Speaker. But the doors still opened behind him a second later—Hap was resistant.

But the guards who entered weren't. He reached a hand up quickly, putting an arm on the Speaker. Halud had been playing the game of survival a very, very long time. "It's okay, First Speaker. Calm deep breaths." He exaggerated his lungs rising and falling rapidly, as though encouraging the demigod to breathe.

He turned to the guards and modulated his voice, lacing soothing and trust into the words. "At ease, gentlemen. A false alarm, I'm afraid. The Speaker became agitated with a particularly visceral video feed. A panic attack, I think."

The guards paused, looking at each other.

"Please, if you would, help him to his private quarters and summon Dr. Davidson. Utmost secrecy about this, gentlemen. The Gods appreciate your service and discretion."

The guards saluted in unison. Hap sputtered as they grabbed him, gently at first, but more firmly as he struggled.

"He's very upset, I'm afraid," improvised Halud. "Do use caution. He carries Strength with him."

The guards nodded and strengthened their grip.   "An honour to serve, Master Poet."

Halud gave them a gracious nod as they carried the Speaker out the door. Hap fought, but the guards listened to Halud over the protests of the Speaker, such was his power. He collapsed in the chair behind him. Subterfuge, politics. These were his game. His friends may be gone, but he was left. If one still stood, the cause was not lost.

And he knew what he had to do.

Quickly, he leapt up from the chair. He nearly jumped down the circular staircase. Joyce turned at the clamour, a slick grin in her eyes. "Halud?"

He nodded at her as he walked by.

"Very stressful news for the First Speaker, it seems." She smiled sweetly.

Halud had no time, no interest in distraction. He had to do this now while there was still the fire within him. He carried on, as fast as decorum would allow, through the halls and out of the complex. He broke out into the centre square. For the first time, he dared to walk right up to the carved circle, the one that had caught his eye from its surreptitious location etched high on one of the surrounding buildings, where only someone looking would see it. The two parallel lines pointed to an alleyway.

Heart racing, he went to the alley, pushing through the crowds. There, another circle, carved into the stone. Tiny and low on the wall, looking like nothing more than shadow to the casual observer. He ran to it, following the clues to another circle, and another and another. He arrived, panting, at a door with an almost imperceptible symbol carved into in the bottom corner.

There was no answer to his simple knock. Instead he twisted the knob and pushed the door open. Down a dark staircase and into a hidden lair. He entered the room and suddenly bodies were everywhere, moving, rapidly aiming laz-rifles at him.

Rebels.

He took a deep breath. "My name is Halud DeGazo, Poet Laureate of the Gods. I have information for you. The tyranny of the Speaker's must be stopped."

TWENTY-FOUR

Sarrin stepped cautiously into the bright room. Kieran had lain in the hypobaric chamber, unmoving, for three days, but now he was awake, and he wanted to see her.

Machines let out loud beeps, both irritating and comforting at the same time. Her eyes landed first on Hoepe, sitting in the corner. Across the room, Leove worked at a computer console.

She took in the high tech hospital, cataloguing the array of medical instruments she couldn't put a name to if she tried. Finally, her eyes fell on the single occupied bed.

Kieran sat up, looking at something in his hands. He turned his head a fraction, wincing. He covered it with a laugh.

She didn't notice the movements it took to get her across the room. He reached a hand out, and she took it willingly, before she had a chance to think about it.

A smile spread on his face, despite the burns. The touch started to tingle with intensity—a hum coming from her bones—and they both let go.

"Doc says I'm gonna live," he said, his voice strained and scratchy. "But I'm no genetically enhanced super human, so it's gonna take a while."

How was it that his smile never faded?

"Might be a few weeks before I'm up and about again. I guess I'll have a few scars, same as everybody else on this rock." He glanced up. "Sorry, Cordelia."

The planet-woman appeared. She smiled graciously and waved it off with something suspiciously like a giggle.

Kieran's voice turned serious, as he turned back to Sarrin. "I hear I've got you to thank for my life."

She looked away, but he reached for her again. His fingers wrapped around her arm, where she felt both the hot press of his hand and the zing of energy that passed through them.

"Thank you, Sarrin." He squeezed once, and pulled away, too soon. "I have some good news for you." He lifted up a sleek tablet that she hadn't noticed siting in his lap, as though she hadn't already heard the best news he could possibly provide. "Before... everything"— his eyes dropped just a little, the corners tight with pain—"Cordelia made something like what we use at home for our research. I've been feeling well enough to go through the data from the last few days." He handed her the tablet. "Here."

A vid was queued and she pressed the stylized play symbol. Halud appeared interviewing what looked like a doctor. He finished with a sermon about the power of the Gods. "Old footage," she said, handing the tablet back.

He shook his head, his entire face lighting up despite the stretching, shiny new skin. "No, keep watching."

She took the tablet back, staring at it intensely.

"There," said Kieran, suddenly reaching out and pausing the scene. "See it?"

"Gods," she gasped. The camera angle shifted, the new camera zooming in. And in that second before he turned his gaze to follow his audience, his right side was highlighted. On the temple was a scar. A scar she recognized. A scar he earned falling, hitting his head, as an old freightship launched from Selousa amidst a torrent of laz-cannon fire. From the day he rescued her. Her hand flew to her mouth. "He's alive."

Kieran gripped her arm again, squeezing. "And he's on Etar. Cordelia can take us there."

She gripped him back. Her eyes stayed stuck to the tablet and it's slightly blurry frozen image.

Halud was alive. He was on Etar. They were going to get him back.

* * *

Galiant Idim stood stiffly on the pristine white floor, surrounded by glowing white consoles. The new 'starship' was sleek, fast, and incredibly high tech.

A gentle buzz shook in his ear. "Yes," he answered.

"*Everything looks green down here, Cap'n. Cordelia says she's ready.*"

Gal shook his head. For all the time he'd spent trying to keep them away from Cordelia, here she was posing as a starship for them. Complete with a super-charged FTL drive.

Beside him, Cordelia smiled knowingly. She'd donned some type of white uniform, with brightly-coloured circles splashed over the entirety of her person.

"What are you wearing?" he said.

Her smiled broadened. "You need more colour in your life, Gal."

He sighed. "Thanks for doing this."

She shrugged. "If this works, I can use this type of travel to reach my home."

That was the deal they had made. Show her how to travel, if she helped them get to Etar. Not that he wanted to be anywhere near Etar. "Still, thank you."

She flushed gently. "This is going to be fun. I've never been on a journey with so many people."

They were headed for the heart of it, to the centre of the Central Army's empire.

"Do you think it's safe?" she asked. "Will anyone tell?"

He felt the weight across his heart, the importance of his promise to her. "No, Cordelia. Not this time. And if they do, you'll be long gone."

She squealed with glee. "Oh, that's right!" Then she shuddered, as though she were cold. "I just hope nobody thinks to put a bomb on me."

Gal swallowed hard.

No one had said anything. There was no telling how much they knew, if anything. It was all so hectic. But Rayne knew. He glanced over to where she studied her console intently. He hadn't meant to. Didn't know what he was doing. But still he had hurt her. The one person he thought he would never hurt was the one he hurt the most.

A voice whispered in his ear, "They're going to find out sooner or later, Gal." Aaron. "At least you can't wire a bomb into this ship."

He faced his eyes front. The hallucinations still haunted him. Demons sat quietly across the back of the starship's bridge.

"What will they do when they find out, I wonder."

Go away, he told the voice.

"What will they say?"

Just a hallucination. Remnants from the addiction.

"They'll find out it was you."

He stared hard at the view screen.

"And you wrote the letters. And you started the war. And everything that's ever come to pass is your fault."

"Gal, are you okay?" asked Cordelia.

He took a stilted breath. "Yes." He forced a smile. "Are you ready?"

She nodded, her eyes bright. "Setting a course for Etar."

The Story Continues....

Human by C R MacFarlane
Red Fever Book 3
Now available on Amazon
Visit <u>viewbook.at/Human</u>

In the third and final instalment in the Red Fever trilogy, Galiant Idim must return to the place where it all began, to the planet he used to call home. Once, made of vast farmland and forests, Indaer has become Etar, and the Central Army's cities cover most of the world in slate. Except a small forest preserve that holds more secrets than Gal himself—a place the Speakers will do anything to destroy.

Knowing nothing of the planet's hidden history, Sarrin arrives with a singular focus: find and free Halud. She expects the danger in the city where Army patrols and folk alike are keenly vigilant. What she doesn't expect is the danger in the forest preserve that may hold the key to her very soul.

Scan this QR Code with your phone
to buy your copy of Human on Amazon

Have You Enjoyed This Book?

Thank you for reading Augment, the first book in the Red Fever Trilogy. If you enjoyed the story, or even if you didn't, I hope you'll take the time to leave a review. A review means a huge amount to a self-published author like myself, and I would be extremely grateful if you'd consider writing one. It's a good way for us to communicate (yes, I read every single one!), for you to tell me what you liked and where I need to keep improving, and it helps other readers know if a book is one they should pick up or pass by.

Don't forget to join my author newsletter at thewritable.com to hear about new projects and releases (plus pick up some sample chapters and a free short story).

Scan this QR code with your phone
to access the author newsletter!

About Charlotte R MacFarlane

Oh, hey there!

It's cool you want to learn more about me.

I am an award winning author of short stories and poetry, a writing coach, editor, and lover of fiction. I also teach people about happiness and authentic living at happy-ology.com.

Probably the best way to truly learn about me is to read the words on the page, but here's a few things you might not know:

1) I have a wicked sense of humour, and a passion for coming up with irregular sayings ("well, float a log down the stream, you've probably already seen in this in the writing)

2) I love to read and write science-fiction and fantasy novels (duh!) To me, they're more than fiction. The

alternate worlds provide a perfect way to make commentary on the human condition using vast and interesting metaphors. For the same reason, I love Star Trek.

3)   I am a classic over-achiever. With awards in writing, horseback riding, math, physics, leadership, and all-around good-person-ness, I often don't know when to stop.

4)   I don't like TV (the one exception being Star Trek). It's not tactile enough for me, and doesn't stimulate my imagination as much as a good book.

5)   I hate socks, but they are a necessity here in the frigid North, which I also have a love-hate relationship with.

6)   I am most afraid of.... Pomeranians. As a former veterinarian, these are some of the hardest dogs to read their body language and hold onto, meaning I've had more tangles with Poms than any other breed. They are cute though, I guess....

Thank you for checking out my fiction, and I hope you'll leave a review and sign up for the newsletter (and buy more books!) It's an honour for a writer to be able to share their thoughts, and I'm so glad I got to share them with you.

More of Charlotte's work can be found at

www.thewritable.com

@CharlotteRMacFarlane

www.ingramcontent.com/pod-product-compliance
Lightning Source LLC
Chambersburg PA
CBHW031134260626
47153CB00021B/284